ALL EYES ON YOU

ALL EYES ON YOU

Sam Frances

ACCENT

First published in 2025 by Headline Accent
An imprint of HEADLINE PUBLISHING GROUP

1

Cataloguing in Publication Data is available from the British Library

Paperback ISBN 978 1 0354 1841 1

Typeset in Sabon by CC Book Production

Printed and bound in Great Britain by Clays Ltd, Elcograf S.p.A.

Headline's policy is to use papers that are natural, renewable and
recyclable products and made from wood grown in well-managed forests
and other controlled sources. The logging and manufacturing processes
are expected to conform to the environmental regulations
of the country of origin.

HEADLINE PUBLISHING GROUP
An Hachette UK Company
Carmelite House
50 Victoria Embankment
London EC4Y 0DZ

The authorised representative in the EEA is Hachette Ireland,
8 Castlecourt Centre, Dublin 15, D15 XTP3, Ireland
(email: info@hbgi.ie)

www.headline.co.uk
www.hachette.co.uk

For my wolf pack:
Tom, Matilda, Beatrice, Douglas, Olive,
Maggie and Molly

Prologue

The seed was planted the minute he saw her, finally putting a face to the name he knew so well. Everything he'd wanted – was owed – was finally within reach.

Hot water ran over his hands until the skin was raw, eyes fixed on the rising steam as it blurred his reflection in the bathroom mirror. The rhyme he'd tried to erase from memory a thousand times spewed from his lips before he even noticed he was making the sounds. 'Left hand, right hand, wash them every day. Left hand, right hand, wash the dirt awa— No!' he shouted, so guttural his throat burned.

He snatched a small white towel from the rack, colour draining from his knuckles as he twisted the material.

There wasn't time for that.

Droplets of water from his cheeks sank into the cotton as he patted his face dry. This would be different to the others. The stand-ins. The placeholders. As if taking out everything he'd lost on those vacuous shells would ever fill the hole.

This time would mean something.

He walked to the bedroom and looked at her picture again, fingertip tracing the soft contour of her chin, down the side of her neck, and across her exposed collarbone.

The heat from the water lingered. His skin tingling. But it was like it came from her now, radiating through the image and igniting the simmering embers in the pit of his stomach. Bare floorboards creaked as he approached the freshly made bed, sheets pristine until creases shot out from under him like cracking ice as he lay down, excitement pulsating.

He would get this right. He'd had enough practice. Learned from the best.

This was his chance.

And nothing, no one, would get in his way.

1

You'd think I'd be better at lying, after eight years in the job listening to criminals of all breeds do it right to my face like their lives depended on it. But Tess's insistence on buying me breakfast this morning – a service reserved for only the direst circumstances – was a clear sign she wasn't quite convinced I was fine about what happened.

And I *was* fine. Absolutely fine.

We were sat at our usual table in Gilly's café. Tess talking. Me listening. Fuelling up on carbs and coffee before another day of graft at the station. What could be more back to normal than that? I stared out the misted window on to the road. The scalloped edges of the emerald green awning fluttered in the breeze, mirroring the movement of the multi-coloured bunting that zigzagged down the cobbled street towards Market Square.

Tess clicked her fingers inches from my face. 'Hello? Earth to Alice! Are you even listening to me?'

I picked at my half-eaten almond croissant. 'Savouring every syllable, my love, carry on.'

The garish earrings Tess had bought for a pound at the church craft fair poked through the tight black curls framing her face as she cocked her head. 'You sure you're all right? I don't mean to kick a girl when she's down, but you look like shit.'

Dad's detective motto hummed in my ears. *Eyes are the windows to the soul, kid. Give people away every time.* Clearly the mighty Chief Superintendent Mick Washington was never wrong, and the out-of-date concealer I'd found down the back of the sofa was no match for the dark puffy rings flanking the bridge of my nose like a pair of overcooked soufflés.

Thanks for nothing, Maybelline.

The thought of telling Tess the truth came and went in an instant. 'I'm not *down*, thank you very much, just a bit tired.' It wasn't a total lie. Last night's attempt to get the recommended eight hours had turned into the now familiar pattern of two hours' sleep and six hours of mental flagellation.

Tess eyeballed me before summarising what I'd missed during my leave from work. 'Well, there was *another* argument about perimeter fence line ownership up at Highedge Farm that ended in a brawl; Mavis Mulberry's grandkids shoplifting bottles of mead from Crow Hill Shop again; a couple of quad bike theft jobs; and a report come in yesterday from that author who lives in the manor by the reservoir, someone following her, sending her weird pictures or something. But other than that, it's been pretty quiet.'

She licked her fingertip and dabbed at the stray golden flakes of pastry on my plate, her perfectly shellacked burnt-orange nail varnish complementing her light brown skin. I slapped her hand away. 'Since when does Fortbridge have a resident author?'

'Since last month. Camilla Harton-Gray,' Tess said, putting on her best snooty accent. 'She's from here, but just moved back from London. I'm sure it's nothing anyway, like, she's a celebrity, she probably gets weird stuff sent to her all the time. Roy's picked it up, nothing for you to worry about.'

Roy. *Fuck's sake.* 'Oh, great, because Roy never causes me any managerial problems at all, does he?'

Tess downed the last of her apple juice. 'He's been behaving himself while you've been off, promise. And when I say behaving himself, of course I mean trawling Facebook and playing Solitaire.'

'Sounds about right, Roy being a lazy twat while Fortbridge lives up to its reputation as Wessex Constabulary's very own *Sin City.*'

Tess's impish smile pushed her cheeks into her eyes as she tucked her forearms under the table and hunched forward. 'Are you sure I can't tempt you with a last-minute holiday? My cousin's been trying to get me to visit her place for months. We should go. It's right on the beach, you could chill out, get some sun on those pasty beanpoles.' She poked each of my knobbly knees in turn under the table. 'Look at you, you're practically translucent.'

She wasn't wrong. Vitamin D was probably just what I needed. And a nice bit of sea salt in my hair to bring some life back to what'd once been a somewhat stylish French bob now accidentally grown out, sitting dark and lank against my shoulders. I chewed the inside of my mouth in feigned interest. 'Caribbean cousin, or Weston-super-Mare cousin? 'Cause those are two very different offers, my friend.'

Tess kicked my shoe. 'Funny. Seriously, why not?'

I pressed a finger to my chin. 'Hmm, I dunno, those pesky little things we have called jobs.'

She shrugged. 'I've still got some leave to use before April, and anyone would understand if you needed a bit more time off – it's only been a couple of weeks since ... well, you know.'

I looked at my watch, squinting to differentiate between the minute hand and the crack in the screen. It had been two weeks, one day and thirteen hours. Give or take. Not that I was counting. Not watching each second tick by, hoping the more that passed, the less the screams that had filled the ink-black sky above the village green that night would reverberate inside my skull. 'I don't need a holiday, OK? And you've gotta remember,' I said, not sure if it was Tess or myself who needed the reminder, 'police time is more like dog years than human ones. So theoretically it's been ages, more like four months.' And did I honestly think even my pretend time gap would be enough to forget about what happened? To forget about the mistake? My mistake. I shoved the last piece of croissant into my mouth like a plug to stop what I was really thinking from bursting out.

'Even so,' Tess said, 'I know you lot deal with some horrible shit, but it's worse, isn't it, when it involves kids.'

The pastry stuck in my throat. Children and animal cruelty were most coppers' kryptonite, but you still had to get on with it. I forced the food down with a mouthful of lukewarm coffee. 'Honestly, I'm fine. And yeah, some jobs get under your skin, but . . . hey, what can you do?'

'OK, but remember you're not a robot, and I know I'm just sat behind a desk all day so I don't know what it feels like . . . but you know you can talk to me, yeah?'

Ah, *talking*. That old magic medicine. I appreciated the sentiment, but talking about your feelings got you nowhere in this job, certainly not on the list for promotion. As much as she tried, Tess would never truly get it. The difference between being a civilian police researcher and a cop. It's one thing to know the ins-and-outs of crimes, incidents and offenders on paper, through the filter of a computer screen. It's quite another to deal with them all in the flesh. 'Yes, idiot girl, I know.' I balled up a napkin and threw it at her. 'But I hate to break this to you, I *am* a robot. We all are, haven't you seen *RoboCop*? That's why they'd never let you join, too many organs. Now, come on.' I nodded towards the door, licking the remnants of icing sugar off my teeth. 'Let's get out of here before Gilly sees your puppy dog eyes and comes over with a tiny violin.'

The early March cold snap slapped my cheeks as I pulled the café door open and held it for Tess. I was about to follow her on to the street when she jumped back into me, a stream of frothy water gushing down the pavement where she'd been about to step. I braced myself for the outburst. For all Tess's exterior pink and fluffiness, her wrong side was to be fervently avoided, like a pedigree poodle with a flick knife tucked into its diamanté show collar.

'Woah, watch it! You nearly soaked me,' she shouted as the owner of the fishmongers next door held up an apology with one hand and an empty red plastic bucket in the other.

'Sorry, love, didn't see you there,' the man said.

He carried on talking but I'd stopped listening. Too busy watching the cobblestones, water traversing the crevices that separated the varying shades of grey and tan. Butterflies fought in my stomach. The suds moved faster than the boy's blood had. Jamie's blood. Viscous crimson snakes slithering between the cracks in the courtyard at St Bernadette's Church. I closed my eyes as the voice of Jamie's mum echoed in my head. *He'll be lucky if he can walk again, never mind play football*. Her tears staining the sterile white hospital sheet that covered the sinewy body of her boy. Her broken baby. I bit down on my lower lip, chewing the thoughts away as a deep thud pounded in my ribcage.

'Alice!' Tess's voice jolted me as she shouted from the other side of the street. 'What are you doing, you melon? Waiting for a lollipop lady or something? Hurry up, I've gotta get a metal theft report finished and up to headquarters before lunch. Can't keep those HQ big dogs waiting.'

I threw my bag over my shoulder and walked across the road, legs filling with concrete.

Tess looked me up and down as I came level with her. 'You sure you're OK?'

I paused before replying, my heart raging so loudly in my ears, for a second, I was convinced she could hear it. 'For the millionth time, I'm fine!'

2

Gnarled stems of flowerless wisteria hung above the door to the Post Office, protruding in all directions like the fingers of a corpse. I swerved, avoiding the grasp of one extra-long tentacle as I followed Tess towards the architectural monstrosity that was Fortbridge Police Station. Plonked awkwardly at the end of a small row of medieval stone cottages with chocolate box facades like some uninvited dinner guest, the bland eighties brick building couldn't look more out of place if it tried. Even the hydrangeas someone had stuck in a flower bed to the right of the reception door were the very definition of trying to polish a turd.

We passed through the empty reception and climbed the stairs as the fire door to the CID office swung open, the familiar odour of *eau de detective* erupting across the landing. A weekend's worth of shifts fuelled by kebabs, burgers and abstinence from showering heightened the pungency.

'Here she is,' Roy said, his voice muffled by what smelled like a bacon and egg sandwich, 'the prodigal daughter returns.'

I inhaled as deeply as the stench would allow and went inside. 'Morning.'

Roy finished his last bite of breakfast before pointing at his computer monitor. 'Come look at this.'

I made my way to his side of the bank of desks. A picture of a middle-aged woman stared out from his screen. My stomach clenched. Who was this? Jamie's aunt? His grandma? His favourite teacher devastated by what happened to him? What *I* let happen to him. 'Who's that?'

'It's Trudy,' Roy said.

I looked at him blankly.

'You know, *Trudy*, the one I went to school with?' Clearly I was expected to know her from her first name alone, like Fortbridge's answer to Oprah.

The memory clicked and I let out the apprehensive breath I'd been holding back, appreciating for the first time how little it took to distract him. 'Ah yes, *Trudy*.'

'You were wrong, she does fancy me. Been sending me messages on the Facebook.' His broad chest puffed out as he sat upright, the buttons on his shirt clinging desperately to their holey counterparts like pairs of doomed lovers going down together on the *Titanic*.

'Really?' I said, making my way back to my desk. 'Good for you. How's Karen by the way?'

Roy dragged his tongue across his teeth at the mention of his wife's name. 'No harm in just talking, is there?'

'Depends what you're saying, doesn't it?' I turned my computer on, not sure if he hadn't heard me or was just pretending, as the phone on his desk rang in a well-timed interruption.

I sat down and tried to remember my log-in details. At

least Roy was acting normally, like nothing had happened. I didn't know why I'd expected anything else. He'd probably already forgotten Jamie's name. Was that what I'd prefer? To not give a shit, like Roy? I cared. So what? Not the worst trait a police officer could have.

'Yeah ... yeah ... mm-hmm ...' Roy said, half listening to the person on the other end of the line, trying to close down Facebook as the Inspector's voice rang out from the corridor.

I pressed my index fingers to my temples as an alternative to clicking my heels together three times to take me home. If I didn't have the energy to deal with Roy today, I certainly couldn't be doing with Jane. The waistband of my jeans climbed up my back as I slid lower in my chair.

'Alice?' Jane said as she appeared in the doorway. 'She in yet?'

Shit.

'Aha, the lady herself.' She marched across the office, eliciting her usual reaction, everyone suddenly staring at their screens like they were figuring out a self-assessment tax return, hoping she wouldn't notice them for a bollocking if they didn't look directly at her.

'Morning, ma'am,' I said.

Jane's eyes narrowed, a pursed smile emerging from lips so thin they were barely visible on her face. It disappeared in an instant, as if returning the pleasantry was physically painful. 'Can I have a quick word?' she said, nodding back towards her office. She spun on the heels of her polished loafers before I could answer, long strides taking her across the water-stained carpet still feeling the after-effects of the great ceiling leak of '09.

My heart rate rose by the second, the varying ways Jane could sack me running through my head. *Maybe you should try a new profession, something less taxing. Off you pop now from Daddy's coat-tails, don't trip over my personalised Vivienne Westwood kit bag on your way out.* I followed the trail of bergamot body mist Jane left in her wake, pausing for a second outside her office to compose myself. I walked in and closed the door behind me.

I'd never gotten over how plush Jane's office was compared to the rest of the dilapidated station. Stepping into it was like passing through the wardrobe into Narnia. The damp-stained walls, peeling paint and eighties décor on display everywhere else in the building gave way to a chic and comfortable room that hipsters would describe as a *'work-space'* whilst sipping their deconstructed matcha lattes from recycled jam jars.

'Sit,' Jane instructed, leaning against her large wooden desk. She gestured towards the mustard velour sofa that filled an entire wall of the office. I'd never been invited to touch her precious sofa before. The minions were usually directed to perch on the cheap plastic chairs. 'So,' she said, sitting down beside me, 'good to be back? Ready for action?'

Trick question. Don't fall for it. Keep it simple. 'Yes, ma'am.'

Jane nodded, her stiff black cowlick bouncing across her

wrinkled brow, streaks of grey glinting in the harsh office lighting. 'Glad to hear it. Spoken to your dad recently?'

'Erm –' why on earth was she asking about my dad? '– not really, why?'

Jane never worked directly with Dad before he retired, but neither had most of the people who sang his praises as soon as they heard the surname and saw the green eyes with amber flecks. *You must be Mick's girl*, they'd say, before following it up with some variation of the old adage of apples never falling far from trees. Dad got it too, in reverse. Whispers of me snapping at his heels made their way to him through meet-ups with the old boys at the golf course. His little Alice, showing those legendary Washington instincts, earmarked as a future leader of his beloved Major Crime Unit. And they weren't wrong; I had them. The instincts. Had them *before*, anyway. I'd always been able to read people, know what made them tick.

Jane rested her elbow on the back of the sofa like a chat show host, legs crossed. 'I just wondered if you'd heard the news through the grapevine, about Jim Barker.'

My stomach leapt at the sound of a name I knew well. Dad's protégé and one of the sergeants at the MCU. 'No, what about him?'

'He's retiring.'

My ears buzzed. This was what the last two years in Fortbridge had been building towards. There was no way they'd have let me jump straight in there as a brand-new sergeant, no matter who my dad was. *You need to break*

13

in those chevrons first, DCI Simon Carver had said when the temporary position came up out here. It wasn't ideal, moving from town, but if spending my time supervising investigations about pissed teenagers on a cow-tipping bender with traffic cones on their heads counted as necessary management experience, I'd take it. If that's what it took to get up there, get stuck into some *real* jobs. The process of my entire future flashing before my eyes clearly went on far too long for Jane's liking.

'That's what you want, isn't it? To get up to HQ?' she said.

'Absolutely, ma'am. It's great here, of course, but yeah.'

'Following in Dad's footsteps, eh?'

My well-practised head bob and smile activated on cue. I wasn't in the mood to trot out the song and dance about how my ambition was fuelled by a desire to actually make a bloody difference in the world, and that if I was truly looking to make *Daddy* proud, becoming a police officer seemed like the worst thing I could have chosen. It was clearly the last thing he wanted.

'Well,' Jane continued, clapping her hands together and dropping them into her lap. 'Now's the time. Selection process won't start for a few weeks yet, but it's never too early to start getting yourself prepared. Happy to lend a hand, of course.'

I shifted my weight on the sofa cushion. *Lend a hand?* Jane Josephs had never lent anything to anyone in her fifty-odd-year existence. I started to wonder if I'd been off for two weeks, or if I'd been in a coma for two *years* and

Jane had undergone a personality transplant. 'That'd be, erm, great, ma'am, thank you.'

'Good. Well, go on.' Her demeanour hardened as if the coins in her *be nice* meter had run out. 'Go find some crimes to solve.'

I sprang from the sofa and headed to the door, a fizzing sensation coursing through me.

'Oh, and Alice?' I turned back, Jane looking up at me through thick, dark eyebrows. 'I mean it, about getting yourself, well . . . prepared. Don't forget that Occupational Health referral for counselling.' I pulled my lips back between my teeth. There it was again, the *other* C-word. 'It's still open, if you need it, with Bev.' She held the V sound a second too long, like a snake with a speech impediment. 'There's going to be stiff competition for the job – I know Bret's going for it as well as a boatload of others – and you wouldn't want that, er, hiccup, to affect your chances, would you?'

I dug my fingernails into my palms. *That's* more like it. Classic Jane. The Jane who'd refer to the possibly permanent paralysis of a twelve-year-old boy as a hiccup. The Jane who had a reputation for breaking the glass ceiling, not so she could pull other women up behind her, but because of the pleasure she derived from watching the shards rain down on those below. The Jane desperate to unleash her own little protégé, DS Bret 'Golden Boy' Seaborn, on to the halls of HQ to show off her mentoring prowess. I didn't *need* help. Not from Jane. Not from Beverly 'call me Bev and yes I do love a bevvy' Taylor. What the hell did Bev know about being a police officer anyway, sat behind a desk all day filling in referral paperwork and watering her peace lily?

Well, fuck you, ma'am, was what I wanted to say, but I could only muster the last of the words aloud before walking out, anger burning a hole in my chest.

3

The flimsy office chair groaned under Roy's weight as he leant forward. He re-opened the Facebook tab and scrolled the last few weeks' worth of messages he'd exchanged with Trudy. He paused, eyes sticking on the one where she'd suggested meeting for a coffee next time she passed through Fortbridge. His stomach did a little backflip. Just like it had the first time he'd read it. Before he'd remembered he couldn't meet her for a coffee, or anything else for that matter, because if he did she'd notice his profile picture was a good ten years out of date and would recede faster than his hairline. *That's if she even recognises you at all,* he thought, staring at the picture. He barely even recognised himself. His hair was more grey now than the sandy blond it was back then, the sharp jaw on display almost completely hidden beneath a layer of soft, stubbly flesh.

His eyes flicked between the screen and the hallway, cursor poised over the minimise button in case Jane or Alice re-emerged, ready to click off before they had a chance to jump down his throat. He expected as much from Jane. She lapped up any opportunity to show him who was boss. Long gone were the days they'd happily shared a pint at the dingy bar of the residential police training centre in their early twenties. Clearing their minds of the fog brought on by legislation lectures and comparing bruises from their Personal Safety Training before she shipped off to HQ and was fast-tracked along the road to Inspector. But he'd thought Alice would be different, being the flesh and blood of the legend that was Mick Washington. He was sure coming from that sort of stock would have rubbed off, that she'd get stuck in with the grunt work and not just trample over anyone in her way to get to the upper echelons as quickly as possible like Jane and a few others he could name. Alice had been top of her class. Strong as an ox. Came close to breaking some poor sod's arm in new recruit training, so Roy had heard.

But it hadn't taken long to see she was just like the rest. Those young cookie-cutter coppers. Too busy making fancy PowerPoint presentations about strategic problem-solving plans rather than rolling their sleeves up and getting some real police work done. Roy would never be convinced getting an A* for an essay about public order tactics at university would actually prepare anyone when it came down to it. Dealing with a riot. Face to face with an angry mob hurling Molotov cocktails and being expected to hold your ground. Not that it ever really went that far out here. But you never knew. There'd been those times the Swampy types came over in droves from London and chained themselves to the fence at Dick Lowry's abattoir. Roy was a firm believer in always being prepared for a good old-fashioned rumble when required, even if it was with a bunch of tree-hugging hippies. *The two aren't mutually exclusive, you know; being academic and being prepared to run towards what everyone else is running away from*, Alice had snarked at him more than once. He didn't even know what the hell she meant. Mutually bleeding exclusive? His point exactly! Too many fancy words, not enough action.

The last fortnight had been a case in point. Taking two weeks off because she thought she'd fluffed it? Couldn't make it up with this lot. It'd been a horrible day, of course it had, for all of them. But it's not like she was the only one there. And no one had asked *him* if he was all right. If he needed some self-care pamper time. He was the one who'd held on to the mother's flailing arms like a human straitjacket. He was the one who'd felt the vibrations under his feet as the kid hit the ground in front of him.

Roy jumped at a different type of vibration: his mobile. He took a second to retrieve it, knuckles scraping against the hem of his trouser pocket as it clung to his thigh. He wasn't sure how much longer he'd fit into these. He needed new ones, but he wouldn't know where to start. The screen lit up as the message banner across the top told him he had one new alert. He opened it and instantly wished he hadn't bothered.

NEW MODULE ADDED TO YOUR SILVERSKY PROGRAMME: MY DEPRESSION AND I.

Jesus wept, Roy thought. The thing sounded more like a bleeding Rogers and Hammerstein number than a mental health module. Where did they get this rubbish from? The first few hadn't been as bad as he'd thought, but he knew he'd regret downloading the damn thing the second Laurie – who he should really remind was his daughter and not his mother – made him do it. He didn't mind going through the motions if it got her off his back, but if she bothered to come and visit him she'd see he was fine since Karen left. Nice to have the peace and quiet for once, if anything.

He held the power button down until the screen went black and stuffed the phone back into his pocket before returning to his computer. The damned thing had timed out already and locked itself. He typed his password, fingers hitting the wrong key at least twice. 'Stupid – piece of bleedin' – Tess,' he yelled. 'This thing's broken.'

Tess strode towards him. 'Is it *actually* broken this time though?'

'Well, the screensaving thing isn't going away, is it?'

'Your caps lock's on,' she said as she tapped it off, 'try again.'

Roy jabbed his index finger against the keys and the screensaver disappeared, his cheeks filling with heat.

'See,' said Tess, before she turned and waltzed off across the office.

'Stupid bleedin'—' He was just about to throw an F-bomb tirade at his screen when he noticed a new message from Trudy, stifling a rare smile as he clicked to read it.

4

Roy had disappeared from his desk by the time I came out of Jane's office. *Thank God.* I slumped into my chair and closed my eyes. Who did Jane think she was kidding? She didn't want me to get this job. Just because she'd buggered up her chance of promotion at HQ – and her marriage – by getting caught shagging DCI Carver didn't mean I was going to mess my opportunity up by making it look like I couldn't cope with the hard stuff. And *of course* she'd want Bret sodding Seaborn to get it over me. No chance of him going over there and making a tit of himself. Solid as a rock Bret. Reliable as they come Bret. Does everything by the book Bret. Bret, Bret, Bret, boring bloody Bret.

No. That job would be mine. End of discussion. I'd worked hard for it. I was a good detective. And it would take more than one wobble to knock me off track. If I'd managed to do all right without counselling as a kid after ... well, I certainly didn't need it now.

I shot daggers at the back of Bret's empty chair on the other side of the room until Roy broke my line of sight, passing me before dropping a pile of photograph printouts on to his desk.

'Looks more like a bleedin' photoshoot for *Country Life* magazine than a stalking case, this one,' Roy said.

He splayed the images out and I sat up to get a better look. Candid shots of a glamorous woman walking two large dogs at what looked like Oakham Reservoir on the edge of the village, displaying the sort of effortless countryside chic that made me think she must be one of those annoying people who even managed to look good at the airport. 'That her, then, the author?'

Roy nodded.

My foot was a metronome tapping against the inside of my chair leg. 'Does she know when they were taken?'

Roy shifted his weight from one leg to the other. 'Report came in yesterday but she thinks it's from a couple of days ago, says she didn't see anyone, but don't you think she's *awfully* dressed up to be dog-walking?'

I looked up at him from my chair, squinting as if I was staring straight at the sun. 'What's your point?'

'Bleedin' celebrities, all the same, ain't they? Always trying to drum up a bit of free promo. Especially when they've got some shit to sell.'

I shook my head, wondering if Roy had always been this cynical or if his years in the job had turned him that way.

Tess's Euphoria perfume tickled my nose as she sidled up beside us before peering down at the pictures. A pock-marked face appeared over her shoulder seconds later.

'Morning, Eddie,' I said as Tess shrugged his pointy chin away from her.

'Oh my God, is that Camilla Harton-Gray?' Eddie said.

I nodded. 'Yep, some creepazoid took these and emailed them to her anonymously.'

Eddie leaned forward to get a closer look. 'No way, seriously?' he said, eye-wateringly stale coffee and chewing gum breath following the words out of his mouth. 'Sounds like something straight out of one of her thrillers, does that. In fact . . .' He scuttled across the office and dug around in his rucksack before pulling out some sort of tablet. Confused looks ping-ponged between Tess, Roy and me as Eddie swiped at the device's screen, his eyes squinting in concentration. 'Ah, no, haven't got the e-book version of her DI Tucker series; got the paperbacks and special edition hardbacks, though, I'll have a look when I get home. I swear something like this happens at the start of the first or second one. What if it's a copycat or something?'

Tess tutted before interjecting, 'They're anonymous emails, Eddie – I'm sure that happens in, like, a million stalker stories. Hardly unique, is it?'

'The way she writes makes it feel like it is, she's sooo good. I've got her new book on pre-order, she's amazing. The "Queen of Suspense", they call her,' Eddie said.

I'd never really pegged him as an avid reader. He looked far too excitable to sit down long enough to read anything longer than the message in a fortune cookie. No harm in letting him crack on with his hunch, though, it would keep him occupied at the very least. Stop him getting bored and shredding the loo roll like an Andrex puppy. 'Tess's probably right,' I said, 'but worth a look. You have at it, Eddie.'

'Ah, so she's got a new book coming out, eh?' Roy said.

'Sounds like the Agatha Christie wannabe might be trying to build a bit of suspense of her own, sell a few more copies.' He rocked back and forth from toes to heels like a proud Weeble.

I closed my eyes and rubbed my temples, reminding myself that the little enjoyment Roy seemed to get from life came from being a contrarian. And that being reprimanded for flipping off a subordinate was the last thing I needed. *Calm. Focussed.* 'Funny joke, Roy, hilarious – our very own Dame Vera Lynn keeping all our spirits up. Now, can we move on to taking this seriously, yeah?'

Roy looked down at his shoes and stopped rocking.

'Have you spoken to her yet?' I asked.

'Briefly,' Roy said. 'Going over to take a statement tomorrow.'

Sticky HQ fingers would be all over this when they found out the complainant was famous, and Roy didn't exactly have the most delicate bedside manner. I couldn't let him mess this job up, not now. The bosses would no doubt already be pencilling 'can't keep children safe' on to my MCU application; I hardly needed 'and can't keep her own officers in check' adding to it. 'We'll go and see her together, OK?'

Roy recoiled as if I'd flicked an elastic band in his face. 'No offence, but, er, you don't need to hold my hand. I've been taking statements since you were in nappies, *Sarge*.'

Indignance coated my title like it always did when Roy was finding me particularly annoying. He seemed to have a major issue with me being in a position of authority.

Probably because at thirty I was more than twenty years his junior. Though, I had to admit, pissing off Roy wasn't my least favourite thing in the world. I tapped the edges of the printouts on the desk, nudging them into a uniform pile. 'I'm not sure how my parents' potty-training strategy is any kind of reflection on how good you are at taking statements, but sure, you're taking the statement; I'm coming for damage control.' Roy control, more like. I poked the wad into his chest. 'The press will be all over this if – when – it gets out, I can see the headlines now: *Fear in Fortbridge: Writer Given Dose of Own Crazy Crime Medicine*.' Roy looked at me like I'd farted. 'All right, I'm not a bloody newspaper editor, am I? You get the gist.'

'Fine.' He shrugged, looking less than impressed with my attempt at journalistic flare. He trudged off towards the hallway, presumably to go beat up the vending machine.

Eddie stayed close, buzzing around Tess like a fly on cocaine as usual. I managed to keep my cool for all of twenty seconds. 'Eddie, can you just be still. Or – even better – *be* somewhere else.'

'Sorry, Sarge,' Eddie said, clasping his hands behind his back as if to physically shackle himself. 'Any legwork you need doing on this one, I'm at your service.' He saluted as Tess joined me in a mutual eye roll, perfectly executed like a pair of Olympic synchronised divers. Eddie was well known for shirking the 'Support' part of his PCSO title and spent most of his time hanging around the station trying to chat up Tess, but hell, could we blame the renewed enthusiasm? Everyone loves an attractive damsel in distress with millions of pounds in the bank and a manor house sat on nine acres.

I slung a cardigan around my shoulders, fist fighting against the inside-out sleeve as Eddie continued.

'May be useful to know, Sarge – did you see that profile of her in the paper a few weeks ago?'

'Until this morning I'd never even heard of her,' I said.

'A. J. did a whole spread about her, and what happened to her family.'

I definitely hadn't read it if the words were those of A. J. 'epicentre of gutter journalism' Howden. I hadn't read anything of his before he did the hatchet job on me the day after what happened to Jamie, and I certainly wasn't going to start now. A headline of *Carnage in the Church Yard: Top Cop's Daughter Centre of Review*, complete with a close-up of my face, had been quite enough for me. *Fucking vulture.* A. J. was a classic armchair detective. First on scene with all the bright ideas, only to be found standing behind the actual officers, quivering like a spiderweb in a breeze the second anything kicked off. Even applied to be a cop at one point, he'd told me as he'd come on to me in the pub a week after I'd moved here, but halfway through his training he'd 'realised his intellectual prowess could be put to better use through investigative journalism'. I'd always taken that as code for *didn't like the fighty bits*. The man was about as trustworthy as the label on an allegedly ripe and ready avocado.

Eddie relayed the article highlights, Roy returning

halfway through with his hand shoved into a packet of crisps. Camilla's family killed. Car accident on their way to a wedding. Hit by a lorry driving on the wrong side of the road. A road they wouldn't have taken if not for the detour to pick Camilla up from the train station. Brimming with excitement, fresh from a week in London celebrating bagging her first book deal.

'*The Haunted Author*, A. J. called it,' Eddie continued. 'Anyway, Sarge, just so you know what you're walking into. It's been about ten years, but, still, I imagine moving back here has brought up some memories for her, poor thing.'

Roy nodded. 'I remember that, yeah. Didn't work it – next county over picked it up, Bret's old stomping ground – but it was a nasty one. Didn't make the news like it would now – she wasn't famous then, of course. Ask Bret, he'll probably know more about it than A. J., or have some mates at his old force who do.'

'I don't get the impression Bret does "mates",' I said, 'and anyway, it was a decade ago. Surely he would still have been training at that point – he's about the same age as me, isn't he?'

Roy shrugged. 'I thought he had a couple of years on you.'

Come to think of it, I had no idea how old Bret was. I'd guessed roughly the same age as me, but half the time he dressed like he'd raided the wardrobe of a sixty-two-year-old accountant called Dennis from Milton Keynes. 'I'm sure A. J.'s article contains more than enough of the gory details.' I scratched my forehead and turned my attention

27

back to Eddie. 'Did it happen to say anything about why she's moved back?'

'Not specifically,' Eddie said, his hands cinching in his oversized uniform at his thin waist, making him look ever so slightly less like a kid wearing his dad's kit to a fancy dress party. 'But you don't stay living in Fortbridge for long when you make the *Sunday Times* bestseller list, do you?'

Tess tutted. 'How come you know so much about her? You her number one fan or something?'

'What can I say?' Eddie shrugged. 'You can't beat a good crime thriller. And with what she's been through, woman's an inspiration. Must be bad enough something happening to your family, but then to blame yourself for it too . . .' Eddie shook his head. 'Can't even begin to imagine how guilty she must've felt. Mum, Dad, little brother, everyone gone, just like that.'

The lining of my throat thickened as Tess placed her hand on my shoulder, subtly squeezing before letting it drop away. I leant over and rearranged everything within arm's length on my desk, hoping Tess was the only one who noticed my glistening eyes. She was the only one who knew about the last time they tried to make me go to counselling. And how the feeling of blaming yourself for the death of your little brother wasn't something I had to imagine.

5

The sun had been up hours before he noticed it was day-time. Before he rose from the chair he'd sat in all night and tugged the curtains open, filling the room with a dull grey light. He circled his head. Moving inch by inch. Savouring every pop and crack as pockets of air escaped from their hiding places between each vertebra.

The floor was a mess. He squatted to tidy it, scooping up reams and reams of notes scrawled across pages and pages of paper. Everything he could possibly know about her. Everything *anyone* could know if they looked hard enough. And he'd looked hard. Very hard. All night, in fact. And what a treasure trove he'd found. He often wondered if people had any idea how much could be discovered from their digital footprint. Their favourite places, when they go, who they go with. He'd even come across the name of her Year 9 English teacher. It was all right there. Ripe for picking. And he was only just getting started.

It took every ounce of willpower he could muster to let go of the neat pile of notes and place them down on the chair. He wanted to read them again. And again. Drink in every drop of knowledge. *Later*, he told himself. He pulled on a pair of boxer shorts and a new white vest, then drew his fingertips across his face as he made his way to the bathroom, nails catching on stubble. *This won't do at all now, will it*, he thought as he neatened himself up.

He'd always enjoyed shaving. The precision. The attention to detail. She'd tried to teach him how to do it. Mother. Just like she'd taught him that stupid song to make sure he remembered how to wash his hands properly like he was some sort of baby. He was ten. Father had meant to teach him; he just didn't have the time, she'd said. He was an important man. A *very* important man. She'd used her leg to demonstrate how to put the shaving cream on, how to hold the razor, angled just so to ensure the smoothest run. The memory was as fresh in his mind as the warm red liquid trickling down his neck from where the blade had nicked his jawline. But he didn't gasp now, not like he had then at the sight of blood seeping through the white foam on Mother's knee.

'Don't panic, it's just a bit of blood,' she'd said, smiling, 'I'm not going to bleed to death.'

She'd leant over and squirted foam on to the end of his nose, and before he knew it she was chasing him and he was squealing with delight and they were running from room to room, climbing on and off beds and chairs, more laughing and spraying and laughing and more and more foam until his mother froze.

He could still hear Father's voice so clear and crisp from the top of the stairs. The sound that riveted him whenever he heard it. Caused every muscle in his body to stand to attention in what he'd once thought was fear, but had long since realised was something entirely different. Respect. 'What's going on here then?' his father had said.

Mother had put the cap back on the can and hurriedly wiped the foam from her legs. 'Nothing, just . . . just showing him how to shave, like you said.'

Father had snorted. 'Why would I say that? That's clearly a man's job. And no wonder – look at the state of you. There's more foam on you than there is on the boy's face.'

He'd caught sight of his mother clasping the collar of her dressing gown from the corner of his eye, his stomach clenching as she'd responded.

'You . . . you said you didn't have time to—'

'Course I've got time,' Father interjected as she fumbled her words. 'Always time for my lad, isn't there? Come on, son.' He'd nodded his head back towards the bathroom. 'Let me show you how it's done *properly* whilst your mother cleans up this mess.'

For a second, he hadn't responded to the instruction. He'd wanted to go to Father, to please him, to make everything all right again. But his feet were planted to the spot as if he were a vine that'd grown up through the slim gaps between the old floorboards, deep and unbreakable roots holding him firmly in place by his mother's side. He couldn't deny that what Father had said was true, though. Him and Mother had done nothing but make a mess, and he hadn't learned anything. And *of course* his father had time for him. He should have known Mother was lying. But he didn't know, then, what she was like. The levels to which she'd stoop. He'd torn himself from the doubt and run across the room to Father, that huge palm engulfing the top of his head as he'd reached his side. He could almost feel the weight of it now, wearing the warmth of his father's hand like a crown. Proud. Just like he was about the fact his face bore the hallmarks of Father's distinguished looks. There was little of her in him. And for that, he was thankful.

He wiped his neck and looked down, head tilted to one side as the thin red stream formed a pattern on the wafer-thin tissue paper. He admired it. Like he'd birthed some one-off piece of abstract art. Father's voice rumbled in his head again as he dropped the bloodied tissue into the bin. *Any woman worth her salt prefers a clean-shaven man.* He washed away the remaining streaks of foam and ran his palms across his cheeks. For what she represented, she was definitely worth it.

6

Gravel splayed beneath the car as I pulled on to the driveway of Myrtle Cottage, one of the four well-spaced properties that dotted the hillside overlooking the village, and my own little sanctuary. I pressed my forehead against the steering wheel, the soft leather a cooling compress massaging my brow. The weight of Tess's sympathetic hand from this afternoon lingered on my shoulder. After hearing Camilla's tragic history, I couldn't get Noah out of my head. As if this mess with Jamie wasn't enough.

I didn't think of my little brother often any more, I'd trained myself out of it. *Remember the good times*, people always said. And we certainly had those. Lots of them. We were inseparable. So much so people thought we were twins. The running joke in our family was that we had indeed been in the womb together, but Noah was so lazy he'd decided to have an extended stay after I was born, finally deciding to make an appearance thirteen months later. Noah and I even thought that might be true for a while. It did explain why even at over a year younger than me he was almost double my size. 'Built like a bobby,' Dad's mates would say when Mum brought us to the station. 'And me!' I'd shout, shoving Noah out the way. 'Look, look, Dad, and me, I am too, aren't I?' I'd say as I pulled up my sleeve, bent my elbow and tensed my apple pip of a bicep as tight as I could. Oh, how they'd all laugh, Dad's flat smile only half hiding the fact he never answered the question.

Dad hated when we got competitive. 'You'd get twice as far as a team,' he'd say as we set up another duel to prove who was the number one Washington child based on who could traverse the living room obstacle course made from chairs, side tables, upside-down storage boxes and the ironing board the quickest. As much as our bouts annoyed Dad, I think he was a little impressed that I always opted for the physical challenges, when if I really wanted to win all I had to do was pick any task that involved careful thought or concentration. Noah couldn't think about one thing for more than a minute before he got bored and shot off to chase more exciting, shiny objects like some weird puppy-magpie hybrid. I didn't want to beat him that way. My eyes stung thinking about our final competition, the one we didn't get to finish.

I shook my head to rid myself of the memory and slid my phone from my pocket, typing in the details of the appointment we had to see Camilla Harton-Gray after lunch tomorrow. It was exactly what I needed. Get that detective muscle flexing again. Recalibrate those instincts. A-game time.

The car door slammed louder than intended as black clouds gathered overhead, the threat of rain thickening the air. I rummaged around in my bag for my house keys. Purse.

Empty chewing gum packet. Digestive biscuit crumbs. A pen that definitely didn't work, and approximately thirteen hair grips. No keys. 'Shit,' I yelled. So much for bringing the bloody A-game.

I was assessing the best strategy for breaking in when footsteps bounced across the lane. *Great, just great.* Getting murdered on my own doorstep really would be the mouldy cherry on top of the stale cake that was my day.

'Everything all right over there?' called a voice from a face I couldn't see clearly.

'Yeah, fine,' I replied, 'sorry for the noise, just castigating myself for forgetting my keys.' Castigating? Who did I think I was, Sister Mary bloody Joseph?

A figure appeared at the end of my drive, the motion sensor light revealing a man of two halves. His body clothed in tired athletic wear and well-worn trainers, but a face straight from the big screen of the fifties. A whiter-than-white Gene Kelly-esque grin contrasting against lightly tanned skin and dark hair, neatly coiffed into short back and sides.

'D'you need any help?' he said.

I fumbled around in my bag again, hoping the keys would do me the honour of magically appearing once they remembered how much I loathed small talk with strangers. It turned my brain into that of a fifteen-year-old who's shared a bottle of cider with three friends in a park and is now just talking for talking's sake to convince their parents they are absolutely, most definitely, *not* drunk. 'It's fine, I gave my friend a spare key after the last time I did this,

I'll get her to bring it.' Maintaining an air of nonchalance became increasingly difficult as the sky burst and raindrops bounced off my face.

'Last time? Do this often then?'

'Just the once, but that once did result in me standing outside barefoot in November in nothing but a *Power Rangers* T-shirt and my knickers, so . . .' Why on God's green earth was I telling a random dude in the street about my underwear like this was the start of a low-budget porno movie? 'Anyway, she'll only be like five, ten minutes when I call her.'

'O-K,' he said slowly, 'well, you're more than welcome to come wait in here.' He swivelled and pointed towards The Willows, the small property opposite Myrtle Cottage that had sat empty for months. 'I'm just moving the last of my stuff in so don't have much in the way of furniture set up, but the kettle and tea bags are out, and the heating's on. A slightly better prospect than standing in the street, maybe?' His shoulders rose with his intonation.

Rain seeped through the stitching of my coat, dripping down my arms as I mulled over the options. The prioritisation of tea was a plus. But the inevitable spidey sense tingled at the prospect of going into a stranger's house. At night. Alone. Even as a cop who'd taken down my fair share of men twice my size, the parental motto of 'stranger danger' and the resulting wariness never really went away. But I couldn't just stand there staring like a moron – I needed to make a decision.

I thought about the points system I'd used before with

Tess to get her to see when she'd picked an imbecile to date, which in her case was the majority of times. She had terrible taste in men, going for the type of guys that would make even Hollywood – and its notoriously low bar for well-adjusted romantic male leads – think twice. My instincts might be off, but you couldn't go wrong with the immutable laws of arithmetic.

A checklist formed in my mind and I scanned through it. Had his address already if he tried anything funny. Plus twenty points. He seemed polite, helpful, friendly enough. Plus ten points. I walked towards him. 'OK, as long as you promise not to Buffalo Bill me.' *Wow.* A totally normal thing to say to a complete stranger. I might as well go back to talking about my knickers.

He squinted. 'To . . . sorry, what?'

I'd started now, I had to finish. 'You know. Guy gets girl into van, cuts her skin off, wears it as a dress? Jodie Foster? *Silence of the Lambs*?' My voice jumped an octave with every sentence.

'Oh, right,' he said, 'the film. Haven't seen it, but I *can* promise I'm too squeamish to cut anyone's skin off. Anyway, I'm not sure which box my knives are packed in, so you're good.'

Hasn't seen *Silence of the Lambs*. Raised by wolves surely? Minus five points. Decent recovery joke. Plus fifty points.

I called Tess before following him across the road and up the sloped stone driveway, my nose filling with the sweet herbal scent the rain had shaken loose from the lavender bushes separating the path from the small, unkempt front garden.

He stopped abruptly at the door, turning to face me with his right arm outstretched. 'Sorry, just realised I didn't introduce myself. Dom.'

'Alice.' I shook his hand, the warm skin making my now very cold fingers tingle.

'Nice to meet you, Alice.' He pushed the door open. 'Like I said, still settling in, so apologies for all the boxes.' I followed him inside the small kitchen, welcomed by a wave of heat from a rusted black log burner in the corner. 'Please, go through,' Dom said, pointing towards a stable-style door on the other side of the room.

He filled the kettle as I went. I hovered in the middle of what an estate agent would probably describe as a snug, using the time it took him to make the tea to scan for red flags. There wasn't much to go on; the space was tiny and bare except for a black sofa.

'Sorry about the sofa, it's seen better days,' Dom said as he came in a few minutes later. 'It was already here and – hold on.' He placed the mugs down on the cream carpet before disappearing into the kitchen, returning with a navy tartan blanket. A cloud of citrus-scented fabric softener filled the room as the material unrolled at the flick of his wrists. He laid it across the seat cushions and gestured for me to sit. Considerate to the comfort of others and appreciates the importance of a snuggly blanket. Plus forty points.

'I hope that's enough milk?' he said, handing me a mug.

It wasn't, but I was far too British to say so. 'Great, thanks.'

I forced out small talk waiting for Tess. All the usual bollocks questions no one actually cares about the answers to. 'So, um, what do you do then, job-wise?' I asked.

He took a gulp of tea. 'Physio mostly, and a bit of personal training on the side.'

'Oh, cool, better than sitting behind a desk all day, I imagine.'

'Yeah, yeah, better for the posture, I suppose.' I instantly felt the urge to sit up a little straighter and stop slouching like a geriatric prawn. 'How about you?' he continued. 'Anything exciting?'

Here it comes. The big test. Huge number of points to be lost for jokes about eating doughnuts or even a hint of innuendo about my ability to handle a truncheon. 'I'm a police officer.' I took a sip of tea and braced.

He raised his eyebrows and jutted out his bottom lip. 'Wow, impressive. You won't be in need of my services, then, probably keeps you in decent shape already. Mind, I wouldn't have thought there'd be too much to police in a village like this.'

Jamie's contorted face pierced my brain. *Not now!* 'Hmm, you'd be surprised. And policing involves a lot more sitting behind a desk than people think, especially in CID.'

'You look like you're pretty fit to me,' his eyes widened, 'I mean *physically* fit, like, heart-wise, not in the face ... not that you're not, you know ... OK, I'm just making this worse now, aren't I?'

The smirk slipped across my lips before I could stop it. 'It's fine, and thanks, I think. Glad the outside looks OK. My arteries are probably held together with cheese strings, so . . .'

'Well, I could use some clients until I start at the hospital in a couple of weeks, so if you want to do any sessions, let me know. I might even put on a few free fitness classes, see if I can drum up a bit of interest.'

As tempting as it sounded to watch Dom do push-ups, I hated group exercise. Just the thought of all the unsolicited high-fives from sweaty hands made my upper lip spasm. 'Trust me, you don't want me in your class – the only thing I have the coordination for is running. Tried a BodyCombat session once, punched myself in the nose.' He opened his mouth to speak again but the phone buzzing in my pocket interrupted him. 'That'll be my friend, Tess, I better head off, she must be outside.'

'No problem,' Dom said, leaning over and taking the mug. 'And the offer's there, about the PT, if you change your mind.'

I nodded and slapped my hands to my thighs like a performing seal as we both stood at the same time. 'Right, well, thanks for the tea. Appreciate it. See you around, neighbour.' I doffed a non-existent hat. *Get out now before you embarrass yourself even further!*

'Look forward to it, pard'ner.' He returned the awkward gesture and added a questionable attempt at a Midwestern cowboy accent. Plus ten points.

He showed me out and I emerged from the heat of the

cottage to the jangling of keys. The rain had stopped, but the road glistened with its leftovers.

'Well, well, well,' Tess said, eyeing me up from my driveway. 'What's happening? Why does your face look like that?'

I touched my cheeks that were now burning at the transition from hot to cold. *Sure, that's what that is, the temperature.* 'Like what?'

'I dunno, kinda like how you look when I make my macaroni and cheese lasagne.'

'What, bloated?'

'No, no, similar,' she said. 'Begins with an H. I'm not sure you'd have time to hear it, with your seventy-hour work weeks. *Happy*, I think they call it?'

'Wow, thanks. I'll have you know I'm always happy, a ray of bloody sunshine, me.'

Tess raised her eyebrows and folded her arms.

'What?' I said. 'Just doing my neighbourly duties and having a cup of tea with the village newbie.'

She craned her neck over my shoulder to see into the window of The Willows. 'And would this newbie be a boy neighbour or a girl neighbour?'

Oh God, here we go. I'd done well so far to avoid Tess's mission to set me up with someone. 'That would be Dom, a boy neighbour.'

She was on her tiptoes now, trying to catch a glimpse of him. 'Now we're talking. Come on, what's he like?' she asked, bouncing on the spot.

I shrugged. 'Dunno, barely spoken to the guy. Seems fine,

41

I guess.' I took my house keys and pulled her car door open, gesturing towards the driver's seat like an overzealous valet.

'What? I don't even get any "thank you for the keys" gossip?'

I nudged her towards the car. 'There's no gossip – woman goes into man's house to shelter for ten minutes and drinks half a cup of tea.'

She stuck her bottom lip out and flopped into the car. 'Maybe if you'd had any kind of man-related gossip in the last two years I wouldn't have to save all my intrigue for one go.'

Two years? Try five, more like. Not since Liam. Another area where the apple didn't fall far from the tree with Dad. Married to the job. Jesus, what a cliché. At least Dad had managed an actual marriage as well. 'There. Is. No. Gossip. Now go away, shoo.' I swatted at the air around her like she was a mosquito.

Her pout tugged into a smirk as she started to sing, 'Alice and Dom, sitting in a tree, K-I-S-S—'

The window muffled her voice as I slammed the door. 'P-I-S-S off!' I sang back.

She edged her electric-blue Nissan Micra out on to the lane and gave three short pips of her horn as Dom's outline appeared in the window opposite. His features were largely hidden by the backlighting from the kitchen's glow, the contour of his muscular arm visible as he waved it above his head. I hated waving. Always found it to be an odd gesture. If you waggled any other body part at someone it would be considered weird. I held my keys aloft and opted for a thumbs up in return. Great, much better, and not at all like a cheesy kids' TV presenter.

I thought about Tess's comments on my disappointing lack of dating gossip as I turned and unlocked the front door. Would it kill me to actually put myself out there again? Spend my down time doing something other than eating a whole tub of cream cheese on toast for dinner, sat in a onesie binge-watching *The Vicar of Dibley*? This could be Alice 2.0: being a more stable, well-rounded individual. Another step towards not becoming one of those lonely old coppers who drink themselves into an early grave. What did I have to lose? It had gone OK so far. Dom was well groomed, meant he'd probably washed recently. Plus ten points. Free physio on tap. Plus fifty points. Not terrible looking. Plus ten points. And let's not forget we'd gotten to the topic of human flaying in less than five minutes: the perfect meet-cute.

OK, neighbour, let's see what you've got.

7

A welcome streak of warmth swept across my calves as I hung my coat on the rack. Vince slumped on to my foot, looking at me in the way all cats do; like he was my landlord and I was late with the rent. 'It's all right, no need to get jealous – it was just a cup of tea. You're still my number one guy.' I crouched down and scratched his chin, which he allowed for exactly eight seconds before wandering into the kitchen to ungraciously gnaw at his claws.

I followed him and dumped my stuff on the kitchen island. The reclaimed oak worktop practically groaned with disappointment, letting out its daily cry to be adorned with fresh flowers or a decorative Oliver Bonas fruit bowl. 'Sorry, mate, all I have for you today is a backpack, phone, and maybe an empty pizza box later if you play your cards right.' I patted the grain in condolence. Myrtle Cottage's stylish renovation by the owner deserved a better tenant than me. It wasn't good old Myrtle's fault she was so cheap to rent because subsidence was inching her further and further down the hill.

The house phone screamed from the hallway and my heart drummed. Only one person ever called it. The only person I knew who still rang landlines except for con artists trying to scam pensioners out of their life savings. I held the handset for a few seconds before answering, 'Hi, Dad.'

'Hey kid, how did you know it was me?' he said, just like whenever he called.

'Told you, I'm psychic.'

A pause. Was he thinking about what happened with Jamie? About how psychic skills would have come in handy that night?

'Just wanted to, er, check in . . . see how the big day went.'

'Dad—' I pinched the bridge of my nose. 'I wasn't starting primary school, it was just another day at the office.'

'Yeah, but it's . . . well . . . you know, after having to take time off . . .'

The plastic creaked as I tightened my grip around the phone. 'I didn't *have* to take time off. I had leave to use and it seemed like a good time to take a break, reset, that's all.'

'No, right.' He cleared his throat. Dad didn't know the meaning of rest and recuperation, the force's poster boy for *Keep Calm and Carry On*. Breaking his wrist rugby-tackling a serial rapist who'd rampaged for two years? Back at work bright and early the next morning. No sleep for four days after keeping vigil at the bedside of a woman he'd found barely clinging to life who'd been held captive for months? Nothing a twenty-minute power nap and a shot of instant Nescafé couldn't fix. 'Good, well, glad to hear everything went OK,' he said.

'More than OK, actually – had an interesting conversation with the boss about Jim Barker retiring.' The back of

45

my neck prickled as if a tiny part of me still thought he might be pleased I'd have the opportunity to get a foot in the door at the MCU. That that's what he'd be calling about, to give me the heads up. The chances of Dad not already knowing Jim's plans were slim to none. They saw each other weekly. Never missed their Sunday morning round of golf, come rain or shine.

Dad paused before replying, like a delay on a video call with a faulty connection. 'Right, yeah, he did mention something about that last week. I would have said, but, erm, wasn't sure you still wanted to bother with all that.'

Fire engulfed my face. *All that*? Since when had my life ambition – not to mention Dad's own biggest achievement – been boiled down to *all that*? He, more than anyone, should understand why this was so important to me. Surely he got it? Every single major investigation in the county of Wessex ended up on the desks of HQ in Swindon. The big jobs. The ones where you got the chance to take the worst type of people off the streets. The most violent. Most depraved. It was where you played a part in making damn sure those people never got the chance to do what they did best ever again, make sure no one else would have to endure what they'd put their victims and families through. I pushed my fingers through my hair, a light grease clagging on the tips. 'Yeah, well, not exactly inundated with big jobs out here, are we? Why wouldn't I still want to apply?'

A deep exhale rattled down the line. 'It's just, you know, with what happened the other week – it's a lot, isn't it? You don't want to rush into anything.'

I coughed away the tremor in my voice. 'I told you, I'm fine.'

'Well, OK, kid, but have a proper think about it, yeah? You know you can do just as much good in smaller places – more so, even. There's more to policing than gun fights and organised crime, you know. More ways to make up for . . . well . . . you know what I mean.'

My stomach dropped. Make up for what? Jamie? Or Noah? Dad wasn't exactly the king of displaying affection, and I knew he'd rather I'd picked anything else as a career, but he'd still managed to be there for me, in his own way. 'I know what I want, Dad.' I chewed furiously at a hangnail. 'Actually, sorry, my work phone's going,' I lied, 'gotta go.'

'OK kid, speak later.'

'Bye.' I slammed the phone down, my nostrils flaring as I tried to control my breathing. The best part of twenty years, it had taken. To get Dad's trust in me back after what happened to Noah. And now it seemed it was gone again in an instant.

8

Roy rued the day he'd decided not to bother getting his car radio fixed. There hadn't been so much as a peep spoken between him and Alice on the drive out east from the centre of the village, winding through the patchwork farmland towards Camilla Harton-Gray's rural abode. It was a relatively short journey, but long enough to make it awkward. Nothing a bit of Fleetwood Mac wouldn't have sorted out. 'You all right over there?' he said, flicking his eyes to the passenger side before returning his gaze to the conveyor belt of tarmac zipping beneath the grubby bonnet.

'Yep. Fine.' The word bullets fired from her mouth with two quick pulls of a trigger.

Sounds like it, he thought.

He gave it another go. 'I dunno if Tess mentioned before we left, but there's nothing of note on any systems about Camilla, or the address. The family who were renting it when she was living in London have moved back to France. No reports of anything for the time they lived there, and nothing from before – well, except for the crash, and looks like Camilla moved away pretty sharpish after that.'

'No, I didn't get the chance to speak to Tess – she was

in with Jane when I came in,' Alice replied, her voice softer now, as if talk of work distracted her from whatever she was worrying about. 'D'you remember much about them, Camilla's family?'

'Not really,' Roy said. 'You'd see them around the village from time to time. The brother trained at the rugby club for a bit, I think, but apart from that, they kept to themselves, from what I remember. Didn't really get involved in any community stuff – not that I did either, to be fair, that was more Karen's bag.'

He tensed, hoping the slip of his wife's name out his stupid gob didn't prompt any follow-up questions. Making up stories on the hoof had never been his forte, and he had no plans to rehash the breakdown of his marriage any time in the next half-century. Talking about it wasn't going to change anything. He'd avoided the question with the therapy woman on that pointless app; he certainly wasn't having the conversation with Alice. She nodded and went back to looking out the side window.

Roy took one hand off the steering wheel and scratched his cheek. He didn't want to rile her up again, but he couldn't *not* mention it. He'd already been putting it off all morning. 'I, er, didn't get a chance to say earlier,' he said, 'but that annoying hospital liaison woman called before you came in – they've let that Jamie kid go home now.'

'Oh, really? Bit soon, isn't it?' she replied.

'They're calling him a medical marvel or something – thought he'd be in there for months, didn't think he'd be

SAM FRANCES

able to walk at all, but, well, he's hardly sprinting about the place, but they said he's doing well.'

Roy could see her looking down out the corner of his eye, fingers fiddling with a frayed thread on the inside seam of her trousers. 'You're not still fretting over that, are you?' he asked.

'Fretting?' she said, her eyes drilling into the side of his head. 'He's not an unpaid parking ticket!'

'All right, all right. I'm just saying, can't win 'em all, can you?'

Alice went quiet again and he didn't object. She was really going to have to start getting over this. He wanted to feel sorry for her, but she didn't make it easy. He'd seen it so many times before with these keen beans, all starting out down the same road, bright-eyed and bushy-tailed, thinking they can save the world. Even Roy had been the same back in the day, he'd admit that. He could still remember the first job he'd cocked up. There'd been others since then, but none with quite the same sting in the tail as that one in particular. He wiped his nose with his knuckle and ignored the heat simmering behind his eyes. No use crying over old spilt milk, he reminded himself.

Alice should think herself lucky. The thing with Jamie hadn't even been a cock-up. Not that there was any point trying to tell her. She'd done all the right things. Everyone said so in the debrief. Build rapport. Don't interrupt. Listen to what they've got to say. Open up to them; all textbook negotiation skills for dealing with a suicidal person. Not that Roy had done the course, but he'd seen it in a film. She

50

thought she had him, thought she'd talked the kid down. Roy thought so too. He'd listened to every word over the radio. All seventeen minutes of it, craning his neck up, the boy's mop of blond hair visible as he stood on the ledge of the church roof above the courtyard. Roy remembered he'd just started to unclench his shoulders, a wave of relief making its way through him. Until the scream. The kid's mother bursting from his arms. A sudden surge of strength, overpowering him like a lioness protecting her young from a pack of hyenas when Jamie jumped.

Roy side-eyed Alice as the black gates he was looking out for, set in the long perimeter wall, came into view. He wasn't sure what else Alice thought she could have done, short of having superpowers that would let her reach out and catch the lad. And who prepares for that anyway? Who wants to live in a world where you have to know what to say to a twelve-year-old who wants to throw themselves off a building?

She'd done everything right, except let the bleeding thing go and move on. He clicked on the indicator and pulled up outside the entrance to Bertram Manor.

9

I bounced off the headrest as the car jerked to a halt outside the manor. The hair bobble doing a half-arsed job of holding my hair out of my face dug into the back of my skull, so I re-tied it as Roy wound down his window, leant towards the wrought-iron railing and prodded the button on the intercom.

The speaker crackled to life, a woman's voice emanating from it. 'Hello?'

'Morning, Detective Constable Roy Briar from Fortbridge Police Station – is that Mrs Harton-Gray?'

A beat passed. '*Miss* Harton-Gray, yes, speaking.'

Roy looked at me and rolled his eyes at the correction. 'My apologies, *Miss* Harton-Gray,' he said, mimicking her emphasis. 'I'm here with my colleague, Detective Sergeant Alice Washington – we spoke on the phone, about the photographs. Can we come in?'

The gates jolted, slowly parting to reveal a sea of ivory-coloured pebbles. We rolled on to the driveway. It bent sharply to the left and our mouths dropped open as the house came into view.

'Blimey,' Roy said, leaning closer to the windscreen.

Two second-floor stone balconies jutted out from the wall of Georgian sash windows like a pair of eyes. A large matt black front door was framed by white stone columns, each one flanked by precisely trimmed evergreens. Only one thing threw off the symmetry: a small security camera fixed to the inside of one of the pillars. It swivelled to face us, scanning as we pulled up alongside the beautifully landscaped front lawn.

'There's probably a bleedin' dress code to get in there,' Roy said. 'We're in the wrong job—'

Excellent. One of Roy's *woe is me* rants. Just what I needed. I rolled my neck and prayed it would be a short one.

'—slogged me guts out for the best part of thirty years, night shifts, locking up scumbags, and can still hardly afford a week's jolly in soddin' Benidorm. How the other half live, eh!'

I took another look at the house as he cranked the handbrake. He had a point. I'd even sniffed a house like this before, let alone lived in one. The three-bed terraced house in Swindon I grew up in would fit into the footprint of this place five times over. 'Yep. It's pretty fancy pants, but dial it down, yeah? How much money this woman does or doesn't have isn't any business of ours.'

Roy opened his mouth then snapped it shut before unclipping his seat belt.

'Problem?' I asked.

'No problems here, *Sarge*.'

I got out into the freezing air and followed Roy to the

front door. My eyes were drawn to the sprawling orchard which began on the left side of the manor and went back further than I could see. It must be quite something in full bloom, when rows and rows of trees would be adorned with pink-tinged white apple blossom before it fell and carpeted the grass. It wasn't as picturesque as that now, of course, the structures sheathed in bare bark and placed at perfectly spaced intervals looking more like some sort of alien invasion laser beamed down from the sky, playing musical statues to lull mankind into a false sense of security before beginning their attack.

To call Camilla Harton-Gray intimidating was an understatement. Not physically – I was pretty sure I could take her – but aesthetically. She was flawless. Porcelain skin. A rare class oozing from her like a Jessica Rabbit-esque librarian. The hems of billowing palazzo pants grazed her ankles as she led us through the grand hallway, slingback kitten heels tapping the polished concrete. How she was walking in those shoes without faceplanting on to the floor I didn't know, swathes of material dangling about willy-nilly.

I pawed at the hair that had re-escaped my bobble as we followed. Tried to get that weird bit of fringe that curled out to stay down. Played with the belt on my trousers as if it would magically transform the unflattering waistline. But I still looked like crap in comparison by the time we reached the kitchen.

'What can I get you? Tea? Coffee?' she said, her voice deep and rich like an expensive dark chocolate.

'Coffee, please,' Roy and I said in unison.

There was some brief small talk before we got down to business.

'So,' Roy said, 'you mentioned in your report that the photos were emailed to you Sunday night. Can you tell us what happened?' He pulled a wrinkled notebook from his inner jacket pocket, the new electronic versions officers at HQ had been given months ago still waiting to be rolled out to us peasants in the far-flung corners of the county.

She tipped fresh coffee beans into the machine. 'I was up late, writing. I'm normally up until about three-ish, it was just as I was packing up.'

I couldn't get over how someone who claimed to be basically nocturnal could possibly look this glowing and refreshed by noon. She finished making the drinks and told us about the email from *bookfiend05@flymail.com*.

'Right, right,' Roy said as he scribbled, 'and this is the first contact you've had?'

Camilla placed the cups in front of us and leant against the kitchen island. 'From *that* account, yes, I think so.'

He stopped writing and looked up. 'Have there been photos from other addresses?'

'No, no,' she said, shaking her head, 'but, well, I get weird messages all the time. Comes with the territory.'

'And have you reported these to the police too?' Roy said.

Camilla laughed. 'I'm a woman in the public eye. If I reported every creepy message I got on the internet I'd spend my life in a police station.' She looked to me knowingly and I nodded in sisterly solidarity before she turned back to Roy. 'But the pictures . . .' Her eyes dropped to the floor and flicked back again so quickly I almost missed it. 'Well . . . that's new.'

'Probably still worth us having a gander at those other messages,' Roy said.

Camilla scoffed again, 'Sorry, I don't mean to be flippant, but you could spend the next year wading through the crap that gets sent to my social media accounts. I think Chrissy deletes it all, the weird stuff, anyway.'

'And Chrissy is . . .?' I asked as Roy carried on writing.

'Chrissy Marchant, my assistant. She isn't here today, she's been away all weekend.'

Roy took Chrissy's contact details and worked through the statement. I couldn't help but watch as she spoke. The way her long auburn hair lay perfectly wherever it happened to fall on her loose-fitting black jumper as her hands moved like a conductor, rising and falling in perfect alignment with the cadence of her voice.

'I know it's probably nothing,' Camilla said, 'but if I'm honest, it is a little scary, someone wanting me to *know* they're watching.' She shuddered.

I thought back to what I'd noticed on the way in. 'Is that why you had the security camera fitted?' I asked. 'Has something like this worried you before?'

'That? Oh no, no, that was Myles's idea, a condition of me moving back here. I didn't even want it. Hardly in keeping with the aesthetic, is it? And not like it's even any use. I've already checked it, there's nothing out of the ordinary on there.'

'And Myles is . . .?' I asked.

She tucked her hair behind her ears. 'Sorry, didn't I say? Myles Carrington, he's my boyfriend – well, partner – he prefers that. Thinks saying we're *boyfriend and girlfriend* sounds a bit childish when we're only a few years shy of forty. He lives in London. He's an actor so it's more convenient for him being there.' She carried on talking as Roy wrote down the details. 'Ever since I decided to move back here he's been worrying about me being on my own. I told him he was being silly – I lived alone in London, what's the difference? And anyway, Ruby and Bo are better protectors than any CCTV camera ever will be.' Roy's pen hung in the air, poised to write more witness contact information. 'The dogs,' she said. 'They're out back.'

I'd completely forgotten about them. A pristine home and neat clothing with those massive things from the photographs bounding about? Vince was a fraction of their size and I didn't have one single T-shirt free of at least three claw holes from where he'd wriggled out of forced hug time. It was official, she's a wizard.

'Right,' Roy said, 'it's probably worth us looking through that CCTV anyway, just in case.'

'Of course,' she nodded.

'We'll sort that before we go. OK, where were we? Right, so you've moved back here recently then?' he asked.

'Yes, only about a month ago.'

'And do you mind if I ask why?' Roy said.

'No, no, not at all. Nothing exciting. The family who've been renting it for the last few years were moving out and, well, one can only live in London for so long before the novelty wears off.'

I thought of asking about the possibility of someone copying the plot of her book, but decided against it for now. Eddie's theory was little more than a stab in the dark and I didn't want to scare her. I leant forward and rested my elbows on my knees, trying to soften my posture. 'Have there been any problems since you've been back? Any out-of-the-blue contacts from old friends? Partners? Most people who are stalked know the person targeting them, even if it's just a loose acquaintance.'

Camilla blew a puff of air through her lips. 'No, nothing. I haven't really spoken to anyone from the village. We were quite a private family before, well . . . I presume you know what happened, everyone always seems to.'

I nodded, trying to shake loose the thoughts of my own family trickling in. 'Yes, I did hear about that. So sorry for your loss,' I said, wincing as the words fell from my mouth. I hated that phrase. *Your loss.* Like you'd misplaced a car key. So inconsequential. Especially in this case. Camilla's family weren't lost. They were taken. By an idiot driver who couldn't follow the basic rules of the road by staying on their side of it. *A tragic accident*, was how the paper had described it, according to Eddie's dramatic retelling. Same as Noah. Just as incorrect. 'Accident' implied no one was to blame. The skin covering my chest tightened like it was a size too small for my body.

Not now, you're at work! Deal with your shit in your own time.

Camilla shrugged. 'Thank you. It's been a long time, so . . .'

Roy finished up as I took in subtle deep breaths, trying to calm myself with each exhale. 'OK, Camilla,' he said, slapping his notebook closed, 'I think that's everything. If we need anything else, we'll let you know. In the meantime, call us straight away if you get any more emails or notice anything unusual, all right?'

'Of course,' she said. 'Myles is picking me up later to take me back to London with him for a few days. I'll have my mobile with me if you need any more information or have any updates or, well, anything.'

Roy handed Camilla a leaflet containing instructions on how to upload her CCTV footage to the new digital evidence portal before we followed her to the front door. Her shoes clicked across the surface as they'd done on the way in, but the beat was different. Slower. Duller. Her gait less purposeful. She was still smiling as she turned to face us, but it wasn't the same smile she'd worn when we arrived, as if talking to us about things had made them all the more real.

She reached for the doorknob. 'Thanks so much for taking the time to come out here, I really appreciate it. Hope it hasn't wasted too much of your time.'

A pang of pity tugged at me. For Camilla, and for every other woman in these situations who felt obliged to sing along to the familiar tune, different variations on the same old concerns. A verse of *I'm sure I'm just being silly* . . . followed by the choruses of *it's probably nothing, but* . . . just to avoid coming off as overreacting. 'You haven't wasted anyone's time, that's what we're here for,' I said. 'Anytime you don't feel safe, please call us.'

She breathed out, the soft smile returning to her face. 'Thank you. It's a relief knowing there's someone watching out for me.'

10

You look different through a camera, he thought, as he analysed each facial feature in turn. How they moved when she spoke. How they settled when she was silent. They were less defined than in person, giving her skin a grainy texture. Though the quality of the imagery had much improved since the first time he'd seen it used in Father's study. Mother, pixelated but recognisable as she flattened out a striped sheet on their double bed, leaning over and folding hospital corners one by one.

He hadn't understood why Father bought the cameras at the time. He'd done such a good job of helping keep track of his mother's day, taking notes on everything she'd done so Father would know how much of a treat she deserved when he got home, just like he'd asked. Every night they'd sit in his study. Father would lift him on to his lap, stroke his hair and listen intently like his words were all that mattered as he read aloud the day's activity log. 'The milkman came just after you left at 8:02 a.m. "Andrew", Mother called him. They spoke about the weather, Monday's delivery and his wife's new haircut. 8:09 a.m. – she took the milk to the kitchen and washed the breakfast bowls . . .

12:52 p.m. – Nina from next door dropped off a basket of cookies . . . 4:23 p.m. – Mother cleaned the, bathroom, then washed her hands and had some of Nina's cookies, and—'

Father had cut across him, his voice sharp as razor wire. 'How many cookies?'

His heart beat just as fast now recalling the memory as it had that night. How he'd winced at the increased pressure from his father's hand on his head that'd made it feel more like his hair was being pulled out at the roots than stroked. The sensation of his stomach, feeling like it was going to drop out from between his legs when it dawned on him he didn't know the answer. 'I . . . I don't know how many,' he'd replied. Father's body had tensed against him. He'd tensed too. Squeezed every single muscle as tight as he could, like the act would stop time. So he could stay there on that lap. Remain tucked into the cradle of his father's arm that fit so snugly it was like it had been crafted just for him.

Father had been silent for a few seconds before relaxing again. 'That's all right, we can ask her later, can't we? Carry on.'

And he had asked later, right as Mother was plating up the tiramisu just like his father had told him to, at the end of the dinner party his parents had thrown for some of Father's work colleagues.

He'd kicked his feet under the table and fidgeted with his napkin, waiting for Father's nod. The signal they'd agreed on. But when he gave it, the words he'd practised got stuck, blocked by the churning in the pit of his belly telling him it was wrong to say them. That he shouldn't ask the question his father had told him to. But then Father nodded a second time, tension visible in his thick neck muscles, and the question spewed out. 'How ... how many cookies d-did you have earlier?'

His mother's eyes had flicked from his to Father's. 'Only a couple.'

Heat had crawled up his neck and down his spine at the audible tremble in Mother's voice. His instinct had been to reach out and hold on to her index finger, wrap his small fist around it in the way she said she liked because it reminded her of the first time he did it as a baby, but instead he'd jumped as Father interjected.

'Cookies *and* cake, love?' his father had said. 'You should be careful. This lot'll tell you we don't make enough money for me to buy you a whole new wardrobe when you can't fit into the one you've got any more.'

The table had erupted in laughter and the response soothed him like a cooling balm. Because what he'd said must have been all right if everyone was laughing. Even Mother had smiled eventually as she put a plate of dessert on everyone's place setting but her own.

It had been a week later the cameras were installed and his reports became surplus to requirements.

'If you'd paid proper attention like I asked, then I wouldn't have to fork out for all this, now would I?' Father had yelled the next time he'd tried to climb on to his lap to deliver the nightly report.

The memory of Father's dismissal scorched his face as he made fists, pressing his knuckles into the table. He could still remember the feeling of his father shoving him away, the wind knocked from his lungs as he fell off Father's lap and landed flat on his back on to the hard wooden floor. He'd been angry at the time, of course. Angry at Father, but also at himself. If he'd done a proper job like he was supposed to, caught every detail, then maybe his father wouldn't have bought the cameras in the first place. But he understood now, why Father wanted them. Understood the benefits of being able to look at her whenever he wanted. Of knowing what she was doing at any given moment. Her, oblivious. Going about her days like anything she did mattered. And this way, he didn't have to miss a moment.

11

Roy waited for the number four bus to pass so he could pull away from the manor gates. He glanced at Alice. 'Well, I think we already know what the tech lot are gonna say about *bookfiend05*.' The double-decker trundled by and he slammed his foot on the accelerator, the car's wheels churning as they clung to the loose stones for traction.

'What d'you— ow!' Alice yelped as her head knocked the side of the car as he swung the vehicle on to the road.

Uh oh, I'll pay for that later, no doubt.

'Bookfiend05?' he said. '2005? These plonkers always put their date of birth in their emails, usernames, whatever you call them, *Aaron woz 'ere '98.* Bleedin' morons. You see it all the time with graffiti jobs. Can't help themselves. Sounds like we're on the hunt for a teenage lad with a crush and a fancy new camera, if you ask me. Probably nothing to worry about.'

'Oh yeah, no, you're right, because a disgruntled sixteen-year-old boy with an obsession never did anyone any harm,' Alice said.

Abort! Abort! Roy thought. He'd done the whole toxic masculinity dance with her too many times to count. He didn't deny women had put up with some shit over the years, but it almost seemed like being a bloke was the worst thing someone could be these days. He chewed his lip before the temptation to poke the bear got the better of him. 'Teenage girls can be just as bad. Trust me, I know. My Laurie was a nightmare once she hit thirteen. Obsessed with that little turnip from Take That when they come back on the scene, Martin, Mike, whatever his name was. Posters all over the place with lipstick kisses, T-shirts with his face on. Had to pry the things off her to get them in the bleedin' wash. I tell you, she'd have probably stalked him if she knew where to find him, all those hormones flying around.'

Alice snorted. 'You wanna see some hormones on display, go down to any city centre at closing time and you'll see a fuckload of *hormonal* men fighting each other over who gets the last serving of cheesy chips. Oh no, wait, sorry, I forgot testosterone doesn't count as a hormone, does it? It's just the girly ones, the ones that make people all *emotional* that are the problem.'

Touché, he thought.

Roy steered the car around a hedge-lined bend as they reached the bottom of Apple View Lane, trying and failing to think of a comeback before turning on to the main road that took them back into the centre of the village. He'd forgotten the point he was trying to make anyway, if there even was one in the first place. 'All right, what's your assessment, then?'

Alice counted on her fingers, 'One, rejected ex, wants

to reconcile, or go down in "If I can't have you no one can" flames. Two, resentful stalker, someone with a grudge, wants revenge. Those two are the most likely, statistically speaking. Mind, we do have to factor in that Camilla's a celebrity. Which means three,' she said, bending her middle finger so far back Roy worried it might snap off, 'we might be contending with some nutjob who thinks they're in a relationship with her – intimacy-seeking stalker, thinks she's personally communicating with them through her books or something. Either way, I don't think we should hold our breath that anonymous emails is as far as this is gonna go.'

This younger lot loved a good statistic. Pie charts this, percentages that. Roy wondered what happened to good old gut feel. Never did him any harm. Well, most of the time anyway. He shifted in his seat, squirming away from the memory of the job where his gut could not have failed him more if it tried.

He pulled into a free space in the small car park behind the police station.

'You can have the pleasure of doing the Hi-Tech submission form,' Alice said as she got out and slammed the door. Roy groaned. He didn't even want to think about the hours he'd wasted filling in digital paperwork, each tab on the case management system less intuitive than the last. Trying to figure out the new-fangled computer processes they'd brought in over the last few years made his head ache more than the time he'd tried to apply for a variable rate mortgage with only a chat bot for help. They both knew it would be a waste of time. Even Roy's eighty-one-year-old mother could figure out how to hide the origin of an email address using a virtual private network. Unless they were dealing with the laziest or stupidest stalker in history, they'd get nothing of use.

He followed Alice into the station and up the stairs.

'What time did Camilla say she usually walks the dogs again?' she asked over her shoulder.

Roy almost tripped on the top step as he pulled his pocket notebook out. 'Ermmm.' He held the consonant as long as it took him to flip through the pages. 'Ah, here it is – said she usually walks them around the same time, well, her or Chrissy depending on what she's got on, between about three and four.'

Alice looked at her watch, 'Well, would you look at that – perfect timing. Why don't you get yourself down to Oakham Reservoir and see if you can canvass us some witness statements, see if anyone saw a suspicious-looking person creeping around with a camera over the last few days. Dog walkers tend to keep to schedules, don't they, so you never know.'

He wanted to protest, to go get himself a nice hot cup of coffee instead of freezing his bollocks off trudging around the bleeding reservoir for hours, but she was right. Dog owners were generally creatures of habit. He always saw the same people at the same times of day when he took his pup for a run around Kestrel Park. 'All right, all right. At least let me get some gloves first.'

Alice pushed open the door to the CID office, Eddie emerging from it before they had a chance to walk in.

'Afternoon, Sarge, Royston. What's going on out here, then, party on the landing?' His question was followed by what Roy could only describe as a 'raise the roof' gesture.

The plan to punish Eddie for calling him Royston *again* despite the fact he'd told him it wasn't his name about twenty times hit him in an instant. 'Oh, have I got a party for you, young man,' Roy said, rubbing his palms together. 'Get your coat, you've pulled.'

Eddie's hands stopped mid-air. 'W-what d'you mean?'

Roy nudged him back into the office. 'Come on, treating you to an afternoon out. I'm going down the reservoir to see if anyone saw Camilla or the creepy bastard following her, and you get the pleasure of coming with me. So unless you want to freeze to death I suggest you get your coat. Get the gloves out my top desk drawer whilst you're at it an' all.' It wasn't often Roy got to be the one bossing people about. He kind of liked it.

Eddie looked at Alice, clearly hoping she might rescue him, but she left him high and dry.

'Erm, OK, gimme a second,' he said as he turned around.

Alice looked at Roy, her eyebrows raised.

'What?' he said.

She folded her arms across her chest. 'Bold move, isn't it? Voluntary one-on-one time with Eddie?'

Roy shrugged. 'Decent amount of ground to cover, better with two sets of feet. He can do a lap, and I can see if that coffee pop-up place they usually have in the car park's open, might have some CCTV.' *And have a nice hot cup*

69

of coffee when I'm there, win–win, he thought as he tried to keep a straight face.

Alice squinted. She probably knew exactly what his game was, but she got something out of it too, an Eddie-free afternoon. He was a good kid really, but Christ, he was annoying.

'Fine,' she said, 'I'll still be here when you're done, so let me know how you get on. And *don't* forget to do that submissions form when you get back.'

Roy nodded curtly, trying to ignore her determination to piss on his chips in some way, shape or form today.

Eddie returned bundled up like the Michelin Man holding a pair of black gloves. Roy stepped to one side and pointed down the stairs. 'Lead the way, Edwina, I'm right behind you.'

12

The CID office was somewhat peaceful as I sat alone for the next hour, the muted bleeps and static of radios drifting down the corridor from the uniform office acting as white noise. I should probably thank Roy for getting both himself and Eddie out of my hair for a bit, even though I knew it'd been more for his benefit than mine. Get Eddie to do the graft while he had an extended coffee break. As long as the enquiries got done, and done properly, I wasn't fussed who did them.

I hit send on this month's detection rate performance update as Tess appeared in the doorway.

'Yo,' I said. She walked past and headed to her desk, saluting with one hand and carrying a notepad and pen in the other. 'Where've you been hiding?'

She slapped the pad down and rummaged in her top drawer. 'I've had the pleasure of Jane's company all afternoon. Sat next to her on a Teams call with HQ for two bloody hours on the off chance someone asked a question she didn't know the answer to about the metal theft analysis. An excellent use of my time. Aha!' She pulled something out and held it towards me.

I got up and walked to her desk. 'What's that?'

She shook her hand, metal clinking against metal. 'Your house keys, dummy. You'd left them on the filing cabinet and Morag was about to tidy them away somewhere you'd never find them again so I rescued them.' I stuck my hand out just in time to catch them in my palm as she let go of the bottle opener keyring. 'You're weeelcome,' she sang.

How could I be so bloody careless? Everyone knew the golden rule to not get caught out by Morag the cleaner's intensive office sanitation system; desks were out of bounds, but everything else was fair game. We'd learned that lesson the hard way when Roy left a carrier bag full of crime scene exhibits by the door ready to take to court and Morag put them out with the recycling. 'Thanks, I owe you at least twelve drinks.'

Tess looked at her watch. 'In that case, it's gone five. Pub?'

I walked back to my desk and sat down, wiggling the mouse to revive my screen. 'Cops can't just swan off at five, part-timer, I'm on till seven today.'

She rolled her eyes. 'OK, quarter past seven then?'

I pulled the shoulder of my jumper up to my face and sniffed it. 'Can we say eight? I need a shower first. I've been in Roy's car today and now I smell like beef.'

'OK, but don't be late,' Tess said. 'You know that new barman fancies me and if I'm sat there on my own he'll come and talk to me again like he did last time.'

'I'll bring my stinky clothing back in a carrier bag, just in case we need to ward him off.'

She wagged her finger at me. 'See, this, this is why we're friends.'

I scrolled through my heaving inbox as Tess swung her coat across her shoulders, the sleeping bag-style black puffer jacket padding out her athletic frame.

'Right, see you later then.' She did her zip up from knee to chin before stopping by my desk on her way to the door, hand held out towards me, fingers slapping open and closed against her palm. 'Almost forgot, gimme.'

'Give you what?'

'Your spare keys. The way you're going at the minute I'd give it a week, max, until you lock yourself out again and need me to rescue you.'

I had no intention of locking myself out again, but you never knew when Morag might go rogue and break the 'no desk tidying' embargo. I dug them out of my coat pocket and gave them to her. She put them into her handbag and turned to leave just as a thought dawned on me. 'Oh wait, did you email me the research pack on the Harton-Gray case?'

'No, sorry, it's still in my queue. Jane asked me to bump up research for Bret's theft jobs, looking like it might be linked to some OCG working out of Swindon. Big money in stolen farming equipment, apparently.'

The urge to protest swept over my face like prickly heat, but I couldn't think of anything to say that didn't make me sound like a petulant child. *You're my best fwiend. You should do my case first, wah wah wah.* I didn't have a leg to stand on. Stalking was taken way more seriously

73

than when I joined, but large scale organised crime groups would still trump most jobs in the priority queue, outside of rape and murder.

I leant back in my chair and crossed my arms high on my chest, half annoyed at Tess, half annoyed at myself. Because I'd be lying if I said the irritation was only about stifling my ability to make sure I did a good job of keeping Camilla safe. There was also the little alarm that chimed in my head as soon as Tess mentioned 'Bret' and 'OCG' in the same sentence. I knew only too well that if he did a decent job, maybe even took down some known names, local coordinators, it would bump him straight to the top of the pile for the MCU job, if he wasn't there already. I didn't know much about his transfer from his previous force given he was about as talkative as Charlie Chaplin, but one thing I did know was he'd come with a glowing reference. I presumed the glittering personality they referred to must have been misplaced in the move, but he had commendations for things like saving puppies from rivers and God knows what other acts of heroism coming out of his arse. Jane practically salivated when she introduced him to the rest of the team. *Shit*. 'Right, well, I need it first thing, yeah? This is important too, you know.'

Tess tucked her chin into her neck and raised her eyebrows. 'I know you're having a bit of a shit time right now, and Bret gets your back up, so I'll let that slide. But *don't* snap at me. I'll get it done as soon as I can. Now, I'll see you at eight o'clock on the dot, OK?'

The door from the stairwell banged open and Roy trudged through it, hands cupping his face as he blew into them.

'Fine. Eight o'clock,' I replied.

'What's happening at eight o'clock?' Roy asked, shrugging off his worn grey overcoat.

'Going for a drink at The Bull,' Tess said. 'See you later.' *You're welcome*, she mouthed at me from behind Roy's head before walking out the door, knowing full well I'd now have the awkward task of avoiding letting him invite himself along.

Roy's eyes burned into the side of my face as I stared at my computer screen.

'No, no, don't mind me,' he said after what felt like a week's worth of silence. 'I'd love to come, but unfortunately for you two, I'm washing my hair tonight.'

'Our loss. Did you forget something?' I asked, keen to change the subject.

He did a one-eighty in both directions as if something in his line of sight would give him a clue as to what I was talking about. 'What?'

'Eddie,' I said, nodding towards the empty chair where he usually parked himself.

'Oh, no, dropped him off home on the way back,' Roy said as he hung his coat up and sat down. 'Got no extra insulation on him, that one, he's frozen up solid like a bleedin' ice pop.'

'Right. Any luck at the reservoir?'

Roy pushed his lips together and shook his head. 'No joy. Spoke to a few people; couple remember seeing Camilla with the dogs, but no one following her. And there's so many people out there taking photos I doubt anyone would stick out anyway. Even in this weather, there's people down there now, posing. Popular spot with tourists for Instagram, Eddie reckons, especially down by the bridge, which is right next to where Camilla's picture was taken. Says he's had loads of "likes" on some of the ones he's shot down there.'

'Well, isn't Eddie full of surprises? First a literary expert, now the next Annie Leibovitz – where will his talents end? Anything with the coffee pop-up CCTV?'

Roy sat back and crossed one leg over the other, a pair of holey socks on display as the action made his trousers ride up his shins. 'Nah, internal facing camera only in case someone breaks in, nothing external. On the plus side, the place does a mean cappuccino.'

Brilliant.

I rubbed my fingers back and forth along my eyebrows. First proper day of investigation: Stalker 1, Alice 0.

13

I pulled on to my driveway, a rumbling in the car persisting after I'd turned off the ignition. I rubbed my stomach. Had I eaten since breakfast? Did I even *have* breakfast? Did a spoonful of Nutella count as breakfast? So much for Alice 2.0; I couldn't even feed myself properly.

Over the course of finishing my work day, stuck listening to endless effing and jeffing from Roy as he wrangled digital paperwork, I'd realised I wasn't in the mood for fending off creepy barmen. But if it'd get me back in Tess's good books after my mini strop, then it was definitely worth doing. Tess was like the weather. She could lift the darkest of moods, her sunny disposition spreading like wildfire. But when a storm rolled in, everyone knew well enough to run for cover.

Speaking of storms, I thought, looking up as I got out of the car, trying to figure out why my surroundings felt darker than usual. I expected to see last night's thick cloud back with a vengeance and ready to soak me. But the sky was clear. Nothing but a navy blanket dotted with winking stars. I realised what was different as movement caught my eye from the doorstep. What should have been a little ginger furball basking in the spotlight shining down on him from the motion sensor light above the door was nothing but a shadowy little blob, given away by the jangling of the bell on his collar as he scratched himself.

'Evening, Vincent,' I said, walking towards him. 'What's happened here, then?' I peered up at the light before waving my hand back and forth in front of the sensor. Nothing. Excellent. Another thing in my life that needed fixing.

I fumbled with the keys in darkness as I heard my name called from across the road. Dom was at the edge of my driveway by the time I turned around.

'Hey,' he said, hands coming to rest on his narrow hips.

I remembered the funky smell of my clothes, clutching my bag to my chest in the hope it might act as an odour barrier if he came any closer. 'Hi.'

'Forgotten your keys again?'

'No, no need for the rescue party today, kind sir,' I said, as if I'd suddenly turned into a court jester performing for the knights of the round table. Why was I like this? 'I just can't seem to get the damn things in the lock; my light's broken.'

He walked over. 'Really?'

Oh bollocks, he was going to smell the beef suit.

'That's weird,' he said as he reached me, looking up at the light and waving at it just like I'd done seconds earlier. 'Mine's gone too. It was fine last night, but when I came home today it was out. Just assumed the bulb must have gone or something, but probably not if yours is dead too.'

'Are the rest of your electrics OK?' I asked.

'Yeah, fine, doesn't seem to be a power outage or anything.'

I thought about Bret's investigation. It wasn't out of the question that whatever group he was looking at were also targeting residential properties, taking out anything that might alert occupants to them skulking around at night. 'Have you touched the light fixture?'

Dom shook his head. 'No, why?'

'There's been a spate of thefts in the area, could be linked – probably worth checking them for fingerprints. If you give me your number I'll get our SOCO, sorry, Scenes of Crime Officers to arrange a convenient time to come out.'

'Oh, OK, yeah, of course.' He told me his full name – Dominic Webb – and number, and I typed it into my phone. 'I must say, that's the most innovative way anyone has ever come up with to ask for my phone number.' He smiled slightly off to one side so that only his right cheek dimpled.

A flush of heat fanned across my face. I let my hair fall forward with a slight tilt of the head, hoping he wouldn't notice. 'I can just leave it if you want, let them come back and steal all your earthly possessions if you'd prefer?'

He held his hands up in apology. 'No, no, not at all, please, do your thing. Not that I have any earthly possessions worth stealing. Except my physio table, it's got a heat pad and everything.'

I was about to fall into a daydream about Dom massaging my shoulders on a warm physio bed when my phone rang in my hand, Tess's name shining out from the screen.

'Sorry, I have to take this. They'll call you in the next couple of days, OK? In the meantime, make sure you keep everything locked up and let me know if you see anything suspicious.'

'Course, have a nice evening,' he said as he turned and walked back to The Willows.

I couldn't help but watch him leave for a few seconds before answering the phone. 'I'm coming!' I barked at Tess before she had a chance to speak.

'Hurry up, I've ignored six of Sleazy Steve's lechy smile drive-bys so far!'

'You do realise you're slowing me down with this very call, don't you?'

'Get here. Soon!'

Dust spurted from a tear in the side of the maroon bench pad as I plonked myself opposite Tess in the booth. She was already halfway through a gin and tonic, my standard glass of red wine waiting for me.

'Jesus Christ,' she said, clasping a hand to her chest. Clearly the hum of chatter and clinking glasses had masked the sound of my approach.

The creepy barman lingered in the distance over Tess's shoulder as I picked up my drink and swirled the dark liquid, peaty grape tones wafting up my nose. 'Managed to keep old googly eyes at bay, then, did we?'

'Only just,' Tess said. 'I've made three imaginary phone calls so far to make myself look too busy to talk to him every time he finds an excuse to walk past.'

I looked over her shoulder again to see him skulk off behind the bar.

'Anyway,' she continued, 'enough Sleazy Steve. You change out of your grumpy pants when you went home?'

'Yeah, sorry about that, I just don't want any more balls-ups on my watch. I need to be all over this, but I know you're busy. And might be about to get busier actually.' I told her about the lights and my encounter with Dom.

'At least you got his number.'

'For official police purposes only, thank you very much.'

'Still, tonight, we celebrate!' she said, holding up her glass.

'Celebrate what, exactly?'

'Your future husband.'

'Oh, do shut up, please.' I touched my cheek instinctively, testing the temperature, begging my skin not to give me away. Tess would sense even the tiniest hint of a crush (which I absolutely did not have), like a shark smelling a droplet of blood in gallons of sea water. I couldn't be arsed to listen to her suggestions for potential wedding venues and children's middle names. 'How about we celebrate the joys of food instead? I'm starving,' I said, in an attempt to distract her.

I went to the bar and ordered two lots of burger and chips. A BLT with extra bacon for me, portobello mushroom for Tess. She's vegetarian. *This month*. A hangover trait from the previous boyfriend, Jasper, who I dismissed as soon as I saw his shark tooth necklace and anklet. I'd never understand the way she absorbed their personalities like she was possessed, as if she didn't think hers was enough on its own. Hopefully, she'd be back to eating her body-weight in prime rib soon enough, I'd just have to give it time. Or pray to the culinary gods that her next boyfriend was a carnivore.

'Come on then,' she said as I sat back down. 'Tell me about your new *friend*.'

Don't set her off. Keep it cool. Breezy. I shrugged and took a sip of wine. 'Not much to tell. Name's Dom. Been here a week or so. Doesn't put enough milk in tea.'

'Don't play games with me, girl. He's fit at least, I could tell.' The straw in Tess's glass gargled as she sucked up the dregs of her drink.

'How can you tell he's fit just from seeing his silhouette through a window?'

'So, he *is* fit.' She nodded boldly like some sort of modern-day Alan Turing after he'd cracked the Enigma.

Call yourself a detective – where the hell is your poker face? 'Fine. He's not grotesque.'

'Careful, that was almost a compliment.'

'He did OK in the points system, I guess.'

Tess flopped forward, patting the table repeatedly with her forehead. 'Give me strength,' she said as she sat up again. 'We're not back to that, are we? You and your points system. It's *dating*, Alice. He's not applying for a sodding visa!'

I paused, thinking of ways to get off the Dom train as the waitress put plates down in front of us. 'Not really sure I've got time for dating right now anyway ...' I told Tess about the MCU job and waited patiently for the squeal of encouragement. But all I got was a view of Tess swirling her finger in the pool of oily water on her plate that had dripped from her sad burger. 'What? What's the matter?'

'Nothing, it's just ... I don't see what's so great about getting in with the ponces up there anyway; bunch of tossers if you ask me,' she said, picking at her bread bun. 'Half the time they care more about getting their faces on the news than they do about the victims they're supposed to be helping.'

'Yeah, well,' I said, scooping up my burger, 'that's part of it, isn't it? If there's a right keeno like me in there then the rest of them'll have to pull their socks up, otherwise they'll look bad.'

Tess lifted her chin, a flat smile on her face. 'Yeah, I can totally see that working; you'll definitely bug them enough to do something, but it might be to murder you rather than change their ways.'

'Yeah, well, joke's on them, isn't it? They'll be the ones who'll have to investigate my death. Think of all the paperwork they'll have to do, a moral victory for me.'

Tess was still smiling, but her eyes seemed to glisten as she finally picked up her burger. 'If you say so. But I'll miss you, won't I, if – sorry, *when* – you get the job up there.'

My cheeks flushed again, not in flirtation this time, but as a result of my selfishness. I forgot sometimes how my desperation to work at HQ made it sound like I wanted to be rid of Fortbridge, and by default in Tess's sensitive big brown eyes, the people of Fortbridge. Last time we'd talked about it properly Tess got wasted and tried to make me get matching Yin and Yang tattoos so I wouldn't forget her. Even after two years of friendship, I didn't understand Tess's aversion to the thought of people leaving her, especially with no runaway dads or dead siblings to speak of.

'It's only Swindon,' I said, putting some of my chips on her plate as a peace offering. 'It's not like I'd be moving halfway across the country; you can still come over and make my dinner and clean up after me.'

'Yeah, but it's not the same as being able to wander over to your desk any time I want, is it?'

'Well, unless I can pull a rabbit out of a hat and impress with this Harton-Gray case, I probably won't get it anyway, so no need to grieve for me just yet.'

'I wish I didn't have every faith in you to get it, but come on, you'll smash it, you always do. And I don't know why you think this Camilla thing is such a big deal. It's probably nothing, some kids being stupid or something. Just leave it for Roy to get on with, then you can really focus on showing them how it's done up at HQ.'

'The woman's being stalked, Tess. How's that *nothing*?'

'Yeah, like obviously it's not cool, but all I'm saying is it's just a few photos, hardly crime of the century.' She pulled a notebook and pen from her bag and tore out a page. 'Here, just to make sure you get your new job, let's make a list, like a Rocky training plan, make sure you're in tip-top shape.'

I dropped my burger on to the plate and watched as she scribbled, nausea rising as the wine and chip fat mingled in my stomach. 'Really, "just a few photos"? You didn't see her, she seemed scared. She tried to hide it, but I could tell. It's really freaked her out.'

Tess stopped writing and wiped the corners of her mouth with a napkin. 'Sorry, I forgot you went to see her today. What's she like, anyway?'

I shuffled the displaced layers of my burger back together. 'She's nice, I guess.'

'Nice? Is that it?'

'Why, what were you expecting?'

Tess shrugged. 'Dunno, don't know the woman. Even when she lived here before, no one ever saw much of her – you don't mingle with the village folk if you don't have to.'

'Yeah, Roy said as much, kept themselves to themselves.'

'Eddie told me all about her books, though – they sound warped. She must have something going on, you know, up there.' Tess tapped the side of her skull. 'She can't just be *nice*. You don't write something like *Follow You Down* if you're just *nice*.'

'Oh, that's her, is it? Think I've actually heard of that one – haven't they made it into a film or something?'

'Dunno, ask Eddie, I'm sure *he'll* know. He hasn't stopped talking about her since yesterday. Camilla this, Camilla that. He's doing my head in.'

I stifled a smirk. Tess clearly didn't fancy Eddie, but a little bit of her liked how much he adored her. She would never admit it, but the ego boost did her no harm. Not that I understood why Tess needed any form of ego boost; she was one of the most naturally beautiful people I'd ever seen in real life. No movie filter required. Like some sort of beach babe plucked from the Californian coast and accidentally set back down in the drizzly greenery of the English countryside. She probably wasn't loving there being another hot woman in the village. Tess hadn't quite made it to the finish line of fourth-wave feminism. She'll *Yas Queen!* the hell out of your no-make-up selfie, but secretly she'll be zooming in on every inch of your face to find some sort of blemish to make herself feel better.

She reached into her bag and pulled out a book, banging it down on the table. A large white image of an eye glared up at me from the neon-orange cover of *Follow You Down*. 'That reminds me, Eddie says you can have this.' She slid it towards me. 'This is the one he was on about yesterday, where it starts with emails and pictures sent to the main character; he said you should give it a read.'

I flipped it over and skimmed the blurb. 'Do we really think someone is using her own novel as a blueprint to stalk her?' I said, thumbing through the pages. 'Surely no one would be *that* stupid, or just outright lazy.' And there was no way the world would be that kind to me, serving up a literal stalker playbook.

'*We* don't think that; I haven't even read the thing. Eddie's the one with the theory.'

'Right, and did Eddie happen to mention how it ends?'

Tess nodded and shook the half-melted ice-cubes in the bottom of her glass, a hint I was going to need another drink for the answer. 'Trust me,' she said, 'you don't want to know.'

14

The combination of the bright white strip lighting glaring at me and Roy rocking my desk as he leant against it intensified my hangover no end. I tried to play it cool while he regurgitated the response from the Hi-Tech Crime Department about the email to Camilla.

'. . . IP address originates in Estonia. A proxy or something. That's it,' Roy said, shrugging. 'Even that tells us bugger all – doesn't even mean it's come from there, could be from anywhere.'

I pressed a finger to my lip, holding in whatever was threatening to burst out. A gasp? A burp? No. Something resembling the noise you make when trying not to vomit in the back of a taxi after a night out because you simply do not have the cleaning fee the driver will charge if you can't keep it together. 'OK, I think Camilla's probably expecting as much, to be honest.'

'I've left her a voicemail – she's up in London with the *actor*,' Roy said, throwing one arm in the air, flicking his wrist like he was presenting some sort of prestigious offering.

'Yeah, right, the boyfriend.' I ran my tongue across the teeth-shaped indentations in the dehydrated flesh inside my mouth. This wasn't an example of me being shit at my job, at least. We had nothing to go on. No suspicious sightings. No grudges. Nothing. Not even Dad would have solved this one just yet. 'OK, what else have we got?'

'I still need to check her CCTV but not holding out much hope for that, like she said, but she did send these through.' Roy slapped some printouts of social media pages down on to the desk. 'She wasn't exaggerating about that online stuff – this is just what's come in since last *week*.'

I scanned a couple of lines of death threats, rape fantasies and an array of sexual propositions before I stopped reading.

Roy folded his arms, shaking his head. 'Honestly, the mind boggles. There's stuff I wouldn't even say to my worst enemy in there. The downside of fame, eh?'

A snort of derision escaped before I had the chance to hold it in. 'You think it's just famous women who get messages like this?'

He shrugged as Tess appeared beside him, the smell of hot lemon and honey floating from her mug. She looked irritatingly fresh. Despite being only two years younger than me, she could still drink like a teenager. She'd looked fine after her full English at lunch. I'd barely kept down a Pot Noodle and a bottle of Lucozade.

She looked at the printouts. 'What's this?'

'A load of stuff sent to Camilla, on her socials,' I said.

Tess scanned the papers. 'Pfft, that's nothing compared to the shit I get. Clearly a more literate bunch – most of mine are just dick pics.'

'You what?' Roy said, fully sitting on the edge of my desk now.

'Oh, Lord,' Tess said as she rolled her eyes, 'there's this one guy, right, calls himself *KingSexy999*, a few months ago he was sending me pictures of himself daily, I'm not even joking. The man needs to go to a urologist. There's definitely something wrong with his bits; I'm not sure why he's so keen to show them to random women on the internet.'

Roy made a noise like a pig snuffling for truffles. 'What on earth would he wanna do that for? You don't half get yourself involved with some weirdos.'

'Involved?' Tess said. 'Never had any interaction with him before in my life. No "Hello, how are you?", or "What's your sign?", just *bang*! Unidentified flying penis straight into my Instagram DMs.'

'Jesus wept,' Roy said, 'disgusting. And they say romance isn't dead.'

'Not really sure it's about romance, Roy,' I interjected. 'It's about power, control, intimidation.'

'All right, all right, I get it,' Roy said as he scooped up the printouts. I was pretty certain he didn't get it, but at least he was trying. 'I'll go through these properly now. See if there's anything worth another look.' He sat down at his desk, Tess taking his place and hovering at the end of mine.

'How you feeling, old lady?' she asked.

'Oh, quite lovely actually, if you ignore the lethal combination of electrolytes and junk food curdling in my intestines.'

'So gross. Your research is done, by the way, I'll email it now.'

'Any zingers?'

'Nothing that's gonna help you solve your case, no, *but*, Camilla's boyfriend might prick a few ears up at HQ.'

My body sat upright of its own accord. 'Why?'

'His dad's the Wessex Police and Crime Commissioner.'

Shit. This was a detail we could do without. 'What, Artie Dingle?'

She nodded. 'Yep, Myles Carrington is only his registered stage name, legal name's still Dingle. Malcolm Dingle.'

Roy chuckled from behind his computer. 'Not got quite the same ring to it as *Bond, James Bond*, eh? Thanks for that – cheered me right up, that has.'

I pulled my lips back between my teeth to stop the laughter slipping out that would only encourage him. 'Stop earwigging, you're supposed to be reading.' A hand appeared in the air that I was ninety-nine percent sure was him doing a Hitler salute at me, but I ignored it and turned my attention back to Tess. 'Any other interesting facts I should be aware of?'

'Couple of old arrests for the boyfriend, one drunk and disorderly, one possession of cocaine. Both of which I'm sure Daddy dearest helped him get out of. Nothing more exciting than that, I'm afraid,' Tess said.

The universe was really not being my friend right now.

As if on cue the door opened from the hallway, Bret Seaborn striding through it two hours early for our shift changeover.

Oh, universe, you really can jog on now, you sadistic bitch.

Bret dropped his briefcase by his desk, hung up his coat and disappeared into Jane's office before anyone had time to take the piss out of the elbow patches on the hideous hunter-green woollen jumper he was wearing, let alone time for me to tell him about the possible line of enquiry on his theft job. Not that I'd tried that hard. Talking to the man made you feel like you were wasting precious seconds of his time even if you were giving him the best news in the world. I'd emailed him the information and Dom's contact number instead, somehow resisting the urge to write it down in a note and leave it on his desk to give myself an excuse to run amok in his meticulously crafted workstation. As if making it messier would set us on level pegging for the MCU sergeant's post on the off chance they happened to consider office tidiness as part of the scoring criteria.

I looked at Roy, his cheek pushed into his eye socket as he leant heavily against a balled-up fist. He used the index finger on his other hand as a pointer to help him scan the lines of Camilla's social media messages like he'd been doing for the last hour.

'Anything?' I asked, pushing my forearms into the table until my bum lifted up off the chair.

'Not yet,' he said without looking up at me.

I plonked back down and opened my emails. My finger scrolled mindlessly as I scanned the latest internal bulletin.

A couple of wanted images, an advertisement for the office bake sale, and a link to a blog post from the Chief Constable with the strapline *The Changing Face of Policing*. That'd be another thing for Roy to rant about when he read it.

'Oh, wait, before I forget,' Tess said, as if we'd been in the middle of a conversation. She pulled something from her handbag. 'You didn't take this with you last night – that's not a very good start, is it?'

She wafted a piece of paper at me, the one she'd torn from her notebook in the pub, now crinkled and stained with wine.

'Oh, for f—' I plucked the paper from between her fingers. 'I was hoping you'd have forgotten about this.'

'Forgotten about an excuse to get you to come to yoga class with me? Doubt it.'

I tried to decipher Tess's drunken scribbles.

Be a Better Alice
1) Improve sleep.
2) Exercise daily.
3) Practise mindfulness/meditation/yoga, etc.
4) Eat vegetables (especially green ones).
5) Drink less alcohol.
6) Get a social life e.g. DATE!

I looked up at her. 'And you're still convinced this is the answer, are you? The regimen that's going to get me my new job? Mindfulness and eating broccoli? Not getting my head together, buckling down? Not impressing the bosses?'

Tess folded her arms and raised an eyebrow. 'You promised. And this *is* getting your head together, remember . . .'

'Please God don't say it again.'

'. . . healthy body, healthy mind.'

I let out a sigh and re-read the list. It wasn't exactly rocket science. And what harm could it do? A bit of a clean and polish, shake away the funk I'd stewed in since Jamie. And I was already ahead of the game with a new possible dating option in Dom. If I did that, Tess would probably forget about the other things on the list anyway. She was convinced I was going to become one of those people who marry their cat in a back garden ceremony and legally change their names to Mr and Mrs Whiskerton-Smythe. And there was lettuce in my burger last night. *Look at you, you'll be making your own granola any day now!* Who needed counselling when I had my own self-help guru?

I stuck my hand out. 'Fine, deal.'

Tess shook it, sealing my fate. 'You'll be a new and improved Alice in no time. How about we start tonight, Wednesday yoga, yes?'

'Come on now, I'm in no state for tying my body up in knots today.'

Tess laughed. 'You are such a lightweight.'

'You're one to talk.' Tess's recovery game was strong, but she couldn't handle her booze in real time. It had taken her all of about fifteen minutes to get drunk enough at our first work drinks to fill me in on all the office gossip. How Terry the station clerk had wanted to join as a cop but failed the entry-level fitness test three times before resorting to

SAM FRANCES

administration. How Bret had declined every single invite to office social occasions since he'd started working there. 'If the man had been in *Reservoir Dogs*, his code name would have been Mr Beige,' she'd slurred.

'Fine,' Tess said, 'well, I'm booking us in for next week, then. Do. Not. Forget.'

'Wouldn't miss it for the world.' I laid my head down on the desk, praying for the end of my shift, and had come dangerously close to nodding off when a shout from Roy's desk almost made me puke on mine.

'Dirty, dirty bastard!' Roy said.

'What, what is it, what's happening?' I said, wiping drool from my cheek.

Roy got up and held one of the printouts up to my face. 'Recognise him?'

I squinted through tired eyes, ignoring the vulgar message sent to Camilla and focussing on the tiny dot of a profile picture and user name of the sender, recognition slapping me like a cold palm. I pulled the paper closer to be sure. 'Oh my God, yeah!' I scanned the message. Nothing overtly about following her or sending pictures, but slimy as hell nonetheless. 'Prioritise looking for other messages from him, see what else is in there. Then we can go pay him a visit, see what he's got to say for himself.'

Roy took the paper back and sat down. 'The pleasure'll be all ours, I'm sure.'

15

The alarm chided me for the fourth time the next morning. Every ten minutes on the dot. My hand flapped around the bedside table in search of the snooze button, the Be a Better Alice list floating to the floor in the commotion. I picked it up.

1) Improve sleep.

I'd had a full night's sleep . . . ish. No nightmare visits from Jamie or his mum. Or Noah. That counted as progress, right? Progress that had almost been spoiled by my inability to get stalker theories out of my head, especially with the interesting little nugget of information Roy had found in the perverted messages sent to Camilla. I went back to the list.

2) Exercise daily.

A jog. I could do that. And who said you couldn't outrun your problems? I rolled out of bed and twelve minutes later peaks of frost-hardened dirt stabbed the soles of my trainers as my feet pounded the mud track that ran from the back of Myrtle Cottage down to the village.

As much as I loathed exercise in general, there was something in the simplicity and consistency of running that I liked. Left. Right. Left. Right. One foot in front of the other. Even *I* couldn't bugger that up. I sucked the cold air in through my nose and powered through the thick morning mist that smothered my usual view of the rolling farmers' fields, the remnants of the fort crowning St Catherine's Hill completely erased from the skyline. Gravity pulled me down the path alongside an empty paddock. The handful of horses it housed during the summer months usually provided the perfect excuse to have a rest after running along the riverbank, stopping to feed them some grass and rub their noses as I trash-talked myself enough to get me back up the incline on the other side.

I tried not to think too harshly of the horses. About how they must be snuggly in their rugs and stables filled with straw as my legs burned. Everything burned, in fact. And somehow I felt ten pounds heavier than when I'd set off. The pumping of my arms did nothing to propel me up the hill, the drag so hard on my muscles I was nigh on orgasmic at the sight of the path levelling out as it intersected the lane that would take me back to my front door.

Thank God!

My run turned into the slowest it could before it was technically walking as Myrtle Cottage appeared up ahead, footfall syncing perfectly with the drumbeat of 'My Hero' blasting through my tinny headphones. I did my utmost to keep breathing while harmonising with Dave Grohl. 'Theeere goes my—'

I saw Dom unloading boxes from the back of a van on the driveway of The Willows too late to stifle the singing.

He turned, cupping a hand across his brow to protect his eyes from the low sun.

'Morning,' he said. 'I wasn't expecting to be ambushed by the dawn chorus.'

'Sorry about that.' I wiped my hands down the front of my T-shirt as if that would magically wipe away the sweat permeating the fabric. 'What you got there?'

Dom scratched his head with one hand, the other resting on his hip like a teapot as he looked down at the boxes. 'Just some work-out stuff, kettlebells, few sets of dumbbells, that sort of crap. You sure I can't tempt you with a free session?'

I gulped, still trying to catch my breath enough to make this conversation sound normal and not like I was doing a heavy-breathing prank call. 'No, thanks though. As you can see, I'm at peak physical fitness already.'

'Right, no, yes, I can see that. In that case, how about you take me out for a drink instead, you know, welcome me to the village?'

'Isn't it customary for neighbours to invite the new person to do something, rather than the new neighbour inviting himself?'

He shrugged. 'Usually, yes, but in my defence it's been almost two days since we met and you haven't so much as brought me a housewarming plant, so I took some initiative. What d'you say?'

The words from the list whispered in my ear, *6) Get a social life e.g. DATE!*

'Fine, why not.'

We agreed tonight was as good as any and exchanged

awkward farewells before I stumbled through the front door. My thigh muscles were jelly as I paced around the kitchen, hands clasped above my head trying to suck in oxygen. Unease germinated in the pit of my stomach. *A date*. I hadn't been on a date since Liam. And even that hadn't involved a period of dating, as such. I'd found my one proper relationship the old-fashioned way: hang around with boys at school because you want to play rugby at breaktime instead of learning the latest Steps dance routine, pick the one who has the best jokes to lose your French kiss virginity to, then invite him to dinner so your mum can cook her famous lemon and pancetta risotto. Bingo. One long-term boyfriend, no dating. Maybe *Heat* magazine should be asking *me* for advice. Want someone to ask you out? Forget the chicken fillet bra inserts, just sing Foo Fighters at them loudly and out of tune whilst reeking of perspiration. Absolutely killing it.

I filled a glass with water and downed it. I could do this. How hard could dating be? Even Donald Trump managed to get more than one person to marry him. My phone vibrated on the kitchen counter. 'Hello?' I said, still struggling to catch my breath.

'It's Roy, just – I haven't, er, interrupted something, have I? Sounds like I've dialled one of those dodgy numbers from the phone box.'

'I've just come back from a run, actually – you should try getting your heart rate over eighty once in a while.' That was harsh; the way that man devoured a fry-up would probably be considered cardio.

'Right, anyway, just letting you know, I haven't been able

to get in touch with Camilla's assistant yet. Her mum says she's away until tomorrow, in Bath with some mates, I've left a message for her to call when she gets back.'

'OK, good, right ...' I was still trying to collect myself, my face stinging from its beating from the cold breeze when Roy cut me off.

'Wait – what ...' His voice was harder to hear as he seemed to pull the phone further from his face. '... oh, God!' The full force of him bellowed down the line, 'There's been another incident at Bertram Manor, according to Twitter – might as well be a soddin' crime reporting system these days.'

My stomach clenched. 'What's happened?'

'I dunno, something to do with Camilla's photos.'

'Get down there, I'll be about twenty minutes.'

I inched the car closer to the manor gates. A crowd of people stood in my path, every single one of them holding their phones in the air, taking pictures. Roy pulled up beside me and wound down his window. I gestured towards the horde. 'What the hell's going on?'

'I told you, it's all over bleedin' social media – not like anyone in this village has anything else to do,' he said, turning his attention to them. 'Police vehicles, move!'

The word 'police' was a red rag to a bull and the cars were swarmed in seconds. I could barely make out the questions, the throng all shouting at once.

'What are you doing about the stalker?'

'Is there a psycho on the loose?'

'Are the women of Fortbridge in danger?'

A fist thudded against the passenger-side window of my car.

'Alice.'

The tightly coiled spring in my stomach twisted to the edge of its breaking point at the nasal voice of A. J. Howden. If I had to run every one of these people over to get away from him, I absolutely would. I revved the engine as a warning but he ignored it and leant forward, his thin, clear-framed spectacles almost bashing against the window. Even through the glass, I could smell the burnt peppermint odour from his vape that always clung to whatever he was wearing.

'Surprised to see you back on duty, Alice. Shouldn't you still be taking some time off? D'you really think you're the best person to be—'

I revved again, harder this time. He stepped back, but not before shoving his camera towards my face. Desperate for the money shot. Like he'd done a thousand times before. Not just to me and other officers or emergency service workers, but to victims. I wasn't so naïve that I didn't understand the need for graphic images in certain areas of journalism. To shine a spotlight on atrocities and be a catalyst for change. But no amount of protestation from the likes of A. J. about 'just doing his job' would ever convince me he was contributing to a better world when he'd taken a close-up image of the woman from the news-agents' bloodied face as she was cut from the wreckage of a car crash before he splashed it across the front page of the *Wessex Star* last year.

I stuck my head out the window. 'Out of the way!' The crowd parted, a chill running the length of my spine as the gates came into view. A collage of the anonymous dog-walking photos were stuck across the railings, fifty of them at least. But they looked different to the printouts Roy had spread across his desk, dark red droplets streaking across them. My eyeline followed the trail upwards towards the source of the stains.

'Jesus Chr—' I heard Roy say through our open windows as I pressed the back of my hand to my mouth to block the vomit.

16

He closed his eyes as her voice played out in his head like a symphony. A light bass tone complemented by her laughter, and the soft percussion of her lips as they formed and shaped words. But it never took long for the notes to sour. To lose their tune as he pictured her face when she realised what was happening, the blame twisting those beautiful sounds into a cacophony of noise. Because they always blamed him in the end. It was always his fault. They took no responsibility of their own. Mother had blamed him, too. For the cookies. She'd never said so to his face, but Father was always straight with him. Treated him like a man. Treated him with respect.

The change in his mother had been obvious from that day. Her grumpiness. Always making excuses to leave the room as he bonded with his father, jealousy oozing from her like oil from the pores in her forehead. Like she begrudged their joy. He'd tried to involve her, he really had. Even told her all about his first crush. The love of his life. Jen. He'd never forgiven Mother for not even trying to muster a fake smile in response to the plan he'd told her about after working it out with Father. He could still see the pathetic tremble of her lips as she made her excuses.

'But you've already asked Jen to be your girlfriend before, love, haven't you? Her mum did mention that to me,' she'd said.

He'd nodded, glad to see the first part of his plan had already been noticed, the effort he'd been putting in recognised. 'Yes. And she will want to eventually; Father says she's just playing hard to get, that's all.'

Mother had even gone so far as to swipe at her cheek before giving her reply, not that he'd actually seen a tear. Probably another one of her tactics to get attention. Father said she did that a lot, something he'd have to learn to look out for if he was going to make sure she didn't get one over on him.

'Now, love,' she'd said, 'don't you think that might be a little bit . . . inappropriate?'

He could still feel his head rattle in confusion at what part of his plan she hadn't got. 'But the school disco is only a couple of weeks away, she needs to say yes before then.'

Mother had reached across and placed her clammy palm on the back of his fist. Another of her tactics. 'But maybe she doesn't want to go to the disco with you. Just because you want her to be your girlfriend doesn't mean she has to. And that's OK, that's absolutely fine, there'll be plenty of other girls who'd like to go with you, I'm sure.'

But he didn't want other girls.

He wanted Jen.

And she wanted him. Father had said so.

He'd cried for hours after that. Cried and cried until his father came home and climbed into bed next to him, holding him tight and kissing his forehead. 'You don't listen to her, d'you hear me? Any girl'd be lucky to have you, eh? My boy. Your mother doesn't have a clue what she's talking about, silly old bat. Isn't she? Go on, say it, silly old bat, silly old bat,' he'd said, putting the words to a tune whilst poking him gently in his tummy and up and down his sides.

In that moment, he'd realised Father was the only one who truly understood him. The only one he needed. And the conflicting emotions that tugged at him, almost splitting him in two time and time again as he watched his parents interact, had been resolved. And by the time his mother opened the door to see what the noise was, they were both bouncing on the bed singing and laughing. He'd pointed at her, from what felt like fifty feet in the air, his body and mind lighter now his allegiance was clear. 'Mummy, you're a silly old bat, silly old bat.' He could barely get the words out, he was laughing so much, his father's deep chuckle harmonising perfectly with his own pre-pubescent cackle.

But Mother hadn't laughed. She'd just reminded them it was way past his bedtime and stormed off in another of her 'sulks', as his father called them.

He missed Father's laugh. And he would never forget how it had been taken from him.

17

Back at the office, I leant over Roy's shoulder while he scrolled through the crime scene images on his computer screen as fast as SOCO could upload them to the system. He zoomed in on the words scrawled across the photographs, daubed in what we now knew to be red paint, not blood.

ALL EYES ON YOU BITCH!

You could forgive the mistake in our initial assessment of the situation, given the animal carcasses we'd seen positioned astride Bertram Manor's spiked gate.

'Totally sick,' Roy said. 'What sort of cracker goes around picking up roadkill to scare someone? Those foxes have been dead weeks if the stink coming off 'em was anything to go by.'

The smell of maggot-infested flesh clung to my nostrils. I pulled a tissue from my pocket and blew my nose violently for the twentieth time in as many minutes. It didn't matter how often you smelt dead flesh; there was no getting used to that fetid yet somehow sweet tang.

I scanned the office. 'Eddie, can you come here, please?' He scampered over, eyes widening as he took in what was on Roy's screen. 'This look familiar?' I said, pointing at the images.

'What? Why would they?'

'Camilla's book, *Follow You Down*, anything like this in there?'

He put his hand to his face, chin resting in the dip between his thumb and forefinger. 'Actually ...' He leant forward, tilting his head as if that might enable him to see something he couldn't when looking at them straight on. 'I could be on to something there.' From the look on his face, I half expected him to straighten and lift his chin so I could hang a gold medal around his neck. 'It's not *exactly* the same, but in the book, after the emails, the next big thing that happens is Lyddie – she's the main character – she comes downstairs one morning and finds her poor little pet rabbits gutted and hanging from a set of pan hooks in her kitchen.'

'Jesus, Eddie,' Roy interjected, 'I haven't had me bleedin' lunch yet.'

All three of us flinched as the phone rang. Roy picked it up. 'Yeah ... all right, Terry.' He nodded his head as he listened to the station clerk. 'OK, be down in two, cheers.' He hung up the phone and stood, almost pushing his chair back into me. 'It's Camilla, she's downstairs.'

Word travelled fast in the social media universe. Despite being over sixty miles away in London, Camilla had been made aware of A. J.'s *exclusive* photographs of her own front gate, posted by the *Wessex Star* digital account, before we'd even made it back to the station.

Camilla stood in the middle of reception, her shoulders in the grip of a tall, well-dressed man with a pained expression on his face. They both turned to look at us as we reached the bottom step. 'Thanks for coming in.' I reached out to shake Camilla's hand as Roy did the same to the man next to her.

'We started heading back as soon as Chrissy called to say what she'd seen online and ... God, sorry—' She covered her face. 'I thought it was my dogs at first, on the gate, and I—' She pulled her hands away and inhaled deeply. 'I don't know what I'd do if something happened to them.' Her usually rich voice was paper thin.

I pushed thoughts of what Eddie said happened next in her book away for now and placed a tentative hand on her shoulder. 'The dogs are fine. Chrissy's mum turned up to feed them when we were there and she's taken them to her house for now – not that we found any evidence of anyone getting further than the gates, but just as a precaution.'

'Thank you, we can pick them up on the way home,' Camilla said.

Her companion shook his head in disbelief. 'Home? You can't be serious, Cam. Surely coming back to London is the best bet right now.'

'Of course I'm going home,' Camilla said, the depth of her voice returning, defiance blooming across her face. 'I will not be forced out by some lunatic!'

Eddie and Terry hovered behind the front desk, both of them doing a terrible job of pretending they weren't hanging on Camilla's every word. And Mavis Mulberry was coming up the walkway, probably to complain about someone stealing her beloved garden gnome, Mr Higgins, for the seventeenth time. 'How about we go through to the mess room, get you both a drink and make you a bit more comfortable, OK?' I shepherded them towards the double swing doors at the back of reception. 'Sorry, sir, I didn't catch your name. Mr ...?'

'Carrington, Myles Carrington. I'm her partner,' he replied. I could almost feel mine and Roy's bodies tense simultaneously as we tried not to snort-laugh at what I knew was going through both our heads. *The name's Dingle. Malcolm Dingle. Shaken, not stirred.*

The desire to laugh disappeared as Myles draped his arm across Camilla's shoulders and she couldn't jerk it away fast enough. 'Myles, please!' she snapped. 'Could you let me breathe for one second.'

A fancy-looking gold watch glinted from his wrist as he held his hands up and let her walk a few steps ahead. He passed close enough for me to notice the flicker along his jaw as though it had its own pulse. Conciliatory on the face of it, but something simmering underneath. I'd seen that a million times before; someone who needs to be in control but doesn't want the world to know it. I recoiled as the cloud of expensive-smelling aftershave trailing him hit my nose.

The glass of water appeared to have a cooling effect on Camilla's temper. Either that or the bright white mess room lighting sucked the flush of anger from her cheeks. 'Take all the time you need,' I said, trying to keep my voice soft

108

and empathetic whilst battling to be heard above the trays of cutlery being bashed about behind me like an orchestra of metallic maracas.

'I'm fine. Really.' I recognised that *I'm fine* snap. It was the same one that kept coming out of my mouth.

'Well, you shouldn't be *fine*, darling,' Myles interjected. He dropped his head forward into his hands for a second before it sprang back like a Pez dispenser. 'Thank God you weren't there, and alone!' He paused, his thick lips pursed as they came to rest against his fingertips.

After a second or two, he pulled his hands away from the mouth that was saying all the right words. Showing all the right concerns. But there was something about his actions that didn't match his exasperated tone. Like they'd been choreographed. Everything thought out to within an inch of its life, the best angles planned and prepared. Was that the actor in him? Or the need for control? He reminded me of someone I couldn't quite place.

The plastic cup Camilla cradled with both hands crinkled, her grip tightening as Myles carried on talking. 'And what if they get into the house, hmm? What will you do? Fight them off with a pair of Manolo Blahniks?'

'I can think of worse weapons,' Camilla said as she took another sip of water.

'This is serious, Cam. I'm just thinking of you here, darling, you could get hurt.' He rubbed his hand across her shoulders.

Myles was a lean man, tall, and I could tell by the way he held himself he was proud of his physique. He ran the other hand through his jet-black hair, every strand springing back into place as his fingers passed along his scalp, as if each one had been given individual instructions on how to behave.

'No one's going to get past Ruby and Bo, are they?' Camilla said.

'Christ, those dogs.' His hand slipped from her shoulder. The gleam of a thumb ring and link bracelet that matched his watch caught my eye as he moved. Mum once told me never to trust a man who wore a lot of flashy jewellery, which probably explained how she'd ended up with Dad, who could barely find a pair of matching socks as he rushed to work every morning. And from my eight years' experience dealing with criminals for a day job, I'd decided she was probably on to something. A smart but functional watch, a wedding ring – fine. But unless you're Jason Momoa or the Pope, it was Mum's view that it was probably best to stop there.

Myles put his arm back across Camilla's shoulders as he started talking again, as if someone might forget they were together if he wasn't physically touching her. 'They are *pets*, Cam, not the Secret bloody Service! Heaven forbid the psycho has enough nous to turn up with two T-bone steaks as a distraction – they'll leave you for dead.' He pinched the skin on his forehead with his free hand. 'Clearly this sicko has no qualms about hurting animals. That's a classic sign, isn't it? You even write about that yourself in your books; psychopaths are known for starting on animals before moving on to people.' The tendons in the back of his hand moved like long, thin insects as he drummed his fingers on the table.

I hadn't wanted to put Eddie's theory into her mind until I'd felt there was more weight to it, but with the similarities in the second incident and what Myles had just said, I couldn't not mention it. 'We wanted to ask about that, actually, if in any of the messages you get anyone has seemed particularly interested in or made reference to *Follow You Down*, because, well, I've been told there may be some parallels to what happens in it.'

'The thing's sold over two million copies; people send me messages all the time, telling me how much they love it or hate it, or pointing out the damn spelling mistake on page ninety-four, but there's been nothing out of the ordinary.'

'Wait, wait a bloody minute!' Myles said. 'Isn't that the one where the killer practises on her pets and then moves on to her? Right, that's it, you're *definitely* coming to stay with me.'

'Look,' I said, 'Mr Carrington, we don't want to alarm either of you, it's just a theory, and it's a red flag, for sure, but there's a big difference between killing a fox and killing a person, and from the looks of those foxes they were dead long before anyone stuck them on the gates – looks like they'd been peeled off the road.'

Myles threw his palms up. 'Oh goody, doesn't actually kill them, just likes to play around with the carcasses, how bloody reassuring.'

Roy chimed in, turning his attention to Camilla, 'I know this is hard, but Mr Carrington does have a point. Even if it's just for a few days, it's probably best if there's somewhere else you can stay, at least until we get results back on the forensics.'

Camilla lifted her chin. 'No. End of discussion. That's my home, and I refuse to be chased out of it.'

I wanted to get up and bang Myles and Roy's heads together. Camilla was a grown woman, more than capable of making decisions for herself. 'That's totally understandable, Camilla,' I said. 'Don't worry, we can give you some advice about upping the security of your property and have a marker put on the address so you can go home, and any calls will be treated as an emergency, OK?'

'If you think that's necessary,' she said. 'Anyway, I want to be here tomorrow when Chrissy gets back – she's just as shaken up about all this as we are.'

'OK,' Roy said. 'If you could also remind Chrissy we'd like to speak to her, she might be able to help our investigation. Assistants are always in the know, the best ones who might have seen something that didn't look right.'

We all flinched as Myles pushed his chair away from the table and stood, metal legs scraping the cheaply tiled floor. 'This is all bullshit. Absolute bullshit. You're just going to *let* her go back there, like some sitting duck? No, I'm sorry, but no, Cam. I've seen the documentaries, the films about people who get murdered by their stalkers because the police don't do enough to catch them.'

'Myles!' Camilla said.

'I'm sorry, Cam, but I'm putting my foot down here. We don't need their help or half-arsed investigation, I can keep you safe myself. We'll get security. Trust me, no one's getting anywhere near you.'

Camilla shook her head in shock and tugged at his sleeve. 'Myles, sit down, you're being ridiculous.'

I folded my arms, trying to remember who it was Myles reminded me of. I couldn't recall, but I'd met a million people like him before in this line of work and outside of it. The ones who force themselves on the world rather than exist within it, who will walk all over you if you let them. 'Mr Carrington, I can assure you this is being taken extremely seriously, and we're doing our very best to keep Camilla safe,' I said, now also standing, pushing my chest out and fully straightening to stretch myself those last few inches I needed to get as near as possible to reaching Myles's six-feet frame.

Myles stared at me. 'And what if your best isn't good enough?' he sneered.

I had no idea if he was referring to policing in general, or if he'd seen the coverage of Jamie and was directing the comment to me personally, but either way, his words slashed like a razor. I cleared my throat before directing my next question back towards Camilla. 'We'll call when we have an update, OK?'

'Yes, yes, of course,' she said, her fist still clutching Myles's sleeve.

Myles shook his head and let out a bewildered laugh, before turning and slamming open the double doors leading back into reception. I could still see him through the window, shaking his head as he waited for Camilla.

'Sorry about him,' Camilla said as she stood and rolled her eyes. 'He's very protective of me. His father works in the police world, and let's just say they have a rather, erm . . . interesting relationship. He'll come round.'

Roy and I followed them back through reception and said our goodbyes to Camilla, Myles already outside and striding halfway across the street.

'What's up his bum, then?' Roy said as he watched them out the window.

I wrapped the fingers of my right hand around the back of my neck and massaged the base of my skull to ward off the brewing headache. 'Police competence, or lack thereof, apparently.'

'The cheek of it! I'd like to see him do a better job. Who does he think he is, bleedin' Batman? Mind you, maybe he's not messing about. He certainly looks like he's got Bruce Wayne money – d'you clock his wrist? That was a Roger Dubuis.'

'A Roger Du-what now?' I said.

'The watch – those things set you back over seventy k brand new, and his didn't look too shabby, that's for sure.'

I couldn't help but look Roy up and down, his pale blue shirt crumpled and only half tucked into a worn pair of navy chinos. 'Since when did you become a connoisseur of men's fashion fineries?'

'Since I seized about fifty knock-off versions of the bleedin' things when some bloke tried to sell them down Market Square a few years ago. Made himself a tidy little profit before we nicked him an' all.'

I let my hand flop back down by my side. 'Yeah, well, with his acting and her books they've probably got quite the disposable income between them, so let's make sure we catch this person before Myles forks out to go all caped vigilante on us. Camilla's the victim here, and she wants us involved even if he doesn't. So, forensics are already in motion; can you ring around whoever develops or enlarges photographs in the area?' It was so easy to order that sort of stuff online these days, but I'd never fail to be amazed by how often you could rely on the stupidity of criminals. 'House-to-house isn't gonna get us anywhere, she doesn't exactly have neighbours.' This was the problem with investigations in more rural locations. If this had been a case I'd worked back in the Swindon office, there'd be more CCTV than we could handle. Ring doorbell footage from neighbours living on top of each other, a zillion traffic cameras. We'd be up to our eyes in, well, eyes. 'What else might have cameras along that road?'

'Just the rugby club, I think,' Roy said. 'I can ask.'

I nodded, thinking back to our visit to Camilla earlier in the week. 'What about that bus that passed us when we were pulling out of there the other day, which one was that?'

'The bus to Tottburn is the only one that runs out that way, but the last one stops about half ten, then doesn't start again until just after seven in the morning, which doesn't help us if someone's done this overnight.'

'OK, see what they've got camera-wise anyway.' Another long shot. Public transport here came around about as often as a deadbeat dad, so even if the handiwork on the gates was done before the bus stopped running, the likelihood of it passing by at just the time we needed it to was unlikely, but still worth a try.

Roy nodded and made his way to the stairs. 'On it.'

I started to follow but stopped as I caught sight of Eddie out the corner of my eye, still hovering behind the front desk with Terry. 'Oi, Eddie, I need you upstairs.'

'At your service, Sarge. What d'you need?'

'A book report. I need to know every key thing that happens in *Follow You Down*.'

116

18

Roy had barely made a dent in the never-ending list of tasks Alice had given him before she dragged him away from his desk when she'd finished with Eddie. He followed her through reception, shoving his hands in his pockets as they stepped outside. Normally he'd be glad to be heading to the pub, but not when he was going for work purposes. And there was no chance of knocking off early for a pint with Sergeant Major in tow.

Alice shuddered before pulling the collar of her jacket tighter around her face. 'I dunno if that shiver is because of the cold or the fact that the details of what happens in Camilla's book are now etched into my brain. I'll never look at a set of pan hooks the same way again.'

Roy stayed quiet in the hope she'd stop talking. He could really do without her rehashing the pet rabbit story, and the fact that the main character's body gets found strung up the same way in the book's grand finale. Why people enjoyed reading stuff like that, he'd never know. Maybe it was because he was used to seeing the real-life version, he didn't feel the need to top up the old memory bank with fictional depravity as well. He'd take Gareth Southgate's autobiography instead any day of the week. Thankfully the walk to The Bull was a short one.

'You wanna take the lead?' Alice said, one hand already braced against the door handle. 'I'd hazard a guess he might respond better to his own kind.'

Roy nodded. 'After you.'

The woman behind the bar looked barely old enough to be serving alcohol. Roy was in half a mind to ask the girl for some ID before she swanned off out the back. With her orange tan and long blonde hair, she reminded him of Laurie when he'd seen her all dressed up for her school prom. The photo Karen had taken of her, anyway; he'd missed the real thing. Had to go to someone's leaving drinks or something. Probably a good job and all. If he'd seen the caked-on face paint hiding his daughter's cherubic features in the flesh, he'd have probably marched her back upstairs to scrub it off and she wouldn't have thanked him for it.

A few seconds later the young woman returned, followed by the man they were there to see. Roy made a curt introduction on Alice's behalf, and one for himself as a formality. Even though this guy had only taken over the pub a couple of months earlier, Roy had still spent enough time in the place that there was no way he didn't already know who he was. 'Mind if we have a word, Mr Cartwright?' he said, nodding to an empty table at the far side of the bar.

'Sure,' the man replied, 'and Steve's fine – Mr Cartwright's me dad's name.' He slung a dishtowel over his shoulder, chewing gum slapping between his yellowed teeth.

Roy crinkled his face in annoyance. He knew what the

women at the station dubbed this bloke. Sleazy Steve. And he'd never really thought much of it, if he was honest. Hadn't done more than order drinks from the man. But now he was up close and paying attention, he could see it. The exact same coating of smarminess Karen's new fella had. Roy went to sit down but paused for a second as he thought about what Alice had meant earlier. *One of his kind.* She'd better have meant 'man' and not 'sleazebag'. He knew he could be a bit of an arse sometimes, but there were lines he wouldn't dream of crossing. Roy looked at her as if her face might tell him the answer, but she was too busy pulling her ringing phone out of her pocket.

'Sorry, gotta take this,' she said, before mouthing *Jane* at him. 'Can you carry on without me?'

He nodded as she got up and walked outside, before focussing his attention back on the barman who was now sat opposite him. 'I won't beat around the bush, Steve, how do you know Camilla Harton-Gray?'

'I don't,' he replied, swivelling so he could stretch out his short legs, one trainer-clad foot crossing over the other at the ankle as he leant back in his chair. 'I mean, I know *of* her, just like most people around here, but I don't *know* her. Probably too high class for a joint like this – she's a knockout, ain't she?' He winked and Roy had to stop himself from jumping over the table and pulling the guy's frigging eyelids off.

Roy usually didn't mind a bit of playing along when questioning people. It was a tried and tested interview technique for getting them onside. Make them feel like they're having a conversation with a mate. But the thought of this pathetic excuse for a man thinking they were the same, that this type of *lads, lads, lads* chat would be right up Roy's street, made his stomach churn. He kept his face as neutral as he could manage. 'Anyone would think you did from the type of messages you send her on Instagram.'

Steve shrugged. 'Just a bit of harmless flirting, nothing more. Come on, we've all done it. She's gorgeous, what does she expect putting pictures of herself looking sexy as hell on the internet?'

The conversation between Alice and Tess rang out in his head. 'She should be able to put whatever she wants on the internet without this type of commentary, frankly.'

Steve sat forward and leant his elbows on the table. 'Is that why you're here? To ask me about flirty social media messages? I thought the police were supposed to be busy these days.'

'We are busy, very busy, trying to keep people safe from malicious communications and potential stalking.'

Steve sat up and lifted his hands in protest. 'Woah, woah, who said anything about stalking? Commenting on her Instagram posts isn't stalking, and I haven't even said anything that bad!'

'We'll be the judge of that, Mr Cartwright.' A dot of spittle followed the last consonant out of his mouth.

'This is stupid, I've never—'

'Where were you last night?'

'What? Here. I was here last night.'

'All night?'

'Until kicking-out time, then upstairs in the flat.'

'And can anyone corroborate that?'

Steve nodded back towards the young woman behind the bar. 'Stayed here last night, didn't you, darling?'

The woman walked over and rested her hand on Steve's shoulder. 'He were here all night, officer, in bed wi' me.'

She giggled and Roy almost retched at the sight of them side by side. The man looked more like a creepy uncle than a love interest.

He needed some fresh air. 'I won't take up any more of your time, Mr Cartwright. But watch it with those messages. Malicious communications is a crime. I suggest you look it up.'

Roy stormed out the pub, almost banging into Alice as she was about to walk back in, phone still in hand.

'Everything all right?' she asked.

'Fine. Dead end, though. He might be a pig but he's got an alibi for last night.'

'Shit. Where was he?'

'In bed with Miss Tropicana back there. I really don't understand how men like that actually get women. He's got *slimeball* written all over him, that one.'

Alice shrugged. 'Your guess is as good as mine. Low self-esteem, maybe? I dunno.'

He wondered what he must have done to Karen's self-esteem over the years to push her down a similar road, but Alice interrupted him before he could come up with an answer.

'Jane wants a full update tomorrow afternoon.'

He harrumphed as they walked back over to the station. Another thing to add to his list.

19

The time for date night with Dom had arrived, so I left Roy in the office. I couldn't figure out if the fizzing in my tummy was nerves, or the sickly leftovers of having to view crime scene images *and* interact with Sleazy Steve, all within the space of a few hours. Whatever it was, I hoped picking up a bottle of Dutch courage from Harper's All Goods would do the trick. I scanned the shelves of the small village shop that truly did seem to sell all goods. Deli meat? Choose from twenty different kinds. New stopcock for your toilet? Pick a colour. I was half tempted to ask the new girl behind the counter if they sold excuses for cancelling social arrangements.

I trudged back across the green towards my car, eyes scanning from left to right in the hope they might see something that would mean I had to go back to the station instead of meeting Dom. A heinous crime that absolutely must be dealt with right that very second for the good of humanity. But all the scene offered up was a group of kids treating the small cenotaph behind the bus stop like their own personal climbing frame and I wasn't sure that was quite enough to whip out the badge. Maybe if I veered closer I'd spot some underage drinking at the very least. No such luck. *Damn you sober children!* I was just going to have to do it. Go home and go on my date like the totally normal adult woman I was.

An hour later I was rummaging through the various collections of grey, black, white, off-white and occasional navy ensembles filling my wardrobe. Between large gulps of wine, I'd landed on a classic: jeans and a nice top. And a jacket. I'd accepted the loss of opportunity to show off my banging arm definition – men liked that in a woman, right? A firmly toned bicep? – because it was freezing, and this wasn't the north-east of England where people are crafted from asbestos and coats are considered blasphemous. I'd gone for my lucky blazer. It was smart, comfortable, and most importantly, easy to wipe clean.

I eyeballed Sleazy Steve as I walked into The Bull ahead of Dom, the young woman who'd given him an alibi earlier now nowhere to be seen.

'Who's that?' Dom asked, my stare clearly not as subtle as I thought.

'We call him Sleazy Steve, he's a bit of a lech.' As if he could feel my eyes on him, Steve looked at me, his glare seeping into the skin on my arms as I removed the blazer. I'd have withheld the show, but the only free table was the one next to the huge fireplace and beads of sweat were already nestling in my eyebrows.

'Oh, OK,' Dom said, 'we can go somewhere else if you want.'

'Trust me, if there was another half decent pub around here there wouldn't be any female clientele in the place.' I hooked my blazer over the back of the chair and sat. 'I doubt he'll be a problem tonight, not while I'm accompanied by a male guardian.'

I carried on watching Steve as we settled ourselves down. Could he be our guy? Sleazy Steve. *Stalker* Steve? It wouldn't be the first time I'd dealt with a fake alibi. If I hadn't had the idea to check a suspect's Apple Watch heart rate and location profile in one of my first jobs in CID, we'd have had no idea our suspect's wife had lied. Telling us he'd been in bed asleep next to her whilst in reality he'd been out ransacking the homes of elderly women in the middle of the night. I let out a sigh, because no, I wasn't lucky enough to pull another find like that out of the bag, and Sleazy Steve was far too obvious. Roy was right, being a creep didn't make him a stalker.

He rubbed a wine glass with a dish towel, twisting it in his hands, eyes now glued to a barely legal patron as she leant over a table to hug her equally young-looking companion. My fists clenched in my lap as I ran through the stalking criteria. The behaviours had to be fixated, obsessive, unwanted and repeated. *Fixated*. Fixating on one person. Sleazy Steve was literally the opposite of that; he'd leer at any woman that came within his line of sight.

'. . . Alice? I don't mind honestly,' Dom said.

Fuck. 'Sorry, what was the question?'

'Drinks, what do you want?'

Concentrate! Stop thinking about work, the world won't

spin off its axis if you have a night off. 'Oh, yeah, erm . . .' I dug around in my bag for my purse.

'Don't worry,' Dom said. 'I'll get them. I was thinking a bottle of red, that work for you?'

I nodded and watched as he walked to the bar. Doesn't feel the need to drink a pint to look macho. Plus twenty points.

Dom came back a few minutes later and placed a bottle of Château Laroque Saint-Emilion and two glasses on to the table. I'd bought a bottle of that stuff for Dad's birthday once; it cost at least £30. 'Oh, erm, I should have said, the house red would be fine. You don't have to buy the good stuff on my account – the wine I drink usually comes from a box.'

'I'd make an excuse about the quality of the grapes or something,' Dom said as he poured a few inches of liquid into each glass, 'but if I'm being totally honest, I don't know anything about wine; I'm just trying to impress you and this looked fancy.'

I liked his honesty. And the wine. Plus fifty points.

'So,' I said, 'I don't think I asked the other night, what brings you to Fortbridge?' I tried to pick up the wine glass like a sommelier instead of a dehydrated sailor.

Dom ran the tip of his finger around the rim of his glass. 'The new physio clinic they're opening at the hospital, mainly. The freelance stuff's been fine, but I needed a bit of stability, salary-wise. And this place is perfect. A nice change of scenery.'

'Yeah, it's not bad around here at all. Much different from where you've moved from?'

126

'You could say that. I've been working in South London for the last few years.'

'Really? You don't sound like a South London boy. Is that where you grew up?'

'No, no, official army brat, so I grew up in a lot of places. Yorkshire, Surrey, a bit of time in Germany. All over the place really. I prefer the countryside though, always find the people to be more friendly.'

'Ha!' I snorted, trying to stop the wine escaping through my nose. 'I'm not sure I'd go that far. It's like anything, isn't it? You get dickheads in all walks of life.'

'True, I've only met a couple of people, but so far so good.' He looked up at me through his eyelashes as he picked up his glass. I bobbed my head and stared at the menu instead of replying. Bit corny, but maybe *I* was just being a dickhead. 'And anyway,' he said, taking his first sip, 'even if the countryside has its own bad apples, so to speak, at least you know there aren't going to be as many. Fewer people, more animals. That sounds pretty good to me.'

I pursed my lips to disguise the smile forcing its way out. Prefers animals to people. *Ding, ding, ding, ding, ding!* Plus five hundred points. Triple score.

The rest of the evening went surprisingly smoothly, and just before eleven the mattress springs twanged as I flopped on to my bed, my stomach expanding with relief when I finally unzipped my jeans. Vince followed suit, his fur grazing my side. I propped myself up on my elbow and tickled his tummy as he stretched himself out like a feline

127

SAM FRANCES

swimsuit model. 'Don't worry, it's just me and you tonight, bud, as usual.'

Overall, Dom had done well. Building his score steadily in the game of Wheel of Alice he didn't know he was playing. He'd gained one thousand points alone by ordering my favourite mozzarella sticks for us to share unprompted, and let me have the last of the odd number. I didn't understand why restaurants did that: dished up food for two and didn't think to base the portion count on each person being able to have an equal share of the goods. I wondered if it was deliberate, a test for new couples, to help them decide if they were compatible early doors based on how they reacted to the issue of 'who gets more of the delicious deep-fried thing'. Dom passed that part of the evening with flying colours. His introduction to Vince, however, had not gone quite as well. 'Have you calmed down now, after your literal hissy fit?' I said, as Vince flipped himself over to block any further tummy access.

I'd never seen Vince hiss at anyone before, not even a drunk Tess when she insists on trying to carry him inside her hoodie like a swaddled newborn. 'You still jealous about the possibility of there being another man in my life, eh? This isn't ancient Egypt, you know – I do have to do things other than just worship you.' He looked up at me before dropping his head to wash his genitals.

OK then. Let's call that agreeing to disagree.

I couldn't really mark Dom too harshly for Vince being a grumpy bastard. He'd already lost some points for not knowing anything about any books, TV shows or films. Not because I thought having that kind of knowledge was a particularly important personality trait, more that it meant he just stared blankly in response to my hilarious jokes, most of which required an in-depth knowledge of late nineties and early noughties entertainment references to get.

Or maybe you just aren't as funny as you think you are?

No, that wasn't it. It was the references thing. Definitely the references.

The pyjamas I'd taken off that morning were on the floor where I'd left them. I pulled them on and crawled into bed. The top corner of the paper that the Be a Better Alice list was written on tore as I yanked it from the jaws of the bull clip holding it to the stem of the lamp on my bedside table. I looked at the points again, my eyes lingering over the last item.

6) Get a social life e.g. DATE!

I'd had a pleasant evening with Dom. I really had. And I hadn't thought about what happened with Jamie once. Or Noah. But was that such a good thing? To forget. Forget how much I'd fucked up? Maybe having that driving me was exactly what I needed. Something to make me work harder. To focus on Camilla's case. Now wasn't the time to be pissing around with my head in the clouds, stomach flipping at a polite goodnight kiss on the cheek. I needed to give this case everything I had and catch whoever was targeting Camilla, before they got too close to her and someone else got hurt on my watch.

20

From the moment he saw the dress in the shop window, he knew it was the one. So acquainted with her body now, having seen it in an array of outfits – in person, in photos and in the footage – he was certain if put to the test he could sculpt a faultless replica from a mound of clay with nothing but his memory for reference. Every curve. Every detail. Down to the very last millimetre. Nothing would ever fit her like the outfit he'd planned. The colour, the cut, the material. It was all perfect.

Clothing says a lot about a person, Father always told him. And he'd been right every time. Those dirty-looking children from the housing estate near Pickford Park weren't to be trusted. It had been one of them who'd put a brick through the window of his father's prized Porsche.

'I saw them, it was those Johnson boys who live next door to the corner shop,' he'd said proudly when Father returned home from his jog, hands on hips in the driveway as he took in the damage. He'd been so pleased with himself, being able to report the perpetrators when the cameras couldn't. They didn't reach that far, trained solely towards activity inside their house.

Father squatted and hugged him tighter than he'd ever done before. 'That's my boy, my clever little man, aren't you? Shame your mother wasn't paying attention, eh?' He'd grabbed him by the shoulders then, still squatting down at his height, turning the pair of them to look back at Mother standing in the doorway. 'Look at her. Probably too busy getting herself all dolled up, trying to get a bit of attention from those horny teenagers. That's why they come down this way in the first place, isn't it? Give themselves a laugh at the old tart.'

He hadn't been sure whether to laugh or not – he'd heard someone at school get told off for calling their teacher that word – but then Father tickled him under his armpits so hard he couldn't help himself. And Mother laughed too, that strange little half-laugh of hers, as if she couldn't be bothered to do it properly, before she disappeared back into the house and didn't come downstairs for the rest of the evening.

It'd barely been a week after the incident with the car when she'd done it again. Put on the same purple tea dress she'd worn that day. The 'tarty' one, as him and Father had started calling it. A Christmas gift from her sister. Her favourite, she'd claimed. But Father's instructions were clear: just because he was out at work didn't mean Mother should be able to disgrace herself like that, especially not in front of company. *Hark at this one*, her friends had said as they'd sat in the living room, him lingering in the doorway with a veil of disapproval draped across his young face after she refused to get changed into something more

131

appropriate, like he'd told her to. *He's going to be a strict one, isn't he? Just like his dad.*

The looks that had followed the comment still confused him, Mother's eyes fixed on the hem of her dress which she twisted between her fingers as knowing glances passed around the other faces in the room. What could they possibly think was wrong with taking after Father? His father had the perfect life. A wife. A handsome son. Lots of important friends. He didn't know what more anyone could want. And he'd told Father as much that night. That had been the last time Mother's friends came to the house, and he'd been glad of it.

Lightning struck his stomach at the feeling of the silk as he skimmed the back of his fingers along the length of the dress. He was afraid to touch it, to hold it properly in case he sullied it.

Everything had to be perfect, just as his father would have liked.

'In my house, we dress for special occasions,' he whispered, leaving the words he'd heard Father say so many times hanging in the air like a delicate perfume as he carefully folded the dress, before placing it back on to the bed of pink tissue paper lining the box.

21

Roy was on the phone when I walked into the office the next morning. 'Forensics,' he mouthed, emphasising every syllable like he was doing face aerobics as he pointed towards a piece of paper on my desk. I read his scrawled message.

Chrissy Marchant – Interview Room 1 – 8:30 a.m.

I checked my watch. 8:36 a.m. *Great.* Roy's attempt at semaphore suggested I needed to make my way downstairs to meet our guest.

The interview room was open a crack, the head of a young girl snapping up from her phone screen as I pushed it wider. 'Chrissy Marchant?' I asked, though I was in no doubt that's who was sitting before me. She was a cookie-cutter Camilla, but a version where the biscuits had slightly burnt around the edges and the consistency of the dough was a little too dry. Tendrils of over-styled hair dyed an unearthly shade of rust fell down the front of her polyester cow print shirt. Both her locks and the material of her top looked like they'd be fire hazards at a bonfire display.

Her hand flew straight in the air like I was calling a school register. 'Yep, that's me.' She looked like she could still *be* at school. It wasn't clear if the flush in her cheeks was from the usual nervousness that accompanied an impromptu trip to a police station, or from having overdone it with the blusher. 'It's Christina actually,' she continued, 'but no one calls me that except my mum, and Gran, but she died last year. Pneumonia. It's fine, though, she was really old, like eighty or something. Gran, I mean, not my mum – she's only forty-two, and that's not *that* old.'

I had no doubt her rambling soliloquy would have continued if not for the wave of panic, her doll eyes doing a full body scan of me, trying to figure out how old I was and whether she'd caused offence. I held my hand out to shake hers. 'Right. Hi. I'm Detective Sergeant Alice Washington. Thanks for coming in. I hope you didn't get the wrong end of the stick from my colleague – we could have come to see you at home.'

'Oh, no, yeah, he did say that, but I've never been here before. I wanted to see what it was like.'

I made a sweeping gesture around the dank room with one outstretched arm. 'You haven't been missing much, I'm afraid. DC Briar who you spoke to on the phone will be down in a minute; he's on a call with the forensics unit.'

'Did they find anything? I still can't believe it.'

'We don't know yet. As much as we'd like it to, it doesn't all happen quite as quickly as it does on *CSI: Miami*, unfortunately.'

She stared back at me, her expression blank. 'CS what?'

Oh yes, I forgot. You're a foetus. I sat down opposite her and wondered if I should have started using Oil of Olay by now. 'Never mind.'

'I went to Miami last year, on a book tour with Camilla. It was a*ma-zing*! She let me fly first class with her. We met Harry Styles in the airport lounge!'

'Wow, that must have been, er, fun. Can I get you something to drink?' *Or anything else to go in your mouth – a ball gag maybe?*

'No, thank you. I'm on a shake diet and I had it on my way in. It's so strict, literally not allowed nothing else, it's a detox cleanse, all very scientific.' Her head nodded at warp speed. 'You can't mess with the levels, or it won't work.'

'Right, the levels, gotcha.' I checked my watch. Where the hell was Roy?

She continued babbling about her miracle shakes.

The door clicked open and Roy lolloped in. 'Apologies,' he said, reaching over the table to shake Chrissy's hand and introduce himself. 'Hope I didn't miss anything.'

Not unless he was interested to hear how many lingonberries and tablespoons of chia seeds she could pack into a 250 ml morning spirit smoothie. I forced a smile and shook my head. 'No, just getting started.' I turned my attention back to Chrissy as Roy sat. 'So, we wanted to see if there's anything you can think of that might help us with our enquiries about those photos that were emailed and then stuck up at the manor.'

'You think it's the same person, then?' she said, eyes wide. 'I knew it.' Roy and I glanced at each other, trying to keep our expressions professional. 'I always thought of myself as a bit of a detective,' Chrissy continued. 'Love all that true crime stuff, that was one of the reasons I was so excited when I got the job with Camilla. I love her books, I've read them all, like, three times each.'

'We think it's a pretty safe bet for us to assume they are linked, yes,' I said. 'So, how long have you worked for Camilla?'

'Technically, I've been helping out since I was a kid. My mum was her family's cleaner before ... well, you know. Then when Camilla was leaving for London she wanted someone local to help look after the place, manage the property and that, so Mum did it, and she'd take me along, you know, in the school holidays and stuff. And when she mentioned she needed an assistant, Mum put in a good word for me. And that was four years ago now, my first job out of school.' She adjusted the layers around her face and exposed a small hair extension clip above her ear. 'I did most of it from here when she was living in London, all her social media and digital stuff. She hates doing all that, but the publisher says it helps with her book sales, so ... I look after her website and her online content now, mostly.' She grinned, her eyes bulging.

'OK,' I said, 'so how much time would you say you spend at the manor, now that Camilla's back living here?'

'Oh, I'm there *all* the time. Like a piece of the furniture, Cam says. Sorry, *Camilla* – I call her Cam,' she said, giggling.

I get it, she's your bestie. 'And can you think of anything you've noticed that seemed out of the ordinary? Anyone hanging around? Unexpected visitors, unscheduled deliveries, anything like that?' Chrissy paused, picking at a chip in IKEA's finest MDF tabletop with a baby-pink fingernail. 'Chrissy? Anything at all, even if you think it's not worth mentioning,' I prompted. 'You never know what might be useful.'

'Well . . . I wasn't sure if it was anything, Myles told me not to say, but . . .'

Mine and Roy's ears pricked up like greyhounds hearing the shot of a starter pistol.

'Go on,' Roy said.

'Well . . . someone rang the intercom last week, then didn't say anything when I answered. I thought the sound weren't working properly so I walked down to the gate, but there weren't anyone there, thought it must have been kids messing around. But then when I was going home later, someone was walking away as I opened the gates. I didn't put the two together, I thought it was someone walking past, but now I think about it . . .'

'OK, and is there anything you can tell us about the person you saw?' I asked.

Her demeanour switched from that of giggly schoolgirl to a toddler who's been told they can't have any ice cream until they finish their vegetables. 'I don't know who he is if that's what you mean.'

'But you think it was a man?' I asked.

Chrissy scrunched up her face. 'I dunno, I just assumed.'

'That's OK,' I replied, 'stalkers are more likely to be male, statistically speaking, but women can be stalkers too.' My mind jumped to intimacy-seeking stalkers, the ones who think they're best mates with celebrities. Chrissy did seem awfully keen to tell us how close her and *Cam* were. Had she really seen someone hanging around? Or was she trying to throw us off? 'We can't just assume it's a man, unless there was something about the person that made you think it was?'

Chrissy shuffled in her seat and readjusted her blouse. 'Sorry, I really don't know, I'm just thinking of the clothes and that.'

'OK,' I said, 'that's a good start – anything about their height, build?'

Chrissy scratched the area around the hair extension clip. 'Umm, no, just the clothes – grey, yeah, definitely grey, I think. It was dark, anyway, like, a tracksuit or joggers or something. They had a hat on, and a scarf, I couldn't see the face.'

If there even was a face to see. 'Anything else?'

Chrissy snorted. 'I said I didn't get a good look. I can't see properly in the dark, I'm not a rabbit!' She looked down. 'Sorry, I don't mean to get all funny. I just wish I could help more, I don't want her to get hurt.'

'That's OK, what you've given us already is really useful. Do you know why Myles didn't want you to tell us about that?'

'I don't want to get him into any trouble; he just said that having the police involved wouldn't help, and that he was going to sort this himself. But it felt wrong, you know, not saying anything.'

'Don't worry, you're not getting anyone in trouble, you've

done the right thing telling us,' I said before Roy chimed in with some routine follow-up questions.

I sat back in my chair and watched as she responded. She was exhausting. Her gestures and expressions were all caricatures of Camilla. There was something mesmerising about her in the sense that you couldn't take your eyes away, but not in the same way as Camilla. The desire to keep watching Chrissy felt more like whatever makes rubber-neckers slow down to get a good look at a mangled car crash on the motorway.

She fiddled. Constantly. With her top. Hair. Earrings. Her hands didn't stop for the entire conversation. Worried about Myles finding out what she'd told us? Worried about what was happening to Camilla? Her boss, her *friend*? Or was it something else? Nerves from knowing more than she was letting on? Or, let's face it, could be the fact the girl has been drinking detox shakes in place of solid food for God knows how long. As if she could read my mind, she somehow managed to bring the conversation back to her diet. 'Right,' I interjected, 'that's been great, Chrissy, thanks again for coming in.'

'No problem. I . . . I'm not in trouble, am I?'

'Why would you be in trouble?' I asked as I stood.

'For not saying, you know, earlier, about the person I saw.'

'No, no, of course not.' I forced a small smile in an attempt at reassurance. 'One more quick thing though, before you go,' I said, 'as you've probably touched the gates a million times, it would really help speed things up

139

with the forensics if we could take your fingerprints to eliminate any marks you might've left behind.'

Chrissy's eyes widened. 'I thought I wasn't in any trouble?'

'You're not,' I said. 'It's standard procedure. We'll be doing the same with Camilla and Myles. We don't want your prints being uploaded to the criminal database by accident, now do we?'

'OK, er, do we need to do it now? I've just had my nails done.'

'Not to worry,' I said, 'your nails will survive.'

'So, what do you think of Miss Marchant then?' I asked Roy as the office door swung closed behind us.

'Miss Mad March Hare, you mean? Absolutely bonkers – given me a right headache with all that jabber.' He sat back in his chair and clasped his fingers behind his head.

That probably had more to do with last night's Laphroaig which I could smell on his breath, but it was true she couldn't half talk. 'Yeah, there's something off about her, isn't there? Her body language is . . . interesting.' I counted on my fingers, 'One, she knows what she's doing with websites, maybe she also knows about fake email addresses. Two, she's got easy access to the house, and three, she's like a Camilla mini-me.'

'Could be *Single White Female*-ing her,' Roy said.

It was a possibility. The way Chrissy's face lit up when she talked about Camilla – was that awe, or envy? There was a fine line. I closed my eyes, waiting for the click I used to get in my head when I was on to something. That spark. But the thought just whirred around and around, the ground-down catch too short to hook on to anything. I cleared my throat, trying to cough up whatever had begun to grip my chest. The instincts would come back, I just needed to give them time.

'You all right?' Roy asked.

'Yeah, fine.' I brushed a strand of hair out of my face. 'Double-check she was actually *in* Bath for the last few days. And we need to see if there's anything in this elusive stranger story as well as anything from the night the gates were vandalised. Any luck with the CCTV enquiries or the photo printing?'

'Not yet,' Roy said. 'Still gotta finish trawling the footage from her doorway, though that's not gonna help us with the gates. Called the bus company and the rugby club yesterday before I left, waiting for a callback. And I'll start ringin' about the pictures this afternoon; there's only a couple of places around here that do it anyway, so shouldn't take long.'

'Right. I think we need to speak to Carrington again, see if he suddenly remembers any mysterious strangers, and maybe he can explain why he told Chrissy to lie to us.'

Roy shrugged. 'I think we already know why, he doesn't want us touching this with a bargepole. We can try, but I'm not sure we'll get much out of him. He doesn't seem to be falling over himself to make friends with either of—' He was cut short by a voice from the doorway.

'Aha! Just the chaps,' Jane exclaimed. 'Can you come through to the office?'

'Hold on to your balls, they're about to get busted ...' Roy whispered when Jane was out of earshot.

'You worry about your own balls, thank you very much.'

We followed Jane through her open door and waited next to it as she answered the ringing phone on her desk, her index finger pointing at us like a withered wand casting a spell of silence. 'Jane Josephs ... yep ... mm-hmm ... got them with me now, sir.' She clicked her fingers and gestured emphatically at the two plastic chairs on our side of the desk. *The minion chairs.* Her gaze drifted back to the phone's cradle as Roy and I looked at each other, our eyes widening in a mutual state of incredulity. 'Mm-hmm ... will do, sir ... yep ... OK.' She hung up the phone. 'So. Author. Stalker. What have you got?' All ten of her spindly fingers drummed on the desk.

Roy updated her on the outstanding lines of enquiry.

'Well, get a move on. That was DCI Carver, he's already fending off calls from the press and the Police and Crime Commissioner's office asking what we're doing about it. You know who her partner's father is, yes?'

'Yes, ma'am,' Roy and I replied in unison.

'He's being a bit standoffish, doesn't really want us involved,' I added in follow-up.

'Well, the father jolly well does, especially after the lovely spread in the paper this morning. I presume you've seen that too?'

We nodded. I'd tried to ignore A. J.'s slant on events on my way past the Post Office, but the headline of *Fortbridge Fox Slayer: Stalker's Deadly Warning to Local Bestseller*, and his assertion that the targeting of *fiery-haired glamour puss Camilla Harton-Gray* was clearly the work of a *psychotic, obsessive fan* was hard to ignore. I should write A. J. a thank you note, get the man a bloody medal. Job solved.

'Well, we aren't going to hear the end of this if you two bugger it up.' *Gee, thanks for the vote of confidence.* 'Keep me posted.' An order, not a request. 'He wants an update as soon as we have one.'

'Yes, ma'am,' Roy and I said in unison. Again.

Jane shuffled some papers on her desk as we awaited further chastisement. 'Well?' she said. 'You're not going to catch anyone sitting around here all day, are you?' She announced she was done with us through three sharp taps on the desk as she aligned a thick stack of reports.

'Ma'am,' we replied, again in chorus like we were channelling the creepy twins from *The Shining*. I pictured Roy in a mid-length brown wig wearing a powder-blue dress as a pink silk bow attempted to contain his paunch.

'Actually, Alice, one more thing,' Jane said as I followed Roy towards the door, not looking up from the paper she'd started to write on.

'Ma'am?'

'The applications for HQ, they'll be opening soon – don't think they won't be watching you like a hawk.'

That was a reminder I didn't need. 'Ma'am,' I said as I continued out the door.

'Don't mess it up, Alice,' she yelled behind me.

Oh, don't you worry, *ma'am*. I won't.

22

Flakes of dried wood fluttered to the rug as I threw another log on the fire, Vince shooting off across the living room like I'd tried to throw *him* in there. Tess bounced as I flopped next to her on the sofa.

'Come on, then,' she said, 'what's the latest on Dom?'

I gave a clinical overview of date night, leaving out the bit about the mozzarella sticks. She'd have taken that as a sign to buy a wedding fascinator.

Her eyebrows danced like a demented clown. 'So far so good, then.'

I hadn't decided what to do about Dom; I didn't need a pile-on from Tess adding weight to the dilemma. Once she had an idea in her head, she didn't let it go. 'Good is maybe overstating it a bit; let's stick with fine for now.'

She shrugged. 'I'll take it, there are worse things a man can be than *fine*.'

'Nice to see you have such high standards for me. Anyway, if we have to talk about love lives then I'm sure yours is far more exciting. Any new targets on the horizon?'

Tess was used to our conversations about men always being one-sided, and not just because I never had anything to contribute. I always thought intimate relationships between two people were exactly that. *Between* two people. Tess respectfully disagreed. With the exception of her first love – who I'd learned very quickly from Tess's mum was completely off limits – she relished in spilling all the gory details about her suitors. An essential part of girl bonding I'd never understand. Maybe that's why I'd never really had a significant female friendship before Tess crowbarred her way into my affections on my first day in Fortbridge. I'd known having her around would make life more interesting when the first thing she asked me, aside from my name, was if it was a good idea to get her heavily pregnant cat Marge to watch *Knocked Up* to help prepare her for labour and life as a first-time mum.

She told me about the latest guy she had her eye on. Nate something. Broad shoulders. Small waist. Chunky thighs. Tess's favourite combo. 'And,' she said, 'he helps his nan every Saturday morning at the church car boot sale. I mean, come on, I'm swooning over here. Man's the full package. I'm going tomorrow to help out and do a bit of recon at the same time – you wanna come?'

I really hoped Nate would live up to this early potential. Tess could do with someone who'd be sympathetic to the fact her mum needed more help now she'd started using a wheelchair. Unlike her ex Freddie, who ended things because apparently Tess's mum's MS was somehow too emotionally draining for *him*. I'd known he was a wrong 'un from the moment I saw his shoes. '*Obviously* helping you attract mates and selling stinky old clothes for 50p a pop

145

are my two favourite things, but can't, sorry. I need to log on and update a couple of bits on the system from this stalking job that I didn't get a chance to finish today.'

'Oh, yeah, right,' Tess said, opening another bottle of wine. 'How's that going – any suspects yet?'

'Nope.' I leant my head back against the grey fleece throw lining the top of the sofa. 'She's got this assistant, Chrissy – there's definitely something off about her, I'm just not sure exactly what. And the boyfriend is like a fucking coiled spring but, I dunno, nothing's firing.'

Tess nodded as she filled our glasses, mine almost to the point of overflowing.

'Oi, watch it.' I nudged her thigh with my heel. 'You're the one who wrote *Drink Less Alcohol* on that bloody list. You're setting me up for failure.'

'Come on, I didn't mean on Fridays!' She put the bottle down and handed me my glass. 'Anyway, this'll help you think. Loosen the mind.'

'I could just be overthinking the Chrissy thing, could just be admiration. I mean, I'm straight and only met Camilla a couple of times and even *I* might be a little bit in love with her.'

Tess choked on her drink. 'I presume you've ruled yourself out as a suspect?'

'God, yes, I haven't got the commitment to be a stalker, seems like an awful lot of effort.'

Tess reached the back of her hand to her mouth to stifle a wine burp. 'Anyone else in mind?'

146

'Roy put the shits up Sleazy Steve for sending pervy messages on her socials, but other than that, nothing yet.'

'Oh my God, yes! My money's on Sleazy Steve. He's so disgusting.'

'I wish it was that easy,' I said before taking a sip of wine, the tannins sending a mini electric shock along my jawline. 'But being disgusting doesn't make you a stalker, unfortunately. And that guy doesn't seem to do anything anonymously – had his real name and profile picture right alongside the messages, not trying to hide a thing, and he's got an alibi for the night the manor gates were vandalised.'

'Hmm, what about the boyfriend then? Isn't it always the boyfriend or the husband?' Tess said, picking at the label on an empty wine bottle.

'That would naturally be the go-to if she'd been attacked or murdered, or if he was an *ex*-boyfriend. But why would someone stalk their current girlfriend? And use her own book as a guide to do it? It doesn't make any sense.'

'Doesn't that freak her out,' Tess said, 'that they're using her own mind against her, in a way? I'd be out of there in a second if someone did that to me, if I knew what was potentially coming.'

'I mean, I don't think she's thrilled about it, obviously, but the woman's got gumption; she's not letting this arsehole dictate her life.'

'Have you tried asking your dad? Maybe he's got some ideas?'

I'd wondered how long it would take for someone to suggest a referral to 'mighty Mick'. What would my dad have done with this job that I hadn't done already? 'Mick Washington doesn't believe in help. He's very much a "stand on your own two feet" kind of man.'

'Don't be daft, he's your dad – why wouldn't he want to help you?'

I regaled her with one of the many stories where my dad left me to it, the time Danny Graham – the resident bully at school – shoved me over after I kicked his arse in the fifty-metre dash on sports day when I was eleven. I didn't remember what exactly caused my switch to flip: the discomfort of parched blades of summer grass bristling against the back of my bare arms, or the sight of Dad just standing there watching. Barely a flinch of reaction. Face neutral. Whatever it was, before I knew it, Danny's tree-trunk body crashed down on to the grass beside me, my shin aching from where I'd swung at his ankles. The other kids chanting, 'Fight! Fight! Fight!' I re-enacted the last part of the story and Tess laughed as I punched the air like a cheerleader with a severe lack of hand-eye coordination.

'You're too hard on him,' Tess said, pointing an accusatory finger. 'Sounds like he was just teaching you to stick up for yourself.'

Or teaching me a lesson more like. For Noah. *Not now!*

Tess dragged her curls into a bun on top of her head. 'I still don't get why you don't just leave this case for Roy to get on with, though. It doesn't really sound like there's enough for both of you to get stuck into.'

'No way, otherwise the latest thing they're going to associate me with at HQ when my application goes in will be

Jamie, and . . .' *Fuck*. The wine was indeed loosening things, just not in relation to the case. I pulled one leg up on to the cushion and hugged it.

She rested her foot against my shin. 'I don't know how many times you need to hear this, but it wasn't your fault. I get it, though, why you can't forget about it – the kid was only twelve, and with what happened to your brother and everything . . .'

My breath snagged. Twelve years old. Three years more than Noah got. 'I'm fine, this's got nothing to do with Noah.'

I scratched the hot itch spreading across my chest. I'd regretted telling Tess about my brother from the second the words slipped out after three bottles of wine. We'd rarely spoken about it since, but in the moments where she was reminded, like the other day with Eddie's retelling of Camilla's backstory, her pity was acid on my skin. I should be grateful pity was all it was. If she'd known the whole story, about why my dad might want to see me take a kicking from Danny Graham, why I really felt so guilty, then even she might not be quite so forgiving.

I pushed myself off the makeshift mattress I'd fashioned on the floor from a pile of pillows, Tess still doing her best impression of a giant starfish across the bed. The top of my spine crunched as I circled my neck before reaching over and slapping her calf.

'Ow!' Tess grumbled, eyes barely opening as she lifted her head. 'What was that for?'

I nodded at her outstretched limbs. 'Sleep well, did you?'

She propped herself up on her elbows. 'Oops, sorry, what time is it?'

'About half nine.'

Tess nearly kicked me in the head as she swung her legs off the bed. 'Shit, gotta go, car boot starts at ten.' She pulled her hoodie on, the silk wrap she slept in to protect her textured hair getting dragged off in the process, and half stuffed her feet into her Converse. 'Right, don't work too hard today, will you? See you Monday.'

'Bye,' I yelled after her.

I was about to relax back on to the pillows when I heard voices as Tess opened the front door. I walked downstairs, following the sound. Tess held the door handle as she looked back at me, her grin so wide it looked like her teeth were multiplying before my eyes.

'Dom. Hi,' I said, suddenly very aware of the pyjama shorts riding up my arse.

'Hi, sorry, I was about to knock, but then the door opened and—' He looked down at his watch. 'I'm off for a run and was going to ask if you wanted to join me. Sorry, I didn't know you had company.'

'Don't you worry about me,' Tess said, 'I'm just leaving.' She looked back again, eyes now competing with her mouth for space on her face.

'Erm,' I came the rest of the way down the stairs and stood beside her, 'I'm a bit hungover, can I take a rain check?'

Tess glared at me. 'Exercise is good for hangovers, actually, and we didn't have *that* much wine.'

Judas. 'Yeah, not quite feeling it this morning, maybe next time,' I said, mentally donkey-kicking her in the shin. I still hadn't decided whether to turn the dial up or down on this potential love interest situation, and it was far too early on a weekend morning to be making important life decisions. Plus, I needed a wee.

'Yeah, sure, no problem,' Dom said. 'I'll catch you later. Feel better.'

He walked backwards a couple of steps before turning and jogging out on to the lane.

Tess looked at me, her jaw hanging so low it seemed barely attached to the rest of her face. 'Are you kidding me? He's *just fine*, is he? He could make a coat from actual kittens and I'd still go out with him. Man, those eyes! And thoughtful too, coming over here like that, inviting you on a little morning date.'

'All right, calm down, the guy asked me to go for a jog. He's hardly the bloody Milk Tray man.'

'But you like running, and dating's on the list, remember?' Tess tilted her head forward and raised one eyebrow. If she had a moustache, she would have been twirling it.

'Yeah, exercise is on the list, and dating is on the list. Two separate items. You can fuck right off if you think I'm doing both at the same time.'

She gave me *the eyes*. 'But you'll go out with him again, yeah?'

'Stop being so nosy. Anyway, you don't have time for this, you've got your own man to snag.'

I lay down on the bed as Tess's car crunched off the

driveway. I needed the rest. If her day went well, she'd be on the phone later giving me Nate's life story. His favourite film, shoe size, greatest fear in life. I had to admit, as full-on as she was sometimes, I was a little jealous of her ability to just go for it when it came to love. Let those walls down without a second thought. Tess claimed to be a real romantic, but there was something to be said for my own parents' approach to showing affection. The look on Mum's face when Dad presented her with an envelope wrapped in a bow on their wedding anniversary one year had stuck with me. I'd peeked my head around the door to see what it was. Coveted theatre tickets? Paperwork for a luxurious all-inclusive cruise? No. Not even close. 'You can't beat the gift of peace of mind,' Dad had said as Mum examined the printout of a life insurance certificate, her pixie nose wrinkled with confusion.

It *was* quite romantic, if you thought about it. Turned out Beyoncé was ill-informed. It wasn't a ring on the finger that showed how much you loved someone. It was the willingness and perseverance required to answer four hundred and thirty-seven questions about your family history of mental health, moles, bowel movements, and every possible ailment, ache and pain over the phone to a complete stranger that really did it. *That's* true love.

I reached for the small white picture frame on my bedside table. Mum's serene face stared back from the photo, her elbow resting on Dad's thigh as she knelt on the floor by his feet, leaning back against the sofa he was sat on. Heat filled my chest. She looked so happy. *Had* been happy. It'd just been part of Mum's life, the visible clench of concern holding her body tight every time Dad left for work, the constant niggle in her mind that today would be the day something would happen to him and he wouldn't come home. The irony wasn't lost on anyone that the qualities that drew Mum to Dad in the first place were the very things that had terrified her. His bravery. His conviction. His refusal to stand by and let injustice happen in front of him. Every time he'd got held up late working, a different nightmare scenario had played out in Mum's mind as she'd secretly wished he'd be just a little bit less of a good man sometimes before it was the death of him, even if that'd made her selfish.

A thin layer of dust coated the photograph. I wiped it with my finger, the full detail of Dad's expression catching in my throat. The way he beamed down at her. That old glow that shone only for Mum. The light that permanently dulled the day she received her diagnosis, prompting his decision to retire, and extinguished completely when the breast cancer took her two years later. 'Just me and you now, kid,' Dad had said through glassy eyes at the hospital as he'd patted me on the shoulder and walked off down the corridor. The rolling tear made it halfway down my cheek before I wiped it away with the sleeve of my pyjama top.

I jumped as my phone made an unearthly metallic noise, vibrating against the base of the lamp. A text from Roy. We were meeting Myles Carrington at nine o'clock on

Monday. I pushed out thoughts of Mum, Dad and Dom, and pulled my memory of Myles's face from the Rolodex in my brain. If he was hiding something, I had to figure out what.

23

Roy and Tess were arguing by the printer when I arrived Monday morning. I didn't need this today. The little sense of relaxation I'd mustered over the weekend in between bouts of mentally overpreparing for the conversation with Myles was already evaporating faster than a shallow puddle in a heatwave.

'Here, will you tell her,' Roy said as he walked over to my desk. 'I've got better things to do than fanny around with office equipment. We've got five minutes till Carrington gets here and I've still gotta follow up with forensics again.' He gestured back towards Tess with his arm outstretched like a prosecutor who'd just disclosed the key piece of evidence to a jury.

It took every ounce of restraint not to smash their heads together. *Breathe and smile.* 'They don't pay me enough to referee you two. Sort it out amongst yourselves, please, children.' Roy stormed off towards the hallway and Tess took his place by my desk.

'Someone needs to remind him that just because I'm not a police officer doesn't mean I'm the friggin' admin assistant,' she said.

155

I turned my computer on. 'Bagsy not.'

I'd already been given the initial low-down on Nate when Tess called after the car boot sale, but she still had plenty of updates to give after they'd gone out for drinks last night. I skimmed my emails for anything urgent as I listened.

'Mate, I can't even tell you, he . . .'

Tess carried on talking but her words turned to mush in my ears as I saw the email about the vacancy for the MCU sergeant's position. It had been sent to everyone who'd put in an expression of interest. All thirty odd of us. Of course Bret was first on the list. Followed by Celeste Augustus, the literal poster woman for the community safety partnership work the Chief bragged about at any given opportunity. Twice she'd headlined on *Police Oracle*. The more recipient names I scanned, the tighter my insides twisted. I needed something to stand out from this crowd of overachievers. The click of Tess's fingers in my face distracted me from the panic.

'Oi! Are you listening?'

'Sorry, yeah, it's just—' We both turned as the door to the office swung open. Bret. Early. *Again.*

I made a point of swinging my arm up to check my watch. 'What you doing here? Mix your shifts up or something?'

He turned his computer on and sat down without taking off his coat. 'MCU job's up today. Want to get my application done before I clock in. Some of us can't rely on our surname to get to the top of the pile,' he said, staring at his screen like he'd just made some innocuous comment rather than hurling a massive insult my way. Bret probably

156

wasn't the only one who thought I'd somehow waltzed through my promotion board because of who my dad was, but what the hell did he know about how much work I'd put in? I was just about to sling a barb right back when he started talking again. 'Got your email, by the way, last week, the porch light thing. But you and your neighbour can stand down. The people I'm looking at are targeting big pieces of kit. Doubt they'd have much interest in swiping your lawnmowers. Probably just some rapscallions getting overexcited playing a game of Knock Down Ginger.'

Rapscallions. *Rapscallions?* It was sometimes easy to forget Bret was quite physically attractive, especially when the man spoke like he hadn't held a conversation with another actual live human since the dawn of the seventeenth century.

Roy came through the door before I had time to respond. 'Carrington's here,' he said. 'You ready?'

I nodded and followed him out of the office. I had more important things to worry about today than Bret Seaborn.

Roy stopped and turned to me halfway down the stairs. 'Before we get in there, I've been on to the hotel where Chrissy stayed in Bath; check-in and check-out is as she says.'

'OK, so that rules her out for vandalising the gates. Let's see what Myles has to say for himself about telling her to zip it about the person hanging around.'

Myles stuck out in reception like a beacon. His matt navy suit folded in all the right places, creases melting perfectly

157

into the fabric as he stood and followed my direction towards the interview room. 'Thanks for coming in,' I said. 'We just need to follow up on a few things.'

Roy came in behind us and closed the door.

Myles sat down hard on the chair, tightly crossing his arms over his chest. 'I'm only here because Camilla practically begged me to speak to you. I'd still much rather deal with all this myself, so I know it's done *properly*.'

He adjusted the collar of his crisp white shirt as his words resonated in my ears. Now I realised exactly who he'd reminded me of when I met him last week. Robin Golding, who'd had the exact same dismissive tone the night he was brought in not long after I moved to Fortbridge. His insistence there was no need for police, sure we all had more important things to be doing than dealing with him and his wife's 'little misunderstanding'. I hadn't even known what he'd been brought in for when I saw him in the custody suite, laughing and joking with the arresting officers about their good old school days, Golding – local lothario turned picture-perfect husband and doting father – centre of attention, a place where he was clearly in his element.

The senses had tingled immediately, like lips after a brush of hot chilli. I'd been the only one not to fall for his act about how those scrapes and bruises reported by a concerned neighbour got on to his wife's face. Too many Proseccos at a friend's hen party my arse. My instincts had been right about Golding, and they'd been what had stopped him being able to drive home to give her another beating as punishment for not covering up the last one well enough. And they were tingling again now, with Myles. *See, there they are! Just needed time.* 'Well,' I said, watching him as he brought both hands to rest on the table, 'we thought it would be a good idea to see if you can have another think about anything out of the ordinary, anything at all, anyone hanging around the manor, something like that. Sometimes things might not seem worth a mention, but you never know.' I clicked the top of my pen.

Myles's deep exhalation curled the fraying edges of my notepad. 'I don't know what you want me to say. I have no idea who's doing this, and even if I did, I'd sort it myself.'

If Myles was anything like Robin Golding, it wouldn't be too difficult to push his buttons. To scratch away the veneer covering his desire for control. People like them didn't react well when you knew something they didn't. Chrissy's little revelation, as useless as it was turning out to be, might be just what I needed. 'Is that why you told Chrissy not to tell us about the person she saw hanging around outside the manor?'

Myles's eyes darted back and forth between me and Roy. 'I don't know what you're talking about.' He leant forward and pressed steepled fingers into the patch of skin between his lips and his perfectly symmetrical nose.

'So you *didn't* tell her to lie?' I asked.

He slapped his palms down on to the table. 'I didn't have to, because she hasn't said anything to me about seeing someone.'

I tried to figure out which would anger him more: realising

Chrissy had defied his order, or Chrissy having information she hadn't told him. Either way, he clearly wasn't happy that he didn't wield the sort of power he thought he did. 'So why would Chrissy say you did?'

Myles frowned. 'You've met the girl, haven't you? Loves a bit of drama. Wouldn't put it past her to have made the whole thing up just to get herself involved. She's always got to be *involved* in everything Cam and I do. She's like a yappy little shadow. She wants to be a writer herself, you know? Good at making up stories, clearly. Did she happen to mention that as well? No, no, I bet she missed that out, didn't she?'

Was he jealous of Camilla and Chrissy's friendship? Was that what this was? Or was he telling the truth? I had wondered the same thing when she so suddenly remembered seeing someone. But now Myles was spouting the theory, I wasn't sure I believed it any more. In fact, something told me not to believe a single word this man said. 'No, she didn't, actually. Myles, do you think Chrissy could have anything to do with what's happening to Camilla?'

He smiled, but only with one side of his mouth. 'She wouldn't dare.'

I leant forward so our faces were closer together. 'Why not? What would she think you'd do if you found out she had?' I replied, deliberately sharpening my tone. Control freaks don't like to be challenged.

He held on to his smile, but only just. I could see the muscles in his face trying to drag it back into a flat line. Men like Myles and Golding were so fucking predictable.

'Are we done here?' he asked, the volume on his voice turned up a notch.

'If you want us to be,' I said, leaning back against my chair. 'You're not under arrest, you're free to leave at any time.'

Myles pressed his knuckles into the desk, using them to push himself to standing. 'I'll be off then, if it's all the same to you. Like I said, I don't know anything, and even if I did, I wouldn't trust you lot with it anyway.'

'Your choice, Mr Carrington,' Roy interjected. 'Just one more thing, though – could we grab a set of elimination fingerprints from you, help us weed out anything of use if we find any marks from the exhibits we recovered from the crime scene? You'll have touched the gates, yeah?'

Myles didn't answer. Just snorted a laugh and walked to the door.

Roy looked at me and gave a 'we can't force him' shrug. And we couldn't. Giving fingerprints was totally voluntary unless we arrested him, which other than the alarm bell ringing in the back of my mind telling me there was something he was hiding, we had absolutely no grounds to do. *Yet*.

I took a final shot at it before he pulled open the door. 'The alternative is that some of your fingerprints might inadvertently get uploaded to the criminal database if we find any on the gates and don't have the elims to rule them out, and we wouldn't want that, would we? Waste of everyone's time.'

He paused before letting out a deep, annoyed breath. 'Fine, I've got nothing to hide.'

Roy took Myles through the elimination print rigmarole before showing him out and coming back to the office.

'Nice chap, what does Camilla see in him?' Roy said as he sat at his desk.

'You mean other than his dazzling personality?'

Roy raised his eyebrows and pushed his lips out. 'Speaking of Camilla, better give her a ring and see if Chrissy said anything to her about this alleged lurker.' He picked up the phone on his desk.

'Good idea,' I said, 'because *someone* is lying, and I want to know who.'

24

The Chrissy or Myles debate stayed in my head for the rest of my shift, and was still hanging on in there as I stood at the kitchen island that evening. Droplets of wine splashed the worktop as I poured a glass, each one a little representation of a red flag about their personalities. His aggressively perfect aesthetic and blatant need for control. A barely submerged rip tide simmering beneath the surface of his bronzed skin. The Camilla doppelganger make-over Chrissy appeared to have given herself. And had she lied about someone hanging around? About Myles telling her not to say anything? That made sense if Myles really did want to deal with this himself, but something else seemed to be going on here. Another reason he didn't want police sniffing around. But why? This wasn't the same as Robin Golding and his wife. There was no sense from Camilla of any fear towards him. I couldn't ignore the uncomfortable feeling he'd given me both times we'd met, but something wasn't adding up. *Or maybe it tallies perfectly and you just can't see it?*

No. None of that today. There was nothing more I could do about it until we went to pay them a visit in the morning, given that neither Camilla nor Chrissy had answered their phones when Roy called earlier. In fact, one by one, every lead in this case was fizzling out. No one in the area who developed or enlarged photos had any record of printing the images stuck up at the manor. There was nothing of use on the CCTV from either Camilla's door or the bus, and the cameras at the rugby club had been broken for over a year. The only thing we were waiting on was possible DNA and fingerprint examination, but I was almost certain you could make out glove marks on the SOCO photos, so the likelihood of getting anything of use from that was slim to none.

I took a large swig of wine and scrolled to the icon of the mindfulness app Tess had downloaded for me on my phone. 'OK, O-K.' I shook my head, exhaling deeply. 'Let's try and leave work at the office for once, switch off the brain, let's go.'

The first instruction was to sit comfortably in a meditation chair. Annoyingly, it didn't specify the difference between that and a regular chair. I went to the living room and sat on the sofa, hit play and closed my eyes tight. A woman's voice oozed from the speaker. She sounded a bit like Camilla. *Stop thinking about work and relax!*

'Notice the feeling of your breath,' she instructed. 'Draw attention to your body . . . feel the bottom of your feet on the ground, feel your hands . . .'

I opened and closed my fingers, still stewing about the case.

'. . . concentrate on your breath, in and out, holding at either end of those breaths, for one, two . . .'

The more she told me to focus on my breath, the more I forgot how to breathe. Suddenly having to think for the first time in my life about which muscles to contract and release, the air stuttering in and out of my mouth like the propeller on a plane about to stall.

'. . . feel the rise and fall of your chest . . .'

Things falling was the opposite of what I needed to be thinking about right now. Because when I thought of falling my mind immediately went to Jamie. Jamie falling. Jamie falling from the church roof.

'. . . and notice if your mind wanders, bring it back to focussing on your breath . . .'

How did people do this *without* their mind wandering? My brain was flitting about more than Marco bloody Polo.

Breathe in.

No amount of breathing was going to fix this, thoughts and memories ricocheting like someone had thrown a bag of ball bearings into the drum of a washing machine.

Breathe out.

Myles. Chrissy. Camilla. Jamie. Dead foxes. Jamie. Noah. *Oh my God, why are you so terrible at this!*

This was pointless. Absolutely bloody pointless. I was thinking about work-related shit more than I was before I turned the stupid app on. I fumbled with my phone until the talking ceased. Scanning the living room, I looked for another distraction. But the first thing my eyes homed in on was Camilla's novel, the neon cover contrasting against the dark grain of the wooden coffee table. It had sat there, untouched, since Tess gave it to me at the pub last week. I picked it up and ran my finger along the embossed title as an image of a large white eye complete with dilated pupil glared at me. Sod it. I was clearly a work-obsessed freak, might as well lean in to it.

I couldn't remember the last time I'd actually sat down and read a book that wasn't the *Blackstone's Police Manual*. Sure, Eddie had already given me the gist, but why was I relying on him? What if he'd missed something? Hadn't read between the literal lines? He wasn't exactly known for his diligent work ethic, and I had a more detailed knowledge of the case than him; maybe I'd see something he hadn't. I curled up on the sofa, five hours passing in no time. The blanket crept further and further up my body like some sort of impenetrable shield to keep me safe from any psycho stalkers that might be prowling my territory, like Arden King from Camilla's book.

The storyline wasn't particularly innovative. She hadn't strayed too far from the old tropes for Arden: the stereotypical school nerd with no friends, idolising from afar the main character, the popular and conventionally attractive Lyddie Harker. A classic case of boy meets girl, boy wants girl, girl doesn't want boy, boy feels personally wounded and vows to seek lifelong revenge for girl's perfectly acceptable decision not to be obliged to go out with every boy who fancies her. *We know the drill*. It started with photos of Lyddie at athletics practice being emailed to her from an anonymous account. And then it got dark. Really dark.

I clasped my mouth, gripping tighter and tighter with

every chapter. I already knew the main events, but actually reading the descriptions was something else. And it was the bits in between that were the creepiest. The sneaking around. The watching her every move. The bits that probably seemed innocuous to Eddie in comparison to the overtly gory bits. I wasn't a religious person, but I prayed to anyone who would listen that Camilla wasn't about to live-action role-play the darkest corners of her imagination.

There was only a couple of pages left of the penultimate chapter when a noise from outside made my hanging mouth snap shut.

I froze.

Held my breath.

Listened.

I inched up from the sofa as slowly as my muscles would allow. There it was again, the noise. Something snapping. Rustling? My heart thudded, every beat pounding in my ears like there were moths trapped inside, flapping their wings against the canal walls, desperate to escape. I stared at the window. It looked out over the back garden down towards the fields. The shutters were folded back away from the pane, leaving an empty black square, just waiting to be filled. My fingers curled around the neck of the wine bottle I'd left on the side table as I crept towards it. Body braced. Waiting for something to burst into view.

The noise had stopped by the time I reached the window. No sound. No movement. My eyes strained, tension tugging as I peered outside. Nothing but my own reflection stared back. I cupped my free hand over my eyebrows and squinted into the darkness, my other hand still holding the bottle.

Nothing.

Just stillness.

Quiet.

Until something sent me reeling, the momentum catapulting the bottle from my hand.

25

Roy put his chicken tikka-stained dinner plate on to the table beside his armchair and picked up the TV remote. He ignored the gurgling in his stomach. At some point he'd have to admit these microwave meals were playing havoc with his insides and he needed to do something about his lack of culinary skills, but today was not that day.

Three months he'd kept himself fed. Clothed. *Alive*. More to show Karen he didn't need her rather than because he'd actually wanted to. He could have sworn he'd seen a tinge of doubt in her face as she'd wheeled that silver suitcase with the broken handle across the threshold of their home for the last time. The same threshold where they'd giggled thirty years earlier after he'd accidentally banged her head on the doorframe carrying her through it after far too many bitters at their wedding. 'Come on,' Roy had said as she'd hesitated. 'Let's stop all this nonsense, sit down, have a cup of tea, and talk this through, yeah? Just like we always do.'

She'd looked at him like he was speaking a foreign language. 'Talk? You want to talk? You haven't talked to me for about fifteen years! You're like a ghost. You don't live in this goddamn house, Roy, you haunt it.'

And with that, she'd left. Down the driveway. Towards *him*. Mr Mid-life Bleeding Crisis sitting there in his bright red Mercedes SL500.

He turned up the volume on the telly to drown out his thoughts and flicked through the channels, surfing from one mindless programme to the next. Had it really been fifteen years? Fifteen years since everything had changed. Fifteen years since Karen had slapped the newspaper down on to the breakfast table, jabbing her bright red fingernail at the front-page story covering the job he'd rather forget and asking him if what she'd read was true. He'd tried to explain it wasn't his fault, hindsight being 20/20 and all that. But she didn't look at him the same way again. The pride she used to have in him, in being a copper's wife, gone. He knew she'd never really forgotten what happened to that woman, and the role she thought he'd played in it. His throat filled with clay. He couldn't have saved her anyway. He was sure of it. Three weeks couldn't have made that much of a difference.

He looked at the photograph on the shelf above the TV. A nine-year-old Laurie stared back, perched on the knee of a much younger Roy. Those were the days. Where he told *her* what to do. Not the other bleeding way around. She thought she knew everything now, that kid. And she wasn't half demanding. He'd done that stupid programme she'd asked him to do and he didn't feel any different. 'Maybe that's because I haven't got bleedin' depression,' he'd told her the last time they'd talked on the phone.

'Or maybe it's because you're not taking it seriously!' she'd barked back.

His cheeks burned at the thought of the last time he'd seen his daughter in the flesh, or heard her slamming the door as she'd left, anyway; he'd been too drunk to actually *see* her. But it had been a Friday night. Who doesn't get drunk on a Friday night? Just because her generation went to coffee shops and vegan cafés instead of pubs didn't mean he had to. He patted the sleeping dog wedged between him and the arm of the chair. 'You listen to me, don't you, eh?'

Something caught in his craw as he looked at the empty tan leather wing-back sitting in what had been Karen's spot, parallel to his, facing the TV and worn on its seat. 'We'll take that down the charity shop this weekend, eh Bobs? More room for us to play with your rope toy thing.' The small whippet barely registered the sound of his voice in its deep sleep. He ran his hand along her pink tummy, the exposed velvety skin soft under his calloused fingers. 'Just the two of us now, girl,' he said, the whisky taking control of his eyelids. His hand pressed against the volume button on the remote, turning it as loud as it went just as the theme tune from *Holby City* kicked in.

'Jesus Christ!' What was left of his drink slopped down the front of him and a little fell on the dog who shot off across the living room. 'Woah, woah, woah, it's all right, I'm sorry, I'm sorry.' He wiped at his jumper with one hand whilst trying to turn off the TV with the other, but nothing happened. 'Come on, for fuck's sake,' he said, moving closer to the sensor and jabbing at the power button. He stopped.

'Hold on a minute,' he said as he noticed a face on the screen. 'Well I never.' Myles Carrington was staring back at him. Not involved in the main action, but being put into a hospital bed in the background. A thought hit him and he pulled his phone from his pocket.

26

Vince scarpered back through the doorway he'd just entered as the wine bottle smashed against the living room wall. One hand sprang to my chest, the other to the arm of the sofa to brace myself. 'Jesus, you scared the living shit out of me, stupid cat!' *Yes, that's the problem here. A cat entering a living room. Not your insane overreaction to it.*

I turned on the big light and went back to the window, the black square still empty. 'Idiot!' I said to my reflection. And now I was talking to myself, great. I stared at the clump of hair knotted up on one side of my head like I'd been styled by a scarecrow. 'Be a *Better* Alice? Jesus Christ. Be a *sane* Alice would be a start.' I tiptoed around the shards of glass and red dregs of liquid spattered across the floor before rummaging through a drawer in the side cabinet, pulling out a bubble-wrap envelope to scoop up the mess. The pieces clinked like windchimes and a small splinter forced its way down the inside of my fingernail. 'Ow, shit!' I held my hand up. A dome of blood formed on the tip of my finger, swelling until it burst, before trickling down and changing direction at the crease in the back of my knuckle.

Paws padded towards me as Vince emerged from his

hiding place, rubbing himself against my side as I sat cross-legged on the floor. He climbed on to me and made himself comfortable across my inner thigh, resting his chin on my knee. 'I'm sorry, bud.' I used my non-bleeding hand to stroke him between the ears, the vibration of his immediate purr a tiny massage. 'That was a bit dramatic, wasn't it?'

I wrapped a strip of bubble-wrap around my finger and let my head fall back against the wall, thinking about what Jane had said on my first day back. About Bev and the counselling. The Chief's blog about *The Changing Face of Policing*. Maybe things *were* different now. Maybe they wouldn't automatically throw my application in the bin because I was having a bit of a hard time. It was cool now, wasn't it, therapy? You couldn't hear a single celebrity talk for more than twenty seconds on a podcast without them mentioning their therapist.

Vince climbed off my leg and stretched out, arching his back in a perfect execution of what Tess had told me was called Puppy Pose in the yoga world. She was going to have me speaking like one of them in no time. And maybe she was right, about all the self-help stuff, and about talking to someone. People would understand. It wasn't every day you saw something like what I'd seen, with Jamie.

But this isn't just about Jamie.

I closed my eyes as my muscles fought against the momentary sense of release. Deep down, I knew I'd done what anyone would have that night on the church roof. I'd replayed it a thousand times in the last few weeks. From the very first word to the last.

'Hi Jamie, my name's Alice. I'm a police officer, and I'm here to listen to you – is that OK, Jamie?' I'd said, holding my voice steady, nerves and the cold night air biting at my throat.

The first five or six questions I'd asked were met with silence, the boy's lips pulled tight, locking away his words. The only noise when I wasn't speaking had been the rustling of leaves, the breeze forcing itself between the branches at the top of the nearby oak tree that'd swayed gently to our right.

No matter what I'd said, Jamie's eyes had remained fixed on his toes. Mine too. I hadn't been able to stop looking at his feet. How small they were. Too small to be up there on his own. Too small to have climbed on to that wall. Too small to have been barely an inch from the edge. It wasn't until I'd taken in the rest of him I'd noticed his replica shirt. 'You into football then, Jamie?' I'd waited a beat. 'Who's that you've got on there, Jamie, Bristol City?' I'd known it wasn't. Dad supported Bristol City, who wore red. Jamie's top had been blue and white.

His eyes had flicked towards mine, just for a second, but enough to make my heart leap into my throat. 'Rovers,' he'd said, his voice barely audible over the breeze and the leaves.

I'd grown in confidence then, but I could still feel the dryness that had scraped my throat. 'D'you go to see them a lot, Jamie, does your mum or dad take you?'

'Mum takes me.' There'd hardly been a gap between my question and his reply. *I'm in*, I'd thought. *Thank God.*

'That's good,' I'd said, resisting the urge to go too far, too

175

fast. All I'd wanted to do was run the four metres between us and grab him and pull him away from that drop. 'And do you play, Jamie?'

He'd nodded.

'Yeah, you any good then, Jamie?' By that point his name hadn't felt like it was a real word any more, I'd said it so much. But that's what they train you to do. Keep saying their name. And I'd thought it was working.

He'd nodded again.

I should have noticed that even though he'd been responding as I kept talking, with nods, shakes of his head and shrugs of his shoulders, the words had stopped. But I hadn't. I was still yabbering on about how talented I bet he was and how I was sure he had a bright future ahead of him and how proud his mum was, when he'd jumped, the blond mop of hair and blue and white shirt gone in a split second. A noise I would have no clue how to explain to a therapist had come out of me like an exorcism as I'd launched myself to the spot where he'd been. Seeing his body splayed down below on the cobbles. Stone scraping through my clothing as my legs had given way and I'd slumped down the wall like a rag doll.

I didn't know the football club was the problem. That that's where the bullying was happening. And I'm sure any therapist would say the same thing if I told them. *How could you?*

But talking to a therapist would also mean talking about Noah. The day *he* died. Therapists dig. That's what they do. It's what they're good at. And what happened that day at the beach was something that needed to stay buried.

The skin on my cheek peeled off the sofa cushion as I lifted my head, woken by the daylight streaming in through the window. I sat up and rubbed my face, wincing as I caught my injured finger. Shaped like a scabby little smile, the cut looked like it was laughing at me, proud as punch of the crusty brown trail it had started that led all the way down the back of my hand towards the cuff of my hoodie. I went to stand, jumping as the soiled piece of bubble wrap that had fallen off during the night popped under the weight of my foot. I needed to get my shit together.

I went to the kitchen and filled a glass with water, glugging down the liquid. Shrivelled organs swelled with each mouthful. I'd finished most of the bottle of wine last night before I'd hurled it across the room. No wonder I was feeling paranoid. Reading Camilla's book and drinking too much wine had put non-existent monsters and stupid ideas in my head. Was that really all it took? Too much Merlot and a scary story? Even if I *had* heard something, it was probably just stupid *rapscallion* kids fannying about in the farmer's field out the back anyway. Probably playing a game of pissed midnight tag around the large hay bales – it wouldn't be the first time I'd caught them doing that.

My phone buzzed behind me on the island, the message icon flashing as well as an alert telling me I had several

other missed calls. I looked at the clock. 10:07 a.m. 'Shit.'
I read the text and the glass almost slipped from my hand.
I ran upstairs to throw on some clothes as Roy pulled up
outside, honking his horn like a maniac.

27

Roy slammed on the brakes, pulling us up alongside the large green veterinary van parked in the driveway of Bertram Manor.

He flung open his door. 'What sort of psycho does that to someone's pet?'

My mind jumped back to Camilla's book. The rabbits. The blood. I let out a semi-sigh of relief that whoever was doing this hadn't gone to the extremes of her fictional stalker. The dogs were alive, at least.

Roy was still ranting. 'It's one thing doing stuff to humans, half of them bleedin' deserve it, but animals? Evil. Absolutely evil.'

A puffy-eyed Chrissy met us at the door, her hand clutching the neckline of a long-sleeved pink top. We followed her to the living room to find Camilla perched on the edge of a tan chesterfield sofa. She was still in pyjamas, her face in her hands.

'Do you want me to get the vet?' Chrissy asked me.

Camilla's head snapped up as if someone had yanked her ponytail. 'No! Leave her, I don't want a second of her attention away from Ruby and Bo.'

Chrissy's gaze went from Camilla straight to the floor.
'It's fine,' I said, 'we can speak to the vet later.'

Camilla's eyes were red and swollen like Chrissy's, but somehow she still looked glamorous. Angry. Very angry. But glamorous. She leant forward and jabbed her finger at a piece of A4 paper lying on a wooden chopping board. 'They left this.'

Roy and I moved closer and peered at the note, squinting to read the words as the blue ink merged with red stains soaked into the page.

THE FINEST STEAKS
FOR YOUR MOST PRIZED POSSESSIONS.

'Blood?' Roy said as he looked at me and then Camilla. 'They said on the phone it was a suspected poisoning, that the dogs had been fed something?'

'They don't have cuts or anything; I presume it's from the meat someone put out for them,' Camilla said. 'Maybe it's that psycho's blood, who knows?'

Roy looked at me optimistically.

No way, that would be too easy. 'SOCO can do a presumptive test, see if it's animal or human, but my money's on it being myoglobin.' All three of them looked at me, waiting for further explanation. 'It's some sort of protein from muscle tissue. You know, when you eat a rare steak, and sometimes it looks like there's blood coming out of it? Well, that's myoglobin. A quick test will tell them anyway. So, the note itself, have you touched it?' I asked Camilla.

'No, just the chopping board. It was already on there; I know I shouldn't have moved it, but I wanted to get it away from the dogs. I didn't want them to smell the blood, or whatever the hell it is, and try to ...' Camilla pursed her lips in what looked like an attempt to stop her face from crumpling in on itself. A single tear rolled down her cheek, dislodged from her eyelashes as she blinked. 'I've left upstairs as it was, my room, it's still there. And out the back ...' She visibly swallowed. 'Can they hurry up and photograph that or whatever they need to do so we can take them down?'

In the commotion with Roy's reaction to the dogs, I'd forgotten about the other parts of the call he'd recited in the car. 'Of course, they'll process it all as quickly as possible. We'll need to take a look, OK?'

We followed Camilla upstairs to her bedroom. She waited by the door. An evening dress lay across the foot of the large oak four-poster bed, another note pinned to it.

THE PERFECT OUTFIT FOR THEIR FUNERAL!

Camilla edged further into the room and shook her head. 'How didn't I wake up? I was lying right there,' she said, her outstretched arm pointing towards the unmade bed, hand trembling.

'Don't worry,' I said. 'The team will go over this place with a fine-tooth comb, and ...' I leant as close as I could get to the paper, '... can't be sure, but looks like there might be some impressions on there, like someone might have written something on the page above it in a notepad. There's tests they can do to see if they can get anything legible, see what they've written – ESDA, it's called. It's basically like a fancy version of rubbing your pencil across a piece of paper to enhance the dents in it. Did you ever do that, when you were at school?'

My attempt to reassure and distract at the same time with a forensics lesson clearly wasn't working as Camilla looked straight past me. 'I thought I'd locked the kitchen door, but ... I presume that's where they got in. I checked the footage from the front door camera and there's nothing.' She cupped her hand across her forehead. 'You can see what they've done outside from here, the window.'

I looked across the rear of the apple orchard, a shiver coursing down my spine even though the radiator was on full and I was still wearing my coat. 'Is that ...' It was only as I pivoted to look at Camilla I noticed the gap in the large wooden chest under the vanity desk opposite her bed. One of the five drawers it should contain had been removed – one of the two narrower ones at the top usually reserved for smaller garments. There was no mystery in what Camilla used the missing one for, as the contents were on full display in the orchard. Several pieces of her underwear hung across the apple tree branches. Crooked little wooden fingers curled around the delicate materials, holding them in place as they fluttered in the breeze like X-rated bunting.

Jesus Christ.

Camilla pulled the silk belt of her dressing gown a little tighter.

Before I could think of what to say, Chrissy appeared at the top of the stairs, scuffing her slippered foot back and forth across the carpet. 'She's finished with the dogs now, Cam.'

We followed Chrissy downstairs and huddled around the vet as she explained her findings.

'What, nothing? Not even paracetamol?' Roy said.

The vet shook her head. 'So far, so good, they seem perfectly healthy. I'll take them in for observation – overnight, I'd suggest,' she said, shifting her gaze from Roy to Camilla, 'just to do a couple more tests. Be on the safe side.'

Camilla nodded vehemently, wrapping her arm around Chrissy's shoulders. 'Of course, whatever they need. God, if anything happened to them, I . . . I don't even want to think about it.'

'I know what you mean,' Roy said, folding his arms. 'Got a whippet myself, Bobby – after Bobby Charlton – absolute gem, she is.'

Roy beamed. I'd never seen him look like that about anything. It was actually quite sweet. *Sweet, Roy? Ew.*

Camilla and Chrissy sat down at the breakfast bar as the vet went to get the paperwork.

'So,' Roy said, 'it was just the two of you overnight, then? No Mr Carrington?'

'No, he went straight back to London after you spoke to him yesterday. Chrissy was staying to help me get ready for some press today,' Camilla said.

Roy smiled. 'Right, bit of a girls' night, then.'

I stifled a tut. Roy was probably envisioning the prospect

183

of these two having a 'gals' sleepover', complete with skimpy pyjamas, pillow fights and massage trains. If only he knew, for most people a more accurate description would involve oversized loungewear, 99p pore cleansing T-zone strips, severely out of tune renditions of the entire back catalogue of musical theatre, with whole Victoria sponge cakes being eaten like hamburgers for sustenance between questionably choreographed dance numbers.

'So, anything out of the ordinary?' Roy asked, his eyes drifting over to Chrissy, 'and we do mean *anything* this time.'

Chrissy shook her head and looked at the floor like a pupil who'd forgotten her PE kit. 'No, nothing at all, I promise.'

I noticed how difficult it seemed for Chrissy to hold eye contact with everyone in the room and wondered when would be the best time to broach the fact that Myles had said she'd made up the story about someone hanging around the gates. I waited.

'No,' Camilla said. 'We were both catching up on some work in the study until about nine, had a nightcap, then went upstairs.'

My phone vibrated in my pocket as I opened my mouth to speak. 'Sorry, will you excuse me for a sec?' I nodded at Roy to continue before walking into the hallway. I looked at the screen. Dom. I pressed the off button until the vibrating stopped. I didn't have time for that right now.

Roy was wrapping up as I walked back in. I interjected, 'There was another thing we wanted to speak to you both about. We did try calling yesterday but couldn't get through to either of you.'

'Sorry, yes, I did see that,' Camilla said. 'I was going to call back this morning but then, well, all hell broke loose here.'

Chrissy said nothing but visibly tensed.

'It's about what you told us, Chrissy, about the person you said rang the intercom and then was hanging around outside the gates,' I said.

The look Camilla threw at Chrissy told me she had no idea what I was talking about. 'What? When? Why didn't you say anything before?' she said.

Chrissy stared at the floor, her lip wobbling.

I spoke softly even though what I really wanted to do was grab her by the shoulders and tell her to grow the hell up. 'You said Myles told you not to say anything, but he didn't even seem to know about it when we asked him.'

Camilla was stood between us now, her head turning left and right from Chrissy's face to mine. 'Will somebody tell me what the hell is going on?'

'I'm so sorry.' Chrissy's eyes scrunched as tears flowed down her cheeks. 'I didn't mean to, I just wanted to help.'

Camilla's hands flew to her hips. 'Didn't mean to what? Help with what?'

I reached out and touched Camilla's shoulder, gently tugging her backwards. 'Do you want to take a seat and let me talk to Chrissy?'

She shook her head and walked off to the other side of the room.

SAM FRANCES

'Chrissy,' I said, 'can you tell me what happened?'

She wiped her face with her sleeve. 'Myles said you wouldn't take it seriously, the stalking, so I thought if I said I'd seen someone you might get more worried, and I didn't want to get into trouble for not saying right away, like – that's withholding evidence or summat – so I just panicked and said Myles told me not to. It was the first excuse that popped into my head, I dunno why I even said it. I'm so sorry, I hope I ain't messed nothing up.'

As much as she was annoying me, I couldn't help but feel sorry for her. 'You haven't messed anything up, Chrissy, but by lying you might have wasted valuable police time.'

'I'm so sorry, I just wanted to make sure Cam was safe.'

I heard a deep sigh from behind me and Camilla appeared by my side. 'It's OK, stop crying, please,' she said as she hugged her.

Roy and I rolled our eyes as Chrissy's sobs turned into a wail, Camilla patting her back like she was her mother.

After finishing up, we followed the SOCO van in convoy down the winding B road away from the manor, rain spitting at the windscreen. The road ahead narrowed, a canopy of large trees blocking most of the remaining grey daylight.

'She's mental, that one, Chrissy,' Roy said. 'Like this job ain't hard enough without people playing silly buggers.'

'We shouldn't be too harsh on her. It's not like her crappy

186

fake description was much use anyway, and she was trying to help, in her weird sort of way.'

'Don't trust her,' Roy said. 'And let's not forget there was no damage to the door lock. So either it wasn't locked in the first place, *someone* unlocked it or someone else has a key to that house.'

I wouldn't go so far as to say I didn't trust her either, but Myles's comment about her wanting to be involved in everything had stuck in my head. 'I dunno, what's off to me is that whoever is doing this didn't actually *hurt* the dogs, or the foxes last time – they were already dead – or Camilla. Like she said, she was lying right there, they could have done anything to her. I read her book last night. I mean, it's grim, and it kinda fits, the photos, the animals, but with none of the actual gore. Like someone's doing a PG version or something.'

'Someone wanting to make a bit of drama without actually causing any physical harm?' Roy said in a knowing tone. 'Hmm, I wonder who we know who seems to have a bit of a flare for dramatic effect. Carrington even said that about the girl, didn't he?'

Despite the fact it had turned out he was telling the truth about Chrissy lying, I wasn't quite ready to go full Team Myles just yet. There was still something off about him too. 'She was practically tripping over herself to tell us how close her and Camilla are at the station the other day; maybe they're not quite as close as she wants them to be. Chrissy could barely look anyone in the eye in there, even before we caught her out in—' My stomach dropped as a thought

187

freed itself from the tangles of my brain. 'Wait, what did Myles say, about someone distracting the dogs with meat, the first night they came into the station?'

'Yeah, he did, didn't he, about them leaving her for dead for a pair of steaks.'

'Well, that's convenient,' I said.

'Bit of an odd strategy, though,' Roy said, not reacting to the hedge scraping the side of the car as he pulled into a passing place to let a massive tractor go by. 'Why would he tell a pair of coppers about it if he was planning on doing it? Could be a double bluff, I s'pose, but I still don't get the point of it. He can be in her bedroom anytime he wants, he doesn't have to sneak in there. That reminds me, actually, I forgot to tell you in all the fuss this morning. Only saw our man on the telly last night, didn't I – Carrington.'

'And?' I said. 'We already know he's an actor.'

'Yeah, but you'd think he was bleedin' Al Pacino with that watch, expensive suits, expensive aftershave. Everything on him's dripping in pound signs, right, but I looked him up on that IMDb thing, he's hardly been in anything – he's more of an extra than a bleedin' actor.' I still didn't see what Roy was getting at, and why Myles's seemingly slim chances of getting a BAFTA nomination anytime soon was of so much concern. Roy looked at me before pulling back out on to the road like his point was obvious. 'Where's he getting all this money from, eh? To live like some sort of playboy? I don't know much about the entertainment business, but I can't imagine playing patient number three in *Holby bleedin' City* gets you much in the way of a pay packet.'

I shrugged. 'Camilla's gotta be loaded, maybe he's a kept man.'

Roy shook his head. 'I thought about that. Had a little gander back through his Instagram page. He's been living it up for years – private yachts off the South of France, villas in the Maldives, all from way before he met her. And we already know his family aren't rolling in it. I mean, his dad's salary ain't one to be sniffed at, but it would still take him a year to pay off that watch alone, they're hardly millionaires.'

'So, what, you think he's into something dodgy?'

'Gotta be. Maybe that's the real reason he doesn't want us sniffing around this case – nothing to do with the fact he doesn't think we'll take it seriously, more like we might stumble across something he doesn't want us to.'

It made perfect sense. He absolutely struck me as someone who'd put covering his own arse in front of all else. I knew it. I knew there was something about him. *Don't get cocky now, Roy put two and two together on this, not you!* Jesus, even Roy was a better detective than me these days. I should have seen it. I wrapped my hand around the plastic door handle and squeezed it like a stress relief ball. A loud crack pierced the air, the handle now loose in the palm of my hand.

Roy did a double take. 'What the . . .'

I stared at the grey lump of plastic. 'Sorry, I – it just came off.'

'Jesus wept, d'you know how many forms I'm probably gonna have to fill in for that?'

'Sorry, I'll ... I'll sort it.'

Roy let out a sigh. 'Look, I don't mean to pry, and I'm keen to keep my head on my shoulders, but are you all right?'

Something my mum told me once popped into my head, about how smiling, even if you don't feel like it, will make you happier. Some sort of hormone or chemical thing that tricks your brain. I peeled my lips back across my teeth and held it. 'Fine,' I nodded, 'absolutely fine.'

28

The sun was setting as I pulled into my driveway later that evening, a mottled collage of yellow, pink and orange puffs of cloud left in its wake. I stared at the sky instead of getting out of the car. There was something soothing about it. The colours. The way the wind dragged them through the air like a slow-moving lava lamp. My head fell back against the seat and I watched, like a baby mesmerised by a musical mobile twirling above its cot.

If I could've forced myself to stay in that state of calm I would have. But it was less than a minute before thoughts of the case took over again as I mused on when the hell logic and rationale were going to kick in, for that good old Washington instinct to sprout roots through the debris and make sense of what was going on with all this.

At least we had some new semi-reasonable lines of enquiry. After SOCO found a possible access point to the rear of the manor's perimeter wall, Roy had the epiphany that Dick Lowry might have CCTV covering the field behind his abattoir, the one that made most sense for someone to cross to reach that part of Camilla's property if they were avoiding being seen on the main road. Reckoned he'd had some installed after getting stick from animal rights activists. And ESDA exams had proved useful in a couple of my previous investigations. I crossed my fingers and hoped the stalker had written their name, date of birth, address and home phone number on their notepad before using the pages underneath to write their threats to Camilla. Make my job a little easier for once.

I closed my eyes, the calming skyline imprinted on the inside of the lids.

Ten seconds of peace was all I managed before something rapped against the window inches from my face. I jumped at the sound before opening my eyes to see Dom's knuckles hovering on the other side of the glass. 'Jesus Christ!'

He stepped back as I pushed the door open. 'Sorry, didn't mean to scare you. I wasn't expecting you to be asleep in your car when you have a perfectly nice house right there.'

'I wasn't asleep, I was just . . . resting my eyes. What's up?'

'Just wanted to see if you fancied dinner tonight? I tried calling earlier but I think it cut off or something.'

'Yeah, I was at work, with a victim – not very professional to be taking personal calls at a crime scene.'

He clapped a hand over his mouth. 'Shit, sorry, I should have thought of that. It wasn't that big stalking case I saw in the paper, was it?'

Great, another new reader for A. J. to fill with shit. 'That's the one.'

'How's it going? Any big leads?'

'I'm not really allowed to talk about it.'

'Of course. Sorry, sounds awful. I didn't get you into any trouble, did I? By calling?'

My stomach rumbled. 'If I say yes, do I get a larger portion of this dinner that's on offer?'

'Well, I am a close personal friend of the chef so I'm sure I could make that work.'

If I stayed home alone, I'd just mull over things I couldn't do anything about yet. And it's not like I was agreeing to marry the man, it was just dinner. 'Sounds good.'

He pushed his dark hair away from his face. 'Casa La Willows it is, then. Half an hour OK for you?'

I nodded. 'Should I bring anything, or . . .?' I instantly regretted the offer. What use would some wilted basil and a mostly empty jar of Biscoff really be?

'No need, I was planning on making a batch of cottage pie so I'd have some left over for the freezer anyway, already got more than I need for just me. I've got us covered.'

Can make homemade cottage pie *and* does batch cooking? That was some proper adulting right there. Plus one hundred points. 'Great, see you in a bit.'

Vince was waiting for me in the hallway. He rubbed himself against my trousers, zigzagging between my legs as I walked to the kitchen. I'd already come to terms with the fact my death certificate would undoubtedly read *Broken neck – felled by feline*. It was the only thing I disliked about living alone, the knowledge I'd ultimately be eaten by my beloved pet if I died unexpectedly. Could be worse, I supposed. There was that time I almost choked on a Fruit Pastilles lolly after the whole thing came off the stick in one go. Imagine the embarrassment, dying because there was no one to Heimlich Rowntree's frozen goods out of your windpipe.

Vince stared up at me from below the counter. 'You do realise if I fall and die, all you'd have to eat until anyone notices are bits of me, and as you can see . . .' I twirled like some novice fashion model doing her first photo shoot in a derelict shopping centre in Croydon. 'I run a tight ship. Not a lot of meat on these bones for you to chow down on.'

Nothing but a slow blink. Sometimes I expected to come home and find him marching up the driveway, Dick Whittington-style bindle dangling over his shoulder, off to find a new home, sick of my shit. I left him to his dinner and went upstairs.

Pausing by the full-length mirror in the bedroom, I looked myself up and down. Twisting from side to side, tucking my T-shirt in, before pulling it out and re-tucking it. *Since when do you give a shit about looking pretty for a boy?* Maybe I should get changed, put on a bit of slap at least. No, I wasn't falling into that trap. I refused to spend the first six months of a relationship setting an alarm to get up an hour before a partner to do my hair and make-up only to sneak back to bed and pretend I'd just woken up. Fuck that. If he didn't like me at my Vicky Pollard, he certainly didn't deserve me at my Marilyn Monroe, or whatever the hell that saying was they ironed on to allegedly empowering crop tops in Primark.

Jittery bubbles swelled and popped in my stomach. I looked over at the picture of Mum and Dad on my bedside table and let myself smile, a real smile this time, before I headed downstairs.

The air in The Willows was thick with roasted garlic and fried meat as a reddish-brown sauce bubbled on the hob. 'Wow,' I said as Dom closed the front door behind me and handed me a glass of red wine, 'that looks amazing.'

His cheeks bunched up. 'Thanks, as do you.'

I hoped the warmth of the room would cover me as my cheeks flushed. 'Very kind of you to say, and probably the only time it might be even remotely true for the rest of the evening; given that I'm wearing a white T-shirt and there's about to be sauce on the go, this *will* get messy.' I realised I was pointing at my boobs a few seconds too late.

He did me the courtesy of pretending not to notice, stirring the sauce before tapping the wooden spoon on the side of the pot. He drained a boiling pan of potatoes through a colander in the sink and got a masher out of the drawer. 'So, how much topping do you want on this thing?' he asked.

'Is "everything you've got" an acceptable answer?' I said before taking my first sip of the wine.

His eyes twinkled as he smiled in response. 'That's actually the perfect answer. Do you know, there are monsters out there who don't eat potatoes? I don't trust them, not one bit.'

I tried to rein in my ever-expanding grin. 'I'd arrest people for that if I could, and people who don't eat bread. I mean, who the fuck doesn't eat *bread*?'

'Probably the same arseholes who are rude to waiting

staff in restaurants.' He returned the steaming chunks of potato to the pan and stirred in lashings of salted butter.

By the time we'd polished off the entire dish, leaving nothing for the freezer as Dom had intended, we'd talked jobs, picked our favourite animals and had a whole plan in place to open Fortbridge's first Michelin-starred restaurant serving nothing but carbohydrates and dairy. Everything would be either deep fried, lathered with butter, or drowning in melted cheese. Dom had yet to convince me he was on to something with his idea it should be pirate themed.

'OK, OK,' I said, 'I get that a theme gives us a unique selling point, but why pirates?' My face hurt from laughing so hard. 'Is it just so we could have a "Boo Box" like they do in *Hook*? That could work, actually, then we'd have somewhere to torture the people who are rude to the waiters.'

'A what box?' he said, almost spilling his wine as he leant closer to me on the sofa.

'Oh, pfft, never mind. I forgot about your non-existent arts, literature and entertainment knowledge. You need to watch a film, read a bloody book, something! Otherwise you're not feeling the full force of my comedy.'

'Don't worry, I think you're very funny,' he said, leaning even closer. He was thinking of kissing me, I could tell. The alcohol and nerves swirled in my head that suddenly felt like it weighed fifty pounds, my neck struggling to hold it in place. 'And sorry, but I'm too busy to read books and watch films with my very important new schedule of designing our prize-winning pirate menu. Wait, can you eat parrots?' he said, pressing his finger into the slight dimple in his chin.

He leant forward again, before immediately jumping backwards. 'Ow, shit!'

A wave of panic rushed me. '*Ow*?' Was my breath that bad?

He stuck his hand into the front pocket of his jeans and pulled something out of it. 'This bloody thing just nearly severed my femoral artery. Sorry, I totally forgot I bought you this; I was meaning to give it to you earlier.'

He held out a closed fist, a red piece of tightly coiled plastic hanging from it.

'O-K, what is it?'

He opened his fingers, exposing even more red plastic attached to a metal clip with a heart keyring. 'So, I got the impression with the fancy wine the other night you might have me pegged as a bit of a flash git, so I thought I'd show you my true colours by buying you the tackiest gift I could find. Ignore the heart bit – I did try and pull it off, but it's, like, welded on there or something. Anyway, I saw it in the petrol station today and thought it might be handy for you to have.'

I took it from him and rolled it around in my palm. 'Sorry, I still don't . . . what is it, exactly?'

'Keys, it's for your keys,' he said, picking up the other end to the one I was holding. 'You clip this end to a zip or something on the inside of your bag, and that end . . .' his hand grazed my finger, a small electric pulse shooting up my arm, '. . . well, that end hooks on to your keys. So you don't lose them again. See?'

My cheeks were on fire now. What was wrong with me, swooning at a plastic keyring? Rosacea. That must be it. I'd suddenly developed rapid onset rosacea. 'Ah, right, OK, thanks, that's really kind of you.'

'They didn't have one without a heart on it, or I would've—'

'Yeah, no, of course.' I couldn't help but think about Dad's gift of life insurance to my mum. No pomp and circumstance. Just what she needed. It may not have been the most romantic thing in the world, but it had worked out pretty well for them. 'Thanks,' I said, looking up to see he'd leant right over to me, his nose no more than four inches from mine. I smiled, the movement highlighting a clump of something stuck between my teeth. *Shit*. 'Erm, can I lip to your noo quickly?' *Jesus*. How much wine had I had? I slapped myself in the face to force my tongue to comply with the instructions I was giving it. 'Sorry, I meant *nip* to your *loo*.'

He moved back to an upright position and pointed towards the door of the snug. 'Course, top of the stairs, first door on your left. Should I make us some coffees?'

Coffee. Yes. *Good idea before you make a drunken twat of yourself.* 'Sure. Thanks.'

The stairs of The Willows were much steeper than the ones in Myrtle Cottage, as if they'd been put in as an afterthought with not enough space to fit them. I couldn't tell if it was the wine or the architecture, but the walls seemed to move, leaning in a few inches closer than they should, the ceiling sagging between thick wooden beams like it might crash down on me at any second.

I tried to rub the drunken fog from my eyes as I went into the bathroom and closed the door. The room was small. Neat. I looked around for something I could use as a toothpick. Nothing. I tried to scrape out what looked like a bit of mince from the tight gap between my teeth with my fingernail, but it refused to budge. Instinctively, I reached for the latch on the cabinet above the sink. My hand lingered before I opened it. *Stop it! What are you doing? You can't just rummage through his cupboards.* I stared into the mirrored door. This was going well. Like, really well. And I didn't want to fuck it up by regurgitating pre-chewed meat into his mouth like some kind of mamma bird feeding her young if he did actually kiss me.

Before I knew it, the magnetic catch clunked and the door swung open. I paused, listening for the shout of 'What are you doing up there?'

It didn't come.

I grabbed a packet of dental floss and worked the bit of mince free, before stepping back out into the hallway. There were two other doors on the small landing; one leading to the room overlooking the front lane, which was closed, and another opposite the bathroom that was open a crack. A desire to look in the rooms took hold like a rash. *Nosy drunk!* I tiptoed towards the furthest. The closed one. *What are you doing? You've been up here so long he's going to think you have bowel issues!* I leant against it as I tried

199

the knob. Locked. Interesting. Was this where he hid his weird stuff? He must have weird stuff. He was too good to be true on paper. *Stop trying to ruin this, not everyone has weird stuff.*

Moving back the way I'd come, I poked my head around the other door. His bedroom. Very minimalistic. A double bed with plain white sheets, a stool as a side table, and a clothes rack in place of a wardrobe. It dawned on me I might end up back in here later. The hairs on my arms prickled with panic. I couldn't remember the last time I'd had sex. Would I even remember how? Just like riding a bike, that's what people said. I ran my finger along the scar in my hairline from where I'd somersaulted over my handlebars when I was fifteen and headbutted a lamppost. *OK, let's hope not.*

I was about to go back downstairs when something caught my eye. Something sticking out of a carrier bag underneath the bed. The door eased open as I nudged it with my shoulder. I scuttled across the room, knelt down and pulled at the handle of the bag, the rustle of the plastic amplified by the silence.

The hairs on my arms prickled again, but for a very different reason.

This time it was at the sight of what was in the bag.

I sobered up in an instant, the realisation an ice-cold waterfall crashing down on top of me. I couldn't breathe. My heart leapt into my mouth, the contents of my stomach threatening to rise up with it.

'Alice?' Dom called from downstairs.

My head snapped towards the door.

'Everything OK up there?'

It was as if I'd forgotten how to speak, mouth gaping. I shoved the bag back under the bed and shot across the room on tiptoes like I was trying to levitate across it. 'Yep,' I managed to push out as I hit the landing.

Stay calm!

I went back downstairs, the steps feeling even steeper than on the way up, like with each one I was falling to reach the next.

'Just fixing my, erm, contact lens.' I emerged back into the kitchen, rubbing my eye for effect. 'Never stay where they're meant to.'

If he noticed the tremor in my voice, he didn't show it. 'Nightmare. Do you take sugar?'

'What?' The word scraped out through parched lips.

'The coffee, do you take sugar?'

'No, sorry, actually, I better be going, this lens, it's ... and I'm knackered, got an early start tomorrow.'

'Oh, OK,' Dom said as I snatched my coat from the back of the kitchen chair. 'Well, don't work too hard. You should make more time for yourself too, you know; you'll burn out if you keep going at it so hard.'

I swung my jacket around my shoulders with such force the zip did an entire rotation of my head and hit me in the face. I barely noticed. Too busy thinking that he'd like that, wouldn't he? If I let this job go, stopped digging into Camilla's stalker. That would work out just swell for him. 'Yeah, well, the harder we work, the faster we catch the person.' The light from the log burner in the kitchen didn't hit his face the same way it had the first night we'd met, when the dancing soft glow had accentuated his chiselled features. Now it just cast writhing shadows, distorting his pronounced bone structure. 'And we *will* catch them.'

'Fingers crossed you do, soon,' he said. 'Well, er, good-night then.' He moved towards me.

I stuck out my arm, not because I wanted him to shake my hand, but to act as a barrier between our bodies so he couldn't hug or kiss me. 'Yeah, night.'

He opened his mouth as if to say something, but I turned and left.

Closing the door behind me, I stepped out into the cold night air, the lavender bushes that had smelt so fresh the other night now sickly sweet, turning my stomach. I kept my pace casual in case he was watching me, until I'd closed my own front door and slid down the inside of it.

29

He stood at the bedroom door. Her scent filled his nostrils as she lay there, moonlight kissing her skin, turning her alabaster complexion an almost extra-terrestrial tinge of blue. She *was* beautiful. Though he'd always found women more attractive when they were asleep. Their faces still. Peaceful. Not twisted in disdain.

I am here now, he thought. Right here. Not outside in the trees like before. He'd never lost the climbing skills he'd mastered as a young boy, and would never forget the first time he watched Mother from the old oak outside her window. The perfect viewing platform. Keeping an eye on her, like Father asked. *For where the cameras don't reach*, he'd said as he ruffled his hair. It was nice to be needed again. To help keep her in check.

She couldn't be trusted. None of them could.

People talked about feeling as though their heart was beating out of their chest. But he'd been terrified his might actually explode that first time. He'd tried to regulate his breathing, but it made no difference. Each thud resonating in his ears. The pace quickening. Volume rising. After that, it became his place of comfort. Stretched across the branch like a lethargic panther digesting a meal. The thick foliage was perfectly placed if he got the angle just right, hiding him from her line of sight, but not her from his. He could've walked right up to that house, into that bathroom, and watched Mother up close. But that wouldn't be the same. There was something about the fact she didn't know, totally oblivious.

It hadn't taken him long to realise that only a minor adjustment in the same spot gave him another unbroken view, this time into Jen's bedroom next door. Flashes of her long, toned legs shot through his brain like bullets. He'd craned his neck to follow her as she'd walked away from the window. *Come back!* he'd begged silently. It had been her return that distracted him. Had she seen him watching? Taking his focus for just a second had been enough for him to lose balance, his foot slipping on the dewy bark.

He opened and closed his fingers as if the pain lingered all these years on from where he'd clawed fruitlessly at the surrounding branches on the way down. His frantic attempt to gain traction to lessen the fall, thwarted by the spongy green moss enveloping the trunk and its lower limbs. He'd crashed hard on to his hip. But the pain had almost immediately been replaced by a new one. A man's fists pummelling his back as he'd tried to get up. Jen's dad. So that's where she'd gone. *Little bitch!* It hadn't taken him long to find other places. Places where he could watch without them knowing. To this day, the desire had stayed just as strong.

Dust floated across the strip of moonlight and peppered the rug like light snowfall, the floor creaking as he made his way to the bed. He scanned the peaks and troughs of the duvet, the dip her head created in the pillow and the arm she placed haphazardly above it. His body tensed as he lay on the mattress, lowering himself as gently as possible so he didn't wake her from her deep sleep. He placed his cheek barely more than a foot from hers. The smell of her so strong now. Overwhelming. He reached towards her, aligning their fingertips. Not touching but only millimetres apart. For a second, he swore he saw electricity jumping between them, like a firing synapse. An image pierced his mind. The two of them, lying there. Limbs entwined. Her skin damp with sweat, head resting on his chest, rising and falling, more content than she'd ever been.

And then he'd tell her.

Blood frothed in his veins as he imagined her face crumbling. The fear. The horror. When she realised what this had all been for.

30

Hair stuck to my cheek, rain-sodden from the dash to my car. I drove the long way to work in a last-ditch attempt to get more time to figure out what the fuck I was going to do about Dom. About what I'd seen. I'd been up half the night thinking about it, so it wasn't exactly clear how the meagre ten minutes added to the journey by turning left out of my driveway instead of right and looping around the back of the school playing fields was going to make much difference, yet here I was.

Meadows undulated as I sped along the lane, before the greenery flattened the closer I got to the centre of the village. Ridges and furrows were replaced with rugby posts and football goals as I grabbed the open can of Red Bull from the drinks holder, chugging it like some kind of magic elixir that would glue the information together in my brain. Make it make sense. Make me sure. Because I'd certainly *felt* sure the second I saw those books. I could see them again now. The neon orange cover a warning signal on top of the pile inside the carrier bag. The white eyeball on the cover of *Follow You Down*. The rest of the bag filled with Camilla's back catalogue. An awful lot of books for someone who didn't read. And why hidden under the bed? Because people hide what they don't want others to see.

The grass in my periphery turned to sandy stone and I slammed the brakes on as the lights changed at the crossing outside Fortbridge School. Drizzle pattered the windscreen, water droplets distorting the neat circumference of the red traffic light through the glass. I'd gone over everything a hundred times last night. The books. Dom's timely arrival in the village. He'd even asked questions about Camilla's case. But had it been a normal number of questions? The number anyone would ask in a small place with not much else going on, or too many? How many *was* too many? And how odd was it that despite me doing every possible open source search I could think of until I'd finally fallen asleep at three in the morning on 'Dom Webb', 'Dominic Webb', 'Dominic Webb physio', 'Dom Webb personal training', 'Dominic Webb whatever the hell else he'd mentioned last night', I'd found nothing more than a private Facebook account which I couldn't even know for certain was his because the profile picture was of a bloody sunset. But not everyone was 'online', were they? *I* didn't even have social media, so who was I to judge?

I could hardly ring the hospital and ask if he was telling the truth about joining the new clinic, unless I was to do so under false pretences. But that was crazy. Was it crazy? Was *I* crazy? Garlic and wine lingered on the back of my tongue, as if I needed proof last night actually happened. That it wasn't just part of some fugue state episode I'd concocted to trick myself into thinking I'd solved this bloody case.

Camilla's books had sold in the millions. Just because he'd bought some didn't make him a suspect.

Movement on the left side of the car distracted me, a stream of teenage boys in sports kit filing through the gates of the sixth form wing. Some in groups, others in pairs, one or two on their own. Tall ones. Short ones. Chubby ones. Lanky ones. A smorgasbord of vessels for teenage angst. I thought back to Roy and Tess's early assessment of the case; the 'young lad with a crush' theory. I scanned each one as they passed. Maybe it *was* one of them. Maybe it was all of them. Everyone. Dom. Chrissy. Myles. Sleazy Steve. A. J. Howden. Fortbridge School's whole bloody Year 12 class. A village-wide stalking conspiracy and my very own *Murder on the Orient Express*. I pressed the heels of my palms into my forehead, pushing the skin up and out as if I could massage the suspicions away, or at least hone them into some semblance of order. You know, exactly the way Hercule bloody Poirot did it.

Could Dom be the stalker? Yes, in theory. Did I have any evidence other than a frigging Waterstones bulk purchase? No. Could this all be an elaborate bit of mental gymnastics to push yet another person in my life away? Yes, in theory. Did I have any proof that's what I was doing? *Your Honour, may I present this bad character evidence.* I had form. Couldn't deny that. Mine and Liam's ten-year anniversary dinner for one. The mouthful of 'Death by Chocolate' hovering in front of his face when I told him it was over. He'd insisted he was happy with our independent but intersecting lives. Evenings drinking wine, eating cheese and playing Bananagrams. But I could see he wanted more. A wife. A family. Traditional. So I'd done him a favour, because he deserved to come first to someone. Cutting a person loose so they could go off and have the life they wanted was one thing. Accusing them of being the village stalker was quite another. Especially if I was wrong. *Again*.

The horn of a car rang in my ears, green light having replaced the red without me noticing. *Shit*. I ground the gears into place, thought I had anyway, but the car jerked forward as the engine stalled. I re-started it, grabbed the gearstick and thumped it into first. 'Move, you stupid piece of crap!' Another, longer beep came from the car behind, before it swerved me, tyres screeching on wet tarmac. The driver gestured wildly before speeding off down the street. The schoolkids laughed as I finally managed to pull away. 'Fuck you, and fuck you, and you and you,' I yelled in the direction of anyone in the vicinity.

More kids broke into a run as they crossed the road up ahead and I realised I was driving like Cruella de Vil. What the hell was wrong with me? Surely I had enough dead or maimed children on my conscience already. I pulled into the next side street and stopped the car.

Breathe, just fucking breathe!

I couldn't turn up to work in this state. I took my phone from my pocket, searched for one of the allegedly calming podcasts Tess recommended and hit play, the introduction to *The Silent Mind* whispering from the speakers.

'OK, come on, just relax,' I said, rolling my shoulders.

Pan flute music filled the car, interrupted by the squeaking windscreen wipers.

'Welcome, friend,' the instantly grating voice said. 'Let's start today's session like we always do, by finding your inner sunshine.' *Inner sunshine?* Jesus Christ. 'Remember to find the sunshine in every day through your intentions—'

No. Absolutely not. I needed more than a bit of sun and good intent today. I batted at the console until the speaker clicked off. The car fell quiet, my own heart roaring in my ears the only remaining sound.

31

I kept my jumbled thoughts to myself all morning, barely talking to anyone until Tess came back from her dentist appointment after lunch.

She wandered over and massaged my shoulders. 'Ooft, someone's tight. What's up with you? You not been doing any of those morning meditations like I told you?'

Remember, just keep smiling.

I looked up at her, my tongue exploring the gumline of my wisdom teeth. 'Actually, I listened to that podcast you recommended on my way in and . . .' I almost told her why I was listening to it before thinking better of it, '. . . well, it doesn't work anyway. And I tried that *Bedtime Yoga* thing the other day and all it made me think was, "Oh, wouldn't it be fun if the instructor got her smug hippie face bitten off by a downward-facing pit bull."'

'Come on, she's not that annoying,' Tess said, slapping my arm.

'The woman's called *Serenity*, for Christ's sake.'

Tess rolled her eyes. 'So you're feeling like a new woman, then?'

'Totally. Zen. As. Fuck.'

Tess rolled her eyes again, so hard this time I was concerned they might become dislodged. 'You can't just do these things once and say they don't work. Would you pick up a guitar and get annoyed you couldn't play it straight away?' She paused, more for effect than to give time for an actual reply. 'No, course you wouldn't. It's called *practising* mindfulness and yoga *practice* for a reason. You'll enjoy it once Rodrigo gets hold of you later. He's the best.' *Shit*. With everything going on – or off, depending how I looked at it – I'd totally forgotten about yoga class. Tess would kill me if I bailed on her again. I nodded as she rounded my chair and leant against the desk. 'And improving your flexibility couldn't come at a better time, with the new man in your life. Come on, what's the latest boy toy update?'

Roy's head popped out from the side of his computer screen. '"*Boy toy*?" What sort of language is that? If I called someone a *girl* toy, you lot would be burning ya bleedin' bras and chucking me on a pyre!'

Tess tutted. 'Fine, boy*friend* then.'

My throat narrowed. 'He's not my boyfriend.'

Roy raised his eyebrows and shook his head. 'I dunno, you millennials and your labels.'

'It's not a labelling problem, he's my nothing. There, that a good enough label for you?'

Tess butted back in. 'He's *trying* to be her boyfriend, and I dunno what her problem is, he looks like an actual fitness model.'

Roy rolled his eyes. 'Oh, what a surprise, another bleedin' pretty boy.'

'Pretty doesn't cut it,' Tess said, fanning her face with a notepad from my desk. 'He's gorgeous.'

Their voices bellowed in my ears like children in a school-yard. 'Can you both just stop! I don't care how gorgeous he is, I . . .'

Careful . . .

'. . . I don't need a boyfriend right now, OK?'

Tess sat on the edge of my desk. 'No one's saying you *need* a boyfriend. But there's no harm in wanting one, is there?'

I pulled some papers out from underneath her bum cheek to get her to stand up. 'Haven't you got work to be doing?'

'All right, tetchy,' Tess said, 'excuse me for thinking talking to you might be more interesting than the super sleuthing I have to do into some of Bret's suspects.'

She turned and walked away, and an idea hit me as she plonked back into her chair. Tess was indeed a super sleuth. She was one of the best researchers I'd ever worked with. I might not have enough evidence to go as far as throwing Dom's name in the hat as an official suspect, but I had the perfect excuse to put her skills to use in another way. The way women all over the world do for their friends every day by turning into FBI-level data mining specialists to find out everything about new love interests, their next of kin, and every person they've ever dated.

I rummaged in my top drawer for something to pass off as a peace offering, the best I could come up with being an out-of-date fruit and nut protein bar. I sloped over to her desk and dropped it in front of her.

She carried on typing, not looking up. 'Bin's over there.'

'Sorry.' I squatted down beside her. 'I didn't mean to snap.'

She pushed her lips out, cocked her head and stopped typing. 'Go on.'

'I'm just a bit in two minds. I barely know him, he could be anyone, right?'

She swivelled her chair to face me. 'Isn't that the point of dating? To get to know people?'

'Yeah, but come on, you know me, I don't like to waste time. I mean, what if I spend weeks getting to know him only to find out he's desperate to have kids, or that he doesn't like animals or, I dunno, he's really into tie-dying his own clothes or something. If only I knew someone with superior social media research skills . . .'

Tess snort-laughed and slapped both hands against her face. 'So that's why you're slinking over here with this tat.' She swiped the protein bar off the table and I caught it just before it hit the floor. 'What's his surname? I'll tell you what he had for breakfast on his eighteenth birthday in twenty-four hours, max.'

'Webb. W. E. B. B. You're the best.'

'Damn straight. One condition, though,' she said.

'What?'

'We're still on for yoga later, yeah?'

I didn't have time for bloody yoga, but I needed Tess's help. 'Yeah, course, said I would, didn't I?'

The door from the landing swung open and DCI Simon Carver strode through it. 'Afternoon all,' he said without stopping, leather satchel bouncing off his thigh as he made his way across the office towards the hallway.

Roy and I looked at each other in mutual panic. This wasn't one of the senior management team's routine monthly visits. Jane always gave advance warning when it was time for whoever had drawn the short straw to trek out to the fringe stations and wave at us like the Queen of Sheba. She'd have told us to 'be presentable' and 'look like we know what the hell we're doing' if she'd had the heads up he was coming.

Roy leant across his desk. 'Is there any chance in a million years we aren't the ones he's here to talk abo—'

'Alice! Roy!' came Jane's voice from her office.

Shit.

I liked Simon Carver. Dad did too, was his inspector for a time. Sure, he looked a bit flashy – a satin sheen to his suit, thinning dirty blond hair forced into trendy tufts with styling clay probably siphoned from his teenage son's collection – but other than that he was known for being a pretty down-to-earth guy. A fair boss. One who kept a protective eye on his flock. But the way he was looking at me now from behind Jane's desk felt more like I was a pedigree puppy who'd done my first shit on the carpet. I squirmed in one of the plastic minion chairs, arms folded, as if that would somehow shield me from his disappointment.

Roy gave them the results we had back from the vandalism of the gates. Nothing of use from any CCTV viewed so far, no useable DNA, and the elimination sets from Camilla,

Myles and Chrissy had ruled out the only fingerprints found worth loading to the database, and they'd been from the gates themselves anyway, not the actual photographs.

'. . . so that's it then, is it, you've got nothing?' Jane said from her throne. Carver lingered behind her, leaning back against the award-filled display cabinet.

'Well, nothing else *yet*, ma'am,' I said, jumping in, worried about Roy's ability to stop himself from snapping back at her. 'We still have outstanding lines of enquiry and forensics from the break-in, and possibly another CCTV opportunity covering the rear access point, the field behind the abattoir, and—'

'And when are we getting those?' Jane interjected, her eyes bulging.

'Soon,' Roy said in support. 'Forensic submission's been fast-tracked and I've left a message with the abattoir about the CCTV, just waiting for a call back.'

'Right, well, in the meantime, DCI Carver's here to review the case file,' Jane said.

My hand flinched. I managed to stop it shooting to my chest to catch my heart before it fell into my stomach. This wasn't the nineties. Everything was stored digitally. There was no reason for him to be physically present to review a case file when he could have done so from the comfort of his seventh-floor HQ corner office. 'With all due respect, ma'am . . .' I looked up at the DCI, 'sir, we—'

Carver pushed himself away from the cabinet. 'Appreciate you've got some irons in the fire, but I'd still like to take a look. No harm in having a fresh set of eyes on it, is there?

And we really need to nip this one in the bud asap. The calls we're getting in, especially after those articles, let's just say the Chief's getting it in the neck as well, so it's in all our best interests to get this sorted sharpish.'

Maybe Roy had a point about how some people changed when they rose in rank. Because the Carver I remembered used to put victims first, not reputations. The words slipped out before I even realised I was thinking them. 'And Camilla's.'

He squinted and folded his arms. 'Excuse me?'

I couldn't suck them back in. I'd said it now. And maybe it wasn't such a terrible thing to remind him that, quite frankly, covering the arse of the Chief wasn't the reason most people were in the job. 'I was just pointing out, it's in Camilla Harton-Gray's best interests, more so than anyone else's, that this gets sorted, so she doesn't have to go through this any more ... sir.'

He pursed his lips and nodded. 'Course it is. That's why I'm here.'

Roy shifted in his seat, and I could have sworn his shoulders were bouncing gently as if trying to stifle a giggle.

'Speaking of the articles,' Jane said, 'we need to put out a holding statement to the press. God knows the public need some sort of official reassurance on this instead of just being pumped full of whatever rubbish the *Wessex Star* wants to churn out next. I've already been on to Pru Bishop in comms; one of her team will draft the release then send it to you for a quote to add in as OIC.'

My mind whirred. What kind of reassurance could I

possibly give at this point? We had nothing. *I* had nothing. Nothing but a bunch of wild suspect theories that didn't even come close to reasonable grounds.

'Problem, Alice?' Jane said.

'No, ma'am. No problem at all.'

32

I wasn't sure I could face an hour of a man called Rodrigo with a Cheetos-orange spray tan banging on about my negative chakra. But it was worth it to keep Tess onside and me out of my own head, stop me reliving the interaction in Jane's office. What was Carver doing out here? Was he checking up on me, or the case? Or was it just an excuse for him to see Jane? Maybe this had nothing to do with their opinions on my investigative capability. And this was a high-profile job, for more than one reason. I'd known from the start they'd be all over it. Would it be any different if Bret was leading it? I didn't recall Carver keeping such a close watch when Bret's arson job at the Mill House B&B hit the national news last year after it was leaked one of the injured occupants was in witness protection. Then again, that case had dropped off the press's radar as quickly as it had entered it. My stomach tightened as I tried to convince myself he'd be getting just as much heat as I was.

Parallel beads of sweat trickled through my hairline and dripped on to the faded red mat as I tried to hold myself in downward facing dog and focus on the positives. The investigation hadn't gone cold. Not yet anyway. And at least

I'd get a proper workout doing this class, not the eight minutes of stretching and fifty-two minutes of pushing Vince off the yoga mat I got when I'd tried at home.

Rodrigo's voice, with an accent I couldn't quite place, floated through the air. 'Pedal out the feets, do whatever movement with the body you need to make yourself feel good . . .'

I dropped down on to my hands and knees and leant across to poke Tess in the ribs. 'Oi, make *myself* feel good?' I whispered. 'Brilliant, I could've stayed home and saved seventeen quid.'

Still in downward dog, Tess twisted her neck and glared at me from underneath her armpit. 'Shh! You're disrupting my flow, you twat.'

Rodrigo's tanned feet padded through the gap between us like a teacher separating naughty classmates as he gave his next instruction, 'Lift your hips high towards the skies . . . feel the releases in the body.'

I pressed my hands and feet into the mat and pushed my bum towards the ceiling, waiting for complaints from my hamstrings. But as it turned out, Rodrigo wasn't talking absolute shit after all. My limbs *did* lengthen. Tension escaped. I could practically feel the endorphins marching around my body, goading me with their little feel-good victory parade. I admitted defeat and did as I was told, focussing on my ujjayi breathing.

Sixty minutes came and went as Rodrigo wrapped up the class. 'And now we'll end this joinings of mind and body in shavasana,' he purred.

Ah, the lying down bit, my favourite. I let everything flop. Arms, legs, ankles, even allowing myself to enjoy the fact my mind no longer felt wound up tight like a ball of elastic bands. This was nice. This was actually nice.

I was thinking of how best to play it cool with Tess, so she wouldn't gloat she'd been right all along about the benefits of yoga, when Rodrigo flipped a switch and a click echoed around the room. Surround sound speakers buzzed and my body melted further into the floor as I waited for my ears to be massaged by some sort of Amazonian rainforest sounds. I was so relaxed it took me a second to compute the actual sound coming from them. The staccato notes of a seagull's long call followed by the rush of water. Waves galloping across sand. Or maybe pebbles. I couldn't tell, my hearing distracted as my other senses jolted to life. The scent of seaweed in the air. The irritation of salt on my skin.

Everything tensed.

It wasn't like I hadn't been to a beach since it happened. I had. Loads of times. This was fine. I was fine. Everything was fine.

'Listen to the waters ...' Rodrigo said.

But it wasn't fine. Because I couldn't just hear the water. I could *feel* it. Flowing through my ears into my head. Filling my lungs on the inside, crushing them from the outside.

'... now hear the waves crashing down as you feels the sensation of your body on the floor ...'

Waves, crashing.

Their force. Pulling.

The air was hot. Thick. Suffocating. My eyes flew open, expecting to see someone sitting on top of me, hands around my throat.

'... wiggle the fingers and let them hang loose, letting go of any tensions in your hands ...'

I stretched out my fingers. Reaching as far as I physically could. To grab him as he jumped. Jamie's face infiltrated my vision. But the image was different this time. The cobbled blur of the courtyard below him now blue. A sea. Protruding rocks dotted around him like tiny brown-tipped icebergs in the water.

Stop!

Large green eyes stared up at me. Pleading for help. Except Jamie's eyes were brown. These weren't Jamie's, nor was the face. The eyes staring at me were like my own. Noah's eyes. Pupils dilated with fear as the sea took him away from me and the safety of the rocks where we'd been scratching our initials seconds earlier.

AW + NW 4 life.

All four of my limbs contracted like the tentacles of a sea anemone recoiling from unwanted contact, as if I could make myself so small the smells and sounds and sensations could no longer find me, touch me, force their way inside me.

'... circle your ankles, before letting your feets relax, remembering to feel every ...'

I rolled on to my side. I'd felt enough. More than enough. Rough edges scratching my knees as I'd knelt on the rock.

Trying to get closer to Noah as he'd drifted. Further and further with each undulation of the water. My skinny arm wrenched from its socket as I'd stretched. Harder. Further. Our tiny fingers inches apart. So close as those big green eyes had disappeared beneath the water. Green with flecks of amber. Just like mine. Just like Dad's.

Gone.

'. . . feel the waves like they is washing over your body . . .'

My eyeballs boiled in their sockets as I pushed myself up. I needed to get out. Needed to run from the other slide in the horror show that had started playing and wouldn't stop no matter how fast I rushed towards the exit. The same arm I hadn't been able to reach, dragged from the water. The body attached to it sprawled on the beach. Noah's bright yellow swimming shorts sticking to his thighs like cling film.

Then shouting.

Screaming.

Waving.

A man I didn't recognise placing his hands across Noah's breastbone. One on top of the other. Palms pounding up and down. Up and down. Pumping to a rhythm no one could hear but him, before stopping to blow air into Noah's mouth. I didn't realise what he was doing at the time. 'Why is that man kissing Noah?' I remembered asking as I'd pulled the wayward strap of my Minnie Mouse swimming costume back on to my shoulder. No one answered. Everyone was too busy. Mum crying. Dad holding Noah's face in his hands, before looking at me, and I knew from his eyes it was all my fault.

Stomach acid rushed up my throat as I stumbled over the bodies strewn on the floor around me, the yoga mat trailing from my fist. The double doors swung back as I burst through.

'Alice? Alice!' Tess's hand was on my back as I bent at the waist, gripping my knees. 'Alice? Can you hear me?'

'Just . . .' I gasped. 'Just give me a second, I . . . fuck, it's hot. It's really hot in there.'

Plastic scraped across the floor.

'Here,' Tess said, pushing a chair towards me, 'sit down.'

A glass appeared in front of my face.

'Drink this,' said Rodrigo.

I gulped the ice-cold liquid, the sudden thirst overwhelming.

'Could you give her a second, please,' Tess said. 'She needs some space.'

I stared at the floor as he went back into the studio.

Tess knelt in front of me, her hand resting on my shoulder. 'What the hell happened in there?'

My heart rate slowed, the taste of foam dispersing. 'I'm fine now, honestly. I felt like I was going to pass out for a second.'

She placed the back of her fingers against my forehead. 'You do feel a bit warm, maybe you're coming down with something?' *Oh, I have something, all right.* 'Come on, let's get you home.'

I handed her the now empty glass. 'Could you top this up for me?' I wasn't still thirsty. I just needed her to focus on something else so she didn't see that I couldn't stop my hands from trembling.

33

It took twenty minutes to convince Tess I was capable of driving home, then another ten sat stationary in the car park to convince myself after she'd left. Grounding techniques, that's what the YouTube video said would help. I drove my knuckles into my eyes, inhaling in through the nose *two, three, four, five, six, seven*, and out through the mouth *two, three, four, five, six, seven*.

I wasn't sure how to tell if it worked, but it got me to the big Sainsbury's in one piece. The trolley rattled as I pushed it down the aisles. I focussed on the produce. The greens of the salad bags. *Green, like Dad's swimming shorts, untouched beside him on the beach towel, his job phone glued to his ear.* Yellows, oranges and reds of the fruit section. *Red, like the sarong Mum was wearing when she left us to get some toffee fudge ice creams.*

The hairs on my arms stood on end as I leant into the freezer to grab a pizza. I straightened, my hand instinctively scratching along the inside of the waistband of my trousers, as if the sand from where Noah had buried me up to my neck would somehow still be there twenty years later. He'd gone too far that day. We'd agreed up to the waist only. But once he'd started going further there was nothing I could do. My pleas falling on deaf ears as he sang the guitar riff from 'Wipe Out' by *The Surfaris* which he'd been parroting on repeat ever since Mum started doing aerobics in the living room to the *Dirty Dancing* soundtrack. I'd hated the feeling. Not being able to move as the sand tomb held me in place. Having no control. The vulnerability of my exposed head. And I'd stewed about it for the rest of the afternoon. Looking for ways to get back at him. *But you didn't mean to . . .*

I threw the ice-covered box into the trolley and clung to the handrail, swinging it around the corner to the next aisle in search of wine. Metal clanged against metal as it clashed with another shopper's cart.

'Alice, hi.'

My jaw clenched. 'Dom.'

'Nice to . . . are you OK?'

I wiped my cheek in case any stray tears remained before looking down into my trolley so he couldn't see my face exposed under the bright supermarket lighting. 'Yeah, fine.'

'Hey, hey,' he said, dipping his head to try and look at me properly, 'come on, you're clearly not, what's wrong?'

Oh, I dunno, the most important investigation of my life is going to shit, I'm not one hundred percent convinced you aren't the one behind it, everyone thinks I'm incapable and I just had a meltdown because Rodrigo, King of the Cheetos, played a recording of some waves and bloody seagulls. 'Honestly, I'm fine, just got stuff going on at the minute.'

'You must be under a lot of pressure. I was reading about

your case online, no wonder it's attracting a lot of attention. A few of the comments on the articles I saw were saying it's a copycat of one of her books – is that true?' He held a hand up before I could say anything. 'Sorry, ignore me, I know you're not meant to talk about it. D'you know – wow, this is a bit embarrassing, but you look like you need cheering up, so, I'll take the hit – I actually bought some of her books to have a read. Thought it might impress you, you know, if I could play detective. And make a start on getting up to speed with all your entertainment references, of course.'

I stared at him. Looked for all the telltale signs of lying. Sweat forming on the upper lip or forehead. Excessive blinking. Licking lips or swallowing hard to deal with dryness in the mouth. Nothing. He just stared back, willing me to respond. Dom scratched the back of his head. 'Honestly, I shit you not, there is literally a pile of her books under my bed right this second.'

'Why under the bed?' The question blurted out before I could stop it.

'I dunno, guess I didn't exactly want you to see them and think I was a loser or something.' His eyes widened. 'Not that I assumed we'd be going into my bedroom or anything ... that we'd be, you know ... I've freaked you out, haven't I? Should have kept that one under the old toupee. Not that I wear an actual toupee ... not that there's anything wrong with ...' His lips vibrated as he blew a full lung's-worth of air through them. 'OK, I'm going to stop talking now.'

It did seem a rather eccentric reason to have bought the books. But it *was* a reason. And he didn't even know I'd seen them. Why make up such a dumb explanation for something he didn't even know he needed to explain? My theory began to fade, but strands of it clung to the tissue in my brain like a tumour. 'It's fine, don't worry about it.'

I was just about to make an excuse to leave when Dom's eyes left mine and looked at something over my shoulder.

'Alice, fancy seeing you here,' came a familiar voice from behind me.

I turned to see A. J. eating crisps from an open family-sized bag he'd placed in the child seat of his trolley. 'I hope you're going to pay for those. I'd hate to have to arrest you for shoplifting.'

He pulled a well-worn wallet from his inside pocket and flapped it at me. 'Surely you haven't got time for that, with much more important things like a stalker still on the loose. Unless you've managed to crack it?' I winced as he leant forward and peered into my trolley. Just when I thought the smell from his vape that clung to his clothing couldn't get any worse, he'd proved me wrong by pairing it with the distinct stale odour of his old leather jacket. 'Celebratory pizza party?'

'You can expect your holding statement tomorrow. Not that it'll make any difference to the shit you've probably planned to write anyway.'

A. J. rubbed crumbs from his hands, his cheeks and upper lip bulging like something was trying to escape his mouth as his tongue ran across his teeth to catch every last morsel of flavour hiding between the enamel. 'Come on now, don't make me look bad in front of your, erm, *friend*.' He looked towards Dom, pushing the bridge of his glasses up his long, thin nose before holding out his hand. 'A. J. Howden, and you are?'

Dom looked at me like he was seeking approval as his hand inched towards A. J.'s. 'Dom, I'm Alice's, erm ... neighbour.'

They shook hands as A. J. squinted, head leaning ever so slightly to one side like he was appraising a rare antique.

I interrupted before either of them could say anything else. 'Right, well, I need to get back, so ...' I nodded at Dom to move his trolley so I could escape the triangular prison we'd formed, blocking the entire aisle.

'Me too,' Dom said, turning his trolley around.

For God's sake, I just wanted to leave. Alone.

'Look forward to the statement, Alice,' A. J. yelled from behind us as we walked towards the till, 'and nice to meet you, Dan.'

Dom nudged me in the side with his elbow and I flinched. He didn't seem to notice.

'Dom. Dan,' he said, 'close enough, I suppose, and not at all a very unsubtle attempt to undermine me. He an ex or something?'

I reached the row of tills and threw my pizza on to the conveyor belt. 'He wishes.'

Dom said something back but I'd stopped listening as I got my card out to pay, thanking the Lord he had a trolleyload of shopping and the checkout man was painfully slow, two factors I hoped would aid my escape. 'See you around then,' I said, grabbing my pizza and powerwalking to the exit before Dom had a chance to protest.

My keys scraped around the casing of the ignition before I found the slot and started the engine. I pulled out of the car park, something rattling deep inside the front left foot-well as the tyres moved from the new roundabout's fresh tarmac on to the weathered country road that ran around the outskirts of the village. Excellent. Yet another thing to add to the list of things in my life that didn't work.

Oakham Reservoir came into view, a reflection of the crescent moon painted on to its glassy black surface. I would miss Fortbridge if I got the job at HQ and moved back up to town. The fresh air. The fields. The sound of birds singing at 4 a.m. instead of arguments between patrons leaving bars and nightclubs interlaced with the wail of police sirens. Maybe it wasn't such a terrible thing if I continued to botch this investigation and ended up staying here. But I couldn't let Camilla down just so I could play *Escape to the Country*. If there was something to know about Dom, to link him to all this, or to eliminate him and put my mind at ease once and for all, I needed to find it. Now.

Before I realised where I was, I found myself climbing the steady incline of Apple View Lane, the road passing Bertram Manor. The red glow of brake lights came into view up ahead as I rounded the bend and the surface levelled out. I couldn't quite tell in the dark, but it looked like the vehicle they belonged to was parked outside the entrance to the manor. The dashboard clock read 9:17 p.m. Why was there a car sat outside Camilla's house at this time of night? It certainly wasn't a marked car doing a welfare check, I could see that from here. I eased my foot off the accelerator, elbows locked out, hands braced against the steering wheel.

There was movement. Two people. Their shapes lit by the ivory interior light. I got closer, a man and a woman coming into view. The man was in the driver's seat, the woman the passenger. A flash of red hair. Camilla. The pair of them were animated. Gesticulating. His hands empty, hers holding what looked like a piece of paper. Myles and Camilla. A lovers' tiff?

My view through their back window disappeared as I pulled alongside them, Camilla and Myles too focussed on their conversation to notice me as I passed. The driver turned and ran his hands through his hair before pressing back on to the headrest. Definitely Myles, but the face of the woman he was arguing with wasn't Camilla.

I craned my neck for one last look.

Chrissy.

I kept watching through my rear-view mirror as they got smaller and smaller, before the car disappeared through the manor gates. What would those two have to argue about away from Camilla? I almost swung the car around to ask them then and there, but thought again when I saw a dot of light to my right. The abattoir. The owner still hadn't returned Roy's call about the CCTV. I could get it now. The sooner we had it, the sooner it might show some evidence of Dom, or someone else, sneaking into the rear of the manor. That was more important right now. And anyway, I had to give Camilla a heads up about the holding statement. I could go there in the morning, mention what I'd seen in front of Camilla and watch them squirm. No time to collude and get their stories straight.

Dense cloud settled over the moon, snuffing out its pale light as I scanned for the turn-off leading to the abattoir's access road, my eyes straining against the darkness before I saw a break in the hedge nestled at the foot of two large oak trees. I turned. The narrow track was pitch-black. My car bounced in and out of potholes for about a quarter of a mile before the beam of my headlights finally hit corrugated metal sheeting bolted between two thick iron fenceposts stopping me going any further. I got out of the car as a stiff wind whipped across the open fields. What sounded like mesh fencing rattled in the distance, not that I could see beyond the range of my headlights. I yanked the rusted latch that sat in a hole cut into the centre of the chipped green panelling. Flecks of rust rubbed off as the metal dug into my palm but it didn't budge.

Shit.

I pulled my phone out and turned on the torch, which lasted all of three seconds before shutting off as the battery died. 'Oh my God, can I catch a break, please! Just one measly little break!' I walked to one side of the gate and ran my hand along the wall, feeling for some sort of intercom so I could get someone to let me in, finding nothing but rough, crumbly stone. I moved to the other side and did the same thing, my hand catching on a small plastic box this time. 'Oh halle-bloody-lujah, finally.' I felt around for a button, found one and pressed it until my finger ached. I almost did a fist pump when the static clicked in, indicating someone else had come on the line. 'Hello?' I said. The only response was more static. 'Is there anyone there?' I thought I heard breathing amongst the crackling but couldn't be sure. 'Hello?' I was just about to press the button again when a gruff voice replied.

'Yeah?'

'Hi, hello, my name's Detective Sergeant Alice Washington, from Fortbridge Police Station. Sorry to bother you so late. We've been trying to call, I think you might be able to help us with an enquiry we have about your CCTV. Could I come through?'

No words. Just another breath. Definitely a breath this time.

I leant a little closer to where I thought the speaker might be, even though I still couldn't actually see what I was talking into. 'Sir, can you hear me all right? My name's—'

'Yeah ... yeah. I'll come get you, gimme a minute.'

'OK, thank you, I appreciate it, Mr ... Mr ...' I racked my brain trying to remember what Roy had said the guy who owned this place was called.

Another pause before he answered, 'Lowry. Dick Lowry.'

'Right, yes, thanks, Mr Lowry, I won't keep you long.'

I stepped back, rested against the bonnet of my car, and waited.

34

Roy had sat still so long in the empty office, even the motion-activated lighting had forgotten about him. He waved his arms and the strips flickered back to life. It had just gone twenty past nine, only another forty minutes to kill before he was out of there. He was getting too old for lates. In theory, he could sneak out now. But Jane had made it perfectly clear before she left he wouldn't be getting a fourth warning about his incomplete information security e-learning module that was three months overdue, so he might as well use the opportunity to get the bleeding thing finished before she had another pop.

He clicked through the pages, not really taking in any of the information, his mind wandering back to the drama with Carver earlier instead. Alice had done well, pushing back like that. He'd half expected her to pander, especially with a job up for grabs. Give it a bit of *Yes, sir, no, sir, three bags full, sir*. But she hadn't. Put Carver right in his place. Not that he understood why Alice was so desperate to work with that lot anyway. Always on the hunt for supposedly bigger and better things. As if the type of insignia on your epaulettes dictated how good an officer you were. Some of the best he'd known had retired as constables.

The bosses could be just as bad as the public these days. Higher the rank, further the ear from the ground. Like one of those stupid talking heads on a vox pop, or those people commenting on police appeals saying helpful things like, 'Why don't they check the CCTV and interview the witnesses, that's what I'd do.' Roy got angry just thinking about it. *Cheers for the tip, Janice from Winchester, that hadn't crossed our minds.* They didn't have a clue. Jane could give the stalking case to HQ as far as Roy was concerned, as if Tweedle-Dum and Tweedle-Uptight would find anything they hadn't already.

He let out a sigh of relief as he finished the training and was just about to turn off his computer when it pinged with a new email.

CASE REFERENCE: SSU-05315-03/2022 ESDA RESULTS

Roy opened it and read. The note left on the chopping board had been too wet with the myo-whatever-it-was-called to test. But there were some impressions on the note left in the bedroom. His excitement waned as he clicked on the attachment and looked at a scanned image of what they'd found before reading it aloud. 'C. L. O. N.' Clon? That could be from bleeding anything. *Clon*ked. *Clon*e. Cy*clon*e. *Clon*dike. Or did that last one start with a K? He wasn't sure, Scrabble had never exactly been his forte.

He banged his hand against the desk. 'Bugger.' Fat lot of

good that would do them, and they were due a win, even just a small one. He didn't hold out much hope for the DNA and fingerprint examination results they had left to come from the break-in either.

The only thing left after that would be the CCTV from the abattoir, and even then the likelihood of it catching someone crossing the fields was small. He looked at the clock. Too late to call now. He opened the browser and searched to check what time it opened in the morning. 'Dick ... Lowry ... Abattoir,' he said as he typed. He sat up as the result under the list of opening times caught his eye. Roy clicked and skimmed the article. *Ah, poor bloke. No wonder he's not answering the bleeding phone. What a terrible way to go and all*, Roy thought as he wondered how Dick Lowry's death three months earlier had managed to pass him by.

35

The wind was doing its utmost to claw through my jacket as I waited, and waited, shuddering and exposed on the open hills. My relief was audible as footsteps finally clomped towards me. A gloved hand poked through the hole in the gate, wrapping itself around the latch before keys jangled in a lock. After a few clinks and one loud clunk, the panelling split down the middle and a heavyset man appeared in the crack between them, wincing and raising an arm to shield his eyes from the headlights. He dragged open one half of the gate then the other. The hinges moaned in protest, clearly well overdue a coat of oil. He gestured for me to bring my car in, stood to one side and waited as I got back behind the wheel. I drove through and pulled up behind a dirty cream Bedford van that looked like it'd seen better days. 'All right to leave it here?' I asked as I got out.

'Fine,' he said, relocking the gates.

The patch of tarmac now housing the two vehicles was just as dark as the other side of the fence had been, but a large floodlight facing in towards the property cast a dull yellow light across a courtyard. What looked like a large,

L-shaped brick barn ran along the right and back of it, with a more residential-looking grey pebbledash dwelling to the left. He walked past me without saying anything and I followed. I presumed he'd turn into the building on the left, lamplight seeping from behind curtained windows, but instead he turned right and heaved open the double-height sliding door to the barn. The space was in darkness. He disappeared to one side, hopefully to turn on a light switch.

'Like I said, sorry to bother you this late, Mr Lowry, and I won't keep you long, I just—'

Switches clicked and bright light burst from large ceiling bulbs seconds before an extractor fan roared. I almost threw up on the spot. Droplets of blood carpeted the concrete floor as far as I could see. A few feet above them, row upon row of at least twenty headless carcasses hung from S-hooks attached to an overhead conveyor system, deep reddish-purple flashes of meat standing out against white fat and bone.

'Not a veggie, are ya?' he said.

I turned to face him, every muscle in my neck flinching in response to finding him stood barely a foot behind me. A theory tore its way through my brain, the stench of iron and sweat coming from him like smelling salts sending my senses into overdrive. Hooks. Steaks. *Camilla?* My heart dropped into my stomach as I stumbled backwards, edging closer and closer to the wall of meat. *Calm down! This is the man's job, for God's sake.* I swallowed hard, trying to regain my composure. 'No.'

'Bit hypocritical, isn't it? Eating meat but not wanting to

see how the sausage is made.' He didn't wait for an answer and walked alongside the line of dead animals. 'This way.'

He stopped and turned when I didn't immediately follow and I finally caught sight of him properly in the light. The full-length black wax jacket he was wearing didn't look like it was big enough to reach over his chest and button up across the white overalls he wore underneath. Mostly white overalls anyway. Large patches were stained pink, just like his almost white wellies. My stomach churned. How could he walk around like that all day, just nonchalantly covered in blood? My hunch was too obvious, surely? Using the tools of his trade on display for anyone to see as part of a secret stalking campaign … The alarm bell in my mind quietened but didn't stop ringing completely, batteries clinging to their last few moments of life.

I dragged my eyes away from the stains and back to his face. Tufts of hair poked out from underneath a dark flat cap and fell across one of his astonishingly blue eyes.

'Office is this way,' he said.

Various bloodstained implements sat on a stainless steel trolley beside a discarded blue plastic apron and a pair of full-arm rubber gloves in the same colour. I tried not to look at them as we walked past. He turned sharply in front of me, revealing a row of smaller hooks with different pieces of meat hanging from them. One looked like an entire liver. Saliva filled my mouth, and not in a good way.

'Don't waste nothin' here, goes out for pet food,' he said over his shoulder as if he could hear my thoughts. 'Trim and forequarter cuts go to make burgers.'

I almost asked what a forequarter cut was but thought better of it as my clothes felt as though they were shrinking. I tugged at the collar of my coat as we passed through a narrow corridor, made even narrower by several columns of dark green packing crates lining the wall to my right from floor to ceiling. He finally stopped and threw his bodyweight against a stiff door at the end of the crates, opening it into a small square office. I followed him inside. He turned a lamp on and pointed towards a worn navy office chair poking out from behind a desk strewn with files and loose papers.

'Take a seat,' he said.

I wiped some crumbs off it before perching on the edge, almost jumping back off it as the door closed and he leant back against it. The office felt small enough when I first walked in; it felt even smaller now.

'Keeps the smell out,' he said, again as if he was reading my mind, though the door would have to be ten times thicker to keep that smell out. 'What d'you need?'

His eyes were less intense in the dimly lit room, but they were still piercing. Small. Disproportionately so compared to his large nose that looked like it had been broken at least once, thick lips, and razor sharp cheekbones, blushed pink like someone who spent a lot of time outdoors.

A sense of unease squeezed the back of my throat. As this was an impromptu visit, I didn't have any of the digital evidence portal leaflets with me, and I really didn't want to have to stay in this place for the amount of time required to explain step-by-step how to upload his footage. Just get

241

a copy in whatever format it's in and get out, that was all
I needed to do. 'I've been told you might have CCTV that
covers some of the surrounding fields.'

'What d'you need that for?'

'We're investigating a break-in over at Bertram Manor,
I presume you know it.'

He looked down to his side and picked at the flap of
his jacket pocket. I hadn't noticed him take his gloves off.
'Not familiar, no.'

'It's the only other property you can see from here, the
one that sits on the orchard. We think whoever broke in
might have come in through a rear access point, and it
might be a bit of a long shot, but if they came from this
direction then your camera might have picked them up.'

'Right. Yeah. Yeah, I see.' He left his pocket alone and
looked up at me, but didn't move.

'OK, so . . .' I scanned the overflowing shelves and sur-
faces around me, seeing nothing that looked like a CCTV
system. He did *have* CCTV, right? I'd said that was why I
was here, didn't I? Did I? Did I mention it on the intercom?
I couldn't remember. I mustn't have. Because surely if I did,
and he didn't have any, he'd have told me so and I'd have
been on my merry way and not wasted both of our time.
'You, erm, you do have CCTV cameras, don't you?'

Again he didn't move. 'Don't you need, like, a warrant
or something for that?'

The alarm in my head trilled louder again. If he had
cameras, what was on them he didn't want us to see? 'I
don't need a warrant to ask, but I can get one if I need to,

Mr Lowry, if you refuse to comply with my request. Is that what you'd like me to do?'

He stared at me for several seconds before replying, 'Don't think that'll be necessary.' The corners of his mouth turned slightly upwards, like he was trying to force a smile he didn't mean.

'Right. Good. Where is it, then?'

He stayed where he was.

'Mr Lowry? As I said, I don't want to keep you.'

'Cameras are only for show.'

The alarm was wailing now. Something was wrong here. Very wrong. 'What?'

'The cameras, outside. They aren't hooked up to anything; I can show you if you don't believe me.'

Then why the hell have you even brought me in here! I almost shouted in his face. Was I right? Was he the one targeting Camilla and I'd walked straight in and made him think we were on to him? A small shiver trickled down my spine as it dawned on me no one knew I was here and my phone was dead. I shifted on the edge of the chair.

'Nice to see what it takes, though,' he said, 'to see you lot taking some action. I'll make sure I'm a celebrity by the next time I need police assistance up here, get you all tripping over yourselves to help.'

I froze, heart drumming. 'I thought you weren't aware of the manor, Mr Lowry.'

He looked at me like he'd been alone and I'd just entered the room, 'What?'

I tried to steady my breath. 'You said you didn't know

what I was talking about when I said I was investigating something at the manor. But now you know a celebrity lives there.'

The feelings of unease I'd tried to keep at bay since the moment he turned on the barn lights rose up in my throat.

He pulled the cap off his head and ran his hand over his face, static flicking his hair out in every direction. 'Course I've heard of her – never out the papers, is she? I meant I didn't know the place was called Burnham or Bertram or whatever you said, that's all. Not a crime, is it?'

'No,' I said as I pushed myself up to standing, planting my feet firmly on the ground, 'but wasting police time is.'

He sniffed hard like he was pounding a line of cocaine, pushing himself away from the door before yanking it open. 'You should probably be getting off then, officer, 'cause like I said, I can't help you.'

Part of me wanted to say something back to him, to let him know messing me around wasn't OK, but something told me to get the hell out of there while I still had the chance. I shot back through the narrow walkway, gulping in fresh air as I hit the courtyard. He followed me as far as the edge of the barn where he leant against the metal frame of the sliding door, staring as I made my way to my car.

I fumbled with the key fob, his eyes burning into my back.

'Suppose you'll need me to do the gate for you an' all,' he shouted, the wind whipping away the ends of his words. He didn't wait for a response as he pushed himself away from the frame and made his way to the gate.

I got into the car, pressing the lock the second the door

slammed closed. He unbolted the gate and I drove through, my headlights sweeping over him like a scanner before he watched me drive off down the road.

The pizza sat cold on the floor next to my bed. Unsurprisingly, I couldn't stomach the Meat Lovers topping. Something was certainly very odd about Lowry, but on the drive back I'd started to feel less sure about what that was. Creepy setting and passive-aggressive vibes aside, could the predilection for raw meat and hanging carcasses on hooks just be a coincidence? Was I reading too much into it? And even with everything that happened at the abattoir, I still couldn't shake off my suspicions about what I'd seen in the moments before that. Myles and Chrissy in the car outside the manor.

I'd run through different scenarios about what the issue could be between them and how it might link to Camilla being targeted. An affair ended? A classic case of jealous scorned mistress? That worked in theory, but as much as I tried to paint Chrissy as the stereotypical bunny boiler, something niggled in the pit of my stomach. She'd been in Bath when the gates were vandalised, but she'd been right there in the house during the break-in. Myles had supposedly been in London for both events. Definitely for the vandalism, because Camilla had been there with him.

Regardless, I had no actual evidence of anything against anyone yet. All I had were feelings. And I could hardly trust those at the moment, let alone take them to the bloody CPS. This had to stop. The constant self-doubt, the replaying over and over again what happened with Jamie. With Noah.

245

It was a constant distraction that hung like a rain cloud above every thought, threatening to burst at any moment. I might have failed at saving them, but that was done now. There was still time to help Camilla, if I could just calm down and focus.

I searched the internet on my phone for some alternatives to what Tess had put on my Be a Better Alice list. Yoga and mindfulness clearly weren't working. I needed something else. Something to get this stuff out of my mind for good, not just moving it from place to place like infected chess pieces. An article about journalling caught my attention. None of this app or therapy bollocks. Just me, a pen and a blank page. I liked it. Simple. Old-school. I read the instructions.

Step 1: Find a quiet place with minimal distractions.

I propped myself up with some pillows and patted the duvet over my legs. Easy. Done. Crushing it already.

Step 2: Think about what impact the event had on your life.

Events. Plural. Check. Done that ad nauseam over the last few weeks.

Step 3: Just start writing – take note of your deepest thoughts, your deepest feelings.

I stretched my arms above my head in preparation before picking up the pen and circling my head. *It's journalling, Alice, not a bloody prime-time boxing match*. My hand hovered over the page. Shaking. I reminded myself they were just words, let out a deep breath, and started to write.

God knows how long I'd been sitting there by the time

I finished and threw the notebook towards the end of the bed like it was coated in hazardous material. I rubbed at the ache in my wrist, writing muscles years out of practice. Did I feel any better? Not really. If anything, committing my thoughts to paper had cemented them. I could see some of the offending words from here, the splayed pages taunting me. *Guilt . . . failure . . . blame.* A pain stabbed deep in my chest, as if a tiny scalpel had mirrored the nib of the pen, each letter etched to the page carving a matching wound on to my heart.

I slouched further into the bed and pulled the blanket over my head, hoping sleep would come before tears.

36

A low mist hung over the grounds of Bertram Manor, smothering the lawn as I pulled up behind Roy's car. I pushed the door open and scanned the trees lining the inside of the perimeter wall as I climbed out, their tops invisible through the fog like a row of soldiers in khaki uniforms still standing to attention despite their decapitation.

Roy emerged with one shirt tail dangling over crumpled trousers.

'Morning.' I pulled my jacket tighter around my neck and gave Roy the lowdown on my adventures at the abattoir and my suspicions about Dick Lowry.

He cupped his fingers under his armpits. 'Can't have been Dick Lowry you spoke to; the old fella's popped his clogs, lung cancer, saw it when I was looking something up last night.'

I froze. 'So who the hell's holed up in that abattoir? 'Cause he *said* his name was Dick Lowry.'

'Blue eyes? Fair hair? Grumpy little sod?'

'Yeah.'

'That'll be Dickie Junior, I imagine. Must be back to take over the family business, probably not too thrilled about it either; last I heard he'd bought his own land up in Scotland or something.'

'That tracks. Happy would be the last word I'd use to describe him. "Creepy as fuck" would be more like it. How well d'you know him?'

Roy turned down the sides of his mouth and shook his head. 'Not well, haven't seen him since the kids left school. He was in Laurie's class in sixth form but I'm sure he went off travelling not long after that.'

'I wanna know what his deal is. He led me right up the garden path last night, bringing me all the way back into the office in that place when he knew damn well he had no CCTV; it was like he was playing with me or something, and I don't like it one little bit.'

'Really? I could've sworn they had cameras up there.'

I pushed my hands deep into my pockets. 'They do, they're just dummies. I wanna know where he was the night of the break-in.'

'Leave it with me. Oh, and before I forget ...'

Roy filled me in on the update he'd had on the ESDA test. 'So, unless anyone knows what the hell "clon" relates to, we're pretty much back to square one evidence-wise.'

'Maybe not,' I said. 'When I was driving past here last night I saw Myles and Chrissy having a barney. Could be nothing, but worth asking the question. You kick off with the heads up about the press release slash welfare check, ask if "clon" means anything to them, then I'll jump in.'

Roy nodded and we walked to the manor.

Myles opened the front door as we approached. His

attire was far more casual than on our first two encounters, his usually pristine hair ruffled and the suave clothing replaced by pyjamas consisting of a slim-fit white T-shirt and baggy black and dark grey checked bottoms. 'What are you doing here?'

'We're here to see Camilla, Mr Carrington,' I said, trying to play nice.

'Let them in, Myles, for Christ's sake!' Camilla called from inside.

He turned, leaving the door open. Roy and I looked at each other, our eyes widening before we followed him to the kitchen where Camilla sat at a large wooden dining table, her oversized dressing gown pulled tightly around her neck. The golden tones of the light failed to hide the ashen hue to her complexion.

'Morning,' Camilla said, her voice hoarse.

'Morning. How are the pups doing?' Roy asked as he took a seat opposite her. I stayed standing. As did Myles, leaning against the doorway.

Camilla sat back, a drop of colour returning to her face at the mention of the dogs. 'They're fine, thank you,' she said. 'The vet kept them in for another night, just to be sure, but didn't find anything unusual in their systems. Chrissy's just left to pick them up.'

Shit. I had hoped Chrissy would be here. I looked at Myles to see his reaction to the mention of her name, but he didn't flinch.

A huge grin spread across Roy's face. 'Great news, really great. And how are you two doing?'

'She's fine—' Myles said before Camilla cut him off.

'I can answer for myself, *thank you*.' Her tone softened as she looked back at me and Roy. 'I'm fine. I could do with catching up on some sleep, but other than that . . .'

A knife would have been hard pushed to cut the tension in the air. Even a hacksaw might have struggled. I moved closer to where Camilla was sitting. 'If you need to talk to anyone, there are helplines you can call, specialist ones, for people experiencing stalking.'

She shook her head. 'No, thank you. It's not the *stalking* keeping me up.'

'Anything we can help with?' Roy asked.

Camilla looked at Myles and then back to us. 'Nothing I can't handle.'

Did she know about Chrissy and Myles's argument? What had she found out that she didn't want to tell us?

Roy turned to Myles. 'Mr Carrington, these things can be hard on loved ones as well. Just so you know, the support services help friends and family, too, if you need someone to chat to.'

Camilla spoke before Myles had the chance. 'I'm sure Myles has plenty of people to chat to already.'

Roy's eyes flitted between them for a few awkward seconds before Myles broke the silence. 'Not necessary.'

'Right, well,' Roy said, 'we wanted to check you were doing all right, but also to give you a heads up that a press release is going out, probably this afternoon. Nothing for you to worry about, no new information, just trying to calm down some of the media attention, OK? And to give the community a bit of reassurance.'

Camilla stood and walked towards the window. 'Do whatever you like. I doubt it'll make any difference, I'm sure that reporter will keep calling anyway.'

I balled my fists in my trouser pockets. 'Who's calling? A. J. Howden?'

She nodded. 'Yes, that's him.'

Bloody hell, A. J.! 'I'll talk to him, OK? It's one thing letting him do his job but it's quite another if he's being intrusive to the point of harassment.'

Her shoulders rose and flopped like she'd tried to shrug and just didn't quite have the energy or the will. 'I doubt that'll make any difference either, but thank you.'

Myles butted in before I could say anything else. 'Again, *officer*, thanks but no thanks. We can sort this ourselves. We done here?'

'Actually, Mr Carrington,' Roy said, 'we did want to check one more thing.' He wagged his finger in the air, channelling his very best Lieutenant Columbo. 'We got something back on one of the tests on the note that was left in the bedroom; the dents on it spelt out C-L-O-N. Does that mean anything to either of you?'

Camilla shook her head. 'Nothing springs to mind.'

'Clon?' Myles said. 'That's not even a word.'

'No, but it could be the start of a word, or middle, or end,' Roy said.

Myles laughed. 'Jesus, is this the level of policing we're relying on? Solving crossword puzzles?'

I took the chance to jump in, catch him off guard. 'We can ask Chrissy too, see if she has any ideas. I was hoping she'd be here this morning, I wanted to check she's OK.'

One side of Myles's lip curled and he folded his arms. 'Why wouldn't she be?'

'So you're not aware of anything that might have upset her?' I asked.

Slowly, he pushed himself upright and crossed the room to sit on the chair that Camilla had just vacated. Did he need a seat, or was he just buying time? Sizing me up? 'Not that it's any of your business, but we had a bit of an argument last night. I'm still not thrilled about her saying I told her to lie.'

Camilla spun around. 'I thought we'd sorted that? She knows it was wrong, she panicked!'

'I know, I know, please let's not go over it again. She's fine, it's done now, I promise.' He looked back at me. '*Now* are we done?'

There was no point pushing him. Whether he was telling the truth or not, that was his story and he was sticking to it. I reminded myself this was supposed to be a victim welfare check, not an interrogation. 'Almost,' I said, turning from him towards Camilla. 'Have you had any dealings with the owner of the abattoir, a Mr Lowry, son of the previous owner?'

Camilla thought for a moment. 'No, not that I know of anyway. Why?'

Myles's eyes were on me. I couldn't ignore his previous threats to handle this situation himself, and I didn't want to be responsible for Dick Junior getting a kicking if he had nothing to do with what had been going on here. 'Not to worry, we just thought we might have had a CCTV opportunity from his property, but unfortunately that's been ruled out. Anyway, that's it from us, we won't take up any more of your time.' Camilla went to move but I held a hand out to stop her. 'Don't worry, we can see ourselves out.'

The sun had eaten through most of the fog by the time we made our way back to the cars, traces of crisp blue sky peeking through the remaining cloud.

Roy looked up, squinting. 'Someone's in the doghouse,' he said. 'What was that all about, then?'

My eyes followed a squirrel as it bounded across the gravel, stopping to look left and right every few seconds as if someone was tailing it. 'Between him and Camilla? Mr Entitled doesn't seem to be getting his way about something by the looks of it. Something they clearly don't want us to know about, anyway. Him and Chrissy? God knows. Give her a call, ask about the argument before he tells her what to say.'

Roy nodded, immediately pulling out his phone and dialling. 'Voicemail.'

I scuffed my boot through the small pebbles, the squirrel darting for cover at the sound. 'Keep trying once we get back to the station.'

He nodded. 'At what point do we have to stop playing nicey nice with this prick? I dunno what's going on with him, but something sure as hell is.'

I stared back at the manor as I pulled open my car door.

'When we have something more solid to go on than him being an arsehole. We'll need a watertight reason to go digging into him, especially with who his dad is.' I looked at Roy before I got in. 'So find one.'

37

Roy and I spent the rest of the afternoon strategising discreetly but got nowhere. By the time I arrived home just after seven, my head was pounding, so I poured myself a glass of water and downed it alongside a couple of paracetamols. A door slammed somewhere outside. If everyone around me could just shut up until the pain relief kicked in, I'd be eternally grateful. I went into the hallway and peered out the window overlooking the road to see where the noise had come from just in time to see Dom bent over at the front door of The Willows. *What the hell is he doing?*

I hadn't been able to shake the uneasy feeling about him since I'd found those books, no matter his supposed reason for buying them. There'd been the distraction of wondering what Myles and Chrissy were playing at, and what was so creepy about Dick Lowry's son aside from the fact he worked in an abattoir, but as I looked at Dom again now, the hairs on my arms prickled all over again. I reminded myself for the umpteenth time heebie-jeebies didn't count as reasonable grounds.

Dom stood and I tucked myself behind the curtain, waiting a few seconds before peeking around the edge to carry on watching as he turned and walked down the drive. From the way he was dressed – shorts, vest, trainers – and the fact he was circling his arms and lifting his knees high as he made his way out on to the lane, I presumed he was going for a run. The realisation of why he'd been hunched over hit me and a curiosity bomb exploded in my mind. He'd left himself a key. He was going out, and his key was under the mat.

I spun away from the window as Dom set off, my heart pounding. It would take no time at all. Nip over there. Use the key. Get in. Get out. See if there was anything to either prove he was our man, or put my suspicions to bed. I tried to conjure some kind of legal rationale for going in there. But there was no disturbance. Nothing to suggest a crime in progress. And I knew damn well no one was home to invite me in willingly. But I couldn't help it. The Willows had transformed into a giant magnet and I was a sliver of metal being dragged towards it as Camilla's novel played out like a movie in my mind. Except Lyddie was Camilla and Arden King was Dom and I couldn't stop him. The watching. The rabbits. The hooks. The body. Like my own personal aversion therapy scene from *A Clockwork Orange* as it refused to let me look away.

Before I knew it I was across the lane and on hands and knees, fumbling under the coarse brown mat, blood rushing in my ears. I pulled the key out. The sight of it in my palm was like the click of a hypnotist's fingers waking me from this insane trance. I dropped it on to the mat and yanked my hand away as if the thing was on fire. Bracing myself against the door, I stood, light-headed. What the fuck was I thinking? I was a police officer, for God's sake. What was I even expecting to find in there? An 'I Heart Camilla' T-shirt and a box of her hair? And even if I did find something, some irrefutable evidence of his guilt, I might as well flush it down the toilet if I'd obtained it illegally.

My chest was heaving now. Tight and burning. I took the deepest inhale I could manage before the air shot back out along with a short, sharp scream as a hand landed on my shoulder.

'Alice?'

I almost tripped over my own feet as I spun to see A. J. standing behind me. 'Wh—wait, what are you doing here?'

'What's wrong with you? You look like you're about to pass out,' he said, staring into each of my eyes one at a time like some sort of doctor.

I shuffled my foot until the key pressed into the bottom of my shoe, safely hidden from view. 'I'm fine, and you didn't answer my question – what are you doing here?'

'New story I'm working on, thought your new man might have some useful insight for me. He in?'

Great, yet another hatchet job on me waiting in the wings, no doubt. 'No. And he's not *my man* either.'

'If you say so. I'll pop back another time, then.'

'I think I can safely say on his behalf he'd prefer if you didn't. Surely you've stuck it to me enough lately; isn't it someone else's turn now? And by that I don't mean more stories about Camilla Harton-Gray. You've done enough to make things ten times worse for her already.'

He tapped the end of his nose. 'Trust me, you'll find out soon enough. Gonna be a corker, I think.'

'If it messes with my investigation or the welfare of my victim, then *you'll* find out I won't hesitate to give Camilla the utmost support and encouragement to report you for intrusion and harassment.'

A. J. laughed and walked off down the driveway back to his car parked on the kerb. 'Just doing my job, Alice.'

I'll 'just doing my job' you, right in the face. I waited for him to pull away before stuffing the key back under the mat and running back to Myrtle Cottage.

I'd managed to play it cool when Tess called seconds after I'd got back in the house, insisting she come over and cook me dinner, and I'd mostly calmed myself down by the time she'd arrived an hour later. Plates and cutlery clinked as she pottered in the kitchen while I got changed. I yanked a hoodie over my head before resting my palms against the deep window ledge, looking out at the vista and willing the tranquil scenery to get me over the finish line back to normal. Or whatever the hell you'd call my resting state these days. The fields were empty. Quiet. Dark greenish-brown sheets with only the metallic food troughs and five-bar gates reflecting the trickle of light from the moon. I threw my work clothes in the overflowing washing basket and went downstairs.

The aroma of roasted meat filled the air, wrapping itself around the contours of my face like a hot flannel. 'That smells delicious.'

259

'Told you, cannot go wrong with Marks and Spencer's aromatic crispy duck,' Tess said as she tore at the meat, thin, succulent shreds falling away from the bone. Normal service had officially resumed with Tess's diet now Nate was on the scene.

I poked at a plate of greenery taking pride of place in the middle of the kitchen island. 'And what, pray tell, is *that*?'

'Spring onions and cucumber batons, to go in the pancakes.'

My top lip curled. 'You do realise, the less vegetables you put in, the more space there is for duck, right?'

Tess's hands sprang to her hips as she switched to parent mode. 'Don't moan about the vegetables; they're on your list, remember? Your lower intestines will thank me one day.'

I rubbed my stomach in an exaggerated circle. 'Intestines talk over dinner, lovely.'

'Speaking of your list, I did a bit of googling on our Mr Webb.'

Breath caught in my throat. With everything going on I'd forgotten about the research mission I'd set her off on. 'And?'

'He doesn't seem to be on socials either, so you two make the perfect couple there, anti-social bastards.'

'It's not anti-social, I just have no desire to talk to people I went to school with fifteen years ago promising me a six-figure salary if I join their bloody pyramid scheme.' And maybe Dom didn't either. Or maybe he was keeping a low profile because he was a psychopath wanted in twenty-four countries. It was a very thin line.

'Anyway, I did find a "DW Fitness" personal training page that could be him. But other than that, no terrifying skeletons in the closet. No tie-dye. No pictures of him proudly holding up a fish like it's catnip for the ladies.'

For a second, I contemplated telling her what I'd been thinking, but I could play out her response without saying the words out loud. She'd pinch the top of her nose, whisper 'Lord give me strength,' then say, 'Let me get this straight, his crimes so far are choosing to move here, showing an interest in you and the work you do, and buying a couple of books?' Then she'd place her hand over mine and pat it like I was an old lady who'd been found wandering the streets in a dressing gown and slippers at two in the morning.

I let my shoulders sag, trying to relieve some of the tension in my chest. *You are literally the worst detective in the world.* How could I possibly have made the leap from vague interest in a case about the village's only celebrity and buying some books to being a suspect? Maybe the apple had fallen much further from the policing talent tree than everyone thought. Dom had done nothing wrong except get involved with me. Making me like him. And when you liked someone, you lost control. Gave a part of yourself over to them. For them to do what they wanted with. And there was nothing you could do to stop it. A little piece of you, trapped and sticking out of the sand. Exposed.

'Where've you gone?' Tess said.

I snapped back to reality. 'Hmm?'

261

'You're worrying me, you know, you're not yourself. You really should think about taking that holiday. All this, it's getting to you, I can tell.'

I leant over and snaffled a piece of duck, trying to act normally. 'Nothing's getting to me, I'm just a little off my game, that's all.'

Tess slid a tray with the pancakes, a small pot of hoisin sauce, and the sad-looking vegetables on it towards me, and picked up another holding the plate of meat as she shook her head. 'Fine, if you say so.'

I was surprised at the limited fight she put up as she turned and walked into the living room. Not that I wanted an argument, but I'd expected more pushback, a bigger attempt at being my saviour. Was I such a lost cause even Tess had given up on me? I picked up the tray and followed her.

Tess wolfed down the first of her evening's two rounds of dinner. She had the metabolism of a five-time Tour de France winner.

'Who arranges a date to start at nine thirty *at night*?' I asked, settling down into my slanket whilst she topped up her MAC lipstick in the mirror.

'It was the only time I could see Nate. He's a paramedic, gotta wait for him to finish saving lives.'

'So when do I get to meet him?'

She pouted at herself and zhooshed up her curls. 'When I think he can withstand your points system.'

I tutted. 'If it's any consolation, he's starting on plus

points for being an emergency services worker – power to the people and all that.'

She threw on her jacket. 'I'm sure he'll be thrilled.'

'Has he passed the Mamma Emmanuel test yet?' I asked.

'Not yet,' Tess said as she wound a green scarf around her neck. 'She's struggling getting about at the minute, otherwise I'm sure she'd be straight down that car boot sale, checking him out.' Guilt hit me like a dump truck. I'd been so busy flitting between suspects it hadn't crossed my mind to ask Tess how her mum had been doing over the last few weeks. She spoke again before I had a chance to apologise. 'You should come over soon, it's been ages since she's seen you. And she prefers you to me anyway.'

'Yeah, course.' I needed to go easy on the man-eater jibes. Tess spent most of her time looking after other people, with her dad working two jobs. Her mum. Her little sister Kylie who'd just hit her teens. And to a certain extent, me. No wonder she was scouring the earth looking for someone to sweep her off her feet, give her a rest for a change.

'Well, enjoy, you deserve it,' I said. 'And I will enjoy my date with my good friend sofa, his partner wine, and as many episodes of *Schitt's Creek* as I can fit in before Netflix starts getting all Judge Judy on me, asking if I'm *still* watching.'

'Later,' Tess said as she whirled from the room, the cushion she'd launched hitting me square in the face. 'Oh,' she yelled from the hallway. 'Vince is at the door, I'll let him in, yeah?'

'Thanks, see ya.' I'd been meaning to get a cat flap installed for two years. There didn't seem much point now – he probably wouldn't use it, having become accustomed to his personal concierge service.

I switched on the TV. I'm not sure how many episodes I made it through before the meat coma kicked in.

My phone beeping from where I'd left it on the kitchen island woke me a few hours later. The fire had almost completely died out, but still it felt unusually cold. I got up, encased in my slanket, freezing air stabbing my face as I walked through the hallway. Jesus, how long had I been asleep? Had we jumped right through from March to December? Why was it so cold? I hoped I hadn't missed Christmas.

I stopped at the kitchen door and stared at the reason for the arctic temperature: the patio door sat gaping on its runners. *Fuck's sake, Tess!* As entertaining as that girl was, she could be a bloody liability sometimes. Easily distracted. I heaved the door shut and picked up my phone before retreating from the cold and heading up to bed. I paused on the bottom step. The new text I had was from a number I didn't have saved in my contacts. I opened it, the words crawling across my skin like ants.

I'd look out for tomorrow's paper – guarantee there'll be something of interest in there for you. You can thank me later. You're welcome.
A. J.

38

Tess flapped a newspaper at me as I walked into the office, Myles and Camilla's secret plastered across the front page.

'You seen this?' she said, throwing it on to my desk as I sat down. A photograph of a petite blonde with a pained look in her saucer-like blue eyes took up a third of the article. Two familiar faces stared back from a smaller photograph embedded amongst the text. Camilla and Myles, arm-in-arm at what looked like some glitzy party.

Roy circled around from his side of the desk and leant over me. 'What we got he— oh dear, oh dear, oh dear. Someone's been a naughty boy.'

I had no idea who the blue-eyed woman was, but the print said it was Helena Knowles, a semi-celeb from some reality TV show. I didn't watch reality telly, would rather rub my eyeballs with a Scotch bonnet, in fact, but I didn't judge people who did. Except for when they called it their 'guilty pleasure'. Sometimes it felt like there was so little pleasure in this dumpster fire of a world that if something brought someone joy, they should cling to it for dear life and not feel embarrassed to do so. I'd told Tess as much the time she tried to shame me for eating knobs of salted butter straight from the fridge.

'Well,' said Tess, 'gotta do something to keep herself accustomed to her new lifestyle. D'you know how much people get paid for these kiss and tells? It's insane, and a hell of a lot more than a nightclub appearance in Bognor Regis, that's for sure.'

A small sense of relief unknotted the tension in my neck at the prospect of a motive more substantial than the dry shit I'd been throwing at the wall recently. But it tensed right back up again as I wondered what this had to do with Dom and why A. J. had been trying to ask him about it. Or was that another story? The next takedown of me he was planning? 'Well,' I said, sliding down in my chair, 'now at least we know what Camilla's laser eyes at Myles were for yesterday, and why A. J. was sniffing around them, probably asking for comment before he went to print.'

'Tess,' Roy said, 'can you do some digging for a contact? We're going to need to pay Miss Big Brother a visit. Could be a woman, this stalker – all equal these days, isn't it? That means women can be mental an' all, you know.'

Tess nodded so hard her earrings jangled. 'I think you're on to something there,' she said. 'The latest stats have women making up at least a good six or seven percent of the murderers in this country. Not quite on the same level as the big boys yet, but we're catching up.'

I knew Roy felt like we were ganging up on him, but sometimes he kind of deserved it. 'Does that mean we get to start a "hashtag not all women" movement soon?' I asked.

'Hash what?' he said, his ears pricking up in some sort of Pavlovian response to the association with fried potatoes.

'Never mind,' I said.

'Well, man or woman, one person we can knock off the suspect list is Dick Lowry Junior,' Roy said. 'I went over to see him yesterday; he was away for the break-in, overnight stay on the far side of Wales for an agricultural trade show. He's got receipts.'

I slapped a palm on the desk. 'Shit.'

'And I wouldn't take his attitude personally. He was arsey as you like with me an' all, amazed he'd been graced with the presence of not one but two coppers, which he says is more than his dad got when he used to put calls in about protesters smashing the place up. According to him, those dummy cameras have done more good than any of our lot ever did for his old man – which is a load of bollocks, I might add. I went to some of those calls; we did what we could, but half the time our hands were tied behind our backs with those sorta jobs. Hardly our fault his dad nearly went out of business.'

I let out a deep sigh at the realisation that Dick Lowry Junior had been playing with me, but not for the reason I thought. He wasn't a stalker, just an angry, grieving son with a grudge to bear about poor police customer service. Excellent. Join the queue, mate.

Roy wandered off as Tess did a little jump, crossing her legs at the ankles and spinning around before walking back to her desk.

'Oi, twinkle toes.' I threw a pen at her back. 'Thanks

267

for leaving my patio door open yesterday. I woke up in the middle of the night freezing my tits off.'

Tess turned to me, her eyebrows gathering at the bridge of her nose. 'What you on about? I didn't touch your patio door.'

'Well, Vince didn't let himself in, did he? He's a clever boy but he hasn't quite figured out how to grow opposable thumbs just yet.'

'Vince came in the front door when I was going out, not the patio door.'

I ran through the night after Tess left. Had I opened it? I didn't remember moving from the sofa. I was set. Slanket, TV remote, wine. *Wine*. Had I gotten up to open another bottle? Maybe I did let Vince back out. I almost chewed through the inside of my cheek trying to pull back a memory, but nothing came. Maybe Tess was right and I did need a holiday.

Two hours later, Roy and I caught the lunchtime train to London. He slept most of the way, the movement of the carriage rocking his head from side to side as we rumbled along the tracks before grinding to a halt just outside of Paddington. Roy snorted himself awake as an announcement told us we'd be delayed for a few minutes as the driver waited for a free platform. I pulled my ticket out of my bag, the plastic key chain from Dom falling out with it.

'What on earth is that?' Roy asked.

I shoved it back into the side pocket. 'It's a keychain.

My neighbour, Dom, bought it for me after I locked myself out of the house.'

'This the pretty boy? What is he, twelve?' Roy said.

'Oh, I'm sorry, is it considered immature to give someone a practical and thoughtful gift? I'll tell him next time I'd prefer half-dead flowers from the petrol station like the ones you get for Karen last minute when you forget her birthday, shall I?'

The train clunked forward and Roy looked like he was resisting the urge to kick me under the table as we pulled into the station. It was the middle of the afternoon, but the Friday post-midday 'get the hell out of London for the weekend' crowd still made it feel like rush hour. The buzz hit me as I stepped on to the platform, the feeling that even the nitrogen particles in the air all had very important places to be. Roy and I broke from the human conveyor belt at one of the smaller side exits. I shook myself off, loosening the instant grip of the city. Roy followed suit and flicked his wrists like he'd touched a piece of dishwater-sodden food in a sink.

'Urgh,' he said, glaring at each passer-by like they'd insulted his grandma, 'not even five minutes in this devil's arsehole of a place and I need a bleedin' deep clean.'

'Hold your nose. She only lives around the corner; we'll be in and out before you know it.'

He followed me across the street as we weaved between the bumpers of back-to-back traffic. 'Still enough time to get stabbed, or robbed, or kidnapped by a yuppie cult,' he said.

We paused at the crossing where Westbourne Grove

bisected Chilworth Street, the stucco-fronted four-storey terrace in front of us hazy behind air thick with exhaust fumes. It was noticeably warmer here, those extra few degrees gleaned from the tightly packed buildings, towering forcefields shielding occupants from the elements. Or maybe the atmosphere was just saturated with droplets of cooking oil from all the takeaway shops.

Roy led the way through a white stone archway into a small mews. The honking and revving of cars from the main road melted behind us as I looked at the narrow houses. Pastel shells, each a different shade, all displaying perfectly manicured window dressings and plantation shutters. It didn't feel like the centre of one of the busiest capital cities in the world. More like a neat bubble of stillness hiding amongst gushing white-water rapids. We reached the end of the row and knocked on the final property's sage-green door. It opened, just a crack, before a sharp blue eye emphasised by an ebony winged liquid eyeliner peeked out from behind it.

'Yes?' the voice cooed.

'Helena Knowles?' I asked.

'Yes?' the woman said again, as if her first answer had been recorded and replayed.

'I'm Detective Sergeant Alice Washington; this is my colleague Detective Constable Roy Briar. Your agent spoke to our colleague Tess Emmanuel on the phone, from Fortbridge Police Station?'

A look of relief flushed her face and the door widened, revealing another ice-blue eye and the rest of her rounded features. 'Thank God, I've been waiting for the paps to come around *again*. I'm sure they'll be back before long.' She leant out and looked up the street. 'Come in, please.'

We followed her up the stairs to her first-floor maisonette that probably cost twice as much as both mine and Roy's houses put together.

'So, Helena – do you mind if I call you Helena?' I asked.

'No, it's my name, isn't it?'

Oh, not today, lady. My patience with this case was already wearing thinner than the paper Helena and Myles's sex scandal was printed on. 'What can you tell me about your relationship with Myles Carrington that I haven't already got from the news?' I'd thought about cloaking my judgement of her, but I didn't have a huge amount of time for people who sold those types of stories. Even if the other party involved could do with being knocked down a peg or two.

Helena shuffled on the edge of her accent chair and looked at the floor. 'Erm, well, I'm . . . I'm not really sure,' she said, scratching at a non-existent stain on the trousers of her black waffle-knit loungewear. I stayed quiet, her discomfort hanging in the air like a bad smell. 'I did say to the woman on the phone, I don't know why I've been brought into all of this. I haven't seen Myles for what must be, God, the best part of a year.'

Brought into it? I started to shake my head but stopped myself. No one made her do that tell-all. I cleared my throat and tried to maintain my composure. 'Helena, I'm sure you understand why we have to follow up with you, with the timing of your newspaper spread.'

271

Her eyes glistened as she flipped her hand over and stared at her nails. 'Look,' she said, so softly Roy and I had to lean in towards her, 'I know what you must be thinking, about me, about the story, but . . .' Her lip quivered.

A twinge of guilt twisted in my gut. I didn't agree with her approach, but I hadn't meant to make her cry about it. 'You don't have to explain yourself to us, Helena – that aspect isn't any of our business – but we do need to follow up on any possible lines of enquiry, anyone with a grudge against Myles or Camilla.'

Her head jerked up, forcing a tear to drop into her lap. '*Me* hold a grudge? Has Myles said that? He should be thankful I—' She pursed her lips as if forming a physical barrier was the only way she could stop herself from finishing the sentence.

'Go on,' I said. Something was coming, I could feel it.

'Oh shit, shit shit shit!' She rose from the chair and ran her fingers through her hair, walking off towards the back of the room.

'Are you all right?' I asked.

She turned to face us, no longer stifling the flow of tears. 'Look, I needed the money, OK? Just because people assume I'm loaded doesn't mean I am. I was going to lose this place, I didn't even know the woman was being stalked till after I'd given the story. Anyway, she should be thanking me, showing her what he's really like; she's better off getting rid.' She wiped spider legs of make-up away from under each eye and sat back down.

I knew it. I bloody knew it. The way he wanted us

272

nowhere near this investigation. The way he talked. The way he was with Camilla. I knew he was hiding something. 'What do you mean, Helena, what he's really like?'

She scoffed. 'I didn't even go that far. The papers only got half of it.'

'What didn't you tell the papers?' My brain was firing now, ready to pounce and start working with whatever she was about to give me.

'I don't know if this has anything to do with what's happening now. I haven't spoken to Myles since I chucked him out and told him never to come back after . . .' Her shoulders rolled in on themselves, transforming her from adult to child in a second. 'He's got this side to him, this, I don't know. Everything was fine until he met *her*,' she said, looking up at us. 'Sorry, I didn't mean it to sound like that.'

Roy was scribbling in his notebook. I kept my eyes fixed on her. 'We'd been seeing each other, on and off; it was normal at first, the *sex*.' She whispered the last word like a conservative grandparent. 'But then one night he brought this, this wig, a long red thing. It was so tacky. I don't know, I thought it was some Poison Ivy kind of thing, you know, so I went along with it, but as soon as I saw her, I knew what he was doing.'

'Saw who? Camilla?' Roy asked, not looking up from his notepad.

She nodded, twisting a lock of short blonde hair at the nape of her neck. 'We all ended up at the same gallery opening. You only had to take one look at her to see the wig was a replica. He was making me a replica of her. Never felt so cheap in all my life.'

My mind jumped to Chrissy. The hair. The clothes. Had she done that herself? Or had Myles taken advantage, seeing someone so young and impressionable, malleable even, and thought he'd hit the jackpot? Had she really been lying about the person she claimed to have seen outside the manor? Had she concealed what she and Myles were arguing about in the car when Roy'd finally managed to get hold of her and she'd confirmed Myles's version of events? 'So what happened then?' I asked.

'I called it off, I wasn't going to keep playing the understudy. Not that he seemed too bothered; he was obsessed with her.'

She told us everything else she could think of about Myles. But I knew I had what I needed. The guy had potentially made himself a little Camilla doll – what could possibly be a bigger demonstration of an obsessive and controlling personality than that? Now I just had to figure out why, so I could see his next move before he did, figure out what he was planning.

Helena folded one leg underneath herself. 'I know how this looks, OK? Bitter ex stalking the girlfriend, but I swear, I've stayed as far away from those two as possible. I really don't know how else I can help you.'

'Thank you, Helena,' I said. 'What you've given us so far is very helpful. And if you think of anything else that might be relevant, let us know straight away, all right?'

She wiped away a tear and nodded before she got up to

show us out, pausing by the front door. 'You don't think he's ... dangerous, do you?'

He was something all right. But I still hadn't quite figured out what, and I didn't want to scare her. I shrugged. 'You know him better than we do.'

She nodded, twisting the door chain between her fingers. 'Right, yeah,' she said, shaking her head as if trying to wake herself from a deep sleep. 'Course, I'm probably overthinking. God, if every man who's treated me badly was dangerous, we'd all be dead.'

We said our goodbyes and walked back towards the station.

39

He had to keep the plan on track. Had to keep his promise. He'd seen what it did to Father when Mother broke hers the first time she tried to leave. Panic spread through his body like a flesh-eating virus as the voice of Mother's sister rang out in his ears, that witch, telling her to leave Father and take him with her. What the hell did she know? She just saw the black eye. She didn't see what Mother did to get it, speaking to Father like that, lying to him.

She'd always been a liar, he could see that now. *Please, son, I can't leave you here with him. If he ever hurt you, I'd—* she'd said, blubbing and crying her crocodile tears. *Hurt me?* he'd scoffed straight into her wizened face. His father would never hurt him.

The thought of letting Father down gnawed at his brain like a rabid rat as he paced the room. Back and forth. Back and forth. He wasn't sure how much longer he could keep up the charade; he'd allowed the mask to slip once or twice already.

He had to get this done. Fast.

40

A small wicker basket with a red and white checked tea towel draped across the top of it greeted me from my door-step as I pulled on to the driveway. 'What the ...' Had I ordered something online after too much wine and for-gotten again? If this was another Le Creuset debacle, then I was going teetotal. I was still paying instalments off my credit card from when Tess introduced me to *The Pioneer Woman* TV cooking show and I over-enthusiastically bought a two-hundred-pound casserole dish online at three in the morning.

I got out of the car and bent down to pick up the small card pinned to the material.

You seemed to be having a rough time the other night, hope this helps. Dom xxx

The relief of not having to take out a small loan lasted barely a second before I remembered what a terrible person I was. I carried the hamper I didn't deserve inside and put it down in the kitchen, flicking back the towel to see an assortment of my favourite foods, the ones we'd talked about over dinner the other night. An array of cheeses, sweet chilli crisps, Maryland cookies and chocolate-dipped flapjacks, all nestled neatly around two bottles of the fancy wine we'd had in the pub.

You are such a dick!

Dom had been nothing but nice to me. Caring. Thoughtful. And I'd repaid the favour by sucking him into my mess of a life. I had to make it up to him. Not that he'd know that's what I was doing, as he'd just gone about his business completely oblivious to what I'd thought him capable of. What I'd almost accused him of. I'd invite him over for dinner this time. Make a proper effort. Maybe even dust off the Le Creuset I hadn't used since buying it.

I put the items away, pushing the two bottles of wine out of sight to the back of the cupboard. Maybe it was time to lay off the booze. It had been going down far too easily in recent weeks and my brain was doing a fantastic job of running amok on its own; it didn't need help to see things that weren't there. Plus, now I thought about it, I *was* getting worryingly close to a full house on the 'clichéd detective from a crime movie' bingo card. 'Who's marked off two fat ladies, childhood trauma, alcoholism and an ass that won't quit? Hmm? Anyone?' I said to Vince as he wandered across the kitchen.

The nerves kicked in about seven seconds after I'd decided to invite Dom for dinner. I had just enough time to fit a quick run in first, blast them away along with the fug of London clogging my pores. It was already getting dark as I pulled on some leggings and a long-sleeved T-shirt, scraped my hair into a high ponytail, and set off down the track behind the cottage. I usually avoided running in the dark, always found it made your body work twice as hard. Not only did it have to pump the arms and legs to keep you moving; it also had to expend energy doing the other task drilled into every woman before hitting puberty: simultaneously clenching and unclenching every other muscle on pervert alert every time you passed an alcove or shadowy corner where some creep might be lurking, waiting to jump out and drag you into the bushes. I held my breath instinctively as I passed the disused bird hide that backed on to a wall of thick privet hedge. The kids from the village mostly used it as a discreet snogging spot, but you never knew.

Empty.

I pushed the air out as I made it past unscathed. The relief always temporary, of course. Another dark corner always waiting around the next bend. Mind, I did sometimes wonder why it was just night-time that got such a bad safety rap. As if the pervs were vampires who turned to dust at the first traces of dawn. There'd been plenty of bright sunshine when a guy on a moped groped my bum as I walked down the high street. An equally sunny day at a university summer barbecue when my housemate and supposed friend Greg followed me into the toilet and locked the door behind us. Huge hands swarming, pulling at my clothing, mouth flapping at my neck and face. His plump lips had made a great target for my fist before blood burst down his prized Tom Ford shirt, distracting him long enough for me to get out of there.

Suspects and motives bounced around in my head as fast as my cadence for the next thirty minutes. Myles exhibited classic narcissistic traits: entitlement, up his own arse, controlling Helena and possibly Chrissy, making everything about him. Chrissy had *Camilla wannabe* vibes written all over her. She was needy, naïve, and infatuation was a definite possibility. Could the two of them have planned something together? Myles the organ grinder, Chrissy the monkey? And Helena, well, she genuinely seemed to want nothing to do with the whole mess. But I couldn't ignore the timing of her little exposé, and if revenge was a factor, she certainly couldn't be ruled out. But what did any of this prove? It was hardly expert insight. Anyone with an AS-level in psychology could have figured out what I had so far. And none of this amounted to actual evidence. Because we had none of that. No description. No useful forensics. No intel. Nothing.

I pushed myself down the mud track back towards the house, my lungs burning as my legs pumped, harder and harder. As if the missing puzzle piece that would make this all fit was just ahead of me and I'd catch it if I ran fast enough. My thighs turned to mush, the investigative muscle in my brain shrivelling and dying along with them.

A metallic film coated my teeth and gums as I turned through the gap in my hedge and crossed the garden. I'd barely made it two metres when I stopped and bent double, hands dropping to my knees, black dots dancing across my vision. I really had pushed myself. *Pushed, or punished?* I took a couple of deep breaths, replenishing the oxygen supply before I stood, arms folded over the top of my head, trying to get more air into my lungs. But my ribcage stopped mid-inhale when I saw it, the dark shape looking back at me from my bedroom window.

41

Roy sat at the bar of The Bull cradling his third whisky in twenty minutes. He wondered if Alice had believed him when he'd said he was meeting friends. Not that it mattered, anyway; everyone already thought he was a loser. The amber liquid burned as it slid down his throat.

'Steady on, old boy,' Sleazy Steve said.

'And what business of that is yours, *sir*?' Roy snarled.

'No issues from me, mate, as long as you're only here to drink and not accuse me of all sorts again. I'll keep pouring if you keep paying for 'em. Just doing my bartender-ly welfare duty. Let me guess, woman troubles?' Roy tried to dislodge the film of phlegm at the back of his throat with no success. The man twirled a small checked towel around his finger. 'Always is, without fail. I see a man drowning his sorrows at the bar, always because of a woman.' The sound of the street poured in as the door to the pub swung open. 'Ooft, now there's a young specimen I wouldn't mind driving me to drink,' Sleazy Steve said as he winked past Roy.

'You'll fall off that stool if you're not careful,' came a familiar voice from behind him. Roy swivelled, nearly fulfilling the prophecy, managing to steady himself in time to see Tess gesturing at him. 'Come sit in this booth,' she said, 'it's closer to the ground.'

'You lucky git,' Sleazy Steve said in Roy's ear.

Roy thought back to the messages this so-called man had sent Camilla, and his blithe insistence that they were innocent. His hands balled into fists of their own accord. 'Oi, less of that. You leave her alone, d'you hear me?'

The barman bared his palms in submission, but the eyes he fixed on Tess as she shuffled into her seat told a different story. 'I get it, she's taken.'

'Slimy twat,' Roy mumbled as he manoeuvred himself off the stool and made his way to Tess. He slumped on to the bench opposite her. 'I've told him to leave you alone.'

'I'm sure that'll make a difference for all of five minutes. It's fine, I'm meeting the paramedic; you can stand guard until he gets here,' she said, scanning his face. 'You OK?'

'Fine. Takes more than a few whiskies to knock me out. I'm heading off soon, anyway; I'll stay until Prince Charming comes. Not that you aren't capable of looking after yourself in the meantime, I'm sure.' Roy's hand missed his forehead in a botched attempt at a salute, flinching as he poked himself in the eye.

Tess smiled.

She reminded him of his own daughter a little, same age, same big brain. As much as it irked him how clever this lot thought they were, he had to admit he was envious of how they absorbed information like sponges. Just plug them in and watch them go. Not like his own pumice stone of a brain, gnarled and impermeable.

'Thanks,' she said. 'While I've got you here, and don't tell her I spoke to *you* about this, but ...'

'What?'

'Alice, I'm worried about her.'

'Why?'

'She's acting weird. Has been since the stuff with that kid.'

Roy shrugged. 'Seems like the normal pain in my arse she has been for the last two years to me.' He took a swig of his drink. He knew that wasn't quite true, but it wasn't anyone's business but hers. 'Jobs like that, they're not easy, you know.' He looked into the now empty glass, willing it to refill.

Tess shook her head. 'She's taking on too much, too soon, what with the case, the job coming up at HQ. You could deal with the stalker thing yourself, don't you think? Maybe suggest she should concentrate on the MCU stuff.'

'Pfft.' Roy caught the dribble before it got far enough down his chin to be embarrassing. 'No way she's coming off that, every bit her old man when it comes to having a bee in her bonnet. She's not letting go of this till it's done.'

'You know her dad, don't you? D'you think it's worth having a word? See if he can talk some sense into her?' Tess said.

'Me? Nah, not really. Know *of* him, worked with him once, sort of ...' *Let him clean up your mess, you mean,* Roy thought. 'But I don't know the bloke enough to call him for a chat.'

Roy had worried when Alice moved to Fortbridge that her dad might have told her about the one time Roy and Mick's careers had overlapped. But there didn't seem to be any recognition on her part when they were introduced. He should have known really. Mick Washington wasn't one for gossip. Didn't play the blame game like other senior officers. Alice wouldn't remember the newspaper articles, the same ones Karen had slapped down on the breakfast table. She must have only been about fifteen at the time. Teenagers had far more exciting things to do back then than read the news.

'Oh,' Roy said, grateful for the interruption as the door to the pub swung open again, 'this your fella?'

Tess turned as a tall, broad-shouldered man scanned the room. 'Nate!' She waved him over. 'Here he is,' she said, a grin spreading across her face as the man walked to their table. She turned back to Roy. 'Look, just keep an eye on her, yeah?'

Roy nodded as Nate reached their booth.

'Hey babe,' she said, reaching up to kiss him. 'This is Roy from work, he was keeping me company.'

Roy stood and smoothed the wrinkles in his suit before adjusting his tie. 'Pleasure,' he said, holding out his hand for Nate to shake. 'Ooft,' Roy nodded towards Tess approvingly, 'good strong handshake, this one, comes from doing a real job, proper day's work, does that.'

Nate smiled awkwardly and sat down beside Tess.

Roy tipped the glass to his lips in another attempt to

finish the whisky he'd already consumed. 'Well,' he said, 'I'll leave you lovebirds to it. Catch you Monday.'

'Bye,' he heard over his shoulder as he shuffled towards the door. He needed the hard slap the cold air gave him as he walked outside.

42

My heart raced as I crept across the kitchen, leaping higher up my throat with each step as the rubber soles of my trainers squeaked on the floor tiles. The shape had disappeared from view as it met my eyes. But the front door hadn't slammed. The side door and back windows hadn't left my sight as I'd run across the garden. Whoever was in my house was still there.

I needed a weapon. Something. Anything. The solid wood pepper mill was the sturdiest object I could get to without opening and closing noisy cupboards and drawers. I grabbed it from the side of the stovetop. The fingers of my other hand curled around the black handle of a large carving knife before I unsheathed it from the block on the counter.

The hallway didn't seem to get any closer as I inched forward, but at the same time it was too close, like if someone were to burst from it they'd be on me. I held my breath and poked my head around the doorframe.

Nothing.

Through to the living room, the nooks and crannies I loved so much about this place now traps. Waiting for me to pass. Waiting to pounce.

Still nothing.

Everything sat exactly where I'd left it.

The stairs loomed to my right, heart thumping so loudly I worried it might give away my position. I took each step softly. Every creak a betrayal. I took a moment, before launching myself through the bedroom door. Nothing but my own reflection in the full-length mirror stared back at me.

I scoured the house for another twenty minutes. In cupboards. Under the bed. The loft. Nothing. I sat on the sofa, my head falling between my knees as I thought back to the heaving in my chest when I'd finished my run. Lungs bursting. Blood gasping for oxygen. I'd run hard. Really hard. No wonder there were little black dots floating across my eyes, I'd done it again, hadn't I? Gone the whole day without eating anything except for the tiny nut snack box Tess had made me take on the train. So much for getting my shit together. Tess's 'healthy body, healthy mind' mantra played on repeat in my head. But I could hardly blame low blood sugar for mistaking some dots for a human intruder, for Christ's sake.

With my weapons of choice safely returned to their rightful places in the kitchen, I shook my head as I leant against the worktop. The knife? Fine. A standard defence response. But a *pepper grinder*? What was I going to achieve with that if I'd found someone in here, over-season them to death? I needed to lie down. Inviting Dom for dinner would have to wait.

I flinched as the phone rang from the hallway. *It's an inanimate sodding object, calm down!*

Two calls from Dad in less than a fortnight? What was this, his new defective daughter outreach programme? 'Hi Dad.'

'You, erm, on your way soon, kid?'

'On my—' My stomach dropped. I looked at the retro wall clock Tess gave me for my birthday, today's date goading me alongside the time. 18th March. *Oh God.*

'If you've got other things on, we can—'

'No, no, honestly, I haven't, just running a bit late, that's all. I'll be there in about forty minutes. You need anything picking up on the way?' I wrapped a thick strand of hair around my finger and pulled until it hurt. Because yeah, sure, picking up a five quid bottle of Pinot Noir would totally make up for forgetting the anniversary of my mum's death.

I definitely broke the speed limit and at least three other traffic laws on the thirty-mile drive to Norton Abbot, the village north-west of Swindon Dad had moved to not long after Mum died. He couldn't bear to stay in our family home with her gone, every surface steeped in memories. Not that he'd ever admitted as much, but it had been written all over his face.

My hand hovered an inch shy of the door knocker. I couldn't remember the last time I'd been to Dad's for dinner. The two of us one-on-one. No buffer. No quick and easy get-out clause of being able to feign bad phone reception. It couldn't be this time last year, could it? Was that really the only reason we broke bread together now? Annually for the last seven years in Mum's memory? I jumped as the door of the next house along on the terrace swung open. Dad's neighbour, Irma Constance, stuck her head out, her cropped silver afro glowing as it caught the light from the exterior lamp fixed to the wall between us.

'Alice!' she said, her voice raspy as ever. I would have refused to believe the woman's claims to have never smoked a day in her life if her skin wasn't so damn smooth. 'I thought that was you pulling up.' Irma was Norton Abbot's Mavis Mulberry. Always watching. All knowing. 'How are you, darling, everything well?'

I was just about to hit play on my 'I'm fine' recording when Dad's door opened.

'All right?' he said to me before turning to give Irma a nod and half-smile. Irma nodded back, her hand looking for something to fiddle with and finding the ruby pear drop earring in her left earlobe. She suddenly looked sixteen instead of sixty, swooning, her dark brown skin hiding the blood that was certainly rushing to her cheeks. As much as I didn't like to think of my dad snogging like some sort of schoolkid, I wasn't opposed to the idea of him having someone. I'd even hinted at it a few times, not that he seemed to take any notice.

The three of us stood in awkward silence before Irma broke it. 'You two enjoy your evening then,' she said, making no move to retreat into her house.

I looked at Dad, widening my eyes, hoping he'd pick up the hint and extend the dinner invite. He either didn't get it or chose to ignore it as he stepped aside to let me in and said goodnight to Irma.

There'd hardly been a word spoken until he'd finished plating up some pasta and sat down opposite me at the small metal dining table that looked more like an office desk in the middle of his kitchen. Just because this was a celebration to honour Mum, heaven forbid we actually *talked* about her. She should be thankful she at least got a dinner. It was more than Noah got. As if he'd never existed.

We clinked glasses, knowing but silent, before I stabbed my fork into the giant mound of spaghetti and twirled the handle between my fingers. 'You should have asked Irma if she wanted to join us, there's enough food for about five people here.'

He tore himself a slice of garlic bread and slapped it down on the table beside his plate. 'Never known you to complain about having too much food. Lost your appetite or something?'

'No, might be nice, though, broaden the conversation.'

'You ever had a proper conversation with Irma? Mad as a box of frogs, that one.'

I tutted. 'Don't be mean. She's nice, and clearly she think's you're ... something.'

His forkful of food stopped short of his mouth. 'Don't start that again, all right?'

'I'm just saying, you could do a hell of a lot worse than—'

The cutlery clanged against the side of his plate as he dropped it. 'Alice, please. Not today. Especially not today.'

My cheeks flushed at the change in atmosphere caused by my own stupidity. What better time to try and set someone

291

up than the anniversary of their beloved wife's death? *Nice going, Cupid.* 'Sorry.'

He mopped up sauce with the bread and shoved it in his mouth. 'How's work anyway? I heard about that job you've got on, with the author, sounds like an interesting one.'

Someone give that man an Oscar for such a seamless and not at all prepared transition. I wondered who he'd been talking to. It was silly of me to think just because I hadn't told him didn't mean he wouldn't find out through other means, especially now HQ had stuck their beaks in.

'Yeah.' Screw it, he'd brought it up, may as well see if there's anything in the archives that might be of use. 'D'you know much about the Police and Crime Commissioner, Artie Dingle?'

Dad stopped mid-chew. 'That's a name I haven't heard for a long time. Can't say I've missed it, to be honest.'

'Why, what's wrong with him?'

'What's *right* with him, more like. Used to run one of the main security businesses in town and had a base out of London as well, basically taking money to run a bunch of thugs dressed up as bouncers, security guards, that sort of thing. God knows who he had to pay off to get elected to PCC. You're not getting stick from those levels already, are you?'

'Not yet, but might be coming my way. His son's the victim's other half, and he's being a pain in the arse. Doesn't want us involved, reckons he can sort it himself. Says it's 'cause he doesn't trust the police to keep her safe, but I reckon it's more than that. There's something not right with him; he doesn't want us sniffing around.'

He took a drink of water. 'You need to tread carefully, kid. Unless his dad's had a mid-life hallelujah moment, Artie Dingle doesn't play nice. It's not too hard to imagine any spawn of his probably doesn't either.'

My mind jumped back to what I'd seen – thought I'd seen anyway – in my bedroom window earlier. Maybe my eyesight had been bang on the money. Was that what this was all about? Myles using Daddy Dingle's resources to get me to back off? I shook the thought away. How stupid. Myles might have connections to a few heavies, but that hardly made him Tony bloody Soprano.

'Don't worry, I can look after myself.'

'I know you can, kid. You just be careful, all right?'

We ate the rest of our dinner and chatted with minimal fallout. Sticking to safe topics like Dad's plans for his new bathroom and what we'd seen on the telly before saying our goodbyes. I got into my car and sat for a moment in the quiet, letting myself decompress. I hated how things never felt relaxed between us, that I needed a recovery period after spending time with him. Whatever had happened, he was the only family I had. And there must be something we could do to make it easier. I instantly dismissed the obvious thing we could do, which was to have an actual conversation about Noah, and turned on the radio, hiking up the volume with the paddle on my steering wheel as I backed out of Dad's drive and headed towards the junction at the end of his street.

Light flashed in my rear-view mirror as a car pulled

off the kerb into the road close behind me. 'Jesus Christ, mate,' I said, squinting. 'Love your full beams so much, try marrying the bloody things instead of blinding me with them.' The roads around here weren't exactly brimming with lampposts, but there were more than enough to see with normal headlights, which the driver thankfully realised before I got around to throwing them a questionable hand gesture out the window.

I hummed along to 4 Non Blondes and a myriad of other songs I didn't know the lyrics to on the drive back to Fortbridge, letting the subtle vibrations of the engine massage my back and legs as I pulled off the dual carriageway on to one of the B roads that wound its way down into the village.

A set of full beams flashed again in my mirror, a much more acceptable use of the feature given this road was pitch-black, but I wasn't too keen on how close this person was driving behind me. I was way under the speed limit, too worried about a fox or some other nocturnal creature running out in front of me at this time of night, and I had no intention of driving any faster than I was comfortable with just because this person thought they were the next Jenson Button. Instead I slowed, pulling as far to the left as I could, giving the other car all the space it needed to overtake before the road narrowed up ahead between the woods. But instead of passing, they copied the movement, braking just enough to slow with me, but not enough to not still be up my arse. I slowed even more. And so did they.

'What the—'

I was about to stick my arm out the window and wave them past when a thought dawned on me. Had I seen the car parked at the end of Dad's street, the one that had pulled out after me, turn off at any point? Could this be the same one? Coincidentally doing an identical journey from Norton Abbot to Fortbridge at gone midnight? I hadn't taken in any details of the car, hadn't paid any attention to make, model or colour after they'd turned off the full beams, and I couldn't make anything out now that I was being blinded again. I thought back to what Dad had said. *Artie Dingle doesn't play nice.*

Had he sent someone to follow me?

As if to confirm my theory the car behind revved, practically growling as it inched closer. My heart thudded and I tightened my grip on the steering wheel, as if the harder I squeezed, the more the dips and blind bends in the road would level out in front of me. I picked up the pace, eyes fixed on the tarmac. I couldn't be more than two miles from the village, where I could pull into the relative safety of the police station. But right now, with this person so close I wondered how they hadn't bumped into the back of me already, two miles felt like a thousand.

I concentrated. Hard. Flinching at everything my headlights cast their beams on to. My eyes ached as they darted from object to object, scanning for something mobile, anything that might come out in front of me and get in the way.

And still the car behind was practically skimming my bumper.

I needed to see who it was. Take in something about

295

them, the driver, the car, anything, but the light scorched my retinas, and staring too long in my mirrors until they adjusted to the brightness would no doubt leave me smashed head-first into one of the huge trees running alongside my route. I flung myself around the next bend before hitting a patch of straight road. But when I finally found a safe moment to look back, I was looking into darkness. The car was gone. Disappeared down one of several side tracks hidden from view by the dense, high hedges lining them. 'Shit!' I yelled, slamming my palm on the steering wheel, a strange concoction of relief and frustration washing over my body.

Why would someone who was following me just stop like that? If they were after me, the middle of a dark and deserted road would be the perfect time to attack. I stifled the sob that was going hell for leather to get out from inside my chest. Because what if no one had been following me? Just like no one had been in my house earlier. Nothing but eye floaters and shitty drivers sending me spiralling, feeling like I was losing my fucking mind.

43

Roy was at his desk when I walked in Monday morning, looking up at me through raised wiry eyebrows.

'Big weekend?' he asked.

I unfurled the striped scarf from around my neck. Once. Twice. The third loop pulled it free before I draped it across the back of my chair. 'Nothing special.' Well, unless I counted the constant back and forth in my brain about whether or not I'd become number one on the Dingle/Carrington family hit list. Crusts of sleep irritated the corners of my eyes, though quite when the particles had the time to accumulate and congeal in the short bursts of shut-eye I'd managed over the last couple of nights was beyond me. I'd been constantly woken as my mind sucked up and spat out random theories and possibilities about what the hell was going on with this case, like a tornado rampaging through Texan farmland.

Roy looked up. I braced for a snarky quip before noticing his eyes were staring past me. I heard her before I saw her.

'What's this?' Jane said, slapping a rolled-up newspaper on to my desk. She let go of it and the twisted baton unfurled to reveal the image on the front page.

'Oh, for f—' I massaged the nape of my neck as a picture of my face stared back. A particularly unflattering angle. Mid-word, to ensure the target looked as dumb as humanly possible. I didn't have to look at the byline; I knew straight away who was behind this drivel. A. J. certainly had a way with words, I'd give him that. If the picture wasn't enough, the headline certainly did it. *Queen of Crime's Stalker Evades Top Cop's Daughter*. I snatched at the paper, the words bursting out before I'd processed what I was reading. 'Washington ... daughter of ... no closer to catching ... *prowling predator*.' I looked up at Jane. 'Get that straight from an alliteration generator app, did he? And why does this guy have such a hard-on for my dad!'

Even though it was bad enough on its own, the picture of me looked doubly moronic in comparison with the one they'd used of Dad alongside it, standing tall and proud at what looked like a press conference outside Swindon Crown Court. A. J. hadn't even bothered to find a recent picture of him, just gone for the first one that usually came up if you searched Dad's name. The one associated with the conviction closest to his heart, that of Patrick Acaster.

Dad had put plenty of despicable people away both before and in the fifteen years since, but with most of them he hadn't spent almost a week sat at their victim's hospital bedside, hearing every detail of what happened to her until she'd slowly slipped away before his eyes. The woman had been too far gone by the time Dad found her locked in Patrick's basement, but if it hadn't been for him pushing the case when everyone had written her off as a runaway, Acaster would never have faced justice for what he did.

Jane's voice dragged me back into this decade. 'How many times do I have to tell you, we don't give that man anything but the party line. He cannot be trusted!'

I didn't even know what to say. This was ridiculous. *I* was the one being slated here. And what was I supposed to do about it? As much of a prick as A. J. was, he wasn't exactly wrong. Dad *was* a better police officer than me. He was a better police officer than most people. I could hardly get A. J. done for libel.

Jane's eyes darted towards Roy like a shark spotting a shoal of fish as he shifted his weight in the chair.

Roy stared straight back. 'Don't look at me, I haven't been talking to anyone.'

Jane leant against the desk, looking back and forth between us. 'You sure, hmm? Not a little slip down the pub? After a few drinks?'

You could drain the River Fort and fill it to the brim with whisky and that still wouldn't be enough alcohol to get Roy to say anything to A. J., even I knew that.

'Absolutely not,' Roy said. 'No way.'

Jane's face relaxed, but not completely. 'Well, load of shit or not, Mr Carver has been on the phone already. He wants something done about this.'

Roy interjected, 'With all due respect, ma'am, we can't magic evidence out of thin air. SOCO went over that place millimetre by millimetre, put everything through on fast-track, and I've had the last of the DNA and fingerprint results through this morning. They've got nothing that's gonna get us anywhere.'

The temperature dropped three degrees as Jane's eyes narrowed. 'I'm not asking you to be a magician. Clearly the holding statement didn't hit the spot. We need to set up a community reassurance meeting. This is Fortbridge, there's literally bugger all else going on except for Bret's theft jobs, and as serious as that might be if it's linked to organised crime, it's not exactly *sexy*, is it? Howden's going to keep riling people up until we put a stop to it. So I suggest you either catch this person, or you call the school to see if we can use their hall Wednesday night. No point trying to do it in the briefing room here, we'll never fit all the nosy nellies in. Understood?'

Roy and I nodded silently and Jane marched off, leaving her newspaper behind.

My lips vibrated as I pushed air out through them and scanned the rest of the column. The bottom right corner displayed a photograph of Camilla at some red-carpet event. I skimmed the words alongside: *Harton-Gray seen just a week before the stalking began in a busty, eye-catching, figure-hugging* . . . 'Jesus Christ, does this guy get paid by the bloody adjective?' I pinched the bridge of my nose and pushed the pages away, shaking my head in utter disbelief. What an absolute hack.

Roy pulled the paper towards him and read the rest of the article. 'You know when the boss says *we* need to do a meeting, she means us, don't you?'

'Yep. And sorry, but you're going to have to sort it.' I

pulled my mobile out. 'I'm gonna go check in on Camilla, see if she's OK. First the Helena bombshell and now this? I'd be amazed if she hasn't seen it already. Chrissy certainly will have.'

I ignored whatever profanities Roy was mumbling as I went to the landing to make the call.

44

Camilla filled the water tank for her coffee machine. Dressed in wide-legged ochre cotton trousers and a matching over-sized roll-neck jumper, the outfit was the polar opposite to the one she'd had on in the photographs printed with A. J.'s article, dwarfing her small frame rather than accentuating it. I hoped this was due to the fact the nights were still chilly and she needed the warming hug of comfortable attire, rather than because he'd made her think her clothing choices were anything to do with why she was being targeted.

I'd have loved to provide even a sliver of reassurance by being able to tell her the bollocking I'd given A. J. down the phone before driving over here would impact his behaviour. But if anything, he'd given the impression his work to date had merely been an appetiser, that this was nothing compared to the next big exposé he was on the cusp of revealing. Some might say it would have been sensible to take the opportunity to remind him of his alleged commitment to journalistic ethics and standards rather than barking back, 'Yeah? The world awaits with bated breath, I'm sure, dickhead!' before hanging up, but hey, I was only human.

The water reached the top of the container and over-flowed, Camilla's stare fixed on the window looking out towards the back of the property.

'Are you all right?' I asked.

She flinched as I put my hand on her shoulder. 'Yes, sorry,' she said, turning the tap off. The tank clunked on to the back of the machine and whirred as she turned it on. 'Thanks again for checking in.' She dried her hands on a bright white towel. 'You didn't need to. This isn't the first time Myles's past has come back to haunt us, and the other stuff, well, I'm just used to it now, I suppose. I'm fine, honestly.'

There it was again. The 'I'm fine' song. Mine and Camilla's favourite. Challenging her on it wouldn't elicit the truth, I knew that better than anyone. 'No problem at all,' I replied. 'You got me out of something at work anyway, and let's be honest, this is a much nicer place to spend time. Such a beautiful house, I can understand why you wouldn't want to leave it.'

Camilla put the towel down on the marbled worktop, her palms taking some of her weight as she steadied herself. 'I love this house. I was so looking forward to getting back here permanently. I've missed it.' She looked around, left and right at the walls as if willing them to protect her, then up towards the large pendant light fixture hanging above us, which watched over her as it cast a glow of nostalgia across her face. 'Mind you, the orchard has slightly lost its appeal, after ...' She pointed out the window. 'You can't really see it now it's getting dark, but there's a tree house in the woods. My father built it; my brother and I used to play in it all the time.' She turned to me, her face solemn. 'This is all I've got of my family. Memories.'

I forced a smile and nodded, trying to swallow the lump in my throat. Like an unchewed piece of meat, dangling and choking me. The physical manifestation of dread at the thought of Noah's death getting as much press attention as Camilla's family tragedy had once she'd become a household name. My inability to save him, splashed all over the front pages. That was one benefit of Dad's stoicism. He didn't talk about it, so no one knew the details of what happened. People were aware he'd lost a son in an accident on holiday but not much else. He went back to work a week after the funeral. Six days, to be exact. And that was that. But this wasn't about me; I needed to focus.

Camilla must have carried on talking as I tuned back in mid-sentence, '. . . he was the star then, of course; I was just starting out with my writing career.'

'Sorry, who?'

She handed me a coffee. 'My brother, Henry.'

I nodded, vaguely remembering the name from Eddie's profile highlights. A. J. had really pulled at the heartstrings with that one. As if the fact that almost an entire family had been wiped out in a needless accident hadn't been sad enough on its own, he'd had to add in those additional juicy titbits. Would it have been any less of a tragedy if Henry wasn't the star of the Under 18s Wessex County rugby team, a budding musician, due to move into a plush

London flat with his girlfriend after he secured a place at the Royal Academy of Music?

The dense stoneware of the coffee mug was hot and hard against my palms. 'That must have been difficult for you.' I parroted the basics of family liaison training as my mind dragged me back to my childhood with Noah. Even with all of the competitions, the arguments, we always ended the day the same way: huddled on the sofa watching something on TV, his head in my lap as I twirled one of his shaggy brown curls around my finger. Until the day we didn't.

Camilla nodded. 'I've lost too many years already, not being here, but after it happened I couldn't stand the sight of the place. Not even just being in this house – the whole village was just ... *them*. But that's what I like about it now; it makes me feel like they're still here, somehow. Myles doesn't understand; he's already made it clear he doesn't want us to set up home here. Thinks there's too many memories to start afresh,' she said, a barely detectable quiver in her voice.

My attention spiked at her mention of Myles, but I let the opportunity to probe further go, for now. It wasn't the right time.

She cleared her throat and continued, 'Well, that and apparently Fortbridge isn't exciting enough for our non-existent children. They'll get bored, *when* we have them, he says. Children should have the stimulation of a bustling city.' She mimicked his deep, authoritative voice. 'I don't know, being raised in the countryside didn't do me any harm. How about you – city or rural child, if you don't mind me asking?' She took a sip of her drink.

'No, not at all. Somewhere in between – I grew up in Swindon. Probably not the best advertisement for it, either.'

'Right, anyway, it's a bit early for all that, in my opinion. We've only been together a year, haven't even lived together yet – not for the want of trying on his part, mind you. And now, with, well, you know ... everything,' she shook her head, 'sorry, you're not here to be my agony aunt.' She turned back to the window.

'Don't worry, it's fine, I—'

The crash of Camilla's mug shattering against the bottom of the ceramic sink stopped me in my tracks, her scream so high-pitched I half expected the window to crack. I lurched from the stool, the steel seat and legs clanging against the floor as it toppled. 'Camilla, Camilla, look at me.' I grabbed her by the shoulders, her body trembling. 'Camilla, what is it?'

She pulled away from me. Away from the window. 'There's someone out there, in the woods. I, I saw someone.'

Adrenaline surged as I flung the back door open. Branches bent before springing back into place as something – someone – rushed through them, twigs cracking under the weight of their footsteps as I took off in pursuit across the narrow section of lawn. I hit the lining of woodland and tree limbs whipped my face. Knotted offshoots yanked at my clothing, conspiring against me like they were trying to protect whoever I was chasing. In seconds, the rustling up

ahead was replaced by scraping. The soles of boots against
the stone perimeter wall.

Then clawing.

Climbing.

Dragging themselves up.

You're going to lose them!

The wall was barely two metres in front of me when I
fell, the sudden presence of wet mud underfoot propelling
me into its solid foundations. My shoulder took the brunt
of the impact. 'Shit!' I wailed.

I rolled on to my back, clutching my arm as a leg wrapped
in dark trousers swung out of sight over the top of the wall.
Their feet hit the ground on the other side and I strained
to listen. Desperate to pick up on the follow-up sound of
sprinting so I could figure out which way they were headed
as they disappeared into the fields. But there were no footsteps. Just silence. I didn't know whether to laugh or cry.

They were right there.

Still.

Waiting.

What were they waiting *for*?

A lump of rock no more than three feet deep was the only
barrier between us. So close I could hear them breathing.
Gasping. Before the silence was broken as they ran away.

A search of the area found nothing. I waited with Camilla
until the patrol car arrived to take her to Myles's flat. Away
from her tainted sanctuary. Away from the reporters who
of course didn't take long to follow the police vehicles

like a pack of bloodhounds, A. J. unsurprisingly leading the charge. I didn't want her to go to Myles, but I had no argument to make right now that would convince her not to. Not like with Robin Golding's wife. Once she could sense I'd seen through him, that I'd believe what she told me, she hadn't needed convincing. If anything, the relief of being free from him had flooded out of her with such intensity I'd had to physically catch her as she fell to the floor.

I reached around to unhook my bra, wincing as I examined the extent of the damage from my fall in the bathroom mirror. There were a few scratches across my neck from the branches, and my shoulder had started to bruise, pinpricks of burst blood vessels making their way down towards my collarbone. I circled the joint before swinging my arm back and forth. Swelling limited the movement, but everything worked as it should. *You'll live.* I rolled down my trousers. Clumps of dried mud littered the cold white floor tiles.

The bath creaked as I lowered myself in. I sat in the quiet. Deep breaths not coming easily as droplets from the leaky tap hit the water's surface. They sounded like a xylophone, the bigger drops creating different notes to the smaller ones. I tucked my legs up to my chest, hugging my shins. Pressing my nose against my knee wasn't enough to shift the smell of dog shit, as if the spores I'd sent hurtling into the atmosphere when I'd slipped on one of Ruby or Bo's mammoth faecal offerings were physically clinging to the tiny hairs in my nostrils. I'd have laughed at the absurdity of the situation if it wasn't for the other smell. The one I'd thought about all the way home. The tiniest hint of something familiar, for a split second as I'd gotten closer to them, just as I'd fallen. Before it was overpowered by the stench of animal excrement. I trawled my brain trying to recognise it, to form a link to where I'd smelt it before. I leant back and dunked my whole head under the water, holding the baptism before re-emerging, gasping as I pushed the sodden hair back from my face.

Think.

I wasn't sure how long I'd been sitting there before I gave up. The more I thought about it, the more I questioned whether I'd even recognised the smell at all. Or whether my senses were so jacked on adrenaline I'd imagined *that* as well. Yet another thing to add to my pile of non-existent evidence. This was getting silly. We had nothing. Literally nothing. How was I supposed to reassure Camilla she could feel safe in her own home when I was no closer to catching this psycho than I had been the first time I'd met her? I might have managed to scare someone off tonight, but she couldn't exactly hire me as a personal bloody security guard. And even if she did, that wouldn't stop the likes of A. J. violating her from afar by plastering her private family business across the papers every five minutes until he'd exhausted all her secrets.

A thought caught me mid-breath. What if he *had* already laid bare all of Camilla's private family business? What if his new story was about someone else? Me. Just how far exactly had he dug into me, to Dad?

What if . . .

Every muscle between my little toe and the crown of my head froze.

No, he couldn't know. How would he? I sat bolt upright at the memory of A. J. turning up when I was looking for Dom's key. He seemed convinced Dom was more than just my neighbour. What did he think he knew? Private information about me? About Dad? About Noah?

Oh God, Noah.

My feet slipped against the bath as I thrashed to get out, dragging my towel from the radiator. I flung open the bathroom door and scrambled around on the bedside table for my phone to call Tess. She was the only one who knew. The only one I thought knew, anyway. I tapped her name at the top of my speed dial and held the phone to my ear with one hand as I tried to dry myself with the other.

She wouldn't. Of course she wouldn't, I told myself as I waited for her to pick up.

'You've reached Tess, sorry I'm not available at—' I growled, throwing the phone on to the bed and pulling on the nearest clothes I could find. She wouldn't spill my deepest, darkest secret *deliberately*. But I'd seen it first hand once she'd had a few. She could be the bloody poster girl for 'loose lips sink ships'. Who had she told? Who'd overheard?

My skin was still wet under my clothes as I hammered on Dom's front door.

He pulled it open almost immediately, eyes wide at the state of me. 'Alice? What's happened? Are you all right?'

I jerked away from the light touch he tried to place on

my arm. 'Have you been talking to A. J. Howden about me? Has he been asking you things? Personal things?'

He shook his head and closed his eyes for a second like he was resetting his face. 'Sorry, who? Asking what?'

'A. J.,' my voice echoed down the lane, 'the guy from Sainsbury's, he's a journalist, and he seems to have convinced himself you might have some insight into me for his next big story, because there's nothing that man loves more than digging into other people's shit.'

'What? No, of course not, I haven't spoken to anyone about you. And what would I even tell him anyway? No offence, but you're not exactly the most open person in the world, and I don't think me telling him your favourite flavour of crisps is going to make the front page.' He let out a laugh with the last word and I knew he was just trying to bring down the temperature of the conversation, but I couldn't help myself. I just wanted to yell. At someone. Anyone.

'This isn't funny, Dom. This man's causing chaos with my investigation, he's pestering the victim, he's making us all look like morons and—'

'OK, OK, I'm sorry, I didn't mean to upset you. Why don't you come in, take a breath, have a coffee.'

'I don't want a fucking coffee, Dom! Just stay out of my business, OK?' I yelled before storming back home.

Dom called after me but didn't follow. I was glad he didn't. Because I honestly didn't know what I'd have done if he did.

45

I dosed myself up on painkillers to dull the throbbing in my shoulder and arrived at the office before anyone else the next morning: 7:13 a.m., according to the black and white clock by the noticeboard. I'd been awake since four. No callback from Tess. She was usually the only other person in this early. I'd wanted to collar her before Roy and the others piled in from the café. *Shit.*

The printer chugged, spitting out the case file documents. I clung to the hope that looking at tangible copies rather than staring at characters and pixels on a screen might make something stand out. I fanned it all out across my desk and the floor in chronological order. The email. The photographs. The press articles. Veterinary examination results. Notes from the conversations with Myles and Chrissy. Images from the ESDA examination. Helena's story. All of it.

Myles sneered back from the kiss-and-tell spread. I pulled the paper closer to my face and thought of what Camilla had said about him wanting them to live together. The CCTV camera she didn't want. His desire for kids, to get her away from Fortbridge. So he could watch her in person? All the time? Show her off to his friends? 'Is that what this is, you controlling shit?' I stared into his almost black eyes. 'She won't come willingly, so you'll force her out?' Was that why Camilla hadn't actually been hurt in any of this? Scared shitless, yes, but not physically attacked.

My moment of realisation was short-lived; it couldn't have been Myles in the woods last night. He was in London when Camilla called him. Unless, of course, he was playing some sick version of puppet master, keeping his hands clean, sending Chrissy or one of his – or his dad's – meatheads to do the job for him. I scraped my fingernails across the lines in my forehead, making a note to check where Chrissy was last night. The thought of that scent I still couldn't place twitched and squirmed. If I was right, I'd met the puppet somewhere before. I let the newspaper fall to the desk and sat back in my chair. Theories were great and all, but I needed proof. I lashed out at the wastepaper bin with my foot, toppling it before I noticed movement in the corner of my eye.

Tess stood in the doorway gawking at the spread of paperwork. 'Everything OK?' She placed her bag on the desk tentatively.

'Yeah.' Papers rustled as I scooped the printouts into a pile. 'I tried ringing you last night – why didn't you call me back?'

'Out with Nate after his shift, sorry,' she said, walking over. 'What's up?' She nodded towards where the documents had been strewn, her arms folded.

'Nothing. Erm, look,' I pushed myself up and walked over to her, no time to put this delicately, 'you haven't, you know, said anything to anyone about what I told you, about my brother?'

'Your brother? No, why would I?' she said, her eyes wide with concern.

'You sure – not in the pub, not, I dunno, anywhere?'

'Alice, I'd never do that.'

The hurt look that spread across her face made me realise how much of an idiot I was. Of course she wouldn't. A. J. probably had no idea what happened to Noah. His new story was likely just more of his usual trash. What the hell was wrong with me? Chatter and chortling from the stairwell cut off the conversation as Roy and one of the other DCs stumbled through the door, followed by Morag armed with a hoover. A loud bang echoed around the office as Roy tripped over the metal bin now lying on its side in the middle of the walkway from where I'd kicked it. 'Jesus wept! What's that doing there?' he said, leaning down to rub his shin. 'Nearly broke me flippin' neck.'

Tess placed her hand on my shoulder and whispered in my ear. 'How about we go get some breakfast, yeah? Before you go on a rampage.'

Tess placed a cinnamon bun and latte in front of me as we sat down at Gilly's. I picked at the caramelised sugar crust.

'You are acting really weird,' Tess said. 'Is there something you want to tell me?'

I tore off the first layer of pastry and shoved it into my mouth, the sugar stinging my cracked lips. 'Like what?'

Tess sat back. 'If I *knew* I wouldn't have to ask.'

'People asking if I'm all right every five minutes isn't helping.' I kept my eyes on my plate, tearing the bun into tiny pieces but not actually putting any of them in my mouth.

Tess picked up a chunk and ate it. 'Look, if you don't want to talk to me about it, at least talk to someone. How about Dom? You two seem to be getting on well.'

The look on his face from last night flashed across my eyes and it all spilled out. Why I'd tried to call her. My theory about A. J.'s story. How Dom got the short straw by proximity when she didn't answer and frustration had poured out of me like grain escaping a moth-eaten sack. The bell above the door to the café tinkled before Tess had a chance to respond. I looked over her shoulder to see Dom walk in. 'Shit.' I wondered what the opposite to the expression 'saved by the bell' was.

'What? What's wrong?' Tess said as she turned around. 'Oh, hi Dom.'

He looked back at the door like he was hoping he could dash straight back through it. Realising there was no subtle way out, he made his way to our table. 'Hey, you OK, after, erm . . .'

'Yeah, sorry about last night. Bit of a rough day, shouldn't have taken it out on you. And thanks for the basket . . . hamper . . . thing. I didn't get a chance to say . . . you know, last night.'

'Don't worry, it's fine. Even from just those three precious minutes in Sainsbury's I could tell that A. J. guy has a knack for getting under people's skin. And that was exactly why I

315

didn't answer the door when he came knocking yesterday, which I would have told you if you'd given me the chance.'

So A. J. *was* trying to dig up more dirt on me. I was going to build a cross and nail the bastard to it. 'I'm sorry. He shouldn't be harassing people like that, and I shouldn't have ... well, you know.' I said nothing further and just smile-nodded, conscious of my audience, Tess's face so enthralled in the conversation I considered pausing to ask if she'd prefer sweet or salted popcorn to go with today's cinematic experience.

'It's OK. Right, well, I should be getting off,' Dom said, 'only stopped in to grab a takeaway coffee, so ...'

'Yeah, maybe see you later.'

He smiled but didn't say anything as he went over to the counter. I could almost see the commentary inside Tess bursting to get out as she waited for him to be served, champing to be unleashed by the chime of the doorbell to indicate Dom had officially left the building.

'That was awfully magnanimous of him. I'd have told you to fuck right off,' Tess said, finishing the last of my bun.

Jane called me and Roy into her office as soon as I walked back through the door. Her eyes flitted between us as we sat down opposite her. 'There's been a complaint lodged,' she said, 'from Myles Carrington.'

I shifted in my seat, blood bubbling. 'What exactly is he complaining about?'

'Your competence to conduct this investigation.'

Roy didn't say anything but made his feelings clear

through a derisive snort, a small cloud of mucus particles dusting the misshapen knot in his tie.

'I'm sorry,' I said, shifting further forward until I was perched on the edge of the chair, 'but is this some sort of joke?'

Jane threw her hands up. 'You got me,' she said, a fake grin erupting. 'I have nothing better to do today so thought a little comedy caper would kill some time.' The smile vanished. 'He's not happy with the progress, or lack thereof. Worried we're not giving it the prioritisation it deserves.'

'With all due respect, ma'am, is he for real?' I said. 'He's done nothing to help this investigation from day one, expressed very clearly he doesn't want us involved, and now he's saying we're not involved *enough*?'

'His complaint is for real, that's for damn sure – got his dad's stamp all over it as well. It was addressed straight to the Chief Constable. She's been on the phone for the last half-hour and though it might surprise you to hear, trying to keep her at bay hasn't been the highlight of my day,' Jane said.

The potential puppet master was smarter than I'd given him credit for. Now that there was a complaint at that level I'd need to be very careful how I played things. 'Ma'am, I'm not sure exactly what's going on with him, but I have a very strong feeling he doesn't want us digging around because he's hiding something, and I think there's a possibility he's somehow behind all this, trying to scare Camilla out of her house so she'll move in with him in London. I can't prove it yet, but I will.'

Jane looked at Roy who shrugged and pushed his bottom lip out in a *maybe*.

317

Her shoulders rose and fell as she took a deep breath. 'Fine,' she said, bringing her eyes back to me, 'but you better tread lighter than a flat-footed soldier trying to cross no-man's-land. Think "catch more flies with honey" instead of "bull in a china shop". Understand?'

'I think we can get something out of the assistant, Chrissy,' I said. 'She might know more than she's letting on if he's roped her into helping him stage this. I mean, she benefits too, right?' I looked at Roy. 'She'd cut her right arm off to live a glitzy life in London.'

A purposeful knock on the door made all three of us jump.

'Yes,' Jane called with no attempt to hide her annoyance at the interruption.

Tess stumbled in, her eyes wide, hand shaking as it rested on the handle. 'Sorry to interrupt, but I erm . . . need these two.'

Roy swivelled in the chair to face her. 'You all right? Look like you've seen a ghost.'

Tess swallowed hard. 'Report's come in. A body. The grass verge outside of Bertram Manor.'

The name of Camilla's home crossing Tess's lips was a flame lighting the fuse as I shot to my feet.

46

No matter what he did to distract himself, he couldn't get the image out of his mind. That look on her face and how it made the rage bubble inside him. *Fuck, fuck, fuck!* The words a pneumatic drill inside his head.

This wasn't supposed to happen.

Not part of the plan.

If he'd ruined this, he'd never forgive himself. He was so close.

Why do they always make me do this! he thought as his fingertips navigated his skull, pressing every ridge in the bone. The words he tried to speak melted to a growl as he pulled his hair as hard as he could, before loosening his grip only to tighten it again, repeating the action over and over until his scalp throbbed.

His hair felt different to hers. Hers had been long. Coarse. Strands of copper wire coiling around his fingers like vines as he'd pushed her face into the ground. He shook his head, as if shaking hard enough would make what had happened undo itself like an Etch A Sketch. Take him back to when everything was going to plan. This was all her fault. He'd tried to explain that it wasn't what it looked like. But she wouldn't listen. They never fucking listen. If she hadn't tried to call the police none of this would have happened.

The mattress springs groaned as he fell on to the bed, his heart booming in his chest. Just like it had last night as he'd chased her. She'd been faster than expected. Made it past the gate, out on to the road. He thumped his fist into the pillow. How had he let her make it that far? He'd accelerated towards her faster than he'd ever run before. Seeing the phone pressed against her ear had been like a drug pumping extra oxygen to his muscles.

He dragged himself up to a seated position and held his hands out in front of him, looking at the grazes on his palm from the rough surface of the rock. It had felt unwieldy in his right hand, held aloft above his head. His rapid breathing meshed with the sound of her attempts to scream, muffled by the long grass as he pressed her face deeper and deeper. He still wasn't sure if the next scream had been hers or his. But after it, there had been only silence.

Air rushed into his nose as he sucked so hard the insides of his nostrils almost touched. He went to the sink and turned both taps on, letting the sound of the gushing water take over. His head hung forward, heavy on his neck. 'Left hand, right hand . . .' He gripped the ceramic, '. . . wash them every day . . .' Tighter now, 'Left hand, right hand, wash the dirt away.' He made a bowl with his palms and splashed his face, washing away any trace of those fraudulent fond memories, before staring at himself in the mirror as droplets trickled down his cheeks.

Everything would work out as he wanted it to. Just as it always had. He was better than this. Better than them.

He grabbed the car keys, clutching them so tightly it hurt as he made his way downstairs. No one liked a loose end. He had to do this now.

47

I swear the drive to the manor took three times as long as it had before. Certainly felt that way. Roy's eyes were fixed on the road, his body hunched forward, a thin film of sweat across his forehead despite the still unseasonably cold weather. Police vehicles lined the closed-off road up ahead.

'You think we were getting it in the neck before, just wait till we get back. The boss'll be off her rocker,' Roy said.

I wanted to slap him. 'There's someone lying dead in a ditch less than a hundred metres in front of us and you're worrying about—' The flashing lights of an ambulance took my attention as it sped past in the opposite direction, away from the manor.

'What the hell?' Roy said.

He swerved on to the grass verge behind the melee. We ran towards the crime scene tent as it rippled in the breeze, its blue canopy contrasting against the black metallic entrance gates some twenty feet behind it.

'Eddie,' I shouted. He was stood on the outer cordon, his neck craned back towards the tent. 'Eddie!' I yelled, louder this time.

His face snapped towards me, looking even paler than normal. 'Sorry, Sarge, I was just ... sorry, morning.'

'What the hell's going on?' I pointed down the road following the trail of the ambulance.

'Yeah, it's mad.' He grabbed the peak of his cap, pulled it off and rubbed his head. 'It's my first one, you know, *a body*.' He whispered the last part as if it might hear him and spring back to life like a zombie. 'We get here, and well, she's only still alive, isn't she? Nearly gave me a heart attack.'

Relief and confusion smashed together like a toxic cocktail being shaken around inside my skull.

'What?' Roy said. 'She's alive? What do we know? Who is it?'

'Adult female, red hair, she wasn't conscious ... she was face down. I didn't see her properly before they sent me over here.'

Roy and I looked at each other, eyes wide. Red hair. Camilla or Chrissy. Had Camilla come home?

A familiar voice from behind Eddie interjected, 'Miss Washington, long time no see.' The dulcet tones of Crime Scene Manager Bernie McGovern. He had the type of Scottish accent where the harsh edges had been smoothed with sandpaper, soothing even in the most horrific of circumstances.

I pointed a finger at Eddie. 'You! Pay attention. A. J. pissing Howden will be here any minute trying to get as many gruesome photos as possible – in fact, I'm amazed he didn't sense this coming and camp out here last night so he'd get a prime bloody vantage point. If he gets so much as one snippet of an image, you can personally explain how he managed it to the Chief herself.' He nodded furiously as I turned away. 'Bernie, what the hell's going on?'

'Nice to see you too, the wife's fine, yes, I know I should've retired by now but here I am, ay,' he said in his usual sarcastic tone. 'How's your da?'

'He's fine, sorry, I— we've got a job going on with the owner of the house.'

'Yes, yes, I know that, well aware of our Miss Harton-Gray. You know Pam, she loves a good crime thriller,' he said, looking over his glasses at me like a teacher. 'It's no' her.'

'Her assistant, Chrissy, she's got red hair too, it's got to be her.'

'Bingo. Driver's licence in the handbag belongs to a Miss Christina Marchant,' he said, the Rs in both words little drumrolls on his tongue.

The confirmation hit me like a drunk driver ploughing into my side at a crossroads. 'Is she gonna be OK?'

Bernie pursed his lips. 'You'll have to ask the doctor that one. She'd been there hours by the looks of it. No wonder the person who found her thought she was a goner – looked it, that's for sure. She's taken quite the knock to the back of the head, just the one hit, I'd guess, but by God a big one. Nothing close by she could have bashed it on when she fell. You're looking for someone with quite an arm, I can tell you that for nothing.'

My vision jarred like a scratched DVD. I resisted the urge to drop my hands to my knees to steady myself as a stereotype of what one of Myles's bouncer-type henchmen might look like flashed into my mind. Short, thick neck. Steroid-pumped biceps. Like Roy said, assistants always know what's going on, warts and all. Someone like Chrissy could clearly only stay quiet for so long. And we'd dangled that fact in front of Myles deliberately. Was this us? Had we put her in the firing line?

Roy let out a sigh like a punctured tyre. 'Only blessing, at least it wasn't Camilla who found her.'

'No, no, some poor chap walking his dog had that honour. It's always the dog walkers, isn't it?' Bernie said, gazing wistfully across the surrounding fields as if he was in a daydream rather than dealing with an attempted murder. 'Anyway, she's on her way here now, apparently, the lady of the manor. You can go and wait for her in the grounds; there's a channel down the side,' he continued, nodding towards the grass verge. 'You can get through without clomping your big old boots through my crime scene, thank you very much.'

'Thanks, Bern, we'll be back for the debrief,' I said.

'Of course you will be, dear, my performances are not to be missed,' he said, wagging a blue latex finger at me.

We made our way to the manor's entrance, scuttling down the side of the scene tape and on to the other side of the hedge to avoid the inner cordon, re-entering the road just before the open gates. Roy strode ahead across Camilla's driveway as I paused, resisting the urge to look back at the crime scene tent. I needed to focus. By the time I'd caught up to him, Roy had reached the front door and was taking a seat on the steps, emitting a loud grunt as his buttocks hit the concrete. I could see his mouth moving, but the words were just sounds as I paced backwards and forwards in front of him, eyes constantly flicking to the gates, waiting for Myles's car to pull through them. *Calm down!*

I let Dad and Jane's words play on repeat: 'Tread carefully' and 'Catch more flies with honey.' I could do this. Needed to do this, to make sure he couldn't hurt anyone else. This was the moment. Pull it all together. Catch him off guard. Just like I'd done with Robin Golding and many other suspects before. I'd managed to stop pacing by the time the tyres of his Range Rover hit the gravel. Roy nodded past me as he saw the car. I took a deep breath. I was ready. The passenger and driver doors opened simultaneously. Camilla was out of view on the other side of the vehicle, but I could see Myles clearly. Too clearly. So clearly, in fact, I could see every inch of his face, including the hint of a smirk tugging at one corner of his mouth.

The fraying thread holding the grenade pin in place inside my chest disintegrated, flames illuminating every occupant in the depths of my brain.

Jamie, falling.

Noah, drifting.

Camilla screaming, her mug crashing.

Open patio doors, dark shapes in windows and manic drivers.

Chrissy. Flashing ambulance lights. Tyres clinging to tarmac.

I don't remember exactly what happened after I lunged

at him. Just the grainy texture of his jacket's leather lapels inside my fists. A series of arms clad in different coloured materials forcing themselves between us to prise me away from him. Shouting. Bernie's tone no longer melodic.

'What the fuck do you think you're doing?' Myles yelled, patting himself down as if I'd set him on fire.

Eddie appeared between us, arms outstretched, eyes wide like a rabbit caught between two apex predators. Hands on my shoulders pulled me back.

'What the hell, Sarge?' Roy said as he marched me through the gates.

An elastic strap crushed my lungs.

'Eddie, get back on that cordon, will ya?' Roy barked. We kept walking, my legs tripping over themselves as we passed Bernie. He was flustered. I'd never seen him flustered before. He didn't get flustered, ever. And he dealt with dead bodies and scraped up blood for a living.

That was a disturbing enough sight in itself. But what really sent me over the edge was the look on Roy's face as he swung me around to face him, his eyes overflowing with panic.

48

Roy's heart rate showed no signs of returning to normal after chasing Alice across the driveway. That was further than he'd run in years, and the loose gravel had sucked his feet into it like a soggy beach. What on earth had she been thinking? It was a good job A. J. hadn't turned up yet; he'd have salivated so much capturing that on camera someone would have had to stop him from drowning in it. He'd never seen Alice like that. Frustrated? What copper wasn't. Angry? Absolutely, she swore more than he did. But out of control? Never. He'd always found her to be too *in* control, if anything. Clenched tighter than a cat's arsehole. Pawing over every detail. As much as she annoyed him, she was a grade A detective, he had no doubt about that.

When it came to telling tales, Roy had an old school attitude, particularly when the ear he'd have to whisper them into was Jane's. In his day, you sorted stuff out between you, no running to the bosses. But he also knew this time, he didn't have a choice. She'd gone for a member of the public. A slimy, up-himself member of the public, but that didn't matter. Of course he understood the urge. He'd felt the same more times than he cared to count, but never acted on it. He'd come close the day Mick Washington brought Patrick Acaster in. He'd wanted to smash the man's face into the cell wall. Over and over. Because of what he did to that woman, and if Roy was completely honest, also a bit for himself. To hammer away some of the regret he felt to this day for letting Patrick get one over on him, for believing his lies.

He'd never forgotten the day he went to the house to make initial enquiries, after Valerie Acaster's family reported her missing. Patrick playing the role of bereft loving husband to a tee, insisting she'd run off and left him for one of the many blokes she'd allegedly been having an affair with. The old *woman troubles* camaraderie. He'd fallen straight for it, not realising Valerie was locked in the basement below his feet. Probably screaming for help. Just like she was when Mick Washington reviewed the case a few weeks later and found her there. Barely alive.

Roy clutched the phone. A bead of sweat dripped from his forehead and landed in the middle of the screen. He really didn't want to do this, but he knew it was the right thing. He let out a deep breath and dialled.

49

The smashed TV and piercing headache confirmed yesterday hadn't been a bad dream. I ran my finger along the cracks in the screen and it all came flooding back: the wine I'd downed to forget about the look on Jane's face as she told me I was suspended, her uncharacteristic softness somehow worse than if she'd thrown the words into my face in her usual drill sergeant style. I hadn't even tried to explain myself. Nothing would have excused why I'd attacked him, no matter what I thought he'd done. I was a police officer. An upholder of law and order. My eyes burned. If he was involved, he was going to get away with it. There was no way they could touch him now, not without something undeniable. And it was all my fault. *What were you thinking?*

The lumps of plastic that used to make up the house phone lay on the floor at my feet where they'd landed after smashing into the TV screen. I'd launched it across the room after trying to call Dad – better he hear the news of my suspension from me – only to find his phone turned off. Straight to the default voicemail. No personalised message required because his phone hadn't been off in about twenty years. Clearly someone had beaten me to it, and he was avoiding me, avoiding the shame. Bad news sure did travel fast. I bent down and picked up the pieces, the irony not lost on me that lying amongst it was also the remnants of the Be a Better Alice list I'd torn up in rabid fury.

I was on my way to the kitchen bin when there was a knock at the door. I shoved everything into the drawer in the hallway.

'Blimey,' Roy said as I opened it.

I squinted, partially at the daylight stabbing my eyes, and also in shock at the sight of Roy at my house. It was jarring, like seeing a teacher outside of school. 'Hi, erm, what are you doing here?'

He held up two small cardboard café boxes and a drinks tray containing two cups, coffee-laced steam floating from the tiny holes in the lids. 'I come in peace.'

Roy hadn't so much as made me a cup of instant coffee in the two years I'd known him, let alone brought breakfast to my door. I stepped one foot outside like a deer tentatively sniffing an unfamiliar scent in the air. 'What's in the box?'

'Don't worry, it's not Gwyneth Paltrow's head. How does a bacon sarnie sound?'

I nodded and stepped back. He followed me inside and without thinking I led him to the living room, remembering the state of the TV a second too late. *Crap.*

'What's gone on in here, then?' Roy said.

'Oh ... the cat, he, er ... knocked it over.'

Roy pivoted between me and the screen, his face a blanket of confusion. 'What is he? A bleedin' parkour ninja?'

I shrugged, unsure how to make the story more believable.

Roy gave me the latest on Chrissy as we ate. Bernie's assessment had been right. Blunt force trauma to the back of the head. Single blow. Powerful enough to fracture her skull. A rock with traces of blood and hair found tossed in the field had been sent to the lab. Some fibres had been recovered from her clothing. Fingernail scrapings taken and sent off. No passing vehicles had seen anything.

'Maybe we should stop knocking her wonder smoothies – must be doing her some good, eh?' Roy said.

I couldn't help but laugh. 'Oh God, she's going to bang on about them even more now, isn't she? She talking yet?'

'No, still under. They'll call when she's ready. Poor kid.' Roy nodded solemnly. 'They're guessing, based on the time you left and by the time the press cleared out, she must have been attacked somewhere between nine and midnight. She was supposed to be staying over for something they were meant to be off to this morning. Camilla's in bits for forgetting to cancel. Tried telling her it's no surprise, with her being shaken up, but she's having none of it. Thinks it's all her fault.'

'And none of the press saw anything before they left? No strangers hanging around?'

Roy shook his head. 'Doesn't seem like it. Confirmed with all of them bar A. J. and the bloke from the *Mail* – they didn't answer their phones. I've left messages asking for a callback, but none of the others saw anything before they headed off, so doubt they will have either. Whoever did this wasn't stupid enough to do anything in front of an audience.'

I ran my hands through my hair, the combination of grease and three days' worth of dry shampoo meaning I could only get halfway. It didn't make sense. Surely whoever I'd chased away wouldn't have come back? They had to know the place would be swarming with police. Unless they'd waited for us to leave? Knowing Chrissy would be on her way, and alone. What did she know that someone didn't want her to tell us?

Roy took a large bite of his sandwich but that didn't stop him from carrying on talking. 'So, erm, what do you want me to do about Myles, then? I know we wanted something more solid before putting in a request for his financials, but, well, we still haven't got anything, and, now that, erm . . .'

I couldn't believe I'd physically attacked someone because of a hunch and a cocky smirk. It was still possible he was involved in all this somehow, all part of some selfish sick plan. But I had zero evidence. And lurking around him now, after what I'd done, would only drag Roy into the shit with me. I stood, interlacing my fingers across the back of my head as I looked out the window. The air I was breathing never seemed to reach any further than the back of my throat no matter how deeply I inhaled. 'Leave it, until I'm back anyway, then let me deal with it.'

A buzz from Roy's pocket interrupted us before he could say anything else. 'Better get that,' he said, before walking into the hallway with the phone pressed to his ear.

I sat on the sofa, listening to the 'yeahs' and the

'mm-hmms', before a bellow of 'You've gotta be joking?'
almost stopped my heart. Roy stomped back into the room.
'Gotta go, turns out there was a bit of glass stuck in that
rock they found in the field near Chrissy, the one with the
blood. They've only found a soddin' print on it and got
a hit!'

Veins bulged from my neck. 'Against who?'

Roy rubbed his forefinger and thumb across his brow.
'That's the problem, it's hit against the Police Elimination
Database, one of ours.'

Every single molecule of water disappeared from my
mouth. 'What? Who?'

'Eddie.'

My mind jumped to his blanched skin at the crime scene
and my blood ran cold.

50

Attempted murder?

No, she couldn't be.

Couldn't possibly be.

He jabbed his finger at the phone screen, bouncing between apps. Newsfeed to newsfeed. They must have it wrong. She was dead. Definitely dead. But there they were, articles and video bulletins everywhere confirming it. *Survived.* He dug his nails so hard into his temples he worried he might pierce his brain. He couldn't tear his eyes from the photographs amongst the text, the girl's gormless face smiling, following him like a rotting stench. Her sobbing parents appealing for information about what happened to their precious baby. She was no *baby.* She knew exactly what she was doing, getting in the way like that. She'd brought this on herself.

There was a brief moment of respite from the panic as he realised the police must have nothing to go on. They wouldn't make the parents do that, put them through the ordeal of flashing lights and live cameras, if they knew it was him. But the moment of peace was snatched away by his next thought. That if she woke up and identified him

335

as her attacker, this was all over. And he couldn't let that happen, especially not now the first part of the plan was complete. He'd already cleared up what he thought was his only loose end. Now he'd have to clean up another.

51

I almost wore a hole in the rug, unable to sit as hours passed like weeks waiting for Roy to call with an update on Eddie. It took all the willpower I had not to throw my last working phone against the wall every second that passed without it ringing.

It seemed obvious now, in theory. Eddie's interest in Camilla's case was in stark opposition to the usual lacklustre approach he had to his job. The way he talked about her could be seen as borderline obsessive. Maybe I'd been on the right track with my theory about intimacy-seeking stalkers, just wrong about who it was who thought Camilla was communicating with them through her books. Not Chrissy, but Eddie.

'Edward "Eddie" Lumsdale's our man? Really?' I said in the hope that hearing it out loud would make it make sense.

My brain rewound, catching and whirring like a tired old VHS tape before re-playing the scene in the CID office when Roy came back after he and Eddie had been witness hunting at the reservoir. Hadn't Roy mentioned something about Eddie taking pictures down there, of the bridge? I pulled out my phone and googled, only having to click on two other Eddie Lumsdales before opening the right Instagram account. I scrolled through his pictures. Eddie hiking. Eddie with a dog in a pub beer garden. Eddie smiling for the camera with his arm tightly hugging the shoulders of an elderly woman sat in front of a 'Happy Seventieth' birthday cake – his grandma, I presumed. So wholesome. Innocent. But how many times before had I come across people whose faces didn't match their crimes? I swiped the tab away, staring at the home screen, willing my phone to ring. For Roy to call and put me out of my misery.

Nothing.

Solidifying muscles in my neck and shoulders crunched as I circled my head. I needed to get out of the house. Do something productive. Something to distract me. Fifteen minutes later, I stopped at Wild Blooms on the edge of Market Square on my way to the hospital. Given the choice, I'm sure Chrissy would have opted for something more flamboyant than a bunch of roses. But she didn't have a choice. Wasn't even conscious yet. *God, Eddie, did you do that? Really?*

The brutalist concrete structure housing the intensive care wing towered over me. Paramedics, nurses, patients and their loved ones all swerved me as they entered and exited the building through large sliding glass doors that opened and closed in front of me every few seconds. A tall blonde woman holding an even taller helium-filled balloon walked past and went inside. I tried to follow, but my feet were bolted to the floor. Because I wasn't thinking about Eddie now. All I could think about was standing in this exact spot a little over a month earlier, watching Jamie's mum lean against the wall, no longer able to bear the sterile grey corridors of the children's ward. A cigarette wobbling as it touched her trembling lips. The anger spread across her face after we'd put Jamie into the ambulance had dissipated with the smoke that blew over it, replaced with something else. Guilt. The same cocktail of sadness and self-punishment I'd seen in my own eyes. Nausea mushroomed from the pit of my stomach.

I couldn't do it.

Couldn't go in.

Couldn't look Chrissy in her bruised and swollen face.

How many people are going to end up in this hospital because of you?

I wasn't sure when exactly I'd dropped the flowers as I stumbled back towards the car, a solitary pink petal snagging in my shoelace as I fumbled with the lock. I slammed the door shut, closing the world out before letting my head fall against the window. But that fixed nothing. Made no difference at all. Because the screaming, the shouting, the voices goading me. They weren't coming from outside. They were all still here with me, festering inside my own mind. Tears streamed down my cheeks and I let them come. I wasn't sure how long I'd been sat there when my phone vibrated, rattling the plastic of the centre console. But it wasn't the call I'd been waiting for from Roy, it was Tess.

I wiped away tears and snot with a tissue from the glove compartment and answered. 'Hey,' I said, the word croaking out despite my best efforts at keeping my voice steady.

'What's wrong?'

'Nothing, it's . . .' I swallowed. Swallowed again. But the bubble filling my throat refused to budge. Swelling and threatening to pop as the tears came again.

'Alice? Alice, tell me where you are. I'm coming to get you.'

I didn't want to see Tess. Didn't want to see anyone. 'No, no, I'm fine, I'm OK.'

'Alice, where are—'

My phone did the job of hanging up for me as my battery died.

I unflipped the sun visor and looked at myself in the small, dusty mirror. The remnants of yesterday's mascara streamed down my face. I wiped it with my thumb. Tried to wipe it, anyway, but all I seemed to achieve was smudging it further across my face like some sad little soldier putting camo face paint on for the first time.

The drive home passed in a daze and Tess was hammering on my door as I pulled in.

She put a palm on either side of my face as I got out of the car, scanning me as if looking for an injury. 'What's wrong? You sounded so weird on the phone – what's happened?'

We went into the house, fell down next to each other on the sofa, and I told her about the hospital. 'I needed to distract myself and it's just made everything worse. It's too much, all this stuff with Jamie, and now fucking Eddie, Jesus.'

'Well, there's nothing I can do about what happened with Jamie, but you can cross Eddie off your list of troubles.

That's what I was calling you about.' She gave the update she'd been trying to give me over the phone and I didn't know whether to be relieved or go down to the station and throttle the life out of Eddie. Turned out the deathlike pallor at the crime scene wasn't because he was worried about getting caught for attempted murder; he was just plain old incompetent and had apparently gotten overexcited at finding the bloodstained rock, picked it up without any gloves on, then panicked at the prospect of getting torn a new one by Bernie for contaminating evidence.

'Idiot. Absolute fucking idiot,' I said as I flopped back into the cushions, partially relieved I hadn't been working alongside a secret stalker, but still stiff with frustration at his utter stupidity.

'I know, right?' Tess said. 'Can't believe his strategy of "put it back where he found it and hope for the best" didn't quite pan out. And good thing he has an alibi for last night or he could've really screwed himself over. On the up side, drinks are on him tonight, for the whole bloody pub, 'cause buying a box of Krispy Kremes isn't quite going to cut it. He's really outdone himself this time.'

'Too right. Well, you can help yourself to my allocation, not really up for drinks tonight.'

Tess tilted her head and squinted as if I'd said something wrong. 'You're not coming?'

'As much as I'm glad to hear Eddie isn't the village stalker, it's not enough to get me to shower and try to make myself look presentable. I'll celebrate with him another time, when I'm back at work.'

'So that's the only thing we're celebrating tonight, yeah?'

This felt like a trick question but my mind was a thick fog. I brushed my hand across my forehead like I could clear it from the outside. 'Erm ...'

'You've forgotten my birthday, haven't you?'

Shit. 'No, your birthday drinks, that's tonight, yes.'

'You don't have to come if ...'

'No, of course, I'll be there. Sorry, it's just with everything going on ...'

'Fine. I forgive you, but on one condition.'

'What condition?'

'That you admit this is getting out of hand now, that you're not yourself at all, and that you're taking a holiday. Get yourself off somewhere, relax, do a bloody pilgrimage – I dunno, just have, a, break!' Her fingers drilled into my thigh to emphasise the last three words.

She was right. And maybe if I'd listened to her in the first place, not rushed back so quickly, none of this would be happening. 'OK.'

Tess's eyes widened as if I'd just told her she'd won the lottery. 'Like, seriously? You'll actually do it?'

I shrugged. 'I'm already suspended – no one's gonna miss me anyway, are they?'

She leant over and wrapped her arms around my neck, pulling me in for a hug so tight my back cracked. My face disappeared into her thick curls and I let my chin rest on her shoulder, the oil in her hair adding a coconutty accent to her perfume that was so strong I could only assume she'd bathed in it.

She pulled back and looked at her phone. 'I'm supposed to be meeting Nate a bit early to grab some food, but I can wait here if you want instead, while you get ready?'

'No, no, you go. I'll see you down there in about an hour.'

'OK, see you later.'

She ruffled my hair and left. As soon as the door slammed I slumped to one side and pulled the blanket from the back of the sofa over my head.

52

The last of the village busybodies filed out of the school assembly hall and Roy couldn't be happier to see them go. Of course he hadn't wanted Eddie to be behind the attack on Chrissy, but there would have been a smidge of a silver lining if he had been; the commotion it would have caused in the office undoubtedly meaning they'd have had to cancel this bleeding community reassurance meeting. These things always riled him. Answering stupid questions that didn't actually make anyone feel safer in the long run.

The only saving grace had been that at least A. J. hadn't turned up so Roy didn't have to put up with being eyeballed from behind the man's notepad for the entire meeting, like a lion stalking an injured impala. He'd have been dying for Roy to trip over a response or say something politically incorrect so he'd have something to print in the paper the next day. *Bad copper*. In bold font. Underlined. He let out a deep sigh, blowing out some of the tension in his back with it. At least it was over now.

He scooped the leftover police contact leaflets from the fold-out desk into his rucksack and slung it over his shoulder. Walking towards the door, he scanned the display cabinets that took up the whole wall on his right as he went. Trophies of all shapes, sizes and colours lined the shelves, interspersed with photographs. Old and new smiling faces. Children and teachers in differing variations of the school's red, green and black colours. Roy hadn't been short of a few trophies himself as a kid with the rugby team. He'd been a hefty lad before he discovered the gym in his late teens. Never thought sport would be for him until he found the game that really did suit all sizes. People told him he was one of the best tighthead props Fortbridge Juniors had ever seen.

The daydream about his former sporting glory was cut short as he reached the final display cabinet, different from the rest. Roy paused and squinted through dusty glass. Instead of awards, the middle shelf contained an artificial wreath spelling out what looked like initials: *HHG*. Roy recognised the face of the young boy in a framed photograph above the floral letters immediately. He was almost identical to Camilla, only with dark cropped hair, a slightly more pronounced jaw, and with an extra half a centimetre width to the nose. Henry Harton-Gray. Camilla's younger brother.

Roy tutted at the thought of the strapping young man's life taken too soon. The framed photograph of Henry sat at the centre of tens of smaller photographs, every one containing him, but accompanied by different people, each with its own handwritten message of condolence. *Miss you Henry xxSadiexx*, scrawled in gold marker across a photo of the boy with a young blonde girl; *Team won't be the same without you, mate, can't believe it, FRFC X* written across another of the boy with his rugby teammates.

He was still reading when footsteps from behind nearly sent him jumping into the cabinet. 'Jesus Christ, woman!' Roy yelled as he spun to see Mavis Mulberry hovering over his shoulder. *Great*, he thought, just what he needed right now. The Jessica Fletcher of Fortbridge; knew everyone and everything. What was he in for this time? A detailed account of her next-door neighbour's overgrown hedge? Her jotter full of registration plates of all the cars that had driven past her house that she thought looked *off-ish*?

'They were inseparable, those two, if I remember rightly,' Mavis said, her eyes peeking over the rim of royal blue winged glasses. She pointed towards another photo of Henry at the back of the shelf. 'Absolutely devastated, that one was, when he passed, poor thing.' Roy's eyeline followed the pointing finger.

'What the—' he said as he wiped the dust from the cabinet window, as if rubbing it away would somehow change the photograph and the face of the person he recognised in it, their cheek pressed hard against Henry's face as the two of them grinned towards the camera.

Roy stared at the picture, an unsettled feeling threatening his stomach, before he pulled his phone from his pocket.

53

I dragged myself off the sofa at the last possible moment, having left barely enough time to shower, dress and get myself to the pub. I did the first two in less than ten minutes and was about to leave when a buzzing came from the living room. My phone. I'd left it on the coffee table to charge. Maybe it was Dad, finally calm enough to speak to me. Or maybe it was Jane calling to say she'd had official instructions to sack me. Fire one last metal bolt into my brain like the cattle up at the abattoir. I didn't have the mental fortitude to deal with either of them. The buzzing stopped as I pulled on my ankle boots and opened the front door. I was about to slam it closed when the noise started again. *Oh, just answer the bloody thing, get this over with.*

Roy's name lit up on the screen. 'Yeah?' I said, turning to walk back into the hallway. 'Come on then, what's Eddie done now?'

'Nothing, erm . . . where are you?' Roy said.

'Home. Just about to leave for Tess's birthday drinks, why?'

'She there?'

'No, I'm meeting her at the pub.'

'Did she ever mention anything about knowing Camilla's brother, Henry?'

'Tess? No, why?'

'Well, 'cause it looks like she did. Quite well, actually, if the photo of them as kids down here at the school is anything to go by.'

'Why wouldn't she—' Something shifted in my brain as if Roy was a horologist reaching inside and delicately placing this snippet of information like a tiny screw, filling the gap and enabling the cogs and wheels to spring to life. Turning. Catching. Finally grabbing hold of the connection I'd reached for since I chased someone from Camilla's home. The smell. The smell I was sure I'd recognised for a split second before it was lost to a cloud of dog shit. The smell lingering in the living room from when she was here earlier. Tess's perfume. The phone slipped from my hand, Roy's muted voice shouting my name from down by my feet.

No. No, it couldn't be. Surely. And even if it was, it must be a coincidence at most. My mind whirred as I paced the living room, re-living every interaction I'd had in the last few weeks with Tess. Eating. Drinking. Laughing. Sharing. Why wouldn't she tell me she knew Camilla's brother? Was close to him? It would have been a natural part of the conversation, wouldn't it? Especially with Tess, who spilled her guts on the regular right here on this sofa about everything, everything except . . .

Her mum's warning repeated in my brain. Tess's first love. Off limits.

Oh God, it was Henry.

My hands flew to my face, trying to rub off the layer of tar smothering every pore. Thinking of Tess's mum also sent another theory spinning. *Clon.* The indentation found on the paper on the note in Camilla's bedroom. I scrambled around on the floor for my phone, hanging up on a still yelling Roy and pulling up the browser, my eyes burning, already knowing what I was going to find before I started typing. *MS MEDICATION CLON.* The search bar suggestion finished my thought for me. *MS MEDICATION CLONAZEPAM.* I'd collected that medication for her before. I should have known. Should have remembered. And if I hadn't been so caught up in my own shit, pretending everything was fine until I could get myself back on track before anyone could notice, maybe I would have.

I made it to the kitchen sink just in time for the vomit to bounce off the backsplash, my throat ablaze. This was why she'd been so desperate for me to take a break. Have a holiday. Leave this silly little investigation to Roy and get the hell out of her way. Not out of concern for me. But fear for herself. Fear I'd find out what she'd been doing.

I burst through the door of The Bull, scanning the wall of people.

'Aliiiiiiiice,' Tess squealed, making a beeline for me, cutting through the crowd of familiar faces. 'I had a horrible feeling you'd change your mind about coming and I'd have to come drag you out.' She grabbed my wrist to pull me towards the table she'd reserved.

I whipped my arm away through the gap between her thumb and fingers as hard as I could. 'Don't touch me,' I said in a voice I barely recognised.

'What . . .' Tess stuttered, the smile on the lower half of her face not matching the alarm radiating from her eyes. 'What the hell is . . .' Then I saw it. The flicker in her face as she realised. The moment the light went on and her bright pink lips went from smile to dropped jaw in slow motion. 'Alice, OK, please, let me explain.'

I snorted in absolute astonishment. 'Explain? *Explain?* Are you fucking kidding me? What could you possibly say to explain any of this?'

A tall man in a red top appeared beside her. 'Babe?' he said. Nate, I presumed. 'Everything OK?'

She nudged him back towards the direction he'd come from. 'Yeah, yeah, fine. I just need a quick chat with Alice first, in private – two secs, yeah?' She turned back to me. 'Can we go outside, please?'

I'd have burst out laughing if rage wasn't boiling me alive from the inside. A quick chat? A quick fucking chat? The words erupted like lava. 'Are you serious right now? This isn't a bad date that we need to have a girly chat over while we powder our noses, Tess! You're a fucking stalker!'

The door banged shut behind me. I spun to see Roy, his broad chest heaving, mouth dropped open as he tried to both catch his breath and process the words he'd just heard come out my mouth.

I turned back to Tess and flung my arms out wide. 'Well,

go on then, explain yourself, I'm honestly dying to hear what you've got to say.'

Tess's lower lip quivered, the glaze in her eyes now trickling down her cheeks. 'You wouldn't understand. Because you never let anyone close enough to actually hurt you.'

I wasn't sure if it was the audacity of Tess somehow trying to twist this around on to me, or Nate's red shirt in the corner of my vision like a flag to a bull, but whatever it was I snapped, launching myself at her. Glasses clattered to the floor as I knocked her into a small table. The hum of chit chat in the room disappeared in an instant as eyes bored into me from every direction.

Heavy hands pulled me back towards the door. 'Sarge, Sarge!' It was Roy, dragging me out of yet another alter-cation.

Tess looked up at me from the floor. 'Alice, please, I'm sorry.'

Roy swivelled me around to face him. 'Sarge, I'll sort this. Please, go home, cool off, yeah?'

I looked back at Tess as Nate helped her up. I writhed away from Roy's grip and ran out of the pub.

Kept running.

All the way home.

I burst through the front door and slammed it behind me before tearing at the buttons on my coat. I ripped it off, throwing it on the floor and slumping down on top of it. I rummaged under myself and pulled my mobile from my pocket, turning it off. My own best friend had been behind all this, right under my nose. And I hadn't suspected her for a second.

My, my, Dad *would* be proud.

54

The handbag Alice dropped in the commotion at the pub hung from Roy's arm as he walked to the petrol station. He normally drove there even though it was barely a mile away. But tonight, he needed the fresh air.

One end of the stupid red keyring from her *not my boyfriend-boyfriend* dangled out of it, slapping his leg with every other step. He was glad her keys weren't attached to it so at least she could get into her house. Roy didn't want to have to go over there and rile her up any more than she already was before he even understood what was actually going on.

He opened the door to the petrol station shop. The whole giving up smoking business had been going all right so far, but if he was going to get through what he had to do next he'd need the nicotine hit. Keeping hold of his cool interviewing Tess was going to be a real test. He walked down the aisle to the counter. 'Evening, mate,' Roy said, scratching the back of his neck with his free hand, 'Benson and Hedges, twenty pack.'

The cashier in a *Jurassic Park* T-shirt about three sizes too small for him turned around and pulled back the sliding door that hid the cigarette shelf. Static hummed inside the large strip light above their heads, and Roy perused the selection of lighters as he waited. Every hue of plastic filled the display board. Block colour. Neon. Floral patterns. Stripes. But it was what hung next to them that caught his eye. A series of coiled keyrings. Three different colour choices: red, yellow and green. He pulled out the one from Alice's bag. It looked the same. Except hers had a heart keyring on it the others didn't. He eyeballed the alien attachment like some sort of professional jeweller, noticing up close that the red of the keyring was a shade or two darker than the rest of the plastic.

Something twinged in his stomach. *Nah, probably nothing,* he told himself. Started to tell himself, anyway. He held the little heart up to his ear and shook it. Roy could have sworn he heard the faintest of rattles, like something inside was moving around.

'Oi, mate, do you want these or not?' the cashier shouted, waving the box of cigarettes in the air as Roy strode back down the aisle towards the door.

55

I stayed slumped against the inside of the front door until my back ached and my sitting bones were numb. What else did I have to do? Even if I hadn't been suspended from work, Tess was my best friend so I wouldn't be allowed anywhere near this investigation. And it hardly felt appropriate for me to just pop on some loungewear, pour myself a glass of wine and watch TV as if my life wasn't imploding.

The events of the last fortnight bounced around inside my head as I heaved myself off the floor. I needed air. Something cold and brisk to slap the thoughts away. I opened the door and stepped out on to the drive, focussing on each individual pebble shifting under my feet as my eyes adjusted to the night. Normally I'd have been annoyed at myself for not getting around to fixing the porch light, but in that moment I appreciated the lack of illumination. No beam of shame shining down on me, drawing more attention to the mess I was in. And Dom didn't seem to have fixed his either, the whole lane in darkness.

Standing there for several minutes, I soaked in the calm before a breeze whipped through the trees and made me shiver. I hugged myself, turning to go back inside when a light flicked on in the small upstairs box room in Dom's house, the one I'd tried to spy in when I snooped around, that at one point I'd envisaged housed all his dirty secrets rather than probably just his boring physio kit. I drew in a deep breath hoping that, as well as the oxygen, the air also carried little particles of courage. Because whilst I couldn't fix whatever the hell was happening with Tess right now, I could certainly make a start with apologising to Dom for my behaviour when I'd hammered on his door the other night. A proper apology. Not the half-arsed version I'd managed in the café yesterday.

I walked over to The Willows and knocked, jolting as the door opened under the weight of my fist. 'Dom?' I said. 'Dom, it's Alice.'

No reply came, just creaking hinges breaking the silence as I pushed the open door a little further.

I raised my voice. 'I come in peace, I promise . . . Dom?' Still nothing. I stopped breathing for a second, not making a sound so I could hear any noise coming from inside. But there was none. No reply. No distant sound of a TV or radio. No pots and pans clinking from the kitchen. Just silence. As if no one was in there.

But the light had been turned on upstairs. *Someone* was definitely in there.

My eyes flicked to the broken motion sensor light above the door, reminding me of Bret's dismissal of my theory about it being linked to the spate of thefts. Maybe I'd been right, and whoever was in there wasn't answering because it wasn't Dom. I clawed at my pocket for the hard bulk of my phone. There was nothing but soft material. *Shit!* Whoever was in there could be out and halfway down the street by the time I went back to get it. There wasn't time.

'Police,' I shouted, 'anyone in there, come out now.' I pushed the door fully open, careful to avoid touching anywhere that might be useful for fingerprints if someone had broken in. 'Hello? Police!'

No panicked footsteps. No response. Nothing.

I entered, scanning the kitchen before making my way to the bottom of the stairs, calling as I went. 'Police, is anyone in here?' I checked the rooms. Downstairs first, then upstairs to the bathroom. Empty. Bedroom. Empty. I ran to the room next door, the one with the light glowing down on to the lane, unlocked this time. I stopped dead in the doorway. An invisible fist punched me square in the gut as I took in the sight in front of me.

56

Roy marched back to the station and dropped Alice's bag on the front desk. 'Here, Terry,' he said, ringing the buzzer to get the attention of the station clerk, or 'Support Services Administrator', as he was calling himself these days. Terry seemed proud of his new title, but Roy would take some convincing that rather than being a bump in status, it was actually just an excuse for the bosses to get him to do more stuff for less money. Front Desk Clerk. Property Officer. Odd Jobs Manager. You name it, if it didn't require a badge they had Terry doing it. Not that Roy cared about that at the minute, because all he wanted was a screwdriver. And one thing you could say about Terry was that he was always prepared.

Terry shuffled over from the back office like a giant penguin. Big body. Little head. Swaying side to side. Chin slightly lifted as if he was afraid his small round glasses would slide straight off his nose if he held it level. He leant both elbows against the small ledge behind the glass partition, clearly tuckered out despite only having moved about four metres.

'You're back an' all, Roy?' Terry said. 'It's like Piccadilly

Circus in here tonight, what's going on? No one'll tell me nuthin'.'

'Not now, Terry mate. You still got that mini screwdriver back there? The slotted one?'

'Erm, yeah, I have somewhere.' He bent down and Roy heard his knees pop through the glass before he dragged himself back up empty-handed. Terry scratched his head, leaving white candyfloss-like tufts of hair sticking up in all directions. 'I need to find the toolbox; it's around here somewhere, so it is.'

Roy didn't have time for this, especially not at the pace Terry moved. Jane was waiting in the interview room for him with Tess. 'Look, do us a favour, find it, and see if you can wedge this apart, will ya?' The key chain dangled from his hand, heart keyring bouncing at the bottom of it like a miniature bungee jumper.

Terry chuckled. 'You're a bit late for Valentine's Day, Roy, and I prefer chocolates.'

Jesus H. Christ, he thought. 'Just see if you can get it open, I swear there's something in there.'

'Ah,' came Jane's voice from behind him, 'there you are, come on.'

She looked like she'd aged about ten years since he'd seen her earlier, not that he was surprised with what he'd told her about the revelations in the pub. He probably wasn't looking too grand himself. A storm set in across his stomach. The keyring was probably nothing, just a timely distraction from what he had to do now. He took a deep breath as Jane marched into the interview room before he followed her.

57

A small lamp illuminated the contents of the room. A wall of eyes glared. All of them familiar. All of them mine. Photographs of me filled two of the four walls. Getting out of my car. Drinking wine in the kitchen. Standing outside the station. Running. My eyes darted from image to image until they snagged on a photograph of me on my sofa, blanket pulled up around my neck, reading what looked like Camilla's book. My mind spun. The noise I'd heard outside the back window and dismissed. The snapping. Someone *had* been there, in the undergrowth. And that someone was Dom. My eyes moved on and wished they hadn't, the next photograph sending a tidal wave through me so strong it almost burst through my skin.

That was me.

Asleep.

In bed.

A close-up.

My mouth filled with hot saliva.

Just below the images sat a computer monitor on the desk, turned on, but in sleep mode. I dragged my feet in the opposite direction to where they wanted to go and walked towards it. My breath stuttered as I shook the mouse, and stopped completely when the screen sprang to life, lit up by what looked like a live CCTV stream. The current time and date ticked over in the bottom left corner of an image of the front of Myrtle Cottage.

Before I could even begin to process the concept of evidence preservation my amygdala took over and the monitor was on the floor, cracking under the heel of my boot. Hip flexors burning as my leg pumped up and down like a piston. Lungs shrinking with each exhale, like two dehydrated raisins, sucking in nothing but emptiness.

What the hell was going on?

Why was I plastered all over his walls?

I needed to get out. Away from the paper eyes staring at me.

The entrails of the screen tripped me as I ran for the door. I stumbled down the stairwell, through the kitchen and out across the road. The thin gravel was quicksand under my feet, eyes fixed on the sanctuary of the cottage that never seemed to get any closer. My head swung back towards The Willows with every other stride as I grappled with my keys, before I threw myself at the front door, opening it and slamming it shut behind me.

No phone on the sideboard. *Shit!* I dashed for the kitchen. Had to call it in. Call *something* in. I didn't know what the hell was going on, but God only knew what this guy was capable of. I stopped by the kitchen island, as if teetering on the edge of a cliff. Still no phone.

Where had I put it?

I looked towards the patio door, the outline of my body reflecting back from the pane of glass. Except the outline I saw wasn't mine. I was a smaller Russian doll, shadowed by the larger frame of the figure standing behind me.

58

Roy watched as Jane fiddled with the ancient recording equipment, before scanning the room as she went through the 'You do not have to say anything' motions and made sure one last time Tess didn't want a solicitor present. Part of him was waiting for someone to jump out and tell him this was all one big prank. That the person sat opposite him wasn't Tess at all, just some joker in a very elaborate mask. He locked eyes with her. She was solemn. Still.

'How did she know it was me?' Tess said before either of them had a chance to ask her anything.

Roy could see from the resigned expression on Tess's face that she wasn't here to play games. She was done. No need for the interview strategy he'd planned in a rush on the walk to the petrol station based on the well-worn framework of asking the right questions at the right time, giving your suspect just enough rope to hang themselves, tie themselves up in knots, before hitting them with something they couldn't talk their way out of. Tess clearly wasn't going to try and talk herself out of anything.

'I dunno what made her certain, but I think I set her off. I called from the assembly hall, at the school,' Roy said, his voice hoarse. 'There's a picture of you and Henry, all lovey dovey. I thought it was odd, you not mentioning you knew him, so I called her to ask and, well, then she hung up on me. Next thing I know you're tearing each other's hair out in the pub.' He thought back to the low-down Alice had given him about the different types of stalkers. From what he could remember, Tess's escapades must fall into the box of the ones who are resentful, or after revenge. A wave of nausea washed over him. He'd never pegged Tess as vengeful.

She smiled, a mixture of reminiscence and heartbreak, nodding gently as tears pooled. 'Thought they got rid of that. No one gave a shit about what happened to Henry after Camilla moved away. They only put it there in the first place 'cause they knew it would get in the papers once that book of hers came out. Bet they thought she'd come down for a photo op. She couldn't even be bothered to do that, got out of here as fast as she could.'

'It must've been hard for her too, you know, it was her family,' Roy said.

Tess's head fell forward, fingers clawing at the back of her neck. 'He'd still be here if it wasn't for her, getting her own way as usual. They wouldn't have been anywhere near that lorry if she hadn't insisted on being picked up, chauffeur driven.'

'It was an accident,' Roy said.

Tess lifted her head and leant back in her chair, staring towards the ceiling to stop tears falling down her face. 'We had it all planned out, flat in London, everything. He was going places with his music. I nearly had a meltdown when I found out he got into that school, thought it meant he was gonna leave me behind. But it didn't even cross his mind. Said he wasn't going unless I went with him. And,' Tess bit her lip to stop the quivering, 'no one has ever treated me the way Henry did, loved me like he did. And he'd have given it all up to come back with me when Mum got sick, I know he would.'

'But what use is revenge?' Roy asked. 'It's not gonna bring him back.'

'This isn't about revenge!' Tess said, the volume of her voice rising. 'No one was meant to get hurt, OK? I just wanted to scare her, that's all, so she'd fuck off back to London, or Timbuk-fucking-tu, I dunno, just, for her to go anywhere rather than be here. I can't bear to look at her, but since she's been back you can't fucking avoid her. Any excuse to have something about her in the paper; twice I nearly bumped into her the first week when I was out running at the reservoir. And it's not like *I* can leave, not with the help Mum needs. I can't take it, it just brings it all back, like it happened yesterday. It's like looking at Henry in a wig! When she came back, I— I just wished she'd stayed away.' She gave up trying to restrain the tears now, flowing fast on to her teal satin top.

Jane interjected, 'And then what? Hmm? You get her to leave again, and all the pain goes away? Out of sight, out of mind, was that how you thought this would work? I hate to break it to you, Tess, but you can't just chase pain away; you have to deal with it.'

Paternal instinct squeezed at Roy as he looked at Tess. She barely filled the chair, mascara running down her face like a little girl caught trying on Mum's expensive make-up. Hope-filled eyes called to him from behind the grey smudges, as if he could make it all better. Make everything go away. A cloak of failure draped across his shoulders as the faces of the women in his own life transposed with Tess's. Karen and Laurie. Jane's words about chasing the pain away replayed in his ears. *Is that what I've been doing?* he thought. Pushing his girls further and further. Every day. Hanging another little ornament filled with his shortcomings somewhere on their bodies, until they were covered in so many they crumpled under the weight. He took a drink from the small plastic cup in front of him, hoping the water would wash away the lump in his throat.

'I'm sorry,' Tess said, looking at Jane and then to Roy as she wiped her runny nose with the back of her hand. 'I didn't mean for any of this to happen. Is Alice coming back? I need to talk to her. I didn't want her involved, didn't want anything to blow back on her. I tried to get her off the job, but she wouldn't listen.'

'I don't think that's a good idea just yet,' Roy said. 'But, I'm not being funny, Alice should be the least of your worries now. The stalking is bad enough, but what about Chrissy, eh? You nearly bleedin' killed the girl!'

Tess shook her head. 'I swear to God, Roy, I had nothing to do with that.'

'What, Camilla's got two stalkers now, has she?' Roy let out an exasperated sigh. He already knew there was little he could do to help her, even less if she wouldn't tell the truth. Lay everything out on the table.

Tess leant forward, hands in prayer, literally begging him to believe her. 'I promise you. I was there that night, OK. I didn't know Alice was going over, I just wanted to scare Camilla. But then after Alice chased me away, I was shitting myself, thought she'd seen me, recognised me. I'm hardly gonna go back and kill someone, am I? I didn't hurt anyone!'

All three of them jumped at a knock on the door, Terry bursting in.

'Sorry to disturb, Roy, where'd you get that keyring? It had this in it,' he said, holding up a white plastic disc the size of a small coin.

'What is it?' Roy leant in to get a closer look.

'I'm no expert, o' course,' Terry said, 'but I've seen these before, when I were manning the exhibits store at the Hi-Tech Crime Unit up at HQ for a time when the usual guy was on holiday, remember? John summat, I think his name were—'

'Get to the bleedin' point, Terry!' Roy yelled.

'Well, it looks like one of those new fangle-dangle tracking device gadget things.'

Roy spun back to face Tess, his eyes wide.

'What's going on?' Jane said. 'Why have you got a tracking device?'

'That's not mine, ma'am, I found it in Alice's bag.'

59

I braced every muscle to fight a second too late. Dom's forearm was a vice clamped across my neck, pressure building in my head like an over-filled balloon. The memory of his muscular arm waving at me from the window the night we met pulsed behind my eyes and I gagged. But I couldn't vomit. There wasn't room, the inner walls of my throat almost touching. Crushing against each other.

No.

Can't let this happen.

Won't let this happen.

His other hand slapped across my mouth. A cloth pad scraped exposed gums as I tried to scream, cry out, something, anything, but the material muffled the noise. I clawed. Pulled. Scratched. Grappled for space between his arm and my chin. Desperate for just a millimetre, anything to leverage the force away from my trachea. Nothing. I flailed, throwing limbs in every direction.

Elbows to ribs.

Heels to shins.

Nails to eyes.

Flashes ripped through my brain. Of Mum. Dad. Noah.

I wasn't thinking about myself any more. If something happened to me, Dad would have no one. *Do something!* My heart beat fast. Too fast. Forcing blood around my body too quickly for the muscles and organs to take what they needed as it whizzed by. Limbs melting. The sweet smell of the material across my face filled my nostrils.

Don't you dare close your eyes!

Cardboard legs. Saturated. Folding in on themselves as I tried to stay upright.

Fight! Fight, for fuck's sake!

Children chanting. '*Fight! Fight! Fight!*'

I was lying on the ground now. Back at my first school sports day. Danny Graham beside me after I floored him. But this time, the other kids weren't laughing. They just walked away. Danny scooped me up and carried me from the sports field as I looked around, trying to spot my dad in the crowd of people walking in the other direction, away from me, away from where Danny was taking me.

He wasn't there.

Dad! I tried to call out, so he'd come, so he'd help me this time, but my throat was raw, barely expelling a squeak.

Everything faded as my eyes closed and a thick dry sponge filled my mouth. I tried to spit it out, but it was my tongue.

60

Dom held the steering wheel so tight it almost crumbled in his hands. Things hadn't gone *exactly* to plan – he could have done with a few more days to prepare – but he would make it work. Had to. For Father. The very least he could do. No one would look for Alice tonight, they wouldn't realise until morning at least, and that was all the time he needed. By then it would be too late. And he'd be gone. A dandelion seed dispersed in the wind. Never to be found. Just like before.

A blaze roared behind his eyes at the thought of the pride and gratitude that would have washed over Father's face if he'd lived to see what he'd done for him. Hear his story. How he'd found her after seeing the botched child rescue in the news. The way he introduced himself that first night, the weather setting the scene. It had been so easy. Like a higher power delivering her on a silver platter, cheering the start of Dom's little game with claps of thunder and the rumbling applause of rainclouds.

He shouldn't have waited for Father's funeral to come back. Should have done this years ago, while he was still alive. So he could see. Dom could have stayed under the radar, like he had at the cemetery. No one knew he was there. No one knew it was *him*. Not after the time passed, his waifish teenage frame and weak jawline unrecognisable in what he'd sculpted now.

Dom wiped his eyes, the one feature that still allowed him to see Father looking back in the mirror. The exit he'd waited for appeared up ahead. Nearly there. After all these years.

Home sweet home.

61

My head lolled to the right. I was incapable of stopping it, neck muscles no longer under my control like when the G-force of a rollercoaster takes over your body. Vibrating metal rumbled somewhere beneath me. We turned. One way then the other. My head following. Was I on a rollercoaster now?

Click – click – click … whoosh!

The turns. The dips. The rises. My body went with them all.

Click – click – click … whoosh!

I wasn't sure how much time passed before the ride ground to a halt. Minutes? Hours? What sounded like doors and locks opened and slammed shut.

What was happening?

Where the hell was he taking me?

Why the hell was he taking me?

Movement again. Warm pressure spread across the centre of my back and behind my knees; I was being carried. I dragged my eyes open. Just a crack. Enough to see a sheet of black above. Tiny white dots coming into focus. Stars. Was I dreaming? Or had Danny Graham actually come back to seek his schoolboy revenge?

But I knew I wasn't dreaming.

The crippling pain in my head and nausea filling my stomach told me this was real. Danny's arms weren't the ones wrapped around me. They were Dom's. Carrying me God knows where. Somewhere dark. Remote. My brain sent the danger signal to my limbs, instructing them to thrash, to kick, to punch. But nothing happened. I hung there. A marionette with severed strings. The only parts that would move were my eyelids, but in the opposite way I wanted them to as they fell shut again, plunging me into a deep, dark hole.

I had no sense of time or place as my eyes reopened, vision and body's playback speed lagging three frames behind normal. Something solid took the weight of my legs and back. I was seated now. Shapes became visible, outlines smudged like abstract paintings.

Where the hell was I? More importantly, where the hell was Dom? And what was that smell? *Jesus, the smell.* Pain shot through my arms as I tried to lift my hands to cover my nose, something hard and thin stopping them, digging into my wrists. I tried my legs next, the same tightness around my ankles, holding me down. I breathed through my mouth but it was too late and the odour knocked me sick. I froze. There was no mistaking it. Not even with the fogginess of my mind and the mustiness in the air. Fetid. Yet sweet. The stench you never got used to no matter how many times you smelt it.

There was something dead in this room with me.

My eyes darted. Left. Right. Back again. A single bare bulb hung above my head, casting a glow that didn't reach the two corners of the bare brick wall in front of me. There was nothing else. No sound, no movement.

Until Dom's voice came from behind me. 'You know, you were so close to messing this up for me.'

I twisted my neck further than my skin wanted to stretch so I could see his face. See what else was behind me. *Who* else was behind me. 'Messing what up? What the fuck is going on?'

His footsteps got closer, followed by a long, deep sigh as he walked around to face me, our eyes locking. He looked different. That Hollywood smile still stretched across his face, but it was only now I noticed it was all mouth, not connected to his eyes.

'Don't worry,' he said, 'this will all be over soon.'

I wanted to scream. So loud it burst his eardrums. I sucked in a stuttered breath. *Stay calm.* 'What will be over soon? What are we doing here? And what the hell is that smell?'

'All in good time, Alice, all in good time.' The muscles in his jaw pulsated, like there was a worm burrowing in his face as he shifted position, folding his arms.

I didn't understand. The photos, the collage of me. None of it made sense. 'What do you want?'

He pushed himself away from the wall. 'What do I want?' He paced back and forth. 'I can't have what I *really* want. So I'll have to settle for the consolation prize. We can't all be like you, getting everything we want when we want it. The little golden girl.'

374

'What are you talking about? Why do you have pictures of me all over your wall?' The display flashed through my mind. It hadn't just been made up of photographs; there'd been newspaper articles too. I couldn't quite make them out, too distracted by the images of me asleep in bed. It was only then it dawned on me that taking photographs may not have been the only thing he did whilst I was asleep, a thought that forced all the air from my lungs. 'I swear if you touched me, I'll—'

'Touch you? Don't flatter yourself,' he said, face perplexed at the accusation. 'You were drunk, I *could* have done anything, but I didn't.'

Fury bubbled through me. 'Wow, thank you. No, seriously, thank you for setting the bar so low for yourself. Bravo on not being a rapist. I'd give you a round of applause if you hadn't strapped my fucking arms to a chair!' My fingers splayed as far as I could stretch them under the restraints. 'I'm sure your parents will be thrilled.'

His head snapped towards me. 'You know nothing about my parents.'

The fear and confusion vanished. I was just angry, pure rage bursting from me. 'Oh, here we go, let me guess – Mummy's fault, is it? Gave you too much attention, did she? Or, no, wait, not enough attention, was it? Which one's your excuse for being a fucking psychopath?' I braced like a human crash test dummy, my eyes closing automatically as he launched towards me. But there was no impact. I opened my eyes to see him squatting in front of the chair, laughing, so hard I could see the pink flesh of his gums at the top of each tooth.

His laughter intensified and he almost fell backwards off his haunches. 'You're all the same, aren't you? Think you're so clever. That stupid girl certainly was, that woman's assistant, had the nerve to accuse me of being obsessed with her boss. I'd never even heard of Camilla what's-her-name until I read about it in the papers. It was her own fault really, what she made me do.'

Chrissy. I wanted to feel relieved. Relieved Tess hadn't been the one to do that to her. But relief wasn't quite something I could muster. My head thumped with a confluence of confusion and the remnants of whatever he'd used to drug me. 'Why did you attack Chrissy Marchant, and why is your room wallpapered with pictures of my face?'

'She was just a case of wrong place, wrong time. I went over there trying to catch the real stalker, and she turned up and thought it was me. I had to shut her up – if she'd gone running to the police it would have ruined everything.' *Real* stalker? I almost laughed as the words came out of his mouth. This was insane. 'I wasn't lying,' Dom said matter-of-factly, 'what I said about buying her books. I *was* trying to figure out who it was. Just not to help you. Quite the opposite, actually. I saw how much it was bugging you, not being able to get it. The old Washington genes failing. Imagine your face if a lowly civilian cracked it before you. You'd have had a meltdown, well, even more of a meltdown than the one you've already been having. Shame I couldn't get that to work, but it was just a bonus, really, not part of the original plan.'

I couldn't compute what he was saying. 'Why do you care so much about making me look bad, and what plan?'

His face soured. 'I know this may be difficult for you to comprehend, but for once, Alice, this isn't about *you*.'

He put his hands to his knees, pressed himself up and walked out, locking the door behind him.

Dom left me alone for what felt like hours. There was no way of knowing. My watch must have fallen off in our fight and I didn't have my phone. All I could tell was that enough time had passed that the constant writhing against the bindings had chafed my wrists and ankles so much they were bleeding. The restraints weren't budging. Sweat trickled down my face from battling to move the chair, but it was too heavy. The few inches it had scraped across the floor were pointless. Even if I could make it move a foot, there was nothing around me. Nothing to grab. Nothing to cut myself free. Nothing to allow me to get up and see what the smell was coming from behind me.

Please be more roadkill, please, please.

I tried to distract myself by thinking about something else. Anything but the smell. How long was he going to leave me here? And what was he planning on doing with me when that time was up? Surely if he was going to hurt me he'd have done it already. I remembered the look on his face when I'd mentioned his parents, when I'd let loose at him. When I thought we'd hit the crescendo as he lunged at me, he hadn't touched me. He was obviously capable of violence, after what he'd done to Chrissy. But if he wanted to kill me, surely that would have been the time. There must be a reason he needed me alive, for now at least.

No matter how hard I thought about it, I had no idea what was going on. This didn't seem to have anything to do with what Tess had been doing to Camilla. So what the hell was it? Why me? I delved into the deepest pit of my mind, panning through the cases I'd worked over the years. Who might want revenge. The most obvious was Robin Golding, but last I'd heard he moved to Marbella to open a bar when he came out of prison with some poor, unsuspecting twenty-something girlfriend. I compared their faces in my head, side-by-side. Other than their *GQ* looks, there was nothing obviously similar about them to suggest any relation. No matching eyes. No similar noses. Nothing hit. Who was this guy? And what did he want with me?

I let out a deep growl as I realised I'd run out of time to think, Dom's footsteps sounding outside the door. He entered behind me and walked into my eyeline. He was all dressed up. A perfectly pressed suit, crisp white shirt. A cloud of aftershave ate its way through the stench already filling the room as my eyes fell on what appeared to be a bright red evening gown draped over his arm. *What the . . .*

'What d'you think?' Dom said, holding his free arm out to the side.

Was this a fucking joke? I said nothing and tried to keep my face still as the hairs on my arms stood to attention.

'Oh come on, this whole thing will be much easier for

you if you play along. I've made us dinner, but you have to be nice to me if you want any,' he said. 'You must be hungry, right? And I'll untie you if you promise to put this on.' He reached the arm holding the dress out towards me.

I wanted to gag even more than I had in the last few hours. There was no way I was going to be able to get myself out of this if I didn't even know what I was dealing with. Who he was. What he was planning. I looked up and nodded, not trusting my mouth enough to open it.

Play his game.

He laid the dress and a small cream tote bag down on to the stained concrete floor and pulled a large knife from his pocket, the serrated edge catching the light as he unsheathed it. I held my breath as he moved closer, my eyes fixed on the blade.

'Don't worry,' he said, 'it's just to cut the plastic, for now.' I pulled my head away, trying to keep my face as far from his as possible as he leant across me, tucked the knife under the ties and began to saw. Forwards and backwards. The motion was violating in a way I couldn't quite put into words. His aftershave doubled in strength now I could smell it directly on him.

Dom stepped back once he'd cut through all the ties, still holding the knife. Poised. 'There, better?' I nodded again, rubbing each of my wrists in turn. 'Good. Well. You get ready, OK? I'll come back and get you soon.' He kept the knife trained on me as he circled back towards the door.

I waited for the footsteps to disappear before I pushed

myself out of the chair. Legs stiff as I forced them to turn me around. They almost gave way as I saw what the smell had been coming from.

My hands flew to my face. A ghoulish wail echoed around the small space. I presume it came from me. Because it certainly hadn't come from A. J., his body slumped in the corner, legs sticking straight out in front of him in a wide V shape. The dark purpleish hands in his lap sat in an unnatural position, fingers defying gravity as they curled up towards his head which was tilted to one side like a broken doll.

'Oh my . . . Jesus Christ.' I gasped at the huge gash in his neck, the blood from it now brown and dried into his jumper. Disgust propelled me as I rushed to the door, reaching out instinctively to where a handle should be, but I was grasping at thin air. 'What the—' The door was completely flat. I skimmed the rough panels with my fingertips as if somehow I'd find another way of opening it. A keyhole. A gap in the grain. Anything I could cling on to. But it was completely sealed.

Oh God.

There must be a way out. A hole somewhere. Because the air was certainly escaping. Oxygen being sucked out faster than I could breathe it in as my vision blurred. I dropped my hands to my knees, skin running hot and then cold on repeat. What the hell did A. J. have to do with all this? I forced myself to stand, to breathe, clasping my hands behind my neck as I circled the room. Think. *Think!* But I didn't think. Just froze as my eyes landed back on the door, noticing now the chips in its dirty white paintwork. That the roughness, the ridges my fingers had fit perfectly into, were not an original feature. They were scratches. Gouges in the wood carved by desperate fingernails.

62

Lead filled Roy's veins as he took in the sight of Dom's front bedroom, his heart almost bursting through his ribs trying to force the blood around his body after his dash to The Willows. He tried not to look at the eyes following him. Alice's eyes. Watching him as he got down on hands and knees and rummaged through the contents of the desk drawers he'd upturned. He held the van rental agreement he'd found as he pushed up to his feet.

Each ring of the dial tone lasted forever, his arm trembling, until someone from the intelligence bureau finally answered the phone. 'Mate, it's Roy, run a vehicle check for me, will ya? Reg is Papa-Lima-One-Nine, Zulu-Juliet-Yankee; it's rented so PNC ain't gonna get you anywhere, have a look at ANPR. And run a name for me . . .' the paper rustled as Roy flipped it back to see the top corner, 'a Mr Dominic Webb, W-E-B-B, date of birth thirteenth January 1989 – call me back.'

Roy hung up and shoved the phone into his pocket. A million questions raced through his mind but no answers came back. Nothing explaining what he'd walked into. He'd believed Tess when she said she hadn't attacked Chrissy. But someone had. Someone strong. Someone angry. 'But what's this guy got to do with Tess,' he hissed, thinking aloud as he almost pulled the hair he had left from his head, 'with Chrissy, with Alice?'

He scanned the walls, eyes stopping as they hit a picture of Mick Washington. '*Mick?* What's this got to do with—' But this wasn't just any old picture of Mick. Roy had seen this one a million times before, no matter how hard he tried not to. Right there. Slap bang in the centre of that old newspaper article Roy couldn't escape, now pinned to the wall in front of him. The Acaster case. Who on earth would be dragging all that up again after all this time? His eyes dropped to the piece of paper he had in his hand, eyes honing in on the first name. *Dominic.* He almost projectile-vomited when his phone rang. 'What have you got for me?' Roy said, trying to hide the wobble behind his words.

'Small white Ford Transit Courier Sport van, clocked on an ANPR camera heading north on the A37 just over two hours ago. And nothing on that name you gave me.'

No, it couldn't possibly be. Could it? 'Try a different name for me, Dominic Acaster, A-C-A-S-T-E-R, same date of birth, I'll stay on.'

The *tick-tick-tick* of fingers on keyboards chattered in the background as Roy moved his mouth away from the speaker to hide his heavy breathing. He repeated the mental reassurance, telling himself it couldn't be possible. That boy was long gone, surely, after what he did.

'Nothing for that date of birth, but there's a record for someone born in the same year, just a different month . . .'

More clicking. Like tiny beetles skittering around Roy's ears. '. . . woah there, this one's an interesting chap. Wanted for murder.' The van rental agreement dropped to the floor as Roy leant over and used his free hand to brace himself against the desk. 'Looks like latest intel on him's from 2007, fled the country.'

Roy forced himself back up straight and cleared his throat. 'I think he might be back.'

'Oh, shit! Have you got a pen? I'll give you the last known address.'

Roy didn't need it. He remembered the house well. As did most people – it had been in the papers enough. Even now, there was still an ongoing battle about tearing the place down after what happened there. 'Hawthorn Hill, Eastfield?'

'Yeah, that's the one, and Eastfield's the stop after where the ANPR camera pinged the van.'

Roy's entire body was on fire. 'Get on to control, I need local response out there. Now!' he shouted and hung up the phone, his legs giving way beneath him.

63

Dom had thought long and hard about changing his first name as well as his second when he went into hiding. Knew he should have. That it was the sensible thing to do. But he couldn't bring himself to go through with it. It was bad enough he wouldn't be able to wear Father's family name with pride – there was no option to keep Acaster – but to give away the name Father picked just for him? The last thing he had of his old life? That was too much. Father had always looked out for him, his Dominic, and now, it was his turn to look out for Father. His memory, at least. Not like Mother. If she'd had her say after what happened with Jen, he would have ended up in one of those juvenile detention centres like those pieces of excrement from the estate.

He looked around the room that was once the hub of their family. The classically tasteful set-up now an empty shell lined with peeling wallpaper. After Mother ruined it all. Driving Father to do what he did. To keep her down there after she threatened to turn Dom in. She'd given them no choice.

His precisely trimmed nails dug into the inside of his fists as he thought of what life with Father could have been like if the others had minded their own business. It had felt like no time at all, just the two of them without having to worry about his mother. Though he couldn't recall exactly how long she'd lived in the room at the back of the basement before the police found her.

Dom unfurled his hands, pressed the fleshy heels of his palms into his eye sockets. A kaleidoscope of dots moved across his vision. He stood, searching for something to smash. To release the tension. He picked up his phone and launched it across the room, the device hurtling through the air before breaking into several pieces as it hit the stone hearth where the fireplace once stood. He didn't need it anyway. Not after this. When he'd start a new life, all over again.

He picked up his rucksack, the same one that had moved with him since he'd run away. From country to country. Place to place. He didn't want to open it. As if every time he did, a tiny piece of all he'd collected escaped. But he could never help himself. Just a peek. He pulled back the toggle on the worn drawstring, the smell drifting up from the opening sending his stomach wild. The fusion of them. Jen's school tights he'd taken from her washing line, the ones he'd wrapped around her neck, the nylon slicing into his fingers as he'd held on tight until she'd stopped moving. His first prized possession now stained. Aged and fraying.

The underwear and necklace he took from the woman in Catalonia.

The earrings – Perth.

The Rolling Stones T-shirt – Bangkok. Or was that from the girl in Vietnam?

Past encounters whirred through his head like a carousel, each rotation spinning faster and faster, the images – their faces – blurred into one. Until they looked like nothing at all. Just a stream of indistinguishable colours and sharp streaks of light.

64

Revulsion replaced the usual thrill of fitting into an unfor-giving dress. Dom knew my size. Perfectly. He'd been in my house, I knew that, but the thought of him rifling through my things made me feel like I was stood in the middle of a crowd completely naked.

I kept my back to A. J., the smell somehow even worse now I'd seen the source. I focussed on the tote bag Dom had left on the floor. It contained a hairbrush and some make-up, like he thought I was his personal geisha. I looked around the room for the hundredth time, as if something useful could be teleported in through sheer willpower alone. Because a lipstick and a blusher brush sure as shit weren't going to get me very far with defending myself.

My stomach knotted as I heard Dom outside.

'Alice?' he called, his footsteps louder as he got closer to the door. 'You ready?'

'Yeah.'

'Remember what we agreed, OK?'

I ground my teeth. 'I'll stay by the chair.'

'I hope so, I don't want to have to end this before you see the big surprise.'

Another rush of rage pulsed through me. What the hell was he talking about?

Play the game, remember.

The door creaked open, inch by inch, before Dom filled the space it left. The knife was still clenched in his right hand.

'Don't you scrub up well,' he said, elevator eyes scanning my body.

The clag of lipstick weighed my mouth down as invisible bugs crawled across my skin. *Keep it together.* 'What's A. J. doing here? What've you done to him?'

Dom looked towards the body as if he'd genuinely forgotten it was there. 'I think what I've done to him is fairly obvious from the state of his neck, *detective.* Turns out the pen is not, in fact, mightier than the sword. Well, knife anyway.' He waggled the blade at me as if he was showing off the latest gadget he'd gotten for his birthday.

My next word barely scraped out of my mouth. 'Why?'

He shrugged. 'Why d'you care? You should be thanking me – no more stories about you, or that stupid author woman. Done. You're welcome.'

My chest began to cave. 'You did this . . . because of me?'

'God, you really do think everything is about you, don't you? Hate to disappoint, but you weren't the subject of his next big shiny story. *I* was. That's why he was knocking on my door, sniffing around me, not to get into your proverbial knicker drawer.'

'What story? What the hell is going on?'

'I've already told you, all in good time.'

I clearly wasn't going to get any answers until he wanted to give them, and I was in no position to bargain with him. I changed tack. 'Why the fancy outfits?'

A smirk crept across his face. 'In my house, we dress for special occasions.'

My stomach lurched. 'And when do I get to find out what this special occasion is?'

'Allow me.' He extended his knife-free arm and hooked it ninety degrees at the elbow, like he was Fred Astaire asking Ginger Rogers to dance rather than a captor escorting his prisoner to a second location.

I edged towards him, disgust curdling, and rested my hand as lightly as I could on his forearm. He led me out of the room, down a small, dark corridor, cold and musty. We were in some sort of basement. The hairs on my forearms pricked as we approached a set of steep wooden stairs leading up to a closed door, a rectangle of warm light seeping through the gaps around its ill-fitting frame. The smell of cooked onions infiltrated the stale air and saliva rushed to my mouth. When had I last eaten? It must have been at least ten hours. I wanted the hunger to go away, but didn't want to eat whatever he'd cooked. He'd already drugged me once today.

Dom unlocked the door at the top of the stairs and opened it on to a large dining room. Miscellaneous bits of furniture and storage boxes were piled high around the sides of the room framing its main feature, a wooden dining table. A candelabra holding four lit candles sat in the middle, and six chairs surrounded it, with placemats set for three.

'Expecting company?' I said.

'You're so impatient.' He turned to face me, a smile crawling up his face. 'We're getting to that.'

My stomach rolled. Was there someone else here? Someone alive? I at least stood a fighting chance if I just had to incapacitate Dom. I was screwed if there were two of them.

'Sit, please,' he said, gesturing towards the table before disappearing through a door to our right. My head snapped around the room. The windows were boarded shut. No obvious signs of anyone else being there.

Dom returned carrying a large tray. 'Lasagne, one of your favourites, I believe.'

I felt a slight relief that the food on offer had all been prepared in the same dish – less chance of it being drugged if he was eating it too. I also needed all the energy I could muster in case my only option became to fight my way out.

'Well?' he said. 'Aren't you going to tuck in? You must be hungry.'

I looked at the table. Plastic cutlery. Not great weapons. 'Are we waiting for someone or not?'

'Fine, I'll get our guest of honour if you aren't going to stop going on about it.' He walked across the room and disappeared into the hallway by the front door that was also boarded shut.

My brain somersaulted, trying to figure out who was about to join the party. Maybe I hadn't been wrong about

Myles after all. I'd always thought he'd had help. Had that help been Dom this whole time? I strained my ears, listening for colluding voices, some other early warning sign. But all I could hear were Dom's footsteps on the cracked parquet flooring. Then another sound. Squeaking. Wheels that needed oiling. Dom came back into view pushing something in front of him and my blood turned to needles in my veins.

65

The tyres on Roy's car clung to the tarmac as the speedometer teetered around ninety, every lump and bump in the road vibrating through his body. Not that he could tell the difference between that and the fact he was already trembling.

He was trying to concentrate, think back to those brief moments on the doorstep years earlier. Summoning Dominic Acaster's teenage face. What he might look like now if Roy was about to find himself stood in front of him again after all these years.

The fact that Dominic had backed up his dad's lies had been the only thing that stopped Roy from getting sacked on the spot when he fucked up the Acaster job. And at the time there was nothing to suggest the boy had any reason to lie about where his mother had gone. They'd only found out he'd been responsible for what happened to the girl from his school afterwards. Roy remembered the headlines. The manhunt launched after Valerie Acaster came around in hospital and everything poured out of the poor woman before she finally let go. Only Patrick had been at the house the day Mick Washington found Valerie. Young Dominic had never been seen since.

Sweat bubbled across Roy's face as the radio crackled in his lap. '6391 Briar receiving,' Roy tried to bark into the speaker, a feather in his throat taking away some of the force. 'You what? What the hell do you mean, there isn't anyone to get out there? This is—' The sign for Roy's turn-off shone in the headlights before zipping past the top of the windscreen. He threw the wheels to the left and veered across the chevrons separating the dual carriageway from the slip road metres before a steep grassy bank. The radio clattered into the footwell. 'Fuck's sake!'

He tried to wipe away his worry with the back of his hand as he hurtled towards the roundabout. He wouldn't let this guy get away with it. *Couldn't* let him get away with it. Not again.

66

'Dad!' I screamed, shoving my chair back from the table. I didn't have the chance to fully straighten before Dom let go of the handles of the wheelchair my dad was strapped to and whipped the knife from his pocket. The silver blade glinted as he lifted it to Dad's throat, his other hand pointing to the chair as I hovered over it.

'Sit. Now,' Dom said.

I lowered myself back down, not taking my eyes off Dad for a second. At well over six feet tall and teetering around the fifteen-stone mark since he'd stopped any form of physical fitness other than golf, the old rickety wheelchair should have looked like a child's toy in comparison. But it swallowed him. His face gaunt. Eyes puffed up like a boxer who's suffered a heavy twelfth round defeat.

'Kid, don't—' Dad croaked before Dom jabbed the knife dangerously close to his carotid artery.

'What did I say? Huh? Shut up,' Dom spat.

Hopelessness flattened me. *Don't you dare let him see you cry!* 'Why are you doing this?'

Dom looked at my dad. 'OK, Chatty Cathy, do you want to tell her or should I?'

Dad coughed, a gut-wrenching mix of blood and spittle dribbling from the corner of his mouth, staining the top of the two thick white straps crossing his body, holding him upright in the chair.

'Fine, I'll go,' Dom said, the knife still honed on Dad. 'Me and old daddy are good friends, aren't we? Well, I wouldn't say *good* friends, but we know each other. Spent the golden years of your career looking for me, didn't you?' Dad's head fell back with nothing to support it. My heart pounded in my throat. *What has he done to you?* 'Don't feel too sorry for him – your precious dad ruined my life, having my father put away. And to see him celebrated in the papers, like a fucking rock star? My mother deserved everything that happened to her. All Father did was try to protect me – if she'd let him, none of this would have happened.'

A bolt of lightning pierced my brain. The claw marks on the basement door. I'd thought they must have been A. J.'s, and maybe the newer ones were. But not all of them. The newspaper articles stuck up with his montage of me. I could see them now, my dad's face amongst the text. The Acaster job. The story so important to tell that Valerie Acaster forced herself awake just long enough in her hospital bed to tell it. To tell Dad what happened to her. Why they'd locked her down there. Her husband, and her son.

'That was you. The son of that guy who locked his wife up,' I said.

'Well, well, she finally figured something out. I'd give you a slow clap but . . .' he looked at his hand holding the knife, 'maybe later.'

My insides felt like they were going to explode. How in the name of all things holy had he come to the conclusion this was all his *mother's* fault? I had a sudden urge to viscerally defend this woman I'd never even met. 'All she wanted was to get you help, after what you did to that girl from your school. She didn't want you to hurt anyone else.'

Dom's face contorted. 'Help? She wanted me locked up! What type of mother would do that to her own flesh and blood? And to think there was a time I felt sorry for her, that I almost let her make me doubt what my father told me about her.'

I clung to the wooden armrests so tightly my finger-nails almost bent back. 'Did you ever stop to think that maybe – and I know this is a bold thought, so do bear with me here – *maybe* she didn't want her psychopathic son to turn out just like his psychopathic daddy. And look at you – she wasn't exactly wrong, was she? Your dad *must* be proud.' I regretted the words as soon as they came out. *He's holding a fucking knife to your dad's throat – are you trying to get him killed?*

But Dom's face returned to neutral. 'Father *was* proud of me. Very proud. I know he was. How about you?' he said, talking to my dad now. 'Proud of this one?' Dom said as he nodded back towards me. 'Such a good detective she couldn't even detect it was me who broke her porch light.'

Our interaction on my doorstep replayed in my mind and turned my stomach. 'That was you?'

'Course it was, I couldn't have our motion sensors going off every time I fancied a snoop in the dark, and I could tell straight away you weren't the type of person who actually fixes things in a hurry.' He turned back to Dad. 'Proud of what a mess your daughter is? Proud of her getting suspended for attacking an innocent man? For letting a kid try to kill themselves? For a poor young woman getting her head caved in because this one couldn't solve a simple stalking investigation? Or ...' Dom said, looking backwards and forwards between us, '... how about my personal favourite, for what she did to your boy. To Noah.'

I was on my feet now. The sound of my little brother's name on his tongue was like a banshee screaming in my ears.

Dom didn't tell me to sit, just dug the knife further into Dad's neck, a small trickle of blood running towards the collar of his jumper. 'How about a little holiday story? Hmm? How about you tell him what happened to baby Washington at the beach? Why don't you tell him what *really* happened?'

Tears rolled down my cheeks, my whole body shaking. 'What are you talking about?'

'Come on, either he gets it from you, or I tell him. The account in your journal didn't half ramble on a bit, but I'm sure I can remember the highlights.'

My legs gave way and I slumped back into the chair, falling so hard I nearly bounced back out of it. 'Why are you doing this?'

'This bit? Just an added little bonus.' He laughed again, teeth bared. 'Well, *you're* the added bonus, really, if you think about it. I was coming for him. To tear your shitty father apart limb from limb. Payback. But then I found out about you in the paper, your little, erm, *faux pas*. What was A. J.'s headline again? *Carnage in the Church Yard: Top Cop's Daughter Centre of Review*. I mean, come on, that was just too good to resist. What is it they call it? Kismet.'

He turned to face my dad, the smile melting to a sneer. 'I thought I just wanted you to die, slowly, then I realised I wanted you to *hurt* first. Like I have. Like Father did for the last fifteen years before he literally rotted to death in the prison cell you put him in. I thought just killing her in front of you would do it, but this one,' he said as he pointed towards me, 'well, she's just the gift that keeps on giving, she really is.'

Dom stood and turned his attention back to me. 'Now, you can hurt him in more ways than I ever could have dreamed with your little revelation, or *I* hurt him by slitting his throat – your choice.'

My mouth gaped, flapping open and closed like a fish on land looking for oxygen.

'Come on,' Dom yelled, 'we don't have all day. Well, *he* certainly doesn't.'

Dad winced as Dom pushed the blade further into his throat.

'OK, OK, just stop!' I held a hand out towards them. 'I'm sorry, Dad. What happened to Noah, it was … it was all my fault.'

Dad kept his eyes on me, not saying anything.

'It was my idea to go down to the rocks, Noah didn't even want to go. I made him.'

'Stop,' Dad said, with as much defiance as he could muster through lips that seemed to be swelling by the second.

'I don't think so, Daddio,' Dom said. 'You're going to listen to every, last, detail.'

He gestured at me to continue.

I'd lost control of my mouth now, the words I'd held in for so long spewing out. 'I dared him to swim to the rocks on the other side; he didn't want to, he was scared ... but ... well, he'd never say that, not to me; I thought it was only shallow, I didn't realise—' I pressed my hand to my mouth, as though if I stopped the words flowing out it would stop them being true. 'He wouldn't have done it if I hadn't goaded him, called him "chicken", "baby"; I wanted to get back at him for burying me in the sand ... it was my fault, Dad. I'm so sorry, I should have saved him, I should have jumped in after – I tried, I just couldn't reach, and I—'

'Stop!' Dad's voice thundered out of nowhere, reverberating around the room.

The juxtaposition of his authority and his pain hit me like a battering ram. Tears streamed down my face as a smile spread across Dom's. He was still going to kill him. And Dad would die hating me, now he knew the whole truth. I'd given Dom exactly what he wanted.

Dad opened his mouth again to continue. I braced myself, waiting for his words to crush me. 'You were ten years old, Alice. *Ten*. A child. None of it was your fault.'

I lifted my gaze from the floor in time to see the smile slide from Dom's face.

'No. *No!*' Dom said. 'It *was* her fault, she just told you what she did. She killed your son!'

'No, she didn't, she was a kid.' Dad was talking to Dom, but his eyes never left mine. '*I* should have gone with them, *I* should have been there. Not sat back at the beach with a phone strapped to my ear, trying to make a good impression at work. It's my fault my son's dead. Not hers.'

Dom stepped backwards, the knife pulling away from Dad as he moved. I thought for a second he might drop it as disappointment drenched his face, his shoulders sagging. But everything in him tensed again as quickly as it had loosened. 'You're pathetic, both of you,' he spat as his head darted between us. 'Looks like we're going to have to come up with a Plan B here then, aren't we, to really get under your skin.' He moved to the other side of Dad's chair and paused as he looked me up and down, a hunger I hadn't seen before spreading across his face.

Dad clearly saw it too. 'You lay so much as a finger on her and regret won't even come close to covering it, just like your lowlife of a father.'

'Don't—' Dom clenched his free hand as if physically trying to quell his rage. 'Don't you dare let another word about my father cross those lips. Or I'll cut them off.'

He side-stepped towards me, one leg crossing over the other like a crab. Both his head and the outstretched arm holding the knife moved as one, slowly, back and forth between us, like a marksman watching his prey through the cross hairs of a rifle.

SAM FRANCES

'Get up,' Dom said as he got closer, the knife now pointing back at my dad, but his eyes fixed on me.

I rose. The unarmed skills training module played on a loop in my head. Balance displacement, pressure points, distraction techniques. I could hear the yelp of a neanderthal on my basic training intake, whose arm I'd come far too close to breaking because his own machismo wouldn't let him tap out of a pain compliance position. A million different tips and tricks, many of which I'd used before. But this wasn't kicking-out time at a fucking Weatherspoons. This was different. And no matter how hard I willed my body to act, nothing happened.

Do something! Anything!

There were no cable ties restraining me now, no more paralysing drugs coursing through my system, but I couldn't move. The air around me frozen in an Alice-shaped cocoon.

67

Roy pulled up alongside the metal chain-link fence as giant raindrops pelted the windscreen. His eyes strained to see the property through the gaps in the array of weathered hazard signs, each printed with different variations of the same message: *Danger – Keep Out.*

He couldn't see much; it was dark and the house was engulfed in a veil of ivy. Not like last time he was here. When every piece of foliage and greenery had been pruned with military precision. He remembered thinking at the time, Mrs Acaster must have been a busy woman before she disappeared. Affairs to have, sons to raise, gardens to keep. It was only now he wondered if she'd been the gardener, or if that had been her husband's doing, wanting full control over all the living things in his domain. Roy flipped the collar of his coat around his face and got out of the car.

Rusted padlocks adorned every entry point as he walked the perimeter. He poked his fingers through the holes in the mesh, a rattle ringing out as he pulled at the links, hoping for some give. The fence held tight. Roy kept walking, his feet squelching as long blades of grass grabbed the bottom of his trousers. He was just over halfway around the fence line when he saw it. The shiny new padlock sticking out from the others like a bright orange buoy floating in a dark sea. 'Hello you,' Roy said as he pushed the rain around his face with the back of his soaking wet sleeve. He peered through the fence, still struggling to see as his eyes adjusted, any illumination from the streetlights on the road now completely out of reach. Roy rummaged in his pocket for the small torch on his keyring. He clicked it on and a dim beam of light scanned the ground, revealing a weathered green tarpaulin stretched out across the grass beyond the fence, rainwater pooling in the centre of the plastic.

Roy held the torch between his teeth and pulled sodden sleeves down over his hands like makeshift gloves before gripping the wire above his head. He wedged the scuffed toe of his shoe into one of the gaps in the fence, took a deep breath, then heaved himself up. His biceps cramped. And the padding of the material did nothing to stop the mesh stabbing into his fingers as his foot slipped. He slammed back to the ground, the impact knocking the torch from his mouth. He picked it up and stepped back, taking in the full height of the barrier and instantly regretting sacking off the gym more than a decade earlier. Forty-year-old Roy would have been up and over that like a rat up a drainpipe. He looked at the house. Totally boarded up. Complete darkness, and not a single trace of breakage in the waist-high grass that surrounded it beyond the tarpaulin.

He headed back to the car to get the radio, to check for links to any other Eastfield addresses, but Roy had barely taken two steps when a gust of wind whipped the rain up around his face. 'Oh, for fuck's—' The corner of the tarpaulin closest to the fence blew back on itself. Roy could see now what was underneath it and his eyes bulged from his head. He looked up again at the top of the fence line, then hunted around for something to prop up against it, something he could climb on. But there was nothing. The rain battered his face, his overcoat now completely saturated, its weight pulling at his shoulders. Roy walked backwards with several long strides. He stopped, balled up his fists and charged, throwing everything he had into his left shoulder as he hit the mesh.

The hollow ground thudded as his weight crashed down, the mangled fence he'd burst through wrapping itself around him. He dragged himself back to standing and threw the broken wiring to one side. Roy looked down at the large pair of cellar-type wooden doors in the ground before putting his hand to his chest as if there was a button he could press to stop him having a heart attack.

68

Dom took a step closer, my inaction eating me alive from the inside. But I still couldn't move. *Scream!* What would be the point? No one would hear me. Even if there was anyone nearby, the rain was drumming hard against the boarded-up windows, so heavy I couldn't hear the pitter patter of individual drops any more, just one continuous stream. A waterfall crashing down on the house.

Every muscle was tensed so tightly I worried the pressure might disintegrate my bones. Turn me to a pile of flakes and dust right there on the floor, leaving Dad completely incapacitated and at the mercy of Dom and his knife.

Come on, you can do this.

The room he'd come from with the lasagne was only a few feet behind me. A kitchen, surely. There must be something in there I could use as a weapon – a cooking utensil, another knife maybe? I looked over Dom's shoulder. *Say something, anything, distract him!* I yelled the only words I thought might throw him off, 'Dad, no!'

I had barely three seconds. The time it took Dom to hear the words, spin around, and see my dad still strapped to the chair, not moving. I threw myself towards the kitchen, scanning the countertop as I bolted through the doorway. An unopened magnum of Bollinger sat next to a single champagne glass. *What the fuck?* I grabbed the neck of the bottle and held it like a bat, spinning back to face the doorway as Dom reached it.

His eyes were so wide it looked like the lids had completely retracted into his skull. Looking at the bottle in my hands and then at the knife in his, he burst out laughing.

'Go hard or go home, eh,' he said between high-pitched hoots. 'Come on, don't ruin my reward; I was saving that, for afterwards, a little celebration.' He stood outside the kitchen in front of the door to the basement he'd brought me through earlier. 'It's over, Alice. You know it, I know it, so why don't you just be a good girl, do as you're told, and put that dow—' The end of the sentence stuck in his mouth as the basement door burst open and smacked him in the face. The knife flew from his grip and spun across the floor out of view as both hands sprang to his nose, blood oozing between his fingers.

'What the fuck?' Dom roared as a figure bounded into the room from the staircase, spikes of sodden hair and grass clinging to his reddened forehead.

'Roy!' I yelled, adrenaline burning a hole in my throat.

The scream I'd been holding in for hours burst out as Dom sized up a tackle. I couldn't get the warning out fast enough as he launched, driving his shoulder hard into Roy's side. The pair tumbled towards me, landing against my shins and knocking me over, the back of my head banging into something solid behind me. I clutched my only weapon to my chest to stop it smashing on to the floor.

They scuffled inches from me. A macabre comic strip of arms and legs flying everywhere. I tried to stand, to help Roy, but I was seeing four of them now, the same fight scene playing out side-by-side as my vision blurred. Something warm ran down the back of my neck. They rolled into the dining room before both versions of Roy broke free, dragging themselves to their feet as the two versions of Dom followed. I crawled forwards. Tried to shake my two lines of vision back together. I made it to the doorway in time to see Roy throwing Dom into the dining table, the lasagne tray and wine glasses crashing to the floor.

Roy looked at my dad. 'Jesus Christ, are you alri—' His eyes widened as his head jutted forward, like he'd been punched in the gut. I scanned his body, down to where his hands met one of Dom's, balled into a fist and pressed against Roy's bulbous stomach.

'No!' I used the doorframe to pull myself up as Roy fell to his knees, now face to face with Dom. They were both still, just for a second, before Roy slumped on to his side. I could see it now, the base of one of the broken wine glasses from the dining table glinting from where Dom's hands had left it sticking out of the bottom of Roy's shirt.

'God!' Dom shouted, pulling himself back to his feet, shaking his head from side to side and blinking. He tapped the bridge of what looked like a broken nose. 'Argh, shit! Why did you make me do that?' he roared, bearing down on Roy before his eyes sprang to me. 'Why did he make me do that?'

The knife sat on the floor barely a metre from where Dom was standing.

His head jerked towards it.

There was no time to think. To assess. To make sure I made the right decision. Before I knew it, I was hurtling towards the knife, champagne still in hand, hanging by my side.

He got there first, like I knew he would.

I paused just long enough for him to bend down to pick it up, and then threw everything I could muster behind my right arm, swinging the bottle up and down again on to the back of his head, the crack of his skull echoing around the room.

Dom crumpled to the floor. Energy pumped through me as I swung the bottle again, an inhuman roar bursting out as I hit him a second time. Then a third. A fourth. I kept swinging until the glass exploded across his head, frothy liquid spewing down the sides of his face.

My arms hung by my side, clutching what was left of the neck of the bottle. Air scorched my throat as I sucked it in. Short, sharp bursts. Chest heaving. I edged closer and kicked his leg, relief flooding me when it flopped back into its natural position. Blood pooled around my feet. But it wasn't coming from Dom, it was coming from behind me. From Roy. 'No!' I looked at my dad, unconscious now, his head slumped to one side. *Shit! Fucking focus!*

Roy stared blankly at the ceiling. I grabbed his leathery

409

SAM FRANCES

hands and pressed them against the wound as best I could with the glass still sticking out of it, warm blood bubbling around our fingers. 'I need you to press on this for me, Roy, OK?' I didn't want him to hear the tremble in my voice. 'Come on, I know you love it when I give you instructions. Can you do that for me, Roy? ... Roy?' His face remained vacant but the tendons along the back of his hands twitched and tightened. 'Good man, you're going to owe me a stiff drink when this is all over and don't you bloody forget it.' My lip quivered as I forced a smile, fighting back tears.

A flicker of light in the corner caught my eye, fragments of yellowish-white shrapnel spitting away from the main glow. It was only then I noticed the lit candles that had been on the dining table were now lying at the foot of the cardboard boxes lining the room.

69

Roy had always wondered about the concept of people's lives flashing before their eyes in their final moments. He thought it was a load of rubbish. 'How can we possibly know what they saw before they popped their clogs? We can hardly bleedin' ask 'em, can we!' he'd sniped at Karen when she got obsessed with those crystal skulls she bought from that hippie at the Market Square craft fair. He understood now, a little anyway. She'd needed something to do when Laurie left for university. Empty nest syndrome, they'd called it. If he could move his legs, he'd literally kick himself for mocking all that business.

He'd give anything for it to be true now, a chance to see them again, even if only in his head. A reminder of the good old times. His fingers tingled. They'd gotten cold since Alice had let go. He tried to push harder on the searing pain in his stomach, but his hands didn't feel like they belonged to him any more.

Roy wondered if the slideshow in his mind would be chronological. *Or maybe you get Benjamin Buttoned?* he thought. If that was the case, he'd prefer if it skipped the last few months. Years, even. He could do without a re-run

411

of those. His passing out parade was something he wouldn't mind seeing again. His wedding day. Laurie's first day of school. He'd like that. A little pre-heaven *This is Your Life*. Knowing his luck, his brain would pick the crap bits. Mundane moments sat in traffic on the M3 or that time he had a dicey fry-up on a stag do in Blackpool and spent all day on the toilet. Maybe that's what he deserved. He hoped he'd see things from his own perspective. He wasn't sure he could stomach seeing it from Karen's, certainly not from Laurie's.

The pressure against his wound was non-existent now. He couldn't even feel the hard object any more, whatever it was that psycho had stuck into him. Roy's hands slid uncontrollably down to his sides as the projector began to whir in his head.

70

The flame snaked up the wall in seconds, its tongue lashing at the cardboard boxes and furniture before devouring them whole. Dom and Roy lay on the floor beside me, Dad slumped against the straps of the wheelchair. All three of them were still. I looked back at the dancing light, no longer just in the corner of the room, now creeping along the walls either side of it. The heat smothered as my eyes followed its path, up towards the fiery head butting against the ceiling of white plaster barely visible under a thickening veil of black smoke.

There were boxes in the opposite corner the fire hadn't reached. I ran to them, tearing the lids, looking for something to break out of here. The first contained nothing but junk. Ornaments and trinkets and other crap that was of no use to me. The second full of cushions and curtains was even less helpful. 'Come on!' I yelled, moving to the next box. I almost burst out crying as I opened it. I'd never been happier to see a toolbox in my entire life. I yanked at the bright orange handle of a crowbar, hammers and pliers and God knows what else falling out with it on to the floor. It was small, but better than nothing.

I ran to the front door and wedged the crowbar into the barely visible gap between the wooden board and the frame, throwing my weight behind it, foot braced against the wall. My hands ached as the thick nails held firm. Eighth pull. Ninth pull. Grip disintegrating. Tenth pull. Eleventh. I flew backwards as the whole thing groaned and came away in one go. Cold air gushed in, tiny pinpricks stabbing my lungs. But there was no time to gulp it down. I stumbled back into the dining room, feet tripping over themselves, limbs taking on a mind of their own. Burning. Everything burning. My hands. Lungs. Eyes. The whole fucking room.

Keep going!

Smoke filled the space. I clamped one hand across my mouth and flapped the other in front of me, fingers outstretched like little antennae. My palm hit against the handles of the wheelchair. I dragged it backwards, Dad's head lolling as I swung him around and pushed him out through the gap where the front door should be.

Back in.

The smoke thickened with every step.

Stay low!

I dropped to the ground, the floor scraping my knees through the paper-thin material of the dress as I crawled, trying to figure out the direction that would take me to Roy. I crashed into a heap, hand recoiling from the damp. Even through the smoke I could see it, the clothing covering his torso saturated with blood.

Tears dripped from my chin on to Roy as I manoeuvred towards his head.

'Oghh,' Roy grunted before a deep exhale took over his mouth.

'Everything is going to be fine, Roy, come on—'

His hand grabbed my forearm. Eyes fixed on mine, his face was calm and pale, the word he'd been trying to say no longer garbled as it rung out loud and clear. 'Go.'

The room was nothing but a thick haze. My eyes and throat burned, partially from the smoke, but also because the blood was draining from Roy by the second. 'Don't be stupid, I'm not going to just leave you here.'

A seam burst open somewhere on the dress as I got myself into a low squat before stuffing my hands underneath his shoulders. He groaned as I dragged him across the floor, elbows hooked under his armpits. Cramp chewed at my muscles, energy leaking like water through a sieve as I tried to move Roy's dead weight.

My legs gave way as the cold of the open doorway hit my back. I fell out on to the concrete under a dilapidated portico, Roy's head heavy in my lap. Heavy, and still.

Come on! Focus!

I needed to get back up.

Stay awake!

Get in there and pull Dom out. Dying was too easy an end for him.

Don't close your eyes!

He needed to face up to what he'd done to the girl from his school. Her family deserved justice. The rest of his mother's family deserved justice.

I screamed, not sure if it was out loud or in my head

as my eyes grew heavy and I found myself back on the rollercoaster. Air rushed past my face. The feeling of weightlessness took over as the cart went over the edge of a precipice.

71

The hospital bed was firm against my back. I needed sleep. But the smell of antiseptic burning the inside of my nose and the litany of intermittent beeping, footsteps, metallic rattling of carts and trolleys had other ideas. I reached out and grabbed the water the nurse had left by my bed, a thousand needles pouring down my throat as I took the smallest sip possible.

I couldn't get rid of the memory of my view from the stretcher that morning after they'd found us. Blue ambulance lights flashing against charred brickwork. The doorway of the house gaping wide like a portal to hell that I hadn't been able to take my eyes off in case Dom had come marching out of there unscathed. His Hollywood grin, his Hollywood hair, all untouched by the flames. 'Don't worry,' the paramedic had said as she'd placed the oxygen mask over my face. 'When he does come out it'll be in a bag.'

Not that the house of horrors was the worst thing I could be thinking about right now. I wasn't sure how long it had been since Jane left me alone. To 'give me time to process' after she updated me on Tess's charges, what she'd told them in the interview. My fingers clawed at the bed sheet.

One minute I wanted to grab Tess by the hair. Shake her. Scream until my lungs exploded that there was no excuse for what she'd done. No matter how hurt she felt. No matter how much pain she was in. Even if Henry's death *had* been Camilla's fault – which of course it hadn't – the thought Tess could do that to someone shocked me in ways I wouldn't know how to express in words if she was standing right in front of me. And that wasn't even taking into account the betrayal I felt, not just as her best friend, but as a woman. Because it was like she'd broken some sort of unspoken sororal covenant, exploiting her access to the knowledge of those extra special violating touches that would scare Camilla so much she wouldn't feel safe in her own home. The underwear hanging from the trees wasn't from *Follow You Down*. That was all Tess. Yet no matter how hard I tried, I couldn't stop myself swinging the other way too, wanting to hug her tighter than I'd ever held anyone before and tell her it was going to be OK. That she was going to be OK. That *we* were going to be OK. I wiped away tears with the back of my hand at the realisation that the latter would never happen as a nurse arrived. Here for more poking and prodding and force-feeding me water. Not that I felt any of it, numbness weighing down every part of me.

The nurse had given me strict instructions not to wake Dad, so I wheeled my drip to Roy's room. I looked at him and wondered what it was about hospital beds that made their occupants seem so childlike. Roy looking peaceful was a new one on me. Some of the colour had returned to his face, more of a rosy pink instead of the angry red that usually adorned his cheeks and T-zone. I grabbed a plastic chair with the hand that wasn't using the drip stand as a walking stick, pulled it closer to the bed and sat down, elbows leaning on the thin mattress.

'It's rude to watch people sleeping without their permission, you know,' Roy mumbled as one eye peeked sideways towards me. 'You of all people should know that.'

Dom's photograph shrine crept into my head, but somehow I found myself laughing. 'Yeah, well, I've learned from the best, apparently.'

Roy winced as he picked at the wads of dressing across his stomach. 'Jokes aside, you OK?'

I placed a hand to my chest. 'Am *I* okay? What about you? You're the one who's had a cocktail reception removed from your insides.'

'Pfft, don't get me started,' Roy said. 'Could've at least jabbed me with something a bit hardier. When that lot down the rugby club find out I got shanked with a piece of John Lewis's finest glassware I'm never gonna hear the end of it.'

'So you don't want to keep it as a souvenir, then?'

'Already asked, bleedin' jobsworths won't let me have it.' Roy shuffled himself further up the bed, and from the way his face scrunched like a Shar Pei, appeared to instantly regret his decision. 'Anyway, stop changing the subject – how you doing?'

'I'm f—' I stopped the word before it tumbled out again. The fake word. The word I thought everyone needed to

419

hear. The word that matched the face I was trying to show the world. 'D'you know what, Roy, no. I'm *not* fine. I'm a detective who didn't notice I was being stalked, or that my best friend was the offender in my own bloody case. Did I tell you Dom is the only person Vince has ever hissed at? I thought he was just jealous of someone else getting my attention, but turns out my cat has better instincts than me, for Christ's sake! To be honest, I feel more incompetent, more useless, more like a waste of space than I've ever felt in my entire life.' Maybe Dad was right and I wasn't cut out to be a cop after all.

Roy's injured gut rose slowly as he took a deep breath in, his head nodding as he let it back out again. He reached over and patted the side of my arm. 'Know the feeling.'

I sat back in the chair, the tube from my cannula tugging as it tangled in the motion of me crossing my arms. 'How did I not see what was happening, especially with Tess?'

'Come on, we know better than anyone how easy it is to put on a happy face, hide what you don't want people to see. Sometimes they make it obvious, don't they, the weirdos in the trench coats and night vision goggles. The ones that look normal should wear bleedin' badges.'

'That would make things easier.'

Roy shook his head. 'What the hell is wrong with these people? You know, Tess, don't get me wrong, she shouldn't have done any of that stuff, but she'd never *hurt* anyone. All for show, weren't it? But that lunatic, and his dad, they're a different breed.' He sniffed, looking down at the sheet covering him. 'I met him before, you know, Dominic, back when he was a lad, when they had the mum down in the basement. I went round there, didn't suspect anything. Maybe if I'd paid more attention then ... I dunno, none of this—'

'Don't, Roy. This wasn't your fault.'

He looked up at me. 'Yeah, well, the thing with Jamie wasn't your fault either, but you know that's not how it feels, no matter what anyone else says.'

As much as it pained me to admit, he was right. This was a classic example of why people say you should talk to yourself as if talking to a friend. Because what I'd just said to Roy wasn't a lie to make him feel better. I genuinely didn't believe what had happened with Dom was in any way his fault. And if Roy had been in my shoes on the church roof with Jamie, I'd never have thought what happened was his fault then, either. 'Fair point. Maybe we should both go a little easier on ourselves for a change, see how it goes.'

Roy attempted a laugh and grimaced simultaneously. 'You sound like my therapist.'

I almost fell off my chair. 'Your what?'

'It's not like a proper one or anything. I don't go and lie down on some chaise longue and tell her about my dreams – nah, it's just an app thing. I type stuff in. Some woman called Annalise reads it and types something back a few days later. I dunno what it's supposed to actually achieve. Laurie got me to sign up to it, you know, worried about the stresses of the job. Maybe you should give it a go.'

One half of my lip curled in an attempt at a smile. 'Oh, I'll need much more morphine for that.' I wiped a tear from my cheek and shook away that bit of the conversation. 'Where is she, anyway? And where's Karen? I must let them know how brave you were getting your war wound.'

The little colour Roy had regained seemed to ebb away again.

'Shit, are you OK, should I get a nurse?'

'No, no, stop making a fuss.' He exhaled deeply through his nose. 'If you must know, me and Karen are separated, pretty much divorced, actually. Just waiting for the paperwork to come through.'

My face flushed at the memory of some of the jibes I'd made in the last few months. 'Oh, Roy, I'm ... sorry, I didn't know.'

'S'all right, long time coming.'

'D'you want me to call her? Surely she'll still want to know you're OK? It's been on the news already.'

Roy shook his head. 'Her new fella's taken her and Laurie on a sailing trip. Flashy git. Much as I'd like to knock the wind out of his sails, I don't wanna ruin the girls' holiday. They deserve it, putting up with me all these years. Can't remember the last time I took either of them anywhere nice.'

His forced chuckle and slight shrug made my heart ache. I turned at the sound of footsteps behind me. The same nurse who'd been using me as a pin cushion stood in the doorway.

'Mr Briar, you've got another visitor here.' Roy and I looked at each other, our brows furrowed, before looking back towards the nurse as she carried on talking. 'A Trudy

McDowell? Shall I bring her in or do you two want to finish up first?'

I looked back at Roy and mouthed the name, the bell of recognition ringing as I remembered him showing me the picture of an old school friend he'd been talking to on Facebook. 'Oh, *Trudy*.' I pursed my lips as my eyebrows danced across my forehead. A wave of panic washed over Roy's face as he wiped the sweat from his brow and tried to adjust his hospital gown. 'Calm down, you look great, especially for someone who just nearly died.' I stood and turned back to the nurse. 'I'm just leaving, send her in.'

She took a stride backwards into the corridor and waved off to the left. A second woman appeared, well, her head and shoulders did anyway as she peeked around the frame.

'Hi Roy,' she said, a small, slender hand waving awkwardly by her cheek.

'Trudy, well, I ... good to see you,' Roy said, his lips pursing and then relaxing as if he was stifling a grin. Probably for my benefit.

Trudy walked a couple of steps into the room and stopped. 'I hope this isn't too weird, just, well, I saw on the news what happened, and I couldn't believe it, thought you could do with a cheer up.' She pulled back the flap of the brown leather handbag hanging at her side, taking out a cardboard box. 'I brought you some cinnamon buns – remember, the ones we talked about, from Gilly's?'

'Ah, ah, ah,' the nurse and her wagging finger interjected. 'He can't eat those.'

Trudy's face went bright red. 'Oh, how silly of me.' She

423

swivelled on her heels holding the box out in front of her like a bomb due to go off at any second. 'I'm sorry, what should I do with it?'

I pointed Trudy towards the seat I'd vacated. 'I'll get rid of those for you.'

Roy gestured in protest but then took another look at Nurse Ratched and gave up the fight.

'Please don't go on my account,' Trudy said.

I patted Roy's hand. 'I need to get back to my room, and anyway, I saw his heroics live; I'm sure telling you about them will be much more fun for him.'

'Don't listen to her,' Roy said. 'She's the one who saved the day, I just got in the bleedin' way if anything.'

I winked at Trudy. 'He's being modest.' I looked back at Roy. 'You listen to what you're told and get better, OK?'

Roy nodded. 'Yeah, and you, Sarge,' he said, my title leaving his mouth with a new ease.

72

Steam from a mug of Earl Grey tickled my nose as I nursed it, gazing out of the spare bedroom window across Dad's back garden. A long but narrow rectangle of grass and nothing else. Plain, but neat. Just like Dad. I'd miss the morning brew delivery, a new tradition he'd started in the last two weeks since we'd left hospital, Dad bringing it up whilst I was still asleep and leaving it on the bedside table as part of the daily service provided in our joint recuperation Daddy–Daughter care package. Nothing quite like a hostage situation to bring the family together. Not that we'd properly talked about what happened. I supposed that was what the tea was a replacement for. I gulped down the last of it and finished putting my things in the open suitcase on the bed, leaning my weight on to the hard plastic surface of the lid and zipping it closed.

Dad had refused to take no for an answer on the topic of driving me back to Fortbridge. That, and hiding my phone so I couldn't take any work-related calls. 'You need an actual break, not a Washington-style break,' he'd insisted. Dom had dwarfed the revelation about Tess in the press. I'd tried to avoid it, the news bulletins, the talking heads, the Ians and Sandras of the village who had absolutely no clue what they were talking about. 'He seemed like such a nice man,' they'd said. Aren't they always?

Despite our best efforts, it was impossible to avoid once it hit the national news. Irma liked to gossip over the garden fence. A lot. She'd been too busy telling me the latest hot takes to read the social cues that I didn't want to talk about it. 'You're lucky, darling,' she'd told me yesterday as she hung her washing out. 'From what they're saying, they think this might not have been his first rodeo ... linked him to other girls who went missing.' We knew it wasn't his *first* rodeo. The question was how many had there been since he'd left. I wasn't the least bit surprised he hadn't stopped after killing the girl from his school – Jennifer Woodman – and getting away with it. He'd travelled around since, fleeing when his dad was arrested. Australia. Southeast Asia. Spain. The list went on. My hands skimmed my face, fingers dragging my cheeks down, away from my eyes. *God, how many more women were there?*

The research they'd found in A. J.'s flat would go some way to helping the new investigation. The man might not have been the best writer, the most ethical operator, but Jesus, he knew how to dig. If only he'd come to the police with his suspicions instead of trying to nab the big scoop all by himself, then maybe he'd be here to tell us how he knew who Dom was.

Seeing the press attention hadn't been all bad. The images of Chrissy leaving hospital had made me smile, Camilla holding her hand as her mum pushed her wheelchair, her

stepdad weighed down with bags and balloons and bou-
quets of flowers. She'd waved for the camera as they helped
her into a car.

Attagirl.

It had also been nice to see I wasn't totally off the mark
with my gut reaction to Myles, just misguided as to why
the police attention made him so nervy. He might not have
been behind what was happening to Camilla, but he *had*
been stealing money from her. Chrissy confirmed it when
she came to, how she'd noticed a problem with the accounts
and confronted him. The real reason for their argument
in the car. She'd been too afraid to say when we asked.
Myles had looped her up in knots about how he would say
Chrissy was in on the whole thing. Even helped him access
the funds. Which there was no evidence of, and wouldn't
explain his income streams before he knew either of them:
Camilla was clearly just the latest in what must have been
a long line of shady money-making schemes. But Myles
could be a smooth talker when he needed to be. Nothing
else would explain how he managed to attract someone
like Camilla in the first place, and Helena, even if the latter's bank balance hadn't ended up meeting his pathetic
requirements.

I made a mental note to visit Chrissy when she was ready
and try to be less of a cynical, judgemental prick than I
had the first time I'd met her. Maybe even let her sell me
some of her wonder smoothies. I owed her one. Her being
prepared to give evidence against Myles over the money
was probably the only thing stopping him from pressing

charges against me, the one bit of work news Dad allowed to pass through. Myles was too busy trying to save his own arse to worry about kicking mine.

The carpet muted the thud of the suitcase as I dragged it off the bed. I picked up the raggedy old Care Bear Dad had retrieved from the loft to give me to take home – Noah's favourite toy, and Dad's own way of confirming he'd never blamed me for what happened. I took a deep breath as I looked into its big brown plastic eyes. Cartoon versions of Tess's. I didn't even know where to start processing *that*. A dark mix of anger, embarrassment and pity clouded my brain every time I even attempted to broach the subject. *One stalker problem at a time, Alice.*

The kitchen and living room were empty when I went downstairs, luggage in tow. 'Dad, you ready?' I called, to no response. 'Dad?' I said again. Still nothing. I left my bags in the hallway and went into the kitchen, the back door wide open. I walked into the garden but there was still no sign of him. 'Dad?'

'He's down the end there, pruning his trees,' came Irma's voice from the other side of the fence.

My brow furrowed. 'He's—' Was that some sort of euphemism? Dad couldn't even grow a moustache, let alone a bloody tree. '—sorry, he's what?'

'Down by the apple trees, in the therapy garden,' Irma said as she popped up, a grey herringbone tweed flat cap perched on top of her head.

I squinted as if the sun had pointed a beam straight in my face, even though the sky was thick with cloud. Dad was right, Irma must be as mad as a box of frogs. 'Therapy garden? Sorry, you've lost me.'

Irma threw both hands in the air, a yellow gardening glove on her left hand and a purple one on the right. 'Oh, sweet baby Jesus and Mary, that man! I tell you, I thought he'd at least have taken you down there. Come.' She waved me towards the back of the garden and followed in parallel along her own fence line.

What on earth was she talking about? Therapy gardens? Apple trees? If this was some sort of pensioner swinger sex thing, I was going to have to gouge my eyes out with Irma's rusty gardening fork. We passed through our respective gates and met on the overgrown path running along the back of their terrace.

'Come on,' she said, picking up on the hesitancy in my body language, grabbing the sleeve of my coat and pulling me towards a small mud trail between mounds of bracken. I wiped my nose with my free hand, pollen hanging in the air as I followed her into a clearing. She pointed towards a large black gate leading to what looked like some sort of allotment. 'See, therapy garden,' Irma said proudly. 'Ten years since I started it, took me a while to get your dad down here, can't tear him away now. He says it's just because sometimes Lawrence Peters brings his border collie Marcy down, but I know the truth.' She smiled and tapped the end of her nose. 'Go on in, he'll be the only one here this early.'

She let go of my arm and nudged me forwards. For some reason it felt like I was walking into a job interview as I left her and went through the gate, following the pebbled path between sectioned-off areas of different types of plants. Big leaves. Small leaves. Some attached to climbing poles, trays of nursery pots with bright green shoots threatening to burst through the soil at any moment. I found Dad at the back, a pair of shears in his hand as he inspected one of two large apple trees. A twig cracked under my foot, Dad turning for a second at the sound before going back to what he was doing.

'It's these dead branches that are the problem, you see, the ones you've gotta get rid of,' he said, not taking his eyes off the bark. 'And these little spindly ones here, growing up the middle, they're no good neither. Stops the air circulation – more likely to get a fungal disease then, aren't you? And you don't want that, infects all the other healthy branches. Canker, they call it.'

I couldn't remember the last time I'd seen Dad do anything he looked comfortable doing since he'd left the job, but he looked at home in his tracksuit bottoms and zipped-up fleece. I came alongside him. 'Canker? Wow, you know the lingo and everything.'

He nodded and twanged one of the thin branches. 'You can't stop them growing – they're always gonna grow where you don't want them – just have to learn to manage them is all.'

'You certainly seem to have learned a lot.'

'Good for you, isn't it, the fresh air and all that. And there's a bloke who brings his dog down sometimes. Excitable little sod, she is, a bit like you when you were a kid, actually.'

'Gee, thanks!' I smiled and scuffed my foot through the grass, the morning dew coating the top of my trainer. 'It suits you. And looks like you're good at it,' I said, pointing aimlessly. I had no idea if he was actually good at it. The tree was bare, buds still in hibernation waiting for some spring sunshine. Or maybe he'd killed it – what the hell did I know about bloody apple trees? He certainly seemed to enjoy cutting bits off it, anyway, and that was good enough for me.

'Only thanks to Irma. She's a pain in the arse, but that woman knows plants. Seems a lot more complicated than it actually is. Irma says as long as you've got your roots sorted you're golden. Good roots, good fruits, she says.'

'What if your roots are knackered?' I asked.

'Well, then you're probably fucked.'

I nudged him with my hip. 'Can't blame the roots for everything, though. I mean, at some point the fruit has to start taking responsibility for itself, make its own decisions, choices, you know, once it's dropped off the tree and rolled off on its own.'

He laughed and scratched the back of his head before looking up at the sky. 'You're not on your own, kid.'

'Sorry, I thought we were still pretending to talk about trees?'

'You should get yourself one,' he said. 'Looking after it'll do you some good.'

'An apple tree? I'm not even home enough to keep a cactus alive.'

He sniffed as if that was exactly his point. 'Well, maybe you should make sure you are from now on.'

431

My shoulders dropped. We'd been doing so well. 'OK, so we're doing this? Right, look, I know you've never thought I was cut out to be a cop, but—'

His scoff interrupted me. 'Is that what you think?'

'You haven't exactly hidden the fact, Dad, that I don't live up to the old Washington name.'

He laughed before rubbing his hand back and forth across his forehead. 'You crack me up, kid,' he said as he leant on the handle of the shears he was now holding like a cane. 'The problem is, you live up to it too bloody much.'

'Sorry, what?'

'When people say you're a chip off the old block, they're not wrong. You carry it around with you, the job, just like I did. Still do, and ... well, bloody hell, this is a bit deep for this time in the morning but, it's too late for me now, what's done is done and all that, but you, you've still got your whole life, your whole career.' He turned to look at me now, his face stern but soft. 'I want you to have both of those things, Alice.'

He coughed away the obvious frog in his throat before I had a chance to respond.

'Now,' he said, handing me his large red shears and picking up a smaller set for himself. 'Let me teach you how it's done. I'm going over the other side to start cutting some of the thicker branches; you carry on getting rid of these bits here, clear it right out, OK? We'll get it done easier if we do it together.'

He patted me on the shoulder as he walked past, just like he'd done all those years ago at the hospital when

Mum died. But his eyes weren't glazed this time. Not red. Or raw. Just relaxed. The flecks of amber floating in the emerald sea shining like glitter.

Just me and you now, kid.

73

Dad pulled out of my driveway on to the lane, the rumble of his engine fading as he sped off around the bend. The door fell shut and the house was quiet. I hoped Vince would forgive me for palming him off on to Jane whilst I was away. Even I'd been surprised at the offer in the hospital. Jane the cat lover. Who knew?

I got changed and headed to the station. The piece of paper I pulled from my pocket as I stood outside the reception was almost illegible. Crumpled, stained and barely held together with sticky tape, the Be a Better Alice list had seen better days. I balled it up in my fist, squeezing tight, before dropping it into the bin outside the entrance.

The door swung open before I had a chance to push it, Jane and Bret striding out deep in conversation.

'Alice, well hello,' Jane said. 'I wasn't expecting you so soon.'

'Not here for work today, ma'am, it's . . .' I paused as I caught Bret's eye, something in me reluctant to mention why I was here in front of him. I pushed the words out anyway; there was no point trying to hide it now. I needed to own my shit. 'It's my occy health appointment.'

Jane's face warmed. 'Right, yes, good. Glad to hear you changed your mind about that.'

I considered regaling them with Dad and Irma's 'good roots, good fruits' analogy but thought better of it and just smiled instead.

Bret nodded in a way that made it look like it was the first time he'd ever attempted the gesture. 'Hope it goes well. I best be getting off. Good to see you back, Alice,' he said before raising his hand in an awkward half-wave and walking away down the street.

Wow, I must look in a really sorry state if even Bret felt the need to be nice to me.

'It works, you know,' Jane said once he was out of ear-shot.

'What does, ma'am?'

'Therapy. Did wonders for me after Oliver was born. Had post-partum depression up the wazoo, not sure where I'd be without it if I'm honest.'

Jesus, was I the only one *not* in some form of therapy? Roy with his app. Dad with his trees. Now Jane. 'Oh ... I ... that's good to know, thanks, ma'am, that it worked, not that you had ... well, you know what I mean.'

Jane nodded and smiled. A proper smile. Not like her usual ones where you can't tell if she's smiling or wincing. It completely changed the contours of her face. 'Quite. Oh and erm, when you're ready, remember the MCU sergeant's vacancy is still open, if you want to chat about your application. Bret's asked me for help with his – only fair you get the same treatment.'

I appreciated the vote of confidence but couldn't help but laugh. 'Thanks, ma'am, but I don't think I'm top of their recruitment list at the moment, roughing up suspects and going to counselling. Maybe Bret's a better horse for you to back this time around.'

'Yes, well, the Dingle issue will have to be dealt with, but the counselling shouldn't worry you. I know if I'd ended up at HQ, I'd rather have had guys and girls in my team that knew how to look after themselves, especially with some of the jobs they have to deal with – that was one of the reasons I chose not to go back there.'

No matter how hard I tried I still couldn't imagine Jane in a therapy session. Even less so the prospect of Jane voluntarily shunning the heights of HQ. 'You *chose* not to go back there? I thought . . .' I wasn't quite sure how to phrase what I thought in a way that didn't make me sound like a dickhead.

She swung her handbag over her shoulder. 'Oh, come on, then, I love this game. Which version of the story did you hear about how I ended up in Fortbridge? The depression? Shagging Carver on the side?'

I shifted from one foot to the other. 'The Carver one, ma'am.'

'Glad to know that old fairytale's still doing the rounds.'

'So you didn't . . .'

'God, no, but don't let actual facts get in the way of a good rumour, eh? There was no affair, and my husband left for all the good old-fashioned reasons. Younger model, perkier tits. I wish I had a less clichéd story for you on that one, honestly.'

I felt terrible. Of course the classic 'woman's plan to get ahead by shagging the boss backfires' rumour was the one that persisted. And I'd believed it without a second thought. *Bad feminist!*

'The truth is,' she carried on, 'after Oliver was born, I didn't want to come back at all, never mind coming back to night shifts and overtime. Wanted something a little easier going.'

'Oh,' I said, not quite sure what to make of Jane's confession, 'right.'

'Yes, I know, surprised myself with that one. I'm amazed I still have two eyeballs in my head the number of times I've rolled my eyes at women who scale back their careers when they have children, and well, here I am, and I honestly wouldn't have it any other way. Funny how things turn out. I don't see the point worrying about it. Whether I went back to work full-time or jacked it all in, either way, if he turns out to be a serial killer, I'm sure it'll be all my fault regardless, so might as well do what makes you happy.'

I thought back to the way Dom had spoken about his own mother. The mental gymnastics he'd gone through to make everything her fault. 'Good point, ma'am.'

'That's why they make babies so damn cute, otherwise no one would bother with the hassle. Should have gotten a golden retriever instead. Anyway,' she said, looking at her watch, 'must dash, I'll drop your cat home later.'

'Great, thank you, ma'am, and thanks again for looking after him.'

I watched her cross the road before I walked through reception, up the back staircase, the smell of takeaway food getting closer and closer as I passed the CID office, before continuing to the top floor and along the corridor. My hand paused for what felt like an age before I summoned three quick raps.

'Yeah?' came a voice from inside the room.

I pushed the door open a little and stuck my head in the gap.

'Ah, morning, Alice. Come in, take a seat.'

A pale streak of sunlight shone through the window, spring finally making an appearance like a laser beam slicing across the desk and floor, resting at my feet. *I swear to God, if she makes a joke about 'following the yellow brick road' I'm out of here.* 'Morning, Beverly.'

The woman's head tilted, blocking the stream of light, her face scolding.

'Come now, we've been through this before. Please, call me Bev.'

Acknowledgements

In the summer lockdown of 2020, *All Eyes on You* started out as more of a rant than a novel. It served a purpose as a cathartic way to process my thoughts on how stalking is rarely taken as seriously as it should be, but my rage ramblings didn't exactly make for a compelling piece of fiction. The proverb 'it takes a village' could not be truer when it comes to this book, and whilst I held the figurative pen and made some shit up, there are so many people I will be forever thankful to for helping me bring Alice's story to life.

Firstly, a huge thank you to the whole Headline team. To my brilliant editors Lucy Dauman, Sophie Wilson and Isabel Martin; your support, vision and invaluable insights helped shape this story into what it is now versus the rather odd hodgepodge of *Bridget Jones* meets *Luther* I started out with. An extra special shout out must go to Lucy for setting the wheels in motion by taking a chance on me in a Twitter pitch event. The day you told me you wanted to publish my book will forever be one of the best days of my life so thank you for very literally making my dream come true. Also a huge thank you to Ana Carter, Lily Birch, and Lisa Horton for all your hard work behind the scenes.

To my wonderful agent Sabhbh Curran at Curtis Brown, thank you for believing in me and my writing, your enthusiasm for my weird little world of Fortbridge and its inhabitants, and for helping me navigate the world of publishing. I'm incredibly lucky to be in such good hands.

A heartfelt thanks to my parents, Sue and Frank, for their storytelling genes (a Mackem and a Scouser – could there be a better combo for spinning a yarn?). You always support me in everything I do, including making me think my childhood poetry was the best thing anyone had written since Maya Angelou even though it was about a hamster called Vinny who was rather skinny. You were wrong, but I appreciate the unwavering encouragement. Sorry for all the swearing.

Much of the background and inspiration for this novel came from my time working in the field of violence against women and girls. Thank you to the fantastic charities and advocacy groups in this sector, for your knowledge and insights, and for the incredibly challenging yet vital work you do supporting victims and survivors. Policing has a long way to go in improving how it deals with cases like the one in this book, however I express my thanks to all the passionate police officers I've worked with over the years who do take these cases seriously, and who tirelessly campaign to raise standards every day. A special thanks to my friend and former colleague Greenie for reading an early draft and answering lots of random police-related questions. Any inaccuracies in procedure are either my own errors, or liberties I've taken for the sake of dramatic effect.

This book is entirely fictional, but I may have gifted Alice and company some personal anecdotes, so a huge thanks to my lifelong friends, Shell and Nicki. Please accept my deepest gratitude for the fun and special memories we've shared over the years, and long may I continue to mine and exploit them for commercial purposes. Any royalties owed will be paid in pea pods and un-milky cups of tea, respectively.

To my writerly friends, both those I know in real life and those I've interacted with through online writing communities, thank you so much for the education and encouragement. This book would have crashed and burned had it not been for those who either shared their knowledge of the craft with me, beta read early versions, helped with random grammar questions, completed straw polls on the most ergonomic way to drag a dead body, came on writing retreats with me, or just generally cheered me on, particularly Kat, Charli, Esme, Megan, Becky, Venetia and Victoria. An incredibly special mention must go to Kat; without my publishing team this book would never have made it into the world, but without you it would never have been written in the first place. Our samosa-fuelled bookish chat in Richmond Park changed my life. For that (and your nachos recipe) I will be eternally grateful.

To my partner, Tom. Thank you for the wake-up coffees, the plot fixing and idea forming walk-and-talks, for coaxing me down from nigh on daily writerly existential crises, and for not immediately packing your bags and leaving after reading my first ever scene that was so bad I'm sure it must have made you regret your life choices. I couldn't have done this without you. Not just because of your support, but also because you act as an excellent climbing frame distraction for the rest of the wolf pack: Matilda, Beatrice, Douglas, Olive, Maggie and Molly. I will not be thanking them as they have done nothing but hinder my writing process by rolling on my laptop and lying across my hands/ arms forcing me to type this entire novel one-handed.

And finally, to the readers of this book. The fact you read my story means the absolute world to me. There are so many, many books out there and not enough time to read them all. I don't take lightly the fact you've spent some of that precious time with mine, and I could not be more grateful. I hope you enjoyed it. And if you didn't, that you at least find another use for it (suggestions include, but are not limited to, paperweight, doorstop or yoga block). Either way, thank you, and I hope you come back to join me on Alice's next adventure.